ORDAINED

ORDAINED
I have chosen you

L.C. Anthony

Singing River Publications, Inc.
Ely, Minnesota

ORDAINED
I Have Chosen You

Published by:

 Singing River Publications, Inc.
PO Box 72
Ely, MN 55731
www.singingriverpublications.com

Cover art: Peggy Orchard
Cover design: Dorie McClelland
Interior design: Dorie McClelland, Spring Book Design
Printed in Canada by Friesens

ISBN 978-0-9822596-1-0

First edition
12 11 10 01 02 03

PROLOGUE
꘏

KELLY MORE AND BISHOP FOLEY sat on her porch drinking iced tea on a cool summer afternoon. Anyone walking by would think it a tranquil scene, but for the two of them, this was a new experience. Up until a few months ago, they were enemies, pitted on opposite sides of a bitter dispute affecting millions of people. Each was anxious to put together the missing pieces of a conflict that had stirred up anger and rivalry between them.

Of average height and slim build, Kelly carried her 45 years well, although she lamented the little time she had to exercise in recent months. Though she was by nature an optimistic woman with a positive outlook on life, the bishop who now sat opposite her had tested this disposition severely.

Patrick Foley's appearance was a contrast to Kelly's. At the age of 54, he had the look of a career churchman, outgoing and friendly on the surface but cautious within, watching for anything that might get in the way of his ambitions or test his authority. His appearance was not unpleasant, especially when he smiled, which he did often. But one had a sense that it might not be quite genuine. It was a cultivated look that had been practiced to suit whatever public occasion he encountered. Kelly sensed he was trying to change. A more authentic self was breaking through, one that was less sure of himself. At the moment, he was in one of his more transparent moods. Kelly was finding her pity for the man dissipating; being replaced with a fondness that surprised her. But how could she tell him about the depth of her feelings? Could she describe the core of her own commitment? Would he be able to absorb and treasure it? This talk would tell.

Kelly took a sip of tea and thought for a moment as she looked at her one-time adversary, wondering where to begin. She reached back in her memory to a poignant event both had witnessed from different perspectives, one that would throw them into a turbulent contest that had only recently been resolved.

Do you remember, Bishop, that night the pope died? It was in the middle of April, two-and-a-half years ago. I can still remember the phone ringing, waking me from a sound sleep. The daughter of an older woman in the parish, Vicky Angstrom, called to say that her mother was dying. Funny how I can remember the conversation. I was surprised that the woman's cancer had progressed so quickly. I had visited her just the week before and she was in good spirits and full of energy.

"So sorry to call this late, Mrs. More, but my mother is not doing very well. She keeps going in and out of consciousness. Just now she woke and asked for you. I didn't want to bother you, but if I wait until the morning, it might be too late. Would you come and give her your blessing, the one you promised her a few days ago?"

"Sure. I'll be right there." Pulling on my robe as I spoke, I was trying not to disturb Tom as I got out of bed. I can still remember the time; it was 2:30 in the morning. Within ten minutes I was pulling the car out of the garage, glad to be doing the work I loved so well, caring for the people of St. Gabriel's. No matter the hour, day or night, this was what I was called to do. Caring for the parishioners was not a job to me; it was my life's work and it fit me, right down to my toes. I doubt you realized how important this was to me and what a terrible loss it was when you took it away from me.

As I drove the mile to Vicky's home on that cool April night, I thought of the many times I had been called to bless those who were dying. I always made sure to tell the sick person and the family that I wasn't doing an anointing as a priest would do. This was not a sacrament of the church. All I would be doing is lead them in the prayers for the dying and then do a special blessing using ordinary vegetable oil. It seemed to have a soothing effect on those present, especially the dying person. It gave comfort to everyone, so much so that they would often ask for me even though a priest might be available from another parish. At the end of the prayers, I would invite the family to put their hands on the person and then say a blessing I had composed, making the sign of the cross in oil on the person's forehead and inviting the family to do the same. I'm sure that you frowned on such a ritual, but at the time it seemed so innocent and so beneficial.

What made that blessing of Vicky Angstrom significant was not what happened in her home that night—she died the next day—but what happened after I left and headed home. It was a cool night, but there was a hint of spring in the air, as if the flowers, which weren't even out of the ground, were beckoning to me to stop and pay attention. As I pulled into our driveway, I stopped short of the garage and listened to the silent expectation of spring, so pronounced at this early hour of the morning. Then, for some unknown reason, I flipped on the radio as I eased the car into the garage.

"I repeat," the announcer was saying, "we have just received word that the pope has died of a sudden and unexpected heart attack. He was finishing his morning audience and collapsed on the stairs leading to his residence. All attempts to revive him failed."

Stunned, I sat in the garage for a long time trying to fathom what this would mean for the church and for our parish in particular. I can remember saying a prayer of hope that this unexpected news might make a difference. The acute shortage of priests was creating a terrible burden for the clergy and a lack of the sacraments for the people. Something had to give. Perhaps his death would bring renewal.

As I entered the house and climbed the stairs to my bedroom, I was praying for new life and direction in the church. "Come, Holy Spirit, and hear the cries of your people," I murmured as I got back into bed, careful not to disturb my husband. "Best not to wake him now," I thought. "I'll tell him in the morning."

It was a long night for me. Sleep would not come. I was too wound up thinking about what had just happened and what the next pope might be like. Would he follow the lead of the last two popes as they tried to maintain what, to my mind, was a narrow, centralized and exclusive definition of church? Not only was it not open to a married clergy, it would not even allow the question of women priests to be discussed! And yet a strong movement was afoot to ordain women without legitimate approval, performed by bishops not officially connected to the church. People were taking matters into their own hands. Perhaps the new pope will be different, more open to change—someone with a whole new perspective and set of priorities. It was exciting just to think about it. Spring was in the air, and I was catching the fever.

I must have eventually dozed, because once again the ringing phone brought me to my senses. Tom was already up; I could hear him in the bathroom. I looked at the clock as I reached for the phone. Oh, no! It's already a quarter to seven and the kids have to leave for school by eight. We're in trouble!

"Good morning," I said, as I picked up the phone, trying to suppress the panic in my voice.

"Have you heard the news? The pope just died." I recognized Deb's voice despite the high, excited tone. "We're going to have a new pope. Can you imagine?!"

"Yes. Thanks for calling, Deb. I did hear about it. I did a blessing for Vicky Angstrom early this morning and caught the announcement just after it happened. I suspect the television is full of the news. We'll have to open the church for people to come and pray if they like. But first I have to get the kids to school. I'll catch you later in the office. Try to settle down. You're going to have a heart attack yourself."

I chuckled to myself as I put the phone back on its cradle. Such a good lady, but moments like this were almost too much for her. You know Debbie. She's the one who took over my job as parish administrator, but I knew her as an energetic volunteer when I first came to the parish five years ago. She caught my attention. In her early forties at the time, she was spunky and good looking, although a bit shy. She had enthusiasm and a quick mind, but she had no idea just how capable she was. Sensing this, I encouraged her to enter the lay ministry formation program in the diocese and she loved it. Two years later I hired her as the director of religious formation in the parish. We made a great team. She was always there when I needed her. She had such a gift for working not only with the younger children, but with the teenagers as well. One thing I loved about her was that whenever an unexpected event like this happened, she got so excited her voice became high-pitched like a chirping bird.

Scrambling to get dressed as fast as I was able, I gave Tom a quick kiss. Hopping down the stairs as I put on my shoes, yelling to him over my shoulder, "Tom—have some big news," and then to the kids, "Everyone up. We're running really late this morning."

Rachel, my youngest, came bounding down the stairs as I headed for the kitchen. She was nine at the time and possessed irrepressible life and energy. I kept seeing myself in her, knowing that I could no longer bounce the way she did, but it kept me young just watching her. "Morning, Mom. What's the big news?"

We reached the kitchen together, she heading for the refrigerator to get some milk and I to the television to learn what was happening in Rome.

"No word on when the funeral will be," the morning show host was announcing, "but the cardinals from around the world are making plans to head for Rome within the next few days. Such a shocking and sudden thing this has been."

Rachel plunked herself at the kitchen counter, looking quizzically at the television. "What's up?"

"The pope just died, Honey. A heart attack. The job must have been too much for him. Run upstairs and make sure your two brothers are getting ready, will you please? I'll fix you some eggs if you like, but be quick about it."

"Sweet!" Rachel replied as she slid off the stool and ran upstairs.

I began making lunches for the kids, watching the television at the same time and thanking God for having three healthy children, one of whom I noticed could run up the stairs like a greyhound. Again the telephone rang, this time in stereo. One was in the kitchen and the other was my cell phone which I could hear ringing in my purse out in the hallway. "It's going to be this way all day, I'm afraid. Guess I'll let the cell go for the moment. Hi. Kelly here."

"It's me, Carol. Just heard the news. It's going to be a busy day in the office. But isn't this earth-shaking news? Must be the work of the Spirit. Maybe our prayers do pay off after all."

You've met Carol. She was the third person in the parish office. She had been the secretary for some twenty-five years by the time I arrived, and we liked each other right from the start. She had the physical qualities of an SUV, substantial yet attractive, pleasant and inviting but strong in her opinions, a person whom you could always count on to speak the truth as she saw it, with no frills or elaboration. What I prized most of all is that she was able to fend off all the smaller crises and disruptions so I could get my pastoral work done. I soon discovered that there was little about the parish that Carol didn't know, and if a job needed to be done, she always found someone to take care of it.

"I've already talked to Deb," I told Carol. "She's going to open the church for our communion service at eight this morning. I suspect we'll have a crowd. Would you bring some rolls and make the coffee for the gathering afterwards? Three or four dozen should do it. I'm running late, so I'll get there just before the service. Not sure what my reflection will be about, but I'll think of something. Gotta run."

Tom, that strong anchor in my life, had come downstairs while I was on the phone and was standing dumbfounded, watching the television. I can still picture his bewildered expression. "What's happened?" His voice was raspy, as if he were not fully awake, which he wasn't. Mornings were always a challenge for my husband. What you see as a gregarious and fun-loving man in the evening is nothing like that in the morning. Still, I have grown to love this six-foot-two-inch marvel when his defenses are down and he's just beginning the day.

"An act of God," I replied, going to give him a big hug from behind. "We'll soon have a new pope. Think about that! Did I wake you last night? I had to do a blessing for Vicky. I think she's on her last legs."

"This could be good news or bad news," Tom retorted, not answering my question, but putting his hands on my arms wrapped around him so that I knew it was okay.

I, too, had ambivalent feelings. "You're right," I replied. "So I guess we'll just have to pray harder. This morning could be a big moment for the church, a *big* moment!"

How little did I realize at the time what an understatement that was and how integrally I would be connected to events that stemmed from the death of this pope.

THE BISHOP TOOK A SIP OF ICED TEA and sat back in his chair, shaking his head. His mind was reeling at how much had changed since that eventful morning.

My experience of that day, Kelly, was quite different from yours. When I turned on the television, I was stunned to hear the news of the pope's death. I loved that man. He was doing everything right and was just hitting his stride. He was getting things back in order, solidifying the work of his predecessor. I didn't care if people left the church. It may be smaller but, by God, it would be the one, true, *Catholic* Church! You remember that I had been appointed bishop of the diocese only weeks before this pope who had just died was elected. I was so proud of myself! I was sure I could do a better job than Bishop Gene. He was a nice guy, and everyone loved him, but the diocese was in disarray. I felt it my duty to clean up the place. If I didn't cause any trouble and made sure there were no unorthodox practices taking place, I could possibly use this position as a stepping stone to a bigger and better diocese. Who knows, I might even become an archbishop; I was that ambitious. Nothing else mattered. I was in tune with the pope and was confident that he would recognize this and promote me. Already I was making the necessary contacts so he would be sure to notice. I was making progress.

But then the pope died suddenly that April morning and everything was thrown into chaos. No one knew who the new pope might be. Would my interests and plans be protected? How could I be recognized and appreciated for all I was doing for the church in this diocese? It was an anxious day for me as I tried to lead the diocese in Masses and prayer services for both the deceased pope and the election of a new one. Inside I was depressed, scared, out of control and alone. On the outside I tried to show sorrow and understanding. That was all a sham. I was afraid of what would happen to me with this transition. I labored to get back in control and make the best of the situation.

Bishop Gene, the one you loved so much, but who was a thorn in my side, called that morning to offer help and support. I thanked him but rejected his offer, feeling that I wanted to do it my way. I can't believe how arrogant and proud I was, how condescending and rude I must have been to that kind old gentleman. Here he was, the retired bishop who knew every inch and corner of the diocese, who knew the people, how they felt and what they needed, and I wouldn't even accept his advice or counsel. I wish I could apologize to him now for that, but it's too late.

When I first came to the diocese I had heard about you and your work at St. Gabriel's. In my last diocese where I was the auxiliary bishop, there were no pastoral administrators. I was suspicious when I first heard you had them here. How could this be—someone other than a priest in charge of a parish? In my mind only an ordained priest could be a pastor. Even if he had to handle more than one parish, he was still the boss. But in this diocese it was different. Although a priest came to say Mass and forgive sins, he was not the one in charge of the parish; the pastoral administrator was. Here was a woman banking the money, running the parish office, doing the pastoral care, overseeing the religious education, even standing next to the priest during Mass. I couldn't picture this happening; it was impossible for me to comprehend.

And yet ten parishes had pastoral administrators, with you being one of the most popular. The way Bishop Gene described it, I sensed you were one of his fair-haired pastoral administrators; you could do no wrong. He praised your work as "pastor" of the parish. The priest who came to preside at the Masses and administer the sacraments was confident in your abilities, and the parishioners loved your pastoral presence. So, I confess, before I ever met you, I resented your position and your reputation. I made a mental note that *you* were one of the first things that needed cleaning up in the diocese. I wanted everyone to know just who was and who was not a pastor in *my* diocese. No woman would ever be called pastor if I could help it. This was not a good precedent; it needed careful attention with clear boundaries and well-defined parameters.

Bishop Gene had described you as—let me see if I can remember his words—a forthright, forward-looking pastoral administrator who encouraged parishioners to take ownership of the parish and to realize their full potential as "called and gifted People of God." He said you had it all: good looks, a pleasant and open personality, a loving husband, a beautiful family, and most importantly—his words stuck in my mind like an irritating commercial—a creative, curious mind. He said all this with great admiration, but I felt only resentment, jealousy and anger. At that very moment I was determined not to come across as second best to any pastoral administrator, especially to a woman.

This is why, before ever meeting you, I tried to make you appear less important. The chance presented itself the first week I arrived in the diocese. I'm sure you wondered why I appointed Father Henry Cimanski to be the priest to say Mass in your parish when Father Mac suddenly became ill and could no longer serve both parishes. I knew Henry from his seminary days where I served as a spiritual director. He was just the opposite of all that you were described to be by Bishop Gene. Henry would put you in your place; I was sure of that.

Father Mac had a reputation for being a kind and gentle priest, but in my mind he was a pushover, always allowing pastoral concerns to override diocesan rules and regulations. I couldn't tolerate that. In my instructions to Father Henry, when he began his new assignment, I made sure that he would be a stickler for doing everything the "correct way." Make sure, I told him, to let everyone know that he was the ultimate boss. Although young, he had a love for the older rituals of the church, including some of the devotions that had fallen into disuse after the Second Vatican Council. Adoration of the Blessed

Sacrament, Benediction, reciting the rosary, doing the liturgy "by the book" were important priorities for him. He introduced these into his own parish, but sensed they wouldn't be welcomed at St. Gabriel's. You probably saw him as rigid and unbending. I, on the other hand, found him malleable and a ready instrument for my plan to put you in your place. He called me regularly with reports, not only about his own parish, but also about St. Gabriel's Parish and the liberties you were taking, Kelly, with the liturgy, the spiritual formation of the children, and the administration of the parish.

"She's a wily woman," I can remember Father Henry saying. "When we walk down the aisle for the start of Mass, she insists on walking right next to me as if we were equals or something. Who does she think she is? And when we get to the altar, she wants to start the Mass with the sign of the cross and the introductions. Wasn't I ordained to do that? And she insists on wearing an alb which, to my mind, blurs the distinction between us. The people don't realize that I'm the priest and she is just a lay person like themselves."

Of course he was threatened by your leadership skills, your candor and honesty, your liturgical presence and pastoral style, and the great love the people had for you. You not only knew everyone, you knew their troubles and pains, their joys and triumphs. It was just too much for him. To be honest, it was too much for me as well. I cringed as I heard him describe his experiences in your parish.

During the weeks following the pope's untimely death, your pastoral attributes came to the fore: the church open both day and night so people could come to pray, the special prayer services and rituals you planned for the election of a new pope, the articles you wrote in the bulletin—all of these reached my desk. Yes, I must admit it. I had spies working for me in your parish. If I were to admit the truth, I was impressed by what you produced. It was better than most of the others parishes in the diocese. But at the time all I felt was spite and rage. My future was in doubt, and here was this woman playing up the election as if it were a new dawn for an emerging church. From my vantage point, there was no telling who the new pope might be, and I was frightened about the prospect of change and new direction. What I sensed from you and your parishioners was more like elation and hopefulness, as if you expected another Pope John XXIII to come along. It was clear to me that you and I were serving two very different churches, and I was determined that *my* church would prevail. I longed for the opportunity to trip you up and show you who was in charge. Little did I know how soon you'd give me that opportunity.

⌒

YOU HAVE NO IDEA, BISHOP, the pressure I felt from your dominant presence in the diocese. It was such a shift for me. Most of the time I was just trying to survive, attending to parish duties and staying out of the limelight.

I don't think I ever told you how I came to St. Gabriel's. I saw an advertisement for the position while finishing my Master of Divinity Degree in Detroit. On a whim I applied for the job, not expecting to get it. To my great surprise, after repeated interviews with Bishop Gene, the parish staff and the pastoral council, they offered me the position. I was caught off-guard. Now I would have to follow through with my spontaneous offer. It seemed to be a clear call from God, and I knew instinctively that it was the right choice at the right time.

It was a huge transition for the whole family, which meant leaving the Detroit area with all that a big city and comfortable suburb could offer, and moving a few hundred miles away to the small town of Sarah in the middle of Michigan. Tom had to rearrange his computer programming business so he could work from home. The move was also difficult for our children, Nathan, Michael and Rachel. Adapting to new schools and finding friends in a completely different environment is never an easy task. To their credit, they took it in stride and adjusted quickly.

I arrived in the diocese three years before your arrival and quickly learned that St. Gabriel's needed a great deal of help. I replaced a seventy-five-year-old priest who had not been well. The parishioners did all they could to fill what was lacking in his pastoring, but they needed a leader, someone who could minister to them, direct their efforts and keep St. Gabriel's in repair. When the elderly pastor retired, the bishop told the congregation that the parish would have to close and merge with a parish to the south of them, some ten miles away. The community protested with such vigor that in the end Bishop Gene relented. He announced that he would appoint a parish administrator, someone who was not ordained but who would be their pastoral leader. "We have to take what we can get," was the stoic reaction from one of the parishioners. She told me long afterwards how angry she was that I had been appointed to be their "pastor." She was sure it would never work. To be honest, I was not so sure myself.

After many months of trying to win them over, the congregation began to see the new arrangement as an asset rather than a liability. I was always present when they needed me. Soon the buildings and grounds took on a new luster, looking cleaner and better managed than they had for years. Parishioners were kept informed in ways they had never experienced. They knew how their donations were being spent and how much money was in the bank. This was a first. Father Mac—that's the only name he ever went by—was the priest who came from the neighboring parish to preside at our single Mass on Sunday morning. I suspect you considered him too accommodating and inept, but the two of us worked well as a team. We alternated preaching at the Masses; one Sunday I read the reflections after the gospel and the next Sunday he presented the homily. Once a month

I went to his parish and preached so he wouldn't have to prepare a homily. This gave him a break and allowed me an opportunity to connect with his parishioners. We complemented each other well. When someone was sick, we both visited the hospital or home. I read the prayers, and he anointed with holy oils. If he wasn't available, then I performed the blessing on my own. The people in both parishes felt that their needs were being addressed, and they enjoyed the way we teased one another about our preaching.

Then you were appointed as the new bishop of our diocese. It had come sooner than we expected. When he reached the age of 75, Bishop Gene had tendered his mandatory letter of retirement to the pope, but we assumed it would take some time before it would be accepted. Within a few months he was out, and in you came. It was a difficult transition for me. I wanted to give you all the affirmation I could muster, but I so loved Gene. He was more than a bishop who had invited me into the diocese to be a pastoral administrator. He became my friend and mentor, someone who taught me how to lead and manage a parish. He supported me and was an advocate when parishioners refused to accept me as "their pastor in the absence of a priest," as my job description read. You saw Gene as weak and ineffective, but he was far from either. In my mind, he was a true leader who brought out the best in each person he touched.

And I too, without knowing you, formed my judgments. You appeared to be excited by your new assignment, but I sensed that you were also cautious about taking any risks or trying anything new that was not approved by the dictates of Rome or the Conference of Bishops. I heard via the grapevine that you felt it was our duty to *clean up the diocese*. I didn't want to believe the rumors, but this remark, if true, saddened and angered me. Those of us who loved Bishop Gene didn't think the diocese needed any *cleaning*. Even now, as I think back to your installation as bishop, with all its pomp and clerical ritual, I can still feel the anger rising inside me. It went against my whole understanding of church as the people of God.

Try as I might to stay in the background when you arrived, it was to no avail. When first we met, the look on your face was telling. Your smile seemed fixed and your handshake insincere. I could feel you evaluating me according to some standard or preconception which I could not identify, judging me before we had spoken. And I was doing the same—measuring you against the yardstick of Gene's leadership and finding you lacking in all areas. I came away from our first meeting shaking my head and thinking, "This is going to be difficult. He doesn't like me and I'm not so sure I can get to like him either." First impressions are often wrong, but in this case, as the next six months unfolded, I realized I was correct, that I should indeed be on guard and heed what I did or said in the parish.

Now, Kelly, let me tell you what my first impressions of you were. On the surface you appeared pleasant and non-threatening, a person I would enjoy getting to know. But what I judged you to be—and it took a long time, more than two years, before I was persuaded how wrong I had been—was a manipulating, conniving, women's libber who was challenging my authority as the bishop. I felt it my duty to rein you in and keep you in your place. Without you knowing it, you were gaining an envious reputation in the diocese. Other pastoral administrators and even some priests were looking to you as a model of good pastoring. It was shortly after the death of the pope and the election of a new one that I found that opportunity.

I had no idea, Bishop, how deep the division between us had been and how far back it went. As long as you brought up the pope's election, I want to tell you what it meant to me. The funeral for the dead pontiff and all the hoopla surrounding the election were in such contrast to the person who was finally elected. No one could have predicted that it would take so many ballots. Weren't you surprised by the outcome? I certainly was. Can you imagine? An Italian! The last person anyone expected. When the white smoke finally came out the chimney and the church bells began to ring, we all thought that an African or Hispanic, perhaps even an Asian pope would step on the balcony. But no, here came this short, lean, smiling Italian. Who ever heard of Giuseppe Castalini? And he was only 66, young for a pope. You and I both underestimated the impact he would have. I must admit I had misgivings until I heard the name he had chosen, John xxiv. I was eating breakfast with my kids. Tom was out of town at a conference, but as soon as it was announced, he called to share the news. When I answered the phone I was surprised at how elated I was. Finally, someone who would take the church in a more progressive and enlightened direction as his namesake who made Vatican II possible. Tom asked me what it all meant and whether the pope might call another Vatican Council.

I remember telling him that I had no idea, but the name alone gave me hope. I also realized that much was riding on how he viewed the church and in which direction it should be heading. My prayers over the next few weeks were, "Dear God, help this poor man. Give him strength to do your will and give us faith and hope in the choice the cardinals have made. There must be some reason for all of this. It has been so sudden and unexpected." I also thought about how Father Henry was reacting to the selection of this pope and his name of choice. Your own sentiments were probably closer to Henry's than mine, something along the line of, "Oh no, not a liberal pope, just as we were getting everything pulled together again! Who knows where this might end?"

Something else happened around the time of the election that made an impact upon me. Debbie, our formation director, and I planned a prayer service for the new pope the day after we heard the news. We didn't tell Father Henry about doing this because it didn't involve a Mass, only a few scripture readings, some words from me, petitions for the pope and the church, and then refreshments downstairs to discuss what the members thought of the new pontiff. The reading was from John 15, "You did not choose me, but I have chosen you. I have appointed you to go and bear fruit, fruit that will be lasting." For some reason, when I read these words to the congregation that evening, although chosen to apply to the new pope, I had a strange impression that these words were spoken directly to *me*. I remember thinking that I should make note of this moment, because it might have some significance. "I have appointed *you*," kept ringing in my ears for the rest of the service.

The prayer service and social ended a little after nine that evening. It's still very clear in my mind. I helped with the clean-up, put on my coat and began the short ten-minute walk home. I must have been preoccupied with what had happened at the prayer service and with that gospel passage which was still running through my mind. What did not catch my attention was where I was walking. As you know, St. Gabriel's is on one of the few busy streets in Sarah. Without looking, I stepped into the street right in front of an oncoming car. I can still see the headlights of that car bearing down on me. It was so close, I was sure it was going to hit me. Just then, in an instant, I felt as if someone had grabbed my jacket from behind and yanked me back to the curb. The car swerved, barely missing me as I tried to keep my balance. Only then did I hear the car's horn blaring.

The next I knew I was sitting on the curb, looking around to see who had pulled me backwards. There wasn't a soul in sight. "I must have imagined that," I thought to myself, breathing hard, my pulse racing. By this time, the car had stopped and a teenager ran toward me.

"You okay, lady?" the girl asked, her face white from shock, her hands shaking. "I don't know how I missed you? I didn't even have time to honk."

"Yes. Yes, I'm fine, really I am," I said in reply, still stunned. "It was my fault. I wasn't paying attention to where I was going. I'll be all right. Don't worry."

I picked up my Bible bag that was lying beside me and with the help of the girl, rose to my feet. "It was stupid of me to be so distracted," I said to the girl. "Thanks for stopping. I'm happy you had such quick reflexes."

The girl returned to her car and drove away. I continued walking, shaken by the experience. All the way I was conscious of how lucky I was to be alive and unhurt. "God help me," I muttered to myself as I made my way home. "I was almost a goner. My kids could have lost their Mom. God, are you trying to tell me something? First the scripture this evening and then that yank that saved my life. What was *that* all about? Life is *so* very fragile. I am one very lucky lady, that's for sure."

That night I gave my three children special hugs and kisses—although the boys hate when I do that. Then I settled down to tell Tom what had happened. After sharing with him the scripture passage about "I have chosen you . . . I have appointed you," I told him about almost being hit by a car.

"Funny thing, Tom," I said, "I felt as if someone had grabbed me by the back of my collar and pulled me out of the way of that car. Isn't that strange? There was no one else around, I'm sure of it. It was like what you did to Rachel when she was little, the time she ran into the street without looking. You grabbed her just as the car went by."

"Thank your lucky stars you're not still lying there on the street," Tom said with obvious relief, pulling me closer to give me a kiss and a hug. "Better add a prayer to your guardian angel for working overtime tonight."

"Yes, I will. I'm not sure I believe in guardian angels, but there was someone looking out for me, that's for sure."

While brushing my teeth that night, I reminisced, as I always did, about what I was grateful for throughout the day. Then lying in bed before turning out the light I counted five blessings, one for each finger.

First of all, dear God, I'm so grateful for being alive. You did save me tonight, I'm sure of it.

Second, our new pope. I have no idea what to expect, but at least it's finally settled.

Third, Tom. Every day I count him as a blessing, especially tonight for being so understanding and not laughing at me when I told him about being yanked from the path of that car.

Fourth, the kids, of course.

And finally, I'm grateful for that wonderful reaction to tonight's scripture. I have no idea why it remained with me so, but I don't doubt it was from you. Thank you for keeping me safe. I really do owe you.

⌒

I CAN SEE NOW, KELLY, what a good woman you are. I ask your forgiveness for being so blind and not seeing this sooner. It's clear that God had specific plans for you that no brush with death could deny. I'm flattered and pleased for all that you are willing to share with me and to take me into your confidence, especially given the way I've treated you. But this is something that you need to write and share with others. I'll help you in any way I can. Take some time, write it while it's still fresh in your mind. I'll find someone to substitute at the parish. I might even come myself if the people will accept me. But write you must; tell us your story. I'm not the only one who wants to hear what happened and how you felt about it. Don't leave anything out, not even our acrimonious interchanges. So why are you smiling at me that way? You're hiding something, aren't you? Father Henry was right, you are a wily woman. Come clean, what is it?

Let me tell you, Bishop, that I, too, have thought about writing an account of these strange events. I hesitated because I felt so inadequate to the task. I'm a pastor, not an author. But I did keep a journal. That's why I could recall the morning the pope died. Part of my daily prayer is to make note of God's blessings and gifts. Thank goodness I still have these notes. They reveal many unusual events that kept happening to me, some I welcomed and others I had great difficulty accepting. At Tom's urging, I began to write my account and have now finished the last chapter, the one that includes the two of us. I called you for this chat to help strengthen our new way of relating and to give you a copy of the manuscript. I plan to send it to a publisher within the month. I can't believe this has happened, that I could ever reach this point. As with everything else these last two years, it comes as a great surprise. I'm only an instrument, a small piece of a much larger plan. But it was an essential piece and I felt compelled to give an account of my experience. This is my gift to you.

Kelly, you humble me with your generous and open spirit. This is a great treasure. May I begin right now? Would it be rude to ask if I could stay right here and read your story? Go about your business; I'll not disturb you. I must learn what you have to say, as I'm sure others will as well. Once again you have risen to meet the challenge. I'm very proud of you and so happy that we have reconciled.

Feel free, Bishop, and I hope you enjoy what you read, although it may be hurtful at times. I was honest with my feelings and they were not always positive, especially with regard to you. Be sure to join us for dinner. You should be well into the story by then. I'm sure you'll feel, as I did while writing it, that God works in strange and wondrous ways.

ONE

THE STORY BEGINS WITH a cast of characters, and they were just that—characters. First, my family, myself, of course, Tom, my husband, and our three children. At that time, Nathan was a junior in high school; Michael, a rambunctious freshman; and Rachel, an energetic fourth grader. Debbie Powers and Carol Enright were the two persons with whom I worked. I was the pastoral administrator at St. Gabriel's Catholic parish in Sarah, Michigan. In effect I was the pastor—that's what the parishioners called me—but the bishop would never allow me to have this title. Only a priest could be called pastor and I was a lay woman filling in because there weren't enough priests. Patrick Foley was the new young bishop, only 54, but he was *old church* in his approach to life and his way of leading the diocese. He was such a contrast to Bishop Gene McGovern who had just retired at the age of 75. Despite his age, Bishop McGovern was younger in attitude and outlook than his successor. Father Jerry Cross was a 62-year-old Jesuit living in Detroit. He was my former theology teacher and spiritual director, as well as a dear friend. Along with Tom, he pulled me through many a dark night. Pope John XXIV, the new pope, also played a part, as did Father Henry Cimanski, the 40-year-old pastor at the neighboring parish who came to St. Gabriel's each Sunday morning to hear confessions and preside at the

9:00 Mass. I was at the altar with him when he led the liturgy, which was my duty as the pastoral administrator. Henry was a traditionally minded priest so I know he was uncomfortable having me there. However, the congregation accepted me as their pastor and they expected my presence next to the priest at the Sunday liturgy.

Father Henry had been coming to say Mass for only a few months when the trouble began. It was my turn to preach. We alternated Sundays; he gave the homily one Sunday and I did the reflection the next. Officially mine was not a homily—only a priest could do that. To the worshipers it was all the same. As I looked over the readings in preparation for my reflection, I liked the gospel for that Sunday, John 14. Jesus said to his disciples: "Do not let your hearts be troubled. Have faith in God and faith in me." But then it continued with "My father's house . . ." "No one comes to the father but through me . . ." "If you really knew me, you would know my father also." "Whoever has seen me has seen the father." Father, Father, Father. That was not my concept of God. I always thought of God as both mother and father all wrapped in one. It's a personal being I pray to, but this being is also the creator of this vast universe. Perhaps I could explore these different perceptions with the congregation on Sunday morning.

That particular Mass sticks in my memory, not only because of my reflections on God as mother in the gospel but because of the first reading as well. It was from the Acts of the Apostles about the Greek widows being neglected which led to the establishment of deacons. I can still hear Agnes Cunningham reading, "Brothers and sisters, select from among you seven reputable persons filled with the Spirit and wisdom . . ." I remember it because of the reaction this caused in Father Henry, who was sitting next to me. He was grimacing, his face caught up in a menacing frown. What's the problem with him, I wondered. I looked around the church, first to the servers and then to the congregation. Nothing. Then I realized that the reader had changed the readings by adding *sisters* to the passage to make it more inclusive. Agnes had also changed the word *men* to *persons*. This is something all the lectors did. The congregation accepted this, but not Henry. He was visibly distressed. I wasn't the only one who noticed it. Tom, my husband, was seated in the third pew. He looked at me with an expression that asked, "What's wrong with Henry? Is he ill?"

My, oh my, I thought, could that be what made Henry upset, Agnes using inclusive language? Well, he'd better get used to it. That's just the way we do things around here. A few years ago the use of balanced language in the liturgy had become a hot issue. Some of the parishioners thought the texts should be changed to reflect both genders. Others contested that no one had the right to change the scriptures. "What is written is written," they contended. After much discussion, soul-searching and sharing of opinions, the congregation finally agreed to the use of inclusive language for all the prayers, songs and readings at Mass. A few irate parishioners complained to the bishop and wrote letters to Rome, but nothing came of it. Bishop Gene McGovern, who was the bishop at the time, ignored the issue, so the practice became a tradition at St. Gabriel's. Some of the disgruntled parishioners acquiesced, others worshipped elsewhere. At the time, I felt bad about losing them. A few later returned, while others never did. By now, using inclusive language had become such a common practice that I hadn't even thought to tell Father Henry about the changes Agnes would be making in the first reading. It never crossed my mind, until I saw the reaction on Henry's face. Tom told me later that he could see my eyes grow narrow and that I was upset. I don't think I was aware of this until I stood to do my reflections after the gospel.

I did not go behind the lectern where the gospel was read. I went to the middle aisle so I could make better contact with the people. I had meant to preach on people's different concepts of God, but

Father Henry's reaction to the inclusive language in the first reading changed all that. I launched into new territory, wondering where it would take me. I don't think I really had a choice. I felt driven. I began by thanking Agnes for doing the first reading so well, and then I said to the congregation, "Take a good look at the first reading from the Acts of the Apostles. A need arose and the Apostles couldn't handle it. They were too few and overworked. Sound familiar? Notice all the discussion that is occurring in the diocese about reducing the workload for priests. They can't do it all anymore. They're stretched too thin. No priest, for instance, was available here at St. Gabriel's five years ago. Instead of closing the parish, the bishop appointed a pastoral administrator. It was like the Acts of the Apostles all over again. A need arose, and the church devised a way to meet that need.

"We now have a new Roman Pontiff, Pope John xxiv. Imagine the problems from around the world that face him. Peter had his hands full, but nothing like this pope. For one thing, the issues of ordination and the shortage of priests are facing him head on. One can only speculate as to how many emails he's already received from people asking that he make changes in those areas.

"More immediately is the question of inclusive language in the readings of the Mass. At the moment, there is a difference of opinion in the church, even among the bishops themselves. That is just one of many issues that have to be addressed by the new pope.

"We've had a custom at St. Gabriel's for the last few years of making sure the language used at our masses is gender inclusive, with no distinction between men and women, from the songs we sing, and the prayers we use, to the scriptures we hear.

"Agnes, you did well in proclaiming the words in Acts where you said, 'Brothers and sisters, select from among you seven reputable persons. . . .' What was in the Book was 'Brothers, select from you seven reputable men. . . .' Most people here didn't even realize Agnes had made that change. It's a simple thing, really, but not to some, especially to the Education and Liturgical Congregation in Rome. 'You can't change the texts!' it said in its statements of recent years. Ironic, isn't it, that Jesus tells us in today's gospel, 'Do not let your hearts be troubled. You have faith in God; have faith also in me.' It's faith in God that sets us free, free from constraints and exclusive thinking.

"My contention is that the Holy Spirit is asking us to use our heads and our hearts and to stand for what we know is right. No one is to be excluded from this church, either in the language we use or in the priesthood numbers we are so badly lacking. This is a very critical moment in the life of *our* church—and it is *our* church.

"Remember what a difficult decision it was for us as a congregation to use balanced language in our liturgy. This is risky business, because we can't operate on our own as if we are not part of the larger church. When Bishop Gene McGovern was in charge of the diocese, he gave us tacit permission to do this. Now the church is in a period of transition, with new leadership in both the diocese and in Rome. Part of our allegiance to these new leaders is to be a prophetic voice in the church, just as Jesus was in his own time. There must be room for everyone if the church is to remain faithful to its founder.

"So pray hard, my friends, that we can continue to believe in this church, one that is always in need of reforming. Pray that it will respond to the Holy Spirit in our midst. And pray as well for our new pope in this critical time."

The congregation nodded in agreement with what I had said as I tried to catch my breath and walk back to my chair. I was very surprised at the words I had spoken and the direction my reflections had taken. That wasn't what I had meant to say at all. One sideways glance at Henry told me immediately that I gone too far. Why, oh why, did I say all that? I had wanted to tread easily this Sunday and to not do anything that would aggravate Henry. It was almost as if someone else had been speaking inside me. It was my voice, my gestures and my energy, but someone else was forming the words that left my mouth.

The rest of the Mass was a blur for me. I went through the motions, but I kept wondering what had happened. While I felt at peace, I also felt a bit concerned, not about Henry's reaction, but about what I had said. Something or *someone* seemed to have grabbed hold of me and would not let me go. Parishioners came to me afterwards and congratulated me on my preaching. They often did this, but this Sunday was different. "Right on, Sister!" Debbie patted me on the back. "Where did you get the gumption to say that? I know you think all of this, but you've never said it out loud in front of the entire congregation. Good for you!"

I could see Tom smiling at me from across the church hall during coffee and donuts after Mass. I kept looking for Father Henry, but he was nowhere to be found. I discovered later that he left right after Mass, telling the sacristan that he had to get right back to his own church and couldn't come down for coffee. When I asked Mildred, the sacristan, how he appeared to her, she remarked, "He seemed upset. But don't worry, he'll get over it. I just loved what you said in your preaching this morning."

When we arrived home from church that morning and started fixing our traditional Sunday family brunch, I noticed the message light blinking on our phone. I pushed the button to listen and was surprised to hear: "Kelly More. This is Bishop Foley. I wonder if you would be so kind as to come to see me tomorrow. I have an opening at ten-thirty in the morning. Call if you can't make it. Thank you."

"End of message," the answering machine announced as I sank into the nearest chair. "What's wrong, Mom?" Rachel asked as she looked up from setting the table for brunch. "Are you sick?"

"No, Honey, just a little worried about that phone call, that's all. You know how people call with problems." Then I searched for Tom so I could talk to him about the phone message. I found him in the kitchen cooking bacon. He stopped when I entered the room. I'm sure he could see on my face that something was wrong.

"The new bishop called," I told him. "He said he wants to see me tomorrow morning. It's my day off and he knows it." I got more and more angry as I spoke to Tom. "What could be so important? I'll bet my wedding ring it was the result of today's Mass. Henry went right home and called him about it. I'm sure of it. How quickly the wheels turn when there's a complaint; how slowly if you want to get something done."

"Whoa, Sweetheart, don't jump to conclusions. You're not sure about that."

"Henry's a frightened man who has to have everyone play strictly according to the rules. He doesn't like us changing the readings to more inclusive language. Can you imagine that, in this day and age? I must really threaten him if he feels he has to go right to the bishop. I suppose he knows he has an ally. Bishop Gene would never have taken him that seriously, but Bishop Foley does. They're cut from the same cloth. I suspect he didn't like me talking about the changes the new pope will be facing either. He's a status quo person all the way. Don't rock the boat. If you do, his fiefdom will be threatened. Then I come along and shake the branches of his little tree house. So he runs to Daddy. That makes me so mad!"

"Sounds like you and Henry aren't exactly cut from the same cloth," Tom said, coming to comfort me as only he could do. "But let's not have this get in the way of our Sunday breakfast. Come on now. Try to relax and let it go. You'll only make it worse for yourself." By this time I could feel the tears of anger and frustration welling in my eyes.

"Tell you what," Tom continued, taking over the breakfast

preparations. "Why not go upstairs and put on something silly, laugh at yourself and this whole crazy business. Don't let this get to you. Besides, you're not much good at making breakfast right now anyway. I'll have it done in fifteen minutes."

I took his advice and went upstairs. I rummaged in my closet to see what strange thing I could wear. There was a funky sweatshirt that Nathan and Michael bought for me last Mother's Day. It was green and purple, and written on the front was "I'm the Meanest Mother in the Whole Damn Valley." On the back was a very ugly looking Mama. This goofy getup was just what I needed to cheer myself.

Before heading downstairs for breakfast, I called Bishop Gene at home. I knew that he would be saying Mass at some parish on Sunday morning. He went around the diocese helping whenever a priest wanted to get away for vacation. The parishioners always loved having their former bishop in the parish for the weekend. It made them feel special. After the beep of his voicemail, I left him a message.

"Hi, Gene, it's Kelly. I know we set a date to get together later in the month, but something just came up for which I need your sage advice. Would you call when you return? I'll be hanging out at home. Thanks, Gene."

The kids were calling to me from the dining room, "Mom! Breakfast's ready."

As I came down the stairs, Rachel yelled. "Why are you wearing that sweatshirt, Mom? It's so gross!"

"Because your sweet brothers gave it to me and it is fun to wear on special occasions—like this delicious breakfast your dad cooked so nicely. Hey, guys, wait for grace before you dig in."

The breakfast was a welcomed diversion for me and I had almost forgotten about the bishop's call until the phone rang in the early afternoon. I knew it was Gene returning my call.

"I think we have a problem," I began after inquiring about his morning. "I seem to be on a collision course with the new bishop. I tried to stay out of his way, but he's shining his searchlight on me. Help me with a little advice as to how to handle this, would you?"

I told him everything I could remember from the morning's Mass. It was all a bit blurred in my mind because my reflection had been a spur-of-the-moment thing. But I did recall Henry's reaction to the changes in the readings and to my reflection addressing the issue.

"Ouch," Gene remarked, although I could sense he was pleased that I had risked speaking my mind. "You landed on this with both feet, didn't you? Times certainly have changed. We could laugh off those complaints when I was in charge. Patrick Foley is a different fish altogether. I suspect he's flexing his muscles to show he's the boss and that things will now be different. No more bending the rules or turning a deaf ear. He wants to appear as if he has everything under control. And for heaven's sake, he doesn't want any complaints going beyond his diocese, to Rome for instance, or worse, to the media. My suggestion, Kel, is to do the humble pie thing for now. I know it doesn't suit you, but do what he says and lay low. Choose your battles carefully. This isn't one of them. Keep your mouth shut and listen to what he has to say. He's a smooth politician. Outwardly he'll appear all smiles and very friendly, but underneath he's sizing you up. Fly under the radar. You're good at that."

"Are you saying to give in to whatever he wants?" I was amazed that Gene would ask that of me. "What if he tells me we can't make any changes in the readings, no more balanced language? I'm not sure I can do that! Most of the parishioners won't go along with it either. I could have a mutiny on my hands."

"Hang on. Let's look at this," Gene interjected, picking up the frustration and anger in my voice. "Suppose he wants Henry to have more say in what changes can or cannot be made in the Mass. That's really the only place he's present in the parish. Could you live with that?"

"Not easily. I'm the pastoral administrator here and that still holds. The new bishop hasn't changed that!"

"Oh, but he *could*," Gene shot back. "He very well could. Do you want that?"

"No. No, I do not." All of a sudden I was beginning to realize what this might cost me. "So what do I do, Gene?"

"What if you had the lectors check with Henry before they do the readings. I'll bet he won't be so strict as long as he has a say. I know the man. I should, I ordained him. He's threatened by anyone who tests his authority. But he's not a bad guy, just unsure of himself. Let him have this one and he may calm down. Oh, and no more preaching in his face, okay? You'll only make it worse."

"So go in there tomorrow and just listen," Gene continued. "Don't try to defend yourself. Think of the parish community. Don't make it any worse than it is now. They'll be the ones who will suffer if you get fired."

"Oh, don't even say that!" I could feel my hand tightening around the receiver. "I have far too much invested here to think about leaving. I like this place! Pray for me, Gene. I'll let you know how it goes when I see you. You've helped me a great deal. You've put this in perspective and encouraged me to stop thinking only of myself. Thanks, Gene. Goodbye."

I hung up, wondering if I really could do what Gene suggested. Keeping my mouth shut was not one of my God-given gifts, especially when I was fuming inside.

"What was that phone call about, Kel?" Tom asked, looking up from the paper. "Oh, it was Bishop Gene. He gave me some advice about my appointment tomorrow morning."

"And?"

"He told me to keep my mouth shut when I'm with the bishop. He's right, of course. I'm getting far too worked up over all this. I think I'm pinning too much hope on this new pope. I want in the worst way for things to change. I have to relax. Being uptight is not my best character trait."

⟋

MONDAY WAS MY DAY OFF and I usually slept late and took it easy. Tom made sure that the kids were ready for school, and someone else led the morning prayer service at the parish. But not this day. I decided to get up at the regular time and join with the prayer. Everyone was surprised to see me.

"What are you doing here?" Margaret, the Monday prayer leader asked as she made room for me in the circle of chairs.

"Yes, I know it's a bit unusual. I don't want to butt in, Margaret. You be the leader like you do every Monday morning. I just need a little extra prayer support this morning. The community can help me with some special intentions I have."

When it came time for the petitions, I included a prayer for my meeting with the bishop. The group was quite attentive when they heard this, and stayed afterwards to ask about my prayer petition.

"Anything special with the bishop?" Margaret asked with some concern. She was aware of the tension between Henry and me at Sunday's Mass.

"Oh, nothing really. I've not had an opportunity to talk with the bishop since he came," I mentioned nonchalantly, not wanting to upset the prayer group, "so this will be a good chance. I'll keep you posted. Have a good day, everyone."

I stayed behind to pray for awhile and then walked home to get ready for the half hour drive to the bishop's office. My mind was filled with conflicting emotions as I reached the highway. What a difference one man can make in such a short time. It's been less than a year since Bishop Foley arrived, but the entire tone of the diocese has changed.

Bishop Gene was such a gift to the people. He trusted his priests and ministers. I definitely don't get that same feeling from Patrick Foley.

My thoughts drifted back to his installation, with all the emphasis on pomp and ritual. He's a likeable and friendly man, but he places such an emphasis on appearances and image. It makes me wonder what's underneath the façade. Strange how the priests and administrators are more on edge and ill at ease than they ever were with Gene.

I began to wonder what would happen at the meeting and what it would mean for my ministry. I hoped he wouldn't clamp down on our liturgies. He'd not even been to visit us. His only basis was hearsay, and not from the best source, I wager.

I arrived just before 10:30, and was led into the bishop's anteroom. Even the offices had changed since my last visit to the chancery. I couldn't quite determine what was different, but they seemed to have a more elegant appearance than in Bishop Gene's era.

"Hello, Kelly," the bishop exclaimed as he strode out of his office and extended his hand. He was smiling and pleasant, but I felt there was a heavy agenda lurking under that pretentious exterior. "Thanks for coming on such short notice, and on your day off besides. I hope this doesn't cause too much inconvenience for you. Is your family well and healthy?"

"Yes, they're all fine," I returned as he ushered me into his office. I noticed the large new desk that dominated the room, and the missing warmth that always filled the office when Bishop Gene occupied it.

"Come in and make yourself comfortable."

I walked into his office, but I was anything but comfortable.

"I've heard all about St. Gabriel's, and that you're doing an excellent job. The people are well-served by your administrating. I must get there one of these days. Father Henry's been telling me about the Sunday liturgy—very responsive congregation, good music, an active group of people."

I nodded, receiving his praise cautiously, realizing that my hunch was correct. Henry had waved the red flag and prompted this meeting. "Yes, they're a wonderful bunch of parishioners."

"I'm aware," the bishop continued, "that some previous liturgical practices had to be curtailed because they didn't conform to Canon Law. Bishop McGovern told me about withdrawing permission for anyone but the priest to read the gospel at the Mass."

I nodded again, remembering how difficult a decision this had been for Gene. When I first arrived, I was allowed to read the gospel on the alternate Sundays when I did the preaching. Then someone— a visitor from out-of-state—complained to Bishop Gene, sending a copy of the letter to Rome. Gene had no choice but to withdraw this concession. The parishioners were not happy, but Gene had to comply. Try as he might, he could find nothing in Canon Law that would permit this practice. So, to keep peace with Rome and not make matters worse in the diocese, he asked me to refrain from reading the gospel. I understood the situation and agreed it was best to accept the Vatican decision.

What touched me most about this incident was what happened the first time I was to preach without having read the gospel. Before Father Mac went to read the gospel, he first came to me and asked *me* for a blessing, just as I had always done with Father Mac before I read. I tried to deny the request but he insisted. With tears in my eyes, I blessed Father Mac as the congregation broke out in applause. That was such a stirring moment for me. It brought the scriptures alive in our midst, especially these words of Jesus, "Lord it over no one. Be the servants of others." Poor Henry could never do that. It wouldn't ever enter his mind. I was afraid that the same might be true for this bishop.

Bishop Foley discussed the Masses at St. Gabriel's. "Father Henry has told me that the lector for the first reading at Mass took liberties with the translation. I'm well aware of their intention to maintain balanced language, but you must realize how sensitive a topic this is just now. The scripture translations are approved texts and are not to be changed by the whim of a lector."

He said all of this in a cordial yet condescending manner, which made it clear that this was not a mutual dialogue, but a mandate issued by a parental figure. I didn't even talk to my own children this way. Although it angered me, I managed to remain silent, just as Gene had counseled.

"Father Henry," the bishop added, "also mentioned that you had some rather strong words in your reflection on the readings that could have been misconstrued to mean that you encouraged unapproved changes in the scripture readings at Mass. In addition, you seemed to have given false hopes to the parishioners that changes in the requirements for ordination might be forthcoming from this new pope. That is not a good precedent for a pastoral administrator. It raises expectations that cannot be fulfilled and puts those of us in authority, Father Henry included, in an awkward position."

The bishop paused, allowing time for me to absorb his words. I tried to stay calm and not let him upset me, but it took a supreme effort. I was so infuriated that I was on the brink of tears. Luckily, I was able to restrain my emotions, trying not to let my expression give me away. I was about to explain the parish's tradition of using inclusive language and the history behind that decision, when the bishop spoke again. I wasn't prepared for what came next.

"Kelly," the bishop went on, still wearing that smile on his face, "I think it best that you not present any more reflections after the gospel. Father Henry will now be doing all the preaching. On alternating Sundays, you may give a short reflection after Communion. That's for your own good, as well as for the congregation's. Otherwise your role as administrator could be in jeopardy. As for the readings at Mass, instruct the lectors to adhere to the texts as written. If anyone has a question about this, Father Henry will be the person to settle any disputes. Do I have your word on this?"

I'm sure my mouth must have fallen open. I couldn't believe what I was hearing. I tried to maintain my composure, but I was dumbfounded. This was completely unexpected. My head was filled with questions. "No more preaching? What will I do? This is my lifeblood, my connection with the community. What will *they* do? How will they respond?" I nodded my head, but it was more a nod of shock than agreement.

"But, Bishop," I stammered. "This is my connection with the community. This is the only place the whole parish gathers together."

"This is my last word on the issue, Kelly," the bishop repeated, rising from his desk to usher me out of his office. It was obvious that the meeting had come to an end. "No reflection after the gospel. No changes to the scriptures."

Before I knew what to say, I was out in the ante-room, shaking hands with the bishop and turning to leave the building. What happened? Was this a dream? In disbelief, I made my way to the car and sat in the driver's seat for a long time, not turning the key in the ignition, just sitting and trying to grasp what had occurred. The clock on the dashboard said 11:00. This had all taken place in less than half an hour. Finally tears of rage began to pour down my cheeks. "God, where are you in all this? How could you let this happen? It's not fair to the people. I don't care about myself, but what about the parishioners!"

The trip home was sobering. I was numb. For a while I felt that I didn't even want to go home. Perhaps I should go somewhere by myself for a few days to sort all this. Then I thought of Tom and the kids. I couldn't disappoint them. Tom will know what to do."

I got home before lunch and found Tom fixing a sandwich for his lunch. He called a greeting to me as I came from the garage. "Want half my turkey sandwich—non-fat mayo?" Then he stopped as he saw my tear-stained face. "Honey, what's the matter? Was it really that bad?"

"Like being kicked in the stomach—no worse, like seeing my *kid* kicked in the stomach. Oh, Tom, it was awful! I'm not sure what I'm going to do."

I sank onto the couch as Tom sat beside me and put his arms around my shoulder. "That bad, huh? Tell me the whole story."

I told him of my "conversation" with the bishop. Tom sighed when I was through.

"It wasn't a conversation; it was an assassination."

"Tom, should I just resign?" I said through my tears. "I'm not sure I can tolerate these restrictions."

"This is not the time for any quick decisions," Tom said reassuringly. "Get some distance. Remember that prayer service you conducted for the election of the new pope. How did it go? 'Faith is the assurance of things hoped for, the conviction of things not seen.' This is the time for some pretty strong faith, my dear. It's out of your hands. Keep hoping and praying for things that seem impossible just now."

"You're right." I sank deeper into Tom's body next to me. After a long moment of his reassuring presence I continued, "Let's have that sandwich and then we can think about the next move. For one thing, I'll need to talk to the Pastoral Council and Liturgy Committee as soon as possible. I'll have to keep them from going to the chancery and stringing up the bishop. At the moment, I feel like supplying them with the rope!"

⌒

"WHAT'S HAPPENING?" Greg, the liturgy chairperson asked as they settled down for prayer. "Why did you call this special meeting, Kelly? Must be important; you've got the pastoral council here, too. Something's brewing."

I sensed the tension and the expectation as I looked around the room. Twenty-one people gazed at me with trusting but quizzical expressions on their faces. I hadn't wasted any time after the bishop's "meeting"/declaration. Almost everyone—staff, council, liturgy committee—was able to gather on Wednesday night. I wanted to share what had happened before the rumor mill began. I was surprisingly calm after a few days of prayer and reflection. The parish and its people are what's important. If I'm an obstacle to them and their faith life, I'd better bow out. Any disagreements between the bishop and me need not upset the parish community, but I understood by the end of the meeting how wrong I was. It was their fight more than it was mine.

After prayer I tried to clarify the conversation I had with the bishop, although "conversation" was hardly an apt description. I saw the stunned reactions as I summarized the implications this would have for the parish liturgies—no inclusive language for the scripture readings, no more preaching by me after the gospel. The leaders could not believe what they were hearing. Some of the men shook their heads, growing angrier by the minute. A few of the women put their hands to their mouths, tears welling in their eyes.

"You mean," Betty, one of the liturgy committee members, asked in disbelief, "you won't be preaching any more?"

"Yes and no. I won't be doing it after the gospel, but I will have time after communion. It won't be the same, but it hasn't been ruled out entirely."

"You're telling us that we can't change the words in the readings anymore?" Larry, a long-time lector asked with bitterness in his voice. "We've done that for five years. It'll sound strange to the congregation to return to the old way, especially now that people realize that God is more than just Father. It's not simply words, it's the way we envision God. You can't change that!"

"I know, Larry, I know," I replied, trying to stem the growing tide of discontent. "But I can't go against the bishop either. That's why I've called you together. I need your support and backing on this. If you, as parish leaders and worship planners accept this, then the rest of the people will also. May I have your word that you won't raise controversy about this? I don't think this is the cause to die for—not yet, anyway."

"Okay, but it's going to be rough," retorted Alice, the pastoral council chairperson. "We'll do what the bishop says, but it won't be easy. I'm not sure how others are going to react. It may not be pretty. How can he do this—no consultation, nothing! Doesn't he know how that will make him seem to the people—like a dictator?"

"That leads to the next thing I'm going to ask of you," I began with some hesitancy. "Not only do I need your support, I need you to quell the reaction of others as well. Be the peacemakers. Discourage any protests, letter writing, or picketing. Let's just swallow this and be ready to fight the really big battles. This isn't one of them. It just means you'll hear me later in the Mass instead of after the gospel. That's not too bad, is it?"

"I don't know," Greg, a council member answered. "It's the principle of the thing. The bishop is demoting you, making you less than the pastor you are. I don't like that. It's not a good precedent. If he gets away with this, what's the next thing he'll take from your position as pastor?"

"Don't worry about that," I said, trying to quiet everyone. "*You* folks are the ones who have made me your pastor, much more so than Bishop Foley. Shifting my preaching from one part of the Mass to another won't change that."

I tried to say this with conviction, but I could feel a lump in my throat. It did indeed feel like a demotion and a threat to my mandate as pastor that Bishop Gene had bestowed upon me five years ago. I glanced at Deb and Carol, my two loyal staff persons, and I could see surprise and anger on their faces. All of a sudden I realized that this was an affront to them as well. We were in this together. They were responding as if the bishop had demanded the same from them. I should have told them about this, instead of waiting until now. I wanted to spare them the burden I felt, but I wasn't very honest or accepting of them. "I'm sorry, you two, for surprising you this way. We'll talk about it later. Please forgive me."

Then I turned to the whole group and said, "Let's do what he says, at least for now, and see how it feels. I'll tell the congregation next Sunday what I've told you. There is no sense hiding anything. In a community of this size everyone will know anyway. And we've always made an effort to be honest with each other."

"Larry, would you please call a meeting of the lectors after Sunday Mass and explain the changes? We have a week's grace period because there's no exclusive language in this Sunday's readings, no 'God the Father' or 'men' without the 'women.' The following Sunday, however, will be a problem. We'll have to help the lectors stay within the text. It will be interesting to see how well they'll do. We may lose some of our best readers, people unwilling to return to where we were a number of years ago. I hope that doesn't happen. You know it's not the end of the world—or of our church. Also, I would appreciate if you would stay quiet about this until Sunday—no phones ringing off the hook or email overloads. That will ensure that everyone will hear the same story. Could I have your word on this?"

The meeting ended early. There wasn't much more to discuss. People gathered in clusters around the room, shaking their heads in disbelief and frustration. Their conversations continued in the parking lot as people walked to their cars. Deb and Carol helped me clean afterwards, hoping to have my complete attention for a moment before leaving.

"Oh dear, oh dear, this is not good!" Deb sighed, as she dumped the coffee grounds into the waste can. "Father Henry could impose his authority here and be highly influential. What would we do then?"

"Stand firm," I retorted, putting my arm around Debbie to ease her pain. "For the moment I'm still in charge around here, at least until I hear otherwise. And the three of us are still a team. But if the bishop decides to take away my pastor's role, the parishioners could get quite upset. That's why we have to play this little game of church politics and be as suave and clever as possible. I'll call Henry in the morning and tell him what's happened, although I'm sure he's well aware of all this."

I walked home that evening with a heavy heart. This was going to be harder than I realized. Dealing with my own emotions was one thing, but coping with everyone else's was another issue. How to prevent the time bomb from erupting would take some effort.

The first thing the next morning I called Henry to tell him about the bishop's requests and the leaders' meeting the previous evening. "Nothing new for this weekend, except the First Communions," I said. "You're doing the preaching. The lectors will all be told to adhere to the texts. I'll take a few minutes at the end when we do the announcements, so everyone knows what to expect at future masses. It only seems fair that everyone be told, and that they hear it from me and not at the local bar or beauty parlor."

I sensed Henry's negative reaction to my candor. However, given the tone of my voice, he knew better than to protest. After all, he now had gained the upper hand. As I hung up the phone I felt a knot in my stomach. Something deep inside told me that this was not going well. It felt as if Henry and I were on a collision course. I had a sudden impulse to call Jerry Cross.

Two

⚜

JERRY CROSS WAS A SIXTY-SOMETHING Jesuit priest presently teaching theology in Detroit. He was a tall, lean, athletic-looking man who exuded a sense of confidence without an arrogant attitude. His eyes were intense, always searching for the inner meaning of things, especially in what someone else was saying. His mouth intrigued me—turned up a bit at the edges so that he always seemed to be smiling, which fit his overall persona quite well. He was sought by both faculty and students for exactly what I needed now—practical and wise counsel. His gift was spiritual direction, helping people see what was happening in their lives, what made sense or no sense, recognizing the graces and the pitfalls. Jerry and I had become good and faithful friends over the years. He once told me, "I get as much direction *from* you as I give *to* you. You're a blessing in my life, a light and solace to my days. Thank you for being *you!*"

I was lucky to catch him in his office when I called. "Hi, Kel," he said with delight in his tone of voice. "What's up?"

"Oh, I'm so glad you're there. Do you have a moment? It's been a rough few days." Saying this, I could see him in my mind's eye settling back in his chair, putting aside his work so he could listen to my concerns. His ability to listen, such a rare gift for a busy person, was one of many things I appreciated about Jerry. I loved this man almost as much as I loved Tom, only in a much different way. This was a mutual relationship—as close as any friendship between a man and woman could be. Jerry touched a unique and vibrant chord within me that no one else had discovered. Even I wasn't aware that it was there until Jerry set it in motion. When we spoke together, there was a joy and ease to our conversation that had no boundaries or limits—heart speaking to heart—and I loved every minute of it, and I was sure he did as well.

I poured out my story of the bishop's demands and the reaction from the parish leadership. He let me speak freely, responding only to ask for clarification of my feelings and reactions to each part of the story. After I had finished he paused.

"You know, Kelly, I have a sense that this is something very important. Watch carefully how events unfold and pay close attention to the little things. They reveal a great deal. Be ready and stay open to whatever is being asked of you. No, no, don't shake your head that way. I can see you right through this phone." Jerry said with a laugh. "The bishop is not a very nice man and he treated you very poorly, that's obvious. But the leaders stood by you, even agreeing to keep the lid on things despite their displeasure. You are the one with real authority there. Use it well. This is the time to rise up and be the pastor you were called to become. Don't be rash; don't be spiteful. Play your cards right; do it for the sake of the people. Let them and the Holy Spirit be your guide." Then he paused again. "Oh, and listen, I have something to share with you."

Forgetting in an instant my own troubles and eager to hear the latest from his busy and eventful life, I blurted out, "What is it, Jerry? Tell me!"

"Well, it's kind of interesting. Just this morning, half an hour before you called, I received an email. It was from an ad hoc committee that is being formed from a coalition of Catholic groups and individuals. They're concerned about the new pope and what he might do about changes needed in the church, especially the ordination issue. You'll read about it in the papers in a day or two. It's just now getting off the ground.

"The word is that Pope John XXIV is not likely to take much initiative on his own. But he does seem to be somewhat responsive to pressure, at least based on stories from his home diocese in southern Italy. So, before the Roman Curia and the conservative block gain a foothold, some American Catholics who feel strongly about the need for a change in the requirements for ordination have decided to hold a huge public rally. They want to manifest this desire for change, show the pope that they are alive and well, and request a hearing on the issue."

"That's great, Jerry! So why did they call you?"

"I'm not sure, really. I guess they think I could lend some credibility to the gathering. They don't want a lot of hotheads making wild demands. Somehow they feel that my reputation as a theologian and a firm believer in reconciliation and common sense might give the rally a legitimacy that will have an impact in Rome."

"Good for you! I quite agree. Did you say yes?" I was now on the edge of my chair as I listened to this good news.

"Actually, I did. I can't believe it," Jerry admitted, sounding somewhat sheepish. "Fool that I am, I felt that I must accept. It just seemed the right thing to do. Somewhere way down inside, I heard a voice say, 'Yes, you can do this.' So I said I would. Ordinarily I would have told them that I would think about it and let them know. Not this time. It could tip the balance for a change I know must happen, and happen soon. Not having enough priests is really catastrophic and I hope this new pope realizes that. If I can persuade him and lend support at the same time, then so be it. I can imagine how alone and beleaguered he must feel about now. We need to show him this is a good change to make, and that he has worldwide, or at least American, support for this."

"Oh, I'm so pleased for you, Jerry, especially that they had the good sense to ask you. I can't think of anyone better suited for the job! So, when and where is the rally?"

"That's the good and bad of it. The good news is that it will be right here in Detroit. The organizers felt that our town was centrally located and had a good convention center facility that was available. It would also serve as a reminder of that historic gathering of bishops and laity in Detroit in 1976 when the people called for a married clergy and women priests. The bishops were so shaken by the people's demands that they tried to put the kibosh on it, but the message was out. And here we are again, calling for the very same thing. This time we will not be denied—the Spirit will not be denied!" I had to pull the phone away from my ear because of how loudly Jerry was speaking. "Sorry, Kel, for getting so excited. Am I getting on my soapbox again?"

"No, actually it's great to hear you speak this way. I love it when you get excited about something. How soon will all this happen?"

"That's the bad news. In order to have the maximum impact, they want to do this quickly. We're talking about *three weeks* from this coming Saturday! Can you believe it? There's an email alert going to thousands of people tomorrow. As soon as they got the approval from the speakers and the confirmation of the hall, they began the arrangements. The organizers are working hard to secure enough hotel rooms for everyone on such short notice."

"The committee—and it's a high-powered coalition of people—is thinking this will stir enough energy and emotion that people will drop everything and come. It's going to last only one day so attendees could arrive and depart the same day, with a follow-up rally scheduled for November. The hope is to keep up the pressure until changes are made. This is more than just talk, Kelly. They really mean business.

"Anyway, the plan is to begin with a monumental opening prayer service in the morning and to finish with a memorable Mass at 4 P.M. Quite a celebration. Plus, since it's going to be the Saturday after Pentecost Sunday, the theme will be "Shaking the Foundations," with the idea that we are in the midst of a new Pentecost. We need enough priests to keep the Eucharistic Body of Christ available for all members of the church, which will only happen if there is a shift in who is eligible for ordination. It made me think of next Sunday's reading from the Acts, 'The rejoicing in that town rose to fever pitch.'"

"I mentioned that same quote at our meeting of the council and liturgy committee Wednesday night," I broke in. "Do you really think it will happen?"

"No doubt about it," Jerry said with assurance. "We could be talking about a very large gathering, perhaps five to ten thousand people. I'm not sure how they're going to pay for it, but I understand some dioceses, with the tacit approval of the bishops, have put up assurance money in case the thing bombs. I don't think it will. I feel in my bones this is going to happen, and it will be very good!

"Now to your part in this . . ."

My ears perked up. What does he mean by that?

"*My* part?" I said with surprise. "I'd be glad to help in any way I can, but this is out of my league. I'll come, for sure, but I'll be more than content to bring my family and perhaps a cake and leave it at that, thank you very much." But I knew he had something more in mind.

"Nice try," Jerry retorted, "but you're a natural. I thought of you as soon as I read the email. What about you and I doing this *together*? You won't need to prepare a thing. I'll just tell your story. I'll talk about there not being any Scriptural impediment to a free and open ordination that includes both men and women. Then I would tell them about your pastoring at St. Gabe's as a symbol and manifestation of what thousands of men and women who are not ordained are doing across the country. You smile, look confident, which you do so well, and the place will go wild."

"Hey, stop right there, mister!" I snapped back. "If, and I mean *if* I do this, which I can't imagine that I will, I'll not just stand there and smile as you tell *my* story. Can you imagine, Jerry, how that would look? If I agree to do this," I said, my annoyance rising with each word, "I will speak, ever so briefly, but I will speak on my *own* behalf!"

"Well, yes, of course. I see your point," Jerry agreed apologetically. "So, as I was saying, the place will go nuts, not because of *you* but because of all the others whom they know are doing what you are doing on a daily basis. There's no reason on earth you shouldn't be acclaimed by your people and ordained by your bishop, as should so many others like you. They will see in you how reasonable and necessary this all is, simple as that!"

"Simple for *you*, maybe," I objected, still trying to comprehend what Jerry was proposing. "But remember, I just got my pastoral wings clipped. The bishop and I are going in opposite directions at the moment, in case you had forgotten. Can you imagine what Patrick Foley would say if he saw me up there before that crowd? I think not. I don't want to lose my job—not yet!"

"I knew you'd resist, Kel," Jerry replied. "It's normal for you to respond this way. It's who you are. You haven't asked for this, you don't hanker for ordination. You're just going about your duties as a pastoral administrator, stepping in to fill a gap that has been left vacant because there are no more priests available. That's precisely the reason you *should* be the representative.

"I don't know," I responded weakly, feeling somewhat cornered. "This has all been so unexpected and so sudden. I just called for a little advice and support and now you dump *this* on me. A lot of help you are!"

"Well, think it over," Jerry said reassuringly. "Give me a call in a few days. Somehow I have the feeling that you know deep inside—and I can say this because you have revealed so many of your thoughts and feelings to me—that this is right for you. It's like the burning bush Moses encountered in Exodus. He was such a klutz and on top of that he stuttered, yet God chose him above all others to lead the people out of Egypt. Kelly, this same God may be making a similar call to you. Don't deny the grace of this moment. The Spirit is in you, clear as anything. Your presence will be the highlight of the rally!"

Feeling worse rather than better, I hung up the phone. The parish was about to explode in open revolt, the bishop was after my hide, the visiting priest despised me and now Jerry Cross wanted *me* to stand in front of thousands of people and say to the pope, "Hey, why not ordain women while you're at it!" Talk about fanning the flames of rebellion.

Throughout the rest of the day my thoughts returned to Jerry's request of joining him at the rally. I was of two minds. Turning him down was by far the more prudent thing to do. My job would not be in jeopardy nor my lifestyle disrupted. On the other hand, there was a prompting toward saying yes. Someone should take the risk of raising the issue and representing all those who served in parishes with little support or affirmation.

I finally decided that the best way to resolve the issue was to ask my family what they thought. If I did say yes it would mean an enormous change for them as well. They should have a chance to share in the decision.

After serving tuna casserole, and everyone started eating, I cleared my throat and announced to the tribe, "Wait until I tell you about my day. You can pass along the 'ultra-crazy' title to your mom. In fact, I really need your help with this. I spent some time on the phone with Father Jerry this morning. He told me about a big rally that is going to take place in Detroit. The purpose is to raise the ordination issue so the new pope will be aware of just how many people are looking for change."

"Can we go, Mom?" Rachel, her mouth full of food, blurted out, breaking the seriousness of the moment. "That is *so* cool. Will this mean I can become a priest when I grow up?"

"Not so fast, Honey. Let your Mom finish," Tom said, obviously concerned about what might be coming next. "I think she has more to share." Then he turned back to me and asked suspiciously, "So what else did Jerry say?"

"Ah, yes, there is more," I continued, not wanting to look Tom in the eye. "Not only did he think we—all of us—should attend, but he also has been asked by the organizers to offer his own ideas about ordination from a theological perspective. And get this! He wants *me* to join him on the stage as a person representing all those who are pastoring parishes without the benefits of being ordained."

"Wow, Mom, that's really something!" Michael broke in. "Are you going to do it? Will there be television and all? What are you going to say?" This was vintage Michael, the great risk-taker, full steam ahead, forget the costs. His bright, freckled face of 14 was full of anticipation.

"Whoa, I've not said I would do it yet," holding up my hand to ward off Michael's questions. "I wanted to discuss it with all of you first. I've not told anyone else. It could be very disruptive to our lives if this thing is a big success and lots of people attend. I have to call Father Jerry back soon with my answer. What do you think I should do?"

"Well, Honey, I'm not so sure," Tom said, trying to get his thoughts together and consider future implications. "You could lose your job over this. Is it really worth it? We've sunk a lot into this town over the last five years. Are we ready to pull up stakes and move?"

"No, Mom, not now," Michael pleaded, a pained look on his face.

"I'm really getting into the band now and I'm finally having some fun in this hick town. I never thought I would say this, but I'm getting used to this place."

"Listen to you, my great protester. When did all this happen?" I laughed at his sudden change of attitude.

"Don't tell anyone," Michael said, looking around at his brother and sister in a beseeching tone of voice, "but I really like it here."

"And you like Jeannie, too," Rachel said with a teasing sneer. "I heard you talking on the phone with her."

"Stop eavesdropping!" Michael shouted, casting a withering glance at Rachel. "Mom, make her stop!"

"Okay, okay, back to the issue. Do I or don't I?"

"What do *you* want to do?" Tom said, trying to determine which way I was leaning. "What feels right to you, Kel? We'll back you up on this." Rachel, Nathan and Michael nodded in agreement.

Nathan, assuming his role as the eldest, simply said, "Mom, it's up to you. Do what you think is best."

"To tell you the truth, I'm not sure what that is. The inclination is definitely there. I suppose if I let Bishop Foley in on it first, not asking permission, but giving him fair warning, it wouldn't go so badly. He won't like it, but it may make him and the diocese look important. I think I can play up to his need to look good and have a wider reputation beyond the diocese. If I did that, and he was at least civil, I might give it a try. I'll only have a minute or so. I doubt I can mess things up too badly in that amount of time."

"I don't know," Tom said, shaking his head apprehensively. "It could go badly, even if it is only a couple of minutes long."

I could feel myself tensing. I think without realizing it, I had already consented to do it. Tom's resistance was difficult to hear. "Tom, I think I need to do this, not just for myself, but for all the others in my position. Do you think I'm crazy?"

"Well, if you put it that way, I guess I must concur," Tom replied, hearing resolve in my voice. "What do you say, kids?"

"Go for it, Mom!" all three chimed together.

Knowing that Tom was not entirely comfortable with this decision, I instinctively asked everyone to join hands around the table and say a prayer. "Loving God," I began, "be good and gentle with us. Help us do what's best. And keep us all safe and sound and pleasing to you."

"Amen," the rest responded, the children somewhat surprised by the serious tone.

Then, in an abrupt change of mood, I announced that to affirm our pact together, I had made apple pie for dessert. I decided, no matter what the decision, we would need to celebrate.

"All right!" the children chanted. As I got up to get the pie, Tom followed me into the kitchen. He gave me an inquiring look.

"This could be big, couldn't it?" he said as he got the vanilla ice cream out of the freezer.

"Yes, very big, and it happens in just three weeks," I reminded him as I cut the pie. "We'll have to turn on the television after dinner to see if it hit the regional news yet."

As Jerry predicted, the Detroit Rally was the third item on the local news. "This is going to be some event," Tom said. "Even I recognize some of the names on the program; not a small fry among them. This makes me even more wary about you saying yes to Jerry."

Neither of us said much more about the rally for the rest of the evening, but I could sense Tom's concern. I delayed calling Jerry with my answer. Preparing for the Sunday liturgy occupied my mind. I was still debating what I would say to the parishioners about the bishop's wishes and didn't have time now to consider the Detroit Rally.

~

MORE PEOPLE THAN USUAL showed up for the Sunday Mass. Perhaps someone on the council or liturgy committee had leaked the information. Greeting people as they entered told me otherwise. They could tell something was amiss but didn't know what was brewing. Perhaps the word had gone out to show up Sunday because something important was going to be announced. A few people had asked if I had seen the news about the Detroit Rally and whether any arrangements were being made to send down a contingent from St. Gabriel's.

Father Henry arrived later than usual and said little to me as we both vested in the sacristy, he in his chasuble and stole, I in my long white alb. He gave a decent homily, and Mass progressed as usual until the time for announcements after communion. The commentator encouraged people to join the first communicants and their families outside for refreshments and pictures, then mentioned the upcoming meetings of both the women's club and the outreach committee. Finally he handed the microphone to me for one further announcement. Everyone was watching closely as I stepped to the front of the congregation, especially the members of the pastoral council and liturgy committee who knew what was coming.

"I will make this brief so we can get to the celebrations that follow," I said with a serious look that was unusual for me. Normally, I liked to make a joke or two during the announcements as a way to keep the congregation attentive and interested in parish events. "I had a meeting with Bishop Foley this last Monday," I began, "and he has made a few requests that will somewhat change our Sunday morning worship."

Those who were putting on their coats in the pews stopped to listen.

"He asked that we not make changes in the scripture readings as we have in the past. As you know, there has been controversy and differences of opinion, even among bishops, over this in recent years. Bishop Foley asked that from now on we abide by the American bishops' directives on this matter." I could see the quizzical looks of the parishioners turning into frowns. Except for a few of the more conservative members of the congregation who had smiles on their faces, the majority was not pleased one bit.

"I assured him that we would comply," I continued. "There will be a special meeting of all the lectors to work out the details this morning right after coffee and donuts. It will begin at 10:30 in the parish hall." People looked at each other as they began to understand my words. "Second, the bishop asked that I not do any preaching after the gospel. Every other week, I will be adding my reflections after communion just before the announcements. Bishop Foley felt this would clarify the distinction between the priest's homily and the pastoral administrator's reflections. I agreed to do this as well."

A ripple of disbelief moved through the congregation, which soon turned to grimaces, shaking heads and low murmurs of disapproval, and their palpable reaction had an unexpected emotional effect on me. With as strong a voice as I could muster, fighting back tears, I continued. "I assured the bishop that the people of St. Gabriel's would accept his wishes and live within these requirements. You are a great group of people. This is a parish of more than just outward observances. It's a faith community of friends and believers. That's what really matters. Let's all make the best of this and grow through the experience. Now let's go outside to celebrate those who have received Jesus in Holy Communion for the very first time." I returned to my chair and tried to keep my composure. But try as I might, I couldn't control the shaking in my limbs.

Father Henry gave the final blessing to conclude the Mass and people filed out of church to the strains of the closing song. Outside, however, the mood was not so festive.

"How could he do this to us?" Frank, the head usher, said to me after everyone had filed out of church. "It's such a slap in the face.

Bishop Gene would never have treated us this way. Isn't there anything we can do?"

"Not at the moment," I responded, putting my hand on his shoulder to console him. I could feel the depth of his frustration. "Let's see how this works over the next few weeks, shall we? We may find we like it better this way, who knows?"

And he was just the first of many. I kept fending off questions and angry comments during the coffee and donuts' social until it was time for the lectors' meeting. Father Henry couldn't attend, since he had to return to his own parish for Mass. He was noticeably distant and unresponsive to me, both before and after the liturgy. Nor did the parishioners make him feel welcome. Somehow they knew he had something to do with this sudden change in the routine.

The lectors gathered in the parish hall, fuming at what I had announced and wanting to register some kind of protest. Ordinarily I would not attend this meeting, leaving these matters to Greg, the person in charge of the lectors. But I came to this meeting to act as a calming agent. I knew how upset everyone would be by this news. Greg began with a short prayer, asking God for patience and understanding. Then he opened the meeting by stating, "As much as you would have liked to have been consulted before this change happened—as would I—such was not the case. Let's face it, folks, this decision will not change, no matter how much we protest. We'll have to live with it and figure out how best to maintain an inclusive attitude towards scripture, even though we will be required to read only what is written in the text."

"Forced, is more like it," Agnes, one of the lectors, chimed in. "I'm not sure I can stand there and read 'men' when I myself am excluded from the reading."

The room erupted into comments from all quarters, resulting in a groundswell to resign *en masse* and not have any readings—just silence. I stood and tried to quell the outbreak, but people were too upset to listen to reason. Then, as people were about to quit and stomp out of the meeting, Henrietta, a lector of many years, stood and waited for the room to quiet. Then she asked me, "What would happen if, when we get to a place where we would ordinarily change a word, we just read what was written and then paused for a moment to let the congregation add their own words? Would that be permitted?" The others perked up to listen, wondering what she had in mind. She continued, "For instance, if the reading said, 'Go out and become fishers of all men,' what if we were to pause while others in the congregation, all on their own, mind you, added 'and women.' Could we do that?"

"Sure, I suppose so," I replied with an inquisitive look that soon turned into a smile once I understood where Henrietta was heading. "I never thought of it, but you certainly wouldn't be changing the texts. Whatever people added on their own would be up to them."

The rest of the lectors clapped their hands and congratulated Henrietta for her ingenuity. They all agreed to give it a try and see if people caught on to what was happening. People began leaving with smiles on their faces, now that they were feeling better about themselves and their new strategy. I held up my hand to get their attention so I could make a final comment.

"Don't be too hard on Father Henry," I cautioned, "or on those parishioners who might welcome this new regulation. They're part of our community as well. You know, of course, that some who attend church here are a bit traditional and had a hard time when we changed the readings to fit what we felt was more inclusive. As for Father Henry, I'm not sure how he'll react. He may think this was all *my* idea. But don't worry, I can handle that. Just don't push this into his face, if you get my drift. Give him some room to maneuver. Be gentle, not vindictive. There are many ways of doing this that are both prayerful and reconciling. There are also ways that could be stubborn and hurtful. Do your best to keep the spirit of the scriptures intact. Remember what it says there, 'Love one another. Love your enemies and those who persecute you.' What do you say?" The lectors all nodded in agreement. "This should be interesting," I added as they got up to leave. "And remember, for some of those attending church, your reading of the scriptures may be their only connection with the Bible for the whole week. Do it well."

I walked home feeling proud of the parishioners and their creativity. I came into the house amid smells of a Sunday breakfast in the making.

"You were good, Mom," Michael said as he flipped some wheat cakes. "But the people weren't too happy. How did the lectors' meeting go?"

"Very well, actually," I said, handing my son an apron to wear over his Sunday best. "You'll be surprised with what they decided. Stay tuned, or better yet, come to church next Sunday and see what happens."

Tom and I went for a walk after the meal to take in the rays of the warm spring sunshine and to sort out the experiences of the past week. "Some people just go for a walk, nothing more," I laughed, taking Tom's arm.

"You, on the other hand," Tom retorted, "have had enough excitement in one week to fill an entire diary. Start with an unsettling meeting with your bishop and a tense meeting with the pastoral council and liturgy committee. Throw in a rather astounding request to address a massive rally in Detroit and cap it off with a near mutiny by your lectors. I'd say you deserve some combat pay."

"That's a lot, now that you mention it," I acknowledged, enjoying this special time with him. We walked in silence, taking in the sights of the cozy neighborhood, people washing cars, clipping bushes, cleaning garages, clearing flower beds for spring planting. But finally Tom said what was on both of our minds.

"I don't mean to be contrary, but I'm concerned for you, Kelly. Speaking at that rally could lead to all your work and ministry being annihilated in one blazing moment of glory."

"Oh, Tom, I know and I'm scared, too," I said, stopping to look into his eyes. "But I just feel I have to do this. I'm not sure why, but I'm drawn to it, like it's my destiny or something."

"Yes, like a moth to a candle, just before getting burned to a crisp. Go easy, gal, go easy with this," Tom cautioned, putting his hand on the back of my neck, which always sent shivers down my spine. "This is all very heady stuff. Your real gift, you know, is being of service here, in this town and to this group of people. Beware of jeopardizing that foundation."

"I won't. At least I hope I won't," I responded, thankful for Tom's touch and concern. "That's why you're here, to keep me honest and clear-sighted. This town is such a pretty place, especially now with all the tulips and daffodils about ready to blossom. Let's keep it that way, no changes, no problems, no long hot summer to follow."

"Yeah, right. Don't I wish. What a dreamer you are," Tom said with his characteristic chuckle. "I don't know why, but this whole thing worries me a lot. It has trouble written all over it."

Although not convinced, Tom was becoming resigned to my decision to participate in the rally, and I could feel his resistance soften as he put his trust in my judgment, flawed though it might be. We walked home arm in arm.

I called Bishop Foley on Monday morning to tell him about my decision to speak at the rally. It went better than I had anticipated. Although he was upset that I was participating in the rally, he must have gotten a few positive calls from other bishops not to interfere. The Catholic Conference of Michigan, which included all the bishops from the State, was not endorsing the rally, but it had agreed to allow it to proceed as planned. The bishops also agreed not to make any negative statements to the press or to tell the parishes that their parishioners were not allowed to attend. When I mentioned that I might be on stage as a representative of all the pastoral administrators, the bishop sighed and said in response, "Why am I not surprised?" That was the extent of what he had to say to me. I took that as a positive response and thought back to what Jerry had mentioned, "Pay attention to the little things."

This is one of those little things that's not so small after all, I thought to myself as I hung up the phone. I guess this means I should go ahead and do it. "Throw caution to the winds and take a leap of faith," I say.

Wednesday morning was the monthly gathering of the ten pastoral administrators in the diocese. All of them were in charge of a parish in the absence of a priest. I headed to the meeting with some trepidation, knowing that the word had spread about the bishop's mandates at St. Gabriel's. It could be a monumental meeting knowing that their futures were on the line. I wasn't sure whether I should tell them about my decision to take part in the rally. There would be so much to discuss already. I didn't want to appear special or arrogant. At the very least I could encourage the others to attend. Maybe we could even hire a bus and make it a party.

As I walked into the meeting, Gloria, one of the administrators, pulled me aside and asked, "What's this I hear about you not being able to preach after the gospel. Is it true? And if so, what's likely to happen to the rest of us? Will we be removed one by one? We need to hear your side of the story. Everyone I've talked to about this is greatly concerned. We've put you on the agenda. Take as much time as you like, Kel. This is too important to keep limited to a short time slot."

"Well, I'll do what I can," I remarked, aware of the woman's emotion. I had been her mentor when she first took a parish a few years ago and she still considered me one of the leaders in the group. "Thanks for giving me some time to discuss it."

As I took my place around the table I noticed that not only were all ten administrators present, but five priests as well. I was happy to see Father Mac, the one who came to celebrate the masses at St. Gabe's before Henry. How nice of him to come, I thought. I waved a greeting to him down the table. I supposed he guessed I would be on the agenda from all the rumors that were circulating.

The meeting was tame until it was my turn to talk. I had everyone's utmost attention. I began by explaining what the bishop had requested, omitting my suspicions that Father Henry was the whistleblower. The reaction from the administrators was similar to that of St. Gabe's congregation. Disbelief, anger, and a resolve to protest filled the room.

"We can't let this go uncontested," one administrator remarked to the affirmative nods of others in the room.

"We'll be next," a religious sister interjected. "This won't stop until each of us is demoted to assistant to the priest who comes in to say Mass. No longer will we be considered pastors. It will quickly return to 'Father knows best,' I'm sure of it."

"I disagree," another stated. "It's best not to make a big thing of this. You didn't say so, Kelly, but I'll bet Henry Cimanski had something to do with all this. We all know how he feels about you being the pastoral administrator and about his lack of control at St. Gabe's. Besides, he's a close buddy of the bishop's—disciple is more the word. At my place, Father Bob wouldn't want to preach at every liturgy. He'd rather have me do it all. He has plenty to handle at his own parish."

The debate continued, until the chairperson called a halt to the discussion. "This is going nowhere," she interrupted. "Let's think and pray about this. Then come back next month with clearer heads to

settle on a strategy about what our next steps might be. In the meantime, Kelly will have a better idea about how it feels, both for herself
and for the parishioners. She's still the pastor at St. Gabe's. Don't forget that! Anything more to share, Kelly?"

"Yes, as a matter of fact I do have something else I'd like to share
about an entirely new topic." I glanced around the table, making
eye contact with each person. "I want to alert you to an Ordination Rally taking place in Detroit in a few weeks. I'm wondering if
any of you was thinking of going and whether we should charter
a bus." Faces brightened around the room with the suggestion. "It
could be a big event," I continued, glad for the positive reaction after
the gloom of the previous discussion. "It would be fun traveling
together. I think my family is going, too, and maybe some parishioners. Anyone interested?"

Hands shot up around the room. It surprised me how eager
they were. "Great idea," the chairperson interjected. "How about a
few of you volunteering to act as a committee to gather names and
arrange for the buses. Those with Saturday evening masses will have
to make arrangements with your Mass priest and the congregation. I
already know people at my place who want to attend, and it was only
announced a few days ago. Talk it up, folks. Let's show Detroit what
we're made of and how much we want the pope to make changes. I
certainly hope he's listening."

Much to my relief, the meeting concluded on a high note. I
didn't want my situation in the parish to depress the entire group.
The rally was just the positive spark the administrators needed to
keep spirits high.

I headed to the parish to start preparing for Sunday's liturgy,
the Feast of the Ascension. The readings talked about spreading the
Good News to the ends of the earth, so fitting for the coming rally.
I looked at the first passage from the Acts of the Apostles. "Men of

Galilee," it said, "why do you stand here looking up at the skies?" It seemed so ridiculous to read that phrase when the scriptures talked about a mixed group of men and women witnessing the Resurrection and Ascension. I wonder what the lector will do with that one. "This should be interesting," I thought to myself.

On Sunday morning Greg, the head of the lectors, had chosen to read, and he did very well until he got to the part that said, "Men . . ." at which point he paused. The congregation looked up, stopped and thought for a moment, and then almost in unison responded out loud, "and women!" Then Greg, a broad smile breaking over his face, continued, "of Galilee . . ."

The congregation smiled back, surprising themselves with their response. I couldn't help chuckling to myself as I looked at Father Henry, who appeared simultaneously glum and nonplused. When it was his turn to read the gospel, he quickly checked to see if there was any compromising language. Relieved that there wasn't, he proclaimed the reading, but was too flustered to make any comments of his own. I made a mental note of this and decided to add something extra to my reflections after Communion.

When it was time for me to speak, I talked about a recent visit I had made to the little Mexican migrant community that lived next to a field some distance out of town. "I was so impressed by their simple and direct faith," I said. "Those are the ones who are spreading the gospel of peace, forgiveness and healing, all against great odds." I could feel the emotion growing in my voice. "They have so much to teach us about family, community living and sharing with one another. We Americans get so absorbed in our own little worlds and tight schedules. We can't live without the latest gadgets and all the extra stuff that fill our lives. We have lost the art of a modest lifestyle and communal bonding. Those Mexican migrants are spreading the good news that Jesus talks about in today's gospel. Each of us is called to simplify our lives, to be a healer to others and to reveal the good news of today's gospel in the way we live.

"In a few weeks there will be a concrete opportunity to do just that. On Saturday, two weeks from yesterday, there will be a large gathering of Catholics from around the country. They will meet in Detroit in a show of unity and solidarity, not only for the new pope but for changes in the church to deal with the shortage of priests. There is a sign-up sheet in the back of church for those who would like to attend. We're planning to charter a bus if there is enough interest. Remember what it says in today's gospel: 'Why do you stand here looking up at the skies?" Folks, it's time to spread the good news! Detroit might be just the place to do that."

I took my seat beside Father Henry and could feel his discomfort. He concluded Mass and walked down the aisle so quickly that I couldn't keep up with him. As I was saying goodbye to the parishioners, inviting them to join us for refreshments in the basement, I could see him trying to get my attention, and, with a nod, I indicated I would meet him in the sacristy in a few minutes.

Those whom I greeted at the door seemed to appreciate my comments, adjusting well to the new format of my reflections after Communion. A few mentioned that they enjoyed filling in the blank spaces during the readings. "It keeps us much more alert," one older woman noted. "I'm going to go home right now and look up next week's readings so I'll be ready. Do you think this is what Bishop Foley had in mind?" giving me a wink as she shook my hand.

By the time I got returned to the sacristy, Henry had taken off his vestments. His face was crimson. "What right do you have to mock the scriptures?" he began in a rage. "You have made the readings into a farce. The very idea of people shouting 'and women' in the midst of the scriptures is mob psychology and you are behind this. I know you are! And then, encouraging people to attend that radical rally in Detroit. This is an abomination! The bishop will hear about this. Yes, he will, and he will not be pleased! I don't know how I can continue to preside in this church so long as you act in such a disrespectful and obstinate manner."

"I'm sorry you feel this way, Henry, really I am. I certainly hope there's room for both of us here at Gabriel's. Today's feast is one of unity, not division."

"Call me by my proper title, if you don't mind," he barked, grabbing his alb and stalking out the side door.

Ouch, I said to myself. That was not pretty. There goes one more reason for the bishop to get angry at me. And I wasn't even the initiator this time. He's going to love seeing me on the stage in Detroit, about as much as Michael likes Rachel teasing him about his girlfriend.

After putting away my alb, I headed downstairs for a cup of coffee and to help with the cleanup afterwards. I'd not told anyone except the family about my part in the rally, not even the other two on staff.

Both Carol and Debbie were greeting people. "Better now than never," I thought, looking for a chance to be alone with the two of them. After everyone had gone, I sat down with them both, something we often did at the end of the Sunday social.

"I've been keeping something from you that you should know." The two of them gave each other a questioning glance.

"My good friend, Father Jerry Cross, is going to be one of the speakers at the Detroit Rally," I began. "And he has asked me to be on the stage with him representing all the non-ordained pastoral administrators from across the country."

"Kelly!" Deb exclaimed, her hand over her mouth. "Are you really going to do it? I can't believe it!" She leaped up to give me a hug while Carol, waiting her turn, started to clap her hands in excitement.

"This is *so* great!" Deb continued. "Why didn't you tell us sooner!

Now the whole parish will want to come. Wait until I get the word out about *this*! You devil, you. What are you going to say?"

"Nothing. I'll just stand there and grin my head off and that will take care of the ordination issue." I laughed as I tried to regain my composure after their outburst. "That way *no one* will want to be ordained! To be honest, I don't know *what* I will say. I only have a minute or so. Jerry will do most of the talking. He's the theologian, the expert they asked to speak. But do you really think it's a good idea to tell the parishioners about this?" I said with a frown. "Henry's already fuming about what happened at Mass this morning."

"Are you kidding!" Debbie interjected. "Yes, of course it is. They *need* to know so they can be as proud of you as we are. This will lift their spirits after what the bishop did to you. Does Foley know yet?"

"Yes, I told him Monday and he was pretty good about it, actually. I think some bishops he admires are behind this. They know better than anyone what a predicament we're in with no priests. I don't think he's very pleased about me being up there, though. He's worried about how I'll come across and how this will affect his image and reputation among the other bishops. I hope to make him—and all of us—proud."

"That you'll do, I have no doubt about it," Carol said with obvious joy and elation. "To think we once knew you when you were a lowly pastoral administrator."

"Stop that!" I shouted.

Just then my cell phone began to chime. When I looked at the number on the screen it was unfamiliar to me. I gave the other two a shrug and pushed the button. "Hello, how may I help you?"

"I took a chance at catching you," the deep voice replied. "It's Bishop Foley. Father Henry gave me your cell number." I grimaced as I sensed a guardedness in his tone. "I'm sorry to bother you on a Sunday, but I was thinking about what you shared with me concerning the rally. I'm wondering whether it might be better that you *not* be on the program. It could be read the wrong way and it might backfire for you and for the diocese as well."

I exhaled, pulling the phone away from my mouth so the bishop would not hear my reaction. "I quite understand your feelings, Bishop," I said, raising my eyebrows as I looked over to Carol and Deb. Both of them had their hands on either side of their faces expecting the worst. "But I'm afraid the die is cast. After talking with you on Monday I gave my consent to Father Cross. I can't go back on my word now." Kelly winked to the other two in the room. "I'll do my best to be a credit to all concerned. Please pray for me."

"Ah, yes. So be it," the bishop responded with resignation in his voice. "I only hope we won't all regret this someday," and he hung up before I could say another word.

THREE

THE WEEKS BEFORE THE RALLY were a whirl of activity. The media coverage was intense. The organizers were doing a good job keeping the controversy before the public's eye, and various reactionary groups were increasing the furor by announcing an anti-rally in Detroit to register their anger and outrage that people who called themselves Catholics would even think of staging such a spectacle. "Didn't the last two popes say women's ordination should never even be discussed?" they asked. "This is a national affront to their memory and teachings."

The *Sarah Sentinel* interviewed me about my appearance on the program and published my picture on the front page, after which strangers stopped me in the supermarket and at the gas station, asking me about the rally and pledging their support. Most seemed to have a positive attitude, although some of the more conservative families in the parish began to ignore me and turned a cold shoulder.

"I don't know where all this will end," I said to Deb one day in the office. "I haven't even said a word yet and already people are quoting me. How can they do that?"

"They're quoting the *concept* of you," Debbie replied. "It's what they hope you will or will not say. You don't even need to show up at the rally. You're already present in their minds, big as life, either as their hero or enemy. By the way, Carol told me that the announcement of a bus going to the rally is getting a huge response. Almost fifty parishioners have registered and already paid in advance. We may need to charter more buses. Isn't that wonderful?!"

"I'm not so sure," I responded with some foreboding. "I'm getting concerned about how fast this is picking up momentum. I somewhat wish I had turned Jerry down. He doesn't have a spouse and three kids to consider. How can I protect my family from all this frenzy? Rachel said last night that kids in her grade school were asking her questions she had no idea how to answer. It's making her feel self-conscious and wary. And that's not like Rachel at all. I think it's cramping her carefree and spontaneous spirit. I'll have to have a talk with the family. I need to prepare them, as best as I can, for what may happen."

That evening around the dinner table I tried to explain to the children what to do when the press called for information, and made them promise they wouldn't volunteer anything, but refer the call to Tom or me. "The less you say the better," Tom remarked. "They can get you pretty frazzled if you're not careful. And one more thing, let's try to pick up after ourselves these days to take the burden off your mom. Everyone will have to pitch in with the housework and the meals. Anything to make it easier for her would be appreciated. Understood?"

"Sure, Dad," the three said in unison.

Tom helped me clean up after supper, wanting the chance to talk about the rally. "I don't know, Tom," I began as I stacked the dishes in the washer. "Do you think I'm stupid to do this? Is it really fair to the rest of you?"

"I wasn't too hot on this in the beginning, but it wouldn't be very fair to all the people rooting for you if you pulled out at this late date. Did you notice how proud the kids are of you? You can see it on their faces. Come what may, we're behind you. Get up there, my dear, and tell your story," Tom said, drying his hands after washing the pans. He took hold of my shoulders and looked me in eye. "Actually, this whole thing is pretty wild. Keep your wits about you, Kel, and you'll be just fine. Just know that when you need someone to lean on, I'll be right there behind you. Don't forget that!"

⁓

SATURDAY FINALLY ARRIVED and the kids were excited. "Do you think the things I chose to wear are going to work, Tom?" I asked, as I was getting dressed. "I'm so nervous about this whole thing. And look at my hair! Wait until I get hold of that Jerry fellow. I'll wait until *after* he talks, and *then* I'll strangle him."

"Go easy. You'll do just fine," Tom said reassuringly. "Jerry knew what he was doing when he asked you to do this. You are the *perfect* person for it. First of all, no one would accuse you of hankering after ordination. At the same time, you were born to be a pastor. You should be given all the tools to do it well."

"Thank you, Thomas," I said, trying to be sincere, but I was too distracted as I ran back and forth between the bathroom and the bedroom. "So, which dress?" holding three candidates.

"Wear the black one," Tom suggested, amused at my lack of focus. "That seems appropriate for the occasion. Come on, now. Hurry! We'll have to hustle if we're going to catch the bus."

We grabbed our food baskets and drove to the church just as people were boarding the buses. Everyone clapped, and those still in their cars honked as they saw us arrive. It was so embarrassing. To make matters worse, a huge banner was stretched along the side of the bus—"Ordination Rally or Bust." Someone had drawn a red X through rally, so that the message was more direct.

"You folks are ready, I can see that," I exclaimed, as I saw the sign. "Only leave me out of it!"

The people responded by shouting, "Kel-ly, Kel-ly, Kel-ly!"

"This is going to be one very long day," I yelled to Tom over the racket.

The bus ride into Detroit was playful, but there was also a sense of purpose, like heading to the foreign mission fields. Some of the parishioners had made signs that they planned to wave while I was onstage.

"Kelly More is our pastor." "Kelly More for priesthood." "Ordain her now—she's our priest."

"Heaven help us," I joked as I saw all the preparations. "This is going to be much harder than I realized."

There were four buses from the diocese filled with pastoral admin-istrators, some priests, parish staff members and parishioners from different parishes, all heading to the rally. St. Gabriel's had by far the largest contingent. Despite my misgivings at all this notoriety, I was very pleased and proud of our parishioners and my fellow ministers.

"What a great crowd," Tom said amid the din of the crowded bus. "This has to make a difference to the pope and the powers that be."

When we arrived in downtown Detroit, the streets were clogged with traffic. It took an hour to travel from the outskirts of town to the parking area. Those with cars had an even more difficult time. All the parking lots were filled with buses or vehicles of those who had come a day early. The parishes around Detroit threw open their doors to accommodate the extra people, as well as providing shuttle service to the convention center.

Those attending the rally were well-behaved; they were mostly just ordinary folks. The police kept the anti-rally protestors at a distance. Their own counter-rally was being held farther out of town, so the number causing a scene at the convention center was minimal.

The five of us bid goodbye to the parishioners and made our way to a special entrance for speakers and special guests. "Wow, Mom,"

Rachel shouted over the noise of the crowd, "this is great. We'll be right up front. Cool!"

"Cool, indeed," I responded, taking her by the hand. "I'm ready to burn up with anxiety and nerves and you say 'cool.' Listen, kids, if we get separated, we'll meet at the bus, okay? You remember how to get there, I hope. Look for the *Sarah #4* in the window."

Music was playing while we were ushered to our seats. The prayer service was still thirty minutes away, but already the massive arena was filling. It had been equipped with huge screens so that those on stage were magnified many times over.

"Good heavens," I gasped. "I'm going to be as big as life up there. Not sure this was such a good idea."

"Not so fast," Jerry said from behind. "I've got my eye on you."

"Oh, hi." I turned to find Jerry sitting right behind us. "Have you been here long?"

"Got here just before you. Hi, Tom. Rachel, you look great. And Nathan and Michael, good to see you could both make the trip." Turning back to me, Jerry added, "Isn't this something! It looks as if it will be bigger than expected. They're setting up screens in breakout areas to take care of the overflow. We're talking 10,000 or more. Can you imagine? This is an event whose time has come. All this in just three weeks. This is what email and the Internet have wrought."

We settled into our seats as one music group after another came on stage. People were in a festive mood, many waving signs and placards, each trying to get a message across and catch the attention of the television cameras. Most of the signs were directed to Pope John XXIV, but a number of groups used the occasion to advocate other causes. What was amazing about the gathering, other than its sheer size, was the spirit of hope and solidarity in the hall. People had a sense that this would make a difference. I wondered whether such hopes were premature. There had been no indication from either Rome or the new pope that any changes were in the works.

"I surely hope," I said to Jerry, turning to talk to him over the din of the music, "this is not an exercise in futility. There will be a lot of disgruntled and alienated people if that's the outcome."

"Kelly," he shouted back in my ear, "the Spirit will not be denied. And there's a whole lot of Spirit alive in this room! Hey, kids. Aren't you proud of your mom?"

"Not so fast, Jerry. I've not done anything yet. Let's wait and see how it all turns out."

Ten o'clock came and went and still no prayer service was in progress. By twenty minutes after the hour, all the music groups were in their places and the prayer leaders were coming onto the stage. It was an ecumenical affair, with people wearing robes and outfits of every variety. Most noteworthy was that the majority of those on stage were women. The woman leading the prayer service approached the podium dressed fashionably and wearing a simple white alb. She addressed the crowd and the hall fell silent.

"My name is Kelly Dolman. I'm the director of prayer and worship at the Catholic Cathedral of Detroit. We've come here together to celebrate a turning of the tide."

That was all it took. The place erupted with emotion. The roar of clapping and cheering took a long time to die down.

"We are here in response to a call from the Spirit," she continued in strong, deliberate tones, "and she will not be denied!"

Another round of extended applause. "My goodness," I shouted to Tom. "This will take a very long time if every sentence has a ten-minute ovation."

Eventually the crowd quieted and the prayer leader described how the day would unfold. "This is a day of prayer and petition," she explained. "We long for the day that the church will open the priesthood so that *all* can be ordained, all those chosen by God, all those called forth by the people of God and blessed by our bishops."

Amidst even louder acclamation, the leader started again, "We will begin with a prayer service. Ordination is an issue shared by all faiths. People are chosen—ordained—to lead and guide, to model and challenge, to celebrate and sanctify."

At this, some of the people in audience stood and affirmed their solidarity by joining hands and raising their arms. The speaker waited until all were again seated and then continued, "Following this prayer service, various areas around the convention center and in the parks surrounding the center have been designated for small group discussions during lunch. You have a map in your programs indicating where each region will meet. Thank God for the excellent weather. Pick a spot, choose a group and speak freely. We need your wisdom and insight. Some of your ideas will be recorded on the Ordination Rally website. This will be our link and solidarity with each other after we leave.

"The afternoon program will start at two o'clock in this hall. The session will last until four o'clock, at which time we will have a celebration of the Lord's Supper together. For anyone who is concerned, this will be a valid Catholic Eucharist, everything according to the proper rules and rituals. And yes, this will fulfill your Sunday obligation."

The place exploded with laughter and cheers.

"Now let us pray," the speaker broke in after a few moments of commotion and the convention center suddenly turned quiet.

The musicians began the strains of "Taste and See, the Goodness of the Lord . . ." The massive crowd of thousands sang as one, lifting their voices in prayer. The singing reverberated from the adjoining rooms where the overflow crowd was watching the proceedings on large television screens.

Estimates of the crowd's size circulating around the hall reached more than 15,000 as more people filed into the convention center. The music created an atmosphere of both prayer and celebration. That, coupled with the infectious spirit of the gathering, created an aura of a new Pentecost. Afterward some remarked that they sensed the foundations of the church shaking and the sound of a mighty force moving through the center.

"How can the pope—how can the church—not respond to this outpouring of the power of God in this room?" I leaned over and shouted in Tom's ear. "I've never experienced anything like this before."

I was pleased and gratified as I saw our children getting caught in the intensity of the moment. Even Michael, not one to get turned on by anything churchy, was singing at the top of his lungs.

Then the music stopped and silence filled the vast hall. There on stage, right in front of me, was my dear friend, Bishop Gene McGovern. Although now retired, he still had a reputation across the country as a progressive bishop, one who sought change for the good of the people and in response to their needs. He came forward to offer a prayer of petition and solidarity. Seeing him, the crowd reacted immediately. They all rose, offering him their respect and affirmation.

"Loving and gentle God," he began, head bowed, "we come to praise you and give you thanks. You are a patient God who has waited so long for a church that will at last live up to your Son's desires. He asked us to be servants of all and not to *lord it over one another*, to treat each other as equals, no one better than another. We come before you today, praying that you will touch the minds and hearts of our leaders. Give them eyes to see, hearts of flesh to feel and ears to hear the cries of your people. Too many are without shepherds to lead them, without priests to celebrate Eucharist with them. Too many are without confessors to guide and heal and set them free. Let this day be another Pentecost, a shaking of the foundations, an igniting of our desires, a proclamation of your deeds, a manifestation of your Spirit in our midst, in our church, in the whole world. And to this we all say . . ."

The center reverberated with a resounding "Amen." Then the people gave him a rousing acknowledgment of applause. He returned to his seat and the prayer service continued. Bishop Gene was not the only bishop on stage but as far as I could tell, he was the only Catholic bishop present.

The prayer service concluded at 11:30, and people started filing out of the hall to locate their discussion groups and have lunch. We headed for a section of the park on Belle Isle, where we knew the people from Sarah, Michigan, would be gathering. We grabbed our food basket from the bus, inviting the bus driver to join us. "We have much more than we can eat," I implored. "Be part of our discussions. You probably have some ideas to share that we've not considered."

"Sorry, can't do it," he said with a smile. "Others are going to be stopping to get their food baskets. I'd better stay here and look after things. But thanks, anyway. I appreciate the offer. I'm not Catholic, but I'm impressed with this crowd of people. Everyone is so friendly. It's kind of like a revival, if you know what I mean."

"Yes, I think you've got that right," Tom said as he stepped off the bus and herded the children to the park.

It took half an hour to get there, but the directions were clear so there was no trouble locating the group of parishioners from St. Gabe's. Already little clusters of people were forming, settling down in groups of about ten, to discuss the prayer service and the issue of ordination. Venders had a field day selling drinks to the thousands camped in the park and surrounding areas.

"This is great," Nathan said, as he helped spread out our blanket. I tried to pass the food to the family but I was so nervous I could hardly function—certainly too nervous to eat.

Others who joined our circle were all from our parish. For most of them, this was their first experience of a large gathering of Catholics. They rarely traveled to Detroit except to board a plane to somewhere else. The first part of our conversation included impressions of the city and the park and the huge number of people. Then slowly the discussion moved in the direction of the ordination issue and what changes they desired.

"I don't know what the problem is," Agnes said as she munched on her sandwich. "There were married priests for centuries and we still have them today since some former Episcopalian priests with families have joined the Catholic Church. Why not open it to anyone who feels the call, married or not?"

"It's a matter of control, I think," Greg interjected. "Imagine trying to move a whole family every six years. Imagine how expensive that would be."

"Well, that's how often my son's family has moved," Carol Enright, the parish secretary remarked. "What's so hard about that? When Kelly's family moved to Sarah, we all pitched in and it didn't cost that much."

"Yes, but the whole family would be included in the decision. The bishop would no longer be able to move pawns around a chess board as happens today," Greg chimed in, still not convinced.

"And what about women being ordained?" Alice spoke up, interrupting her lunch in mid-bite. "Why couldn't we even talk about that before now? How ridiculous!"

I sat listening to all this as I tried to eat my sandwich. I had trouble getting anything down; my stomach was in knots. What more could I add to what people already knew and felt. It all seemed so obvious, so reasonable, so right.

One person was starting to write some of the people's thoughts and to pool their responses. "All of the comments from our group,"

Tom said at the end, "could be summarized in a few words, 'Listen to us, Pope John. Give us more priests. We don't care if they are men or women, celibate or not. We want our parishes and our Masses and the sacraments.' Did I get that right?"

"Yes, indeed you did!" Alice shot back, glad to see such unanimity and candor. Even Greg reconsidered and admitted that the time for change had probably arrived.

The lunch circle began breaking up around one o'clock, so people could return to the convention hall on time. I, on the other hand, wanted to run in the opposite direction. I had trouble getting to my feet as someone pulled the blanket almost out from under me. My legs didn't seem to work as Tom helped me stand. The rest of the family noticed my reluctance. "This is like you dragging us to the dentist, Mom," Rachel said, pulling my arm in the direction of the hall.

"That's exactly how I feel!" I responded, allowing them to maneuver me.

We said goodbye to the parishioners who had joined us for the picnic lunch and made our way to the special entrance for presenters. Father Jerry was already there, looking over some of his notes.

I took my seat with the rest of the family, turning to greet Jerry. "Right now I really wish I had turned you down when I had the chance."

The program for the afternoon started late, just as Jerry predicted. Singing and a few announcements preceded the series of speakers. Each was allotted fifteen minutes. I was surprised to learn that there were only eight in all. Given the wide range of possibilities, it must have been difficult for the organizers to choose whom to speak. Father Jerry, of course, was a natural. He had published books and articles on the history and background of ordination, pointing out that nothing scriptural or theological militated against an all-inclusive priesthood. Only man-made church customs and regulations stood in the way. This had gotten him into some previous trouble with the authorities in Rome, but they had not stopped his writing or prohibited him from speaking on the subject.

I tried to listen intently to each speaker but my mind kept wandering back to what I had prepared to say. I wanted to speak from my heart and not use any notes. Now I wasn't sure this was such a good idea. What if my mind went blank? I would look like an idiot, letting down everyone who was counting on me. The more I tried to prepare, the less sure of myself I became. One of the presenters, a real firebrand, was a religious sister. Another was a sociologist who talked about cultural norms and pressures, a third was a motivational speaker who stirred the crowd to demand change in the church. I began to realize what that reading from the Acts of the Apostles was about. This crowd was definitely at a fever pitch. They were ecstatic!

Just then I felt a tap on my shoulder. "Come on, Kel. It's our turn." I turned to see Jerry's smiling face and beckoning gesture.

How could he look so calm, I wondered? I was in a dead panic. I gave Tom's hand a strong squeeze as I struggled to get to my feet. "I'm sure there must be utter terror written all over my face," I said in Tom's ear as I turned to follow Jerry to the side of the stage where the stairs were located. The audience was being led in a song following the last speaker. When the two of us reached the stairs the music was dying down and the emcee was already announcing our names.

"Reverend Jerry Cross, SJ, needs no introduction. His writings in favor of a more open priesthood are well known. He barely escaped censure from Rome for his most recent book, *Priesthood of the Faithful*. With him is Mrs. Kelly More, pastoral administrator—read 'Pastor'—at St. Gabriel's parish in Sarah, Michigan. Please welcome them to the podium on this most auspicious occasion."

I tried to hide behind the six-foot frame of Father Jerry as he ascended the stairs. I had just started up the stairs when a loud explosion erupted from behind the stage. Everyone who was on the stage instinctively hit the deck. Jerry grabbed me as he fled down the stairs and together we fell to the floor in front of the first row of seats, his full weight on top of me. I'm sure he meant to protect me, but I could hardly breathe. A loud scream arose from those closest to the front, but those toward the middle and rear of the hall were not sure what had happened. Nothing appeared on the large projection screens, only a vacant stage. Someone in the music section on the side of the stage started playing his guitar the first thing that came to mind, "Though the Mountains May Fall . . ."

"Probably not a good choice," he said after the event, "but that is all I could think of at the time. I just wanted to let people know we were still alive and able to function." Others in the ensemble picked up the beat and added their part to reduce the level of panic and fear.

Miraculously, people did not panic. They stayed in their seats, many crouching, heads low. But they didn't rush for the exits. Slowly, people on the stage began to reappear. A man in a uniform came on stage and whispered in the emcee's ear. The music died as the emcee approached the microphone holding up her hands, asking for attention.

"See what a powerful event this is. Even cherry bombs go off!"

The crowd, relieved that all seemed well, responded with applause and a collective sigh of relief.

"It seems that someone got through our security net backstage and set off a firecracker right into a live mike—more sound than fury, I understand," the emcee explained in a reassuring voice. She admitted afterwards that her hands were shaking as she spoke. "No one has been hurt and as far as we can tell, no harm or damage was done. We'll be able to continue the program as planned, thank goodness. Let's all stand and give each other a hug and then we'll hear from our next speakers. This isn't a break you understand, just a moment to give one another a little sign of peace, with the assurance that we're all in one piece."

Jerry slowly rolled off me, visibly shaken by the experience. Thankful for his protection, I was even more relieved to be able to breathe again. Tom came running to make sure I wasn't injured. He helped me to my feet and tried to smooth down my dress that was in a sorry state. My hair was a mess and I could feel blood on my knee. Upon closer examination it was only a scratch from being thrown to the floor by Jerry. With Tom's help, I tried to look as presentable as possible while having completely forgotten what I had planned to say.

The emcee had remained at the podium in an effort to assure the audience that all was well. After a few moments she asked for silence as the two of us again ascended the stairs and walked to the podium. I knew I limped a bit, but nothing seemed to be broken.

"Once again, ladies and gentlemen, despite the brief interruption, please welcome Father Jerry Cross and Mrs. Kelly More."

Jerry began by saying, "Such an explosive atmosphere here. If I didn't know any better, I'd say that the Spirit was setting off a fireworks display to get the pope's attention."

The place erupted with laughter and clapping. As the din receded, Jerry added with impeccable timing, "Wait until you see the Roman candles!"

This set off another round of applause. All this time, I stood beside Jerry trying to smile and look composed. I felt terrible. All I could see in front of me were stage lights and little else; the crowd was invisible. But I wasn't invisible to them. I knew I must have looked as if I had just come in from a softball game, with my bloody knee and wild hair. To steady myself I tried to recall being back at St. Gabriel's, waiting for my turn to speak at the end of Mass. This helped me feel more stable and less concerned about my appearance. I turned to listen to Jerry as he began to speak.

I didn't catch Jerry's initial remarks because I was struggling so hard to gather my thoughts. From what others told me afterwards, he described some of the theological essentials of ordination, such as being called by the assembly and affirmed by the bishop. He explained that marital status and gender didn't have anything to do with ordination.

He continued, "Some of us have direct experience of married men ministering in our midst as priests. A number of our Episcopal brethren who were ordained priests have chosen to become Catholic. Their sacerdotal orders have been affirmed by the Catholic Church. Some of you have also experienced women and men ministering in your midst as pastoral administrators or parish life directors. Whatever the terminology, the reality is the same. They're your pastors!"

"Yes!" a few people shouted from the audience and the crowd applauded its approval. "I have with me today one such pastor. Her name is Mrs. Kelly More, a happily married mother of three. Her husband, Tom, along with children Nathan, Michael and Rachel came with her today and are sitting in front. She's been ministering to the people of St. Gabriel's Catholic Parish in Sarah, Michigan, for the last five years."

When Jerry mentioned St. Gabriel's, a group of parishioners started chanting, "She's our pastor! She's our pastor!" and waving signs from the balcony. Television cameras turned to zoom in on this outburst of support for their leader.

"She's here today to tell her story. Kelly?" Jerry added, stepping away from the podium and offering me the microphone.

I walked to the podium, surprised at the confidence I suddenly felt. Perhaps it was the cherry bomb that did it. Somehow the explosion and temporary disruption gave me a new perspective that made me think of something besides myself. In a strange way it had calmed my nerves. I was no longer afraid. I realized that I was just one person, but I was a good pastor and proud of it. I was ready to speak.

"Thank you, Father Jerry," I began, looking at him next to me, "for giving me this opportunity to stand before this gathering of God's people as a pastor, for in some strange and wonderful way that is what I am. I visit the sick, listen to their stories and tend to their spiritual needs. I anoint them with love and tenderness, but not with sacramental oil. Yet they feel anointed." I could feel myself gaining strength and momentum as I sensed the support and encouragement of the invisible people beyond those lights. "I hear people's confessions, understand their worries and their concerns and forgive them their weaknesses. I grant them pardon before God, but I cannot give them absolution. Yet they feel absolved."

At this the hall broke out in applause, acknowledging both my ministry and its constraints.

"I prepare people for marriage," I went on, "walking with them in preparation for the Sacrament of Matrimony, telling them from my own experience what faithful loving is. When their wedding day arrives, I stand by to support them. I don't officially witness their marriage, but they feel that I'm doing so, nonetheless."

Someone in the balcony shouted back, "Yes, Kelly. Yes!"

"I journey with couples and single parents throughout the birth of a new child," I could feel the emotion rising in my voice as I spoke with more emphasis and conviction. "I help instruct them in faith so they can raise their child as a Catholic. I stand beside the font as the baby is submerged in the waters of baptism. I don't pour the water or anoint the child with chrism, but I do clothe the child in a white robe of holiness and the parents are pleased with my care and tenderness."

The large gathering of people applauded.

"I stand at the altar of Eucharist each week as the priest says the words of consecration, wondering how much longer a priest will be available to celebrate at our parish. When will he—yes, *he*—no longer be able to come to our worshiping community? When he stops coming, I won't be able to take his place and celebrate the Eucharist. And the people of God will be deprived of a central tenet of their faith."

I could hear applause breaking through beyond the blinding lights. I held up my hands to quiet the crowd and as the applause died down, I continued, "I'm a pastor. The parishioners call me this. I'm blessed to be able to minister to them, as they do to me. But something is missing. Something is wrong with this perception. What explosions will have to take place in our church, what conversions in men's—yes, *men's*—hearts must occur before the call of the Spirit is heeded and people of faith, once again, can lay claim to the celebration of the Eucharist which is their rightful inheritance?"

When I said this I could hear a chant rising from the great hall, "How long! How long! How long!"

"'How long?' you ask," I continued, taking my cue from the chanting. "Hopefully, not long. As St. Paul tells us in the Second Letter to the Corinthians, '*Now* is the acceptable time. This *very* day is the day of salvation!' Well, this is *our* day, and this is *the* acceptable time for a change! This Spirit will not be denied. Thank you all for coming and for allowing me speak to you. Thank you. Thank you very much."

At this, Jerry came and took my hand, raising it high in the air. People all over the massive hall stood to applaud, acclaiming the speech. My hands were shaking and my whole body was trembling, but Jerry paid no attention. Thankfully, he guided me to the stairs. I would have been lost without him. People reached to shake my hand as we descended the stairs and I made my way to my seat. The children stood and hugged me, Rachel especially, although my teenage sons seemed unusually congratulatory as well. Tom gave me a big hug and a kiss as the crowd around us stood and applauded. I later noted that when the television cameras panned the audience they came to rest on my face which was flowing with tears of relief. I could do no more; I was completely spent and relieved that the ordeal was behind me.

"Where did all that come from?" I whispered to Tom. "That wasn't quite what I had planned—not like *that*! I've got to get out of here! I can't take much more of this."

Only a few more speakers followed our talk. I had no idea what they said; I was too frazzled to pay attention. I took advantage of the break before Mass to sneak out the side exit. I just needed to be alone for awhile, to be freed from the crush of the crowd. I told my family that I would meet them at the bus.

"Thank God I'm out of there," I said to myself as I found my way through the door and back to the parking lot. I called Tom on my cell phone. "Sorry I ran out on you. I felt I was going to suffocate. I couldn't breathe. I'm not made for this sort of thing."

"No sweat," he returned. "Mass is getting started. Catch you after it's over. Just relax. You've been through a lot this afternoon." I could hear the opening song for Mass over the phone.

When I found the St. Gabriel's bus, the driver was in the back watching the television screen. As I climbed on board, hoping to find a little peace and quiet, he started clapping.

"Why are you doing that?" I asked, somewhat frustrated that I could find nowhere to be alone. I was hoping the bus would be my refuge.

"Because you were so great!" he exclaimed, grinning with esteem and delight. "Well done!"

"You saw it?" I asked with surprise.

"Of course I did. It's being shown live on the local television station. I was watching it on the television in the back of the bus. You were sensational—stole the show. I can't believe you're right here in my bus. You were bigger than life up there."

"Yeah, right," I said with incredulity. Then changing the subject I exclaimed, suddenly realizing how hungry I was, "Say, do you want to share some chicken with me? We have plenty, and I'm starved!"

~

I MUST HAVE FALLEN ASLEEP after having a bite to eat with the bus driver. My energy was completely drained from the exertion of a public appearance, the commotion from the explosion and the effort to speak what was on my heart. I was pleased with the result, but I had no more to give. My entire body ached with weariness.

I was awakened by people filing onto the bus, all speaking loudly. When the first person discovered I was in the back of the bus, she let out a scream of acknowledgment. "Oh, Kelly, you were incredible! Everyone was shouting your name, trying to find where you were hiding so they could praise you for your talk. Look, everyone, here she is."

People poured down the aisle to congratulate me. Much as I wanted to sink into the seats and disappear, I knew I had to acquiesce to their benevolence.

"Thanks, gang. Sorry I split," I said apologetically. "I was just too worn out to stick around. How was the Mass and the rest of the program?"

People clustered around me, wanting to be close to their heroine, something I found both embarrassing and amusing. Debbie sat next to me, gave me a hug and exclaimed, "You were just great, the highlight of the whole show. No doubt about it, you—and that cherry bomb. They caught the culprits. Just some kids looking for excitement. The firecracker wasn't very big but it exploded close to one of the mikes so it was really loud. Lots of wild theories were flying around about who did it, from terrorists to people at the counter-rally who had sneaked in to disrupt the program. But that didn't seem to have been the case. No harm done, other than giving everyone a fright. We could see you and Father Cross tumble down the stairs and hit the floor. We thought you had been shot. We couldn't see much from our balcony seats, so we were relieved when you walked onto the stage. How on earth did you have the presence of mind to give your speech? It was so perfect—brief, to the point and profound. We are so *proud* of you, girl."

I could hardly hear Debbie's comments, although she was speaking directly into my ear. Everyone on the bus was clapping, shouting and singing. There was no doubt that the rally had worked its blessings on these people. They were now ready to flood the Vatican with their desires for change.

Deb went on, her voice full of excitement, "The Mass was stupendous. You should have been there, around the altar with all the other speakers and Bishop Gene, too. I'm not sure who the celebrant was. People led different parts of the Mass. A woman gave the homily—whoops—I mean the reflection. She talked about the first Council of Jerusalem where the followers of Jesus had to decide what to do with non-Jewish converts. And when St. Paul was saying, 'Why are you putting God to the test by placing on the neck of the disciples a yoke that neither our ancestors nor we have been able to bear?' She called for a new Ecumenical Council to remove the yoke of celibate male domination from the back of the Catholic priesthood. Musicians picked up the spirit and everyone was singing and clapping. It was just incredible!"

"I suspect I'll see some of it on television," I replied, still groggy from just waking, but getting into the spirit of the group as well. "Did you see Tom and the kids anywhere?"

Just then I heard Rachel's cry and saw her pushing her way down the aisle. "Mom, you were awesome, just *awesome!* People kept asking where you had gone. Reporters and people with cameras were all around us, mostly asking about you and whether you were hurt or anything. Are you okay?" Rachel said as she picked up my skirt to look at my bruised knee.

"Please, Honey, not here. Yes, I'm just fine," I said, relieved to be reunited with my family. "I sneaked out to get some air. That was just too much excitement for your old Mom."

By this time almost everyone had gotten on the bus and people were opening food baskets preparing for the trip home. The plan had been to skip the evening potluck and head home early. The bus driver was anxious to get moving as soon as possible because the downtown area was turning into a traffic nightmare.

As the doors closed and the bus slowly began its way, people passed plates of food and cold drinks, calling me to the front so they could serve me first as the guest of honor. Tom and the boys were there and glad to see me safe and sound.

"I knew you'd be okay, Mom," Michael said over the clamor of the bus, "but shouldn't you have bodyguards or something? Everyone was worried about you."

"I'm fine, really I am," I said while accepting a hug from Tom who looked much relieved to see me. "It was much better to come here to the safety of the bus." I assured him. "Our driver made sure I was well protected." I put my hand on the bus driver's shoulder as he pulled onto the freeway.

The ride home was pure delight for the parishioners. Everyone was in a good mood, and my nap gave me the energy I needed to enjoy the celebration. The television screen on the bus alternated between the network news and the videos people had made at the rally. People cheered as they watched me give my speech once again. I was pleased that I didn't look as disheveled as I thought I did. My dress covered my bruised knee and my hair looked reasonably in place.

"You looked so calm and collected," one of the parishioners said, staring at the small screen. "How did you do that?"

"It was an act, Frank," I admitted, a bit embarrassed at what I saw. "My knees were shaking. The words weren't mine, believe me. Someone out there was taking good care of me. Thanks for your prayers."

At this point, one of the choir members grabbed the mike and started to lead the singing. By the time the bus arrived at the church's parking lot, the group was worn out from all the celebrating. People piled off the bus and headed for their cars, not wanting to leave but knowing that it was time to break up the party.

"One last round of applause for our pastor," Greg shouted out to the crowd, and the parishioners gave me and my family a rousing farewell.

"Enough, already," I said holding up my hands to quiet the crowd. "The cops will be called because we're disturbing the peace. Right, Harold?" He had been part of the entourage, as well as a member of the Sarah police force. "Good night, everyone. Safe journey home."

The five of us drove the few blocks home, looking forward with longing to our nice warm beds. As we approached, we noticed people standing in front of our house. "What's up?" Tom wondered aloud. "I don't recognize anyone. You don't suppose they're reporters, not at this late hour."

"Yes, my dear, I think they are," I responded, trying to think quickly about what to do next. "Thank goodness there are only a few of them. Too bad we can't just drive by and stay in a motel tonight. Guess we'd better face the proverbial music."

As Tom pulled the car into the driveway, the reporters clustered around us, trying to take pictures and ask questions. The kids thought it was cool, but not Tom or I.

Tom had activated the garage door as we pulled into our driveway, but the reporters blocked our way. I rolled down my window and replied "No comment" to their burst of questions. I asked if they would please let us get into our garage. It was late and the children needed to get to bed. The reporters were insistent, but no amount of probing unlocked my resolve to remain silent, so eventually they let the car pass.

Tom carefully drove through the small crowd and into the garage, closing the door behind him. We unloaded the car and escaped into the security of our house. Once inside with the doors locked, Tom and I gathered our brood in the kitchen for milk and cookies and some reassuring conversation.

"Is everyone okay?" I asked with some concern. "Those reporters outside may be just the beginning. You kids could get some ribbing from your friends at school on Monday. Hopefully by then it will all be forgotten, but who knows."

"Mom, we're good," Nathan spoke with the bravado of the first-born. "You're still our Mom, even though you're a television star."

"That will be enough of that!" I said sternly, holding tightly to Rachel as my youngest drank her milk, more to reassure myself than her. "This is out of my league. You know that I don't relish all this commotion. And look at that blinking answering machine. It's *full* of messages. But that can wait. Come on, kids, let's get to bed. I have to get ready for Mass in the morning. Thank goodness I'm not giving a reflection this Sunday. Poor Henry will have an empty church to preach to in the morning, I suspect."

I put my arm around Tom as we climbed the stairs. "You were great," Tom said, his voice full of admiration, "just magnificent. My heart stopped when I heard the explosion; I couldn't see whether you were okay. Jerry was trying to help but he landed on you pretty hard. I'm glad I was close enough to help you. And you had the presence of mind to stand there and say what you did. It was vintage Kelly More, all the way. You are one strong lady!"

"Oh Tom, that was *not* me up there. Something came over me. It was my voice and my gestures, but those were not my words. I had prepared a delivery, but not like that. There was a force and energy at work there that was way beyond me, *way* beyond."

FOUR

꧁

BED WAS A WELCOME RELIEF and sleep came swiftly despite the reporters on the front lawn. I was sure I would be awake all night, unable to calm down from all the excitement, but such was not the case. When the alarm sounded at six o'clock, it was a sudden and brutal shock.

"It can't be six already. I just went to sleep," I moaned, rolling over to turn off the alarm.

"Fat chance; you were out cold all night," Tom said, struggling to come to consciousness. "But there are parishioners to pastor, my dear. I can help you set up the church if you want."

"No, that's okay. You go back to sleep," I said, sitting on the side of the bed and pushing my feet into slippers. "Oh, wait, on second thought, I could use your help. I hate to do this to you, but you don't think there could be reporters with television cameras in church this morning, do you?"

"Don't count it out," Tom returned, propping himself on his pillows. "They want your hide, you know."

I peeked through the shades to see if anyone was outside, but the coast was clear. I got dressed and headed downstairs to retrieve the Sunday paper. Sure enough, there I was on the front page, my head stuck over the podium giving my impassioned speech. "Look at me,"

I exclaimed out loud. "Talk about a bad hair day. I didn't have any time to tidy up after getting thrown to the floor by Jerry. It looks like I'm coming out of the trenches. Oh well—can't be helped."

Tom and I drove to church, thinking we might have to make a quick getaway afterwards. No one was in sight, not Debbie, not Carol, not the musicians, not the sacristans. "Guess they all slept in," I said to Tom as I unlocked the church and turned off the alarm. "How late was it last night?"

"Around eleven," he replied, "but they were kicking up quite a storm coming home and I have a feeling it didn't end in the church parking lot. It was a pretty energetic crowd, the young *and* the old. Here, I'll get the lights."

Together we set up for Mass as a few people started straggling in to practice the music and set out the songbooks. I began thinking what I might say to the congregation about my role at the rally. Although it was Henry's turn to do the homily, I thought I should say something at the announcement time. People will want to hear my reactions to the rally, especially those who didn't make the trip. What more could I say, I wondered, other than thanking them for their prayers, support and encouragement?"

By half past eight, Father Henry arrived, upset and non-committal. "I saw you on the news last night," he said as he started to vest for Mass. He didn't look at me as he spoke, but I could tell from his cool tone that he was neither impressed nor pleased with my speech.

"I must warn you," I volunteered despite his stoic exterior, "that there were a few reporters at our door when we got home last night. They could show up at Mass this morning. I'm committed to making no comments, but just be ready for anything."

The church was less than half full when Mass started. The singing left much to be desired, not at all like the previous evening on the bus. In his homily, Henry made no mention of my talk nor of the rally, for which I was grateful. Mass progressed as usual—until after communion. No one had noticed that a large truck had pulled into the parking lot during the Lord's Prayer. It was now extending its antenna for a live broadcast.

At announcement time, I rose to thank everyone for all the encouragement and support I had received, both before and after the Ordination Rally in Detroit. The congregation gave me a round of applause which startled me, knowing that some of the parishioners were sympathetic with neither the rally nor the part I played in it. Despite the smaller crowd, the response seemed heartfelt and genuine. It was at this point that I caught sight of the television truck in the parking lot as the ushers opened the doors and took their positions to distribute the parish bulletins.

As Henry and I walked down the aisle during the recessional song, there were cameras at the back door filming our every move. "Oh brother, this is going to be hard to avoid," I thought to myself as I smiled into the lenses. As people left, they, too, were being filmed, some welcoming the experience and others heading for the side exits. The two of us shook parishioners' hands and wished them a good week, trying to ignore the intrusion. As Tom approached, I whispered to him, "Stay with me and see if you can get me out of here."

"Good luck. I think they have you cornered back here," Tom observed as he walked past me. "I'll get the car started. Catch you at the side exit near the sacristy."

"Mrs. More. Mrs. More. Could we have a word?" a well-dressed woman in her thirties confronted me as she moved in with her camera crew.

"I've really nothing to say," I said, still greeting the last few churchgoers. "I have to look after the people in the hall. Would you excuse me?"

"You left the rally early yesterday," the reporter insisted as she stuck a microphone in my face. "Were you injured when the firecracker went off?"

"No, I'm fine. No harm done," I said, backing into church. "I really must run."

"You talked about doing all the duties that a priest does but without ordination," the woman continued, following me into church. "Do you want to become a priest?"

"I didn't say I do all the duties of a priest," I returned somewhat defensively, already saying more than I had planned. "That's why we need more priests. I can't do what Father Cimanski does. He's the priest. Why not talk to him?"

"But are you pushing for the ordination of women?" the woman asked, making every effort to draw me into an interview.

"I really have to go. Sorry," I said, struggling to remain courteous to the reporter and not get rattled. "Feel free to come to the church basement and have some coffee and donuts. I need to go to the sacristy and get out of my liturgical garb. So long."

I escaped back down the aisle and nearly ran to the sacristy to take off my alb and get to the safety of the car. The television crew was filming Henry for the moment and as I looked back, he seemed to be enjoying it. I motioned to Mildred, the sacristan, as she was leaving to explain to everyone why I was not going to be downstairs for coffee. "I'm sure they'll understand. Tell them to smile for the cameras if they come downstairs. Catch you later."

Tom drove me home and to my relief there were no reporters on my doorstep. Instead, the house was filled with the aroma of breakfast, a surprise from my thoughtful children. All three of them were in the kitchen to greet me, bursting with pride both for their mom and what they had done in her absence.

The breakfast was a treat for us as we talked about the rally and all that had happened, the little stories, most of which I missed because I was nervous about my brief appearance and exhausted afterwards. I tried not to let it distract me, but all through the meal I kept thinking about those phone messages waiting to be answered. Tom, aware of my concern, offered to clean the kitchen as the rest of the family scattered to read the paper and enjoy their friends on this bright summer day.

I sat at the kitchen table with pen in hand and started to listen to my messages as Tom put on an apron. Most of the messages were from friends who had seen me on television and offered support and good wishes. A few were from reporters asking for comments and reactions. There was also a message from Jerry congratulating me on my talk.

"I never did get a chance to say goodbye," he said in his message. "You were everything I had hoped you would be and more. Sorry I was so forceful in pulling you to the floor. Guess I was pretty keyed up and that firecracker scared the daylights out of me. You weathered it very well. In a word, you were fantastic!"

One short message among all the others caught my attention. It was from Bishop Gene. "Hi, Kelly. It's Gene. You were great. Give me a ring Sunday or Monday. We have to talk. Thanks."

That's strange, I thought. I wonder what's on his mind. He always calls when he has an idea or a project he wants to share. What will it be this time? I think I'll wait until tomorrow to call him back. I just want to savor the peacefulness of the day.

Then the phone rang.

"Don't answer it, kids," I yelled. "Let's see who it is first."

The answering machine clicked and the voice of Bishop Gene came on. "Hi, Kelly. I can appreciate why you're not answering the phone. The media can be very persistent. Sorry to disturb your Sunday, but I have something that can't wait. Give me a ring and leave a message. We can arrange some time to talk."

I quickly grabbed the phone before he hung up. "Gene, how good of you to call. I just this minute listened to your message. You were so great at the rally. Were you really the only Catholic bishop there?"

"And a retired one, at that," he returned. "Thanks for picking up the phone. I suspect you noticed that the tone of my voice had some urgency to it."

"Yes, I can tell when you have something up your sleeve," I responded with a chuckle. "You had an overly solicitous air about you. What is it this time? You know I'm always glad to help in whatever way I can."

"Yes, well maybe you can. Here's the deal. A number of bishops, some retired like myself, others still active, had been in contact with one another even before the planning of the rally in Detroit. We all agreed that I would be a figurehead at the event. I'm pretty harmless in my old age."

"Yeah, sure you are." I interrupted with some sarcasm. "I was putting off responding to your call because I could sense you were up to no good. Am I right?"

"As I was saying," Gene said, laughing at my perception of him, "and you know me far too well, better than most of the priests who have been in the diocese much longer than . . . as I was saying, this group of bishops—and they're not just the progressive ones—have been concerned that our new pope may receive biased information from the Roman Curia. Those bureaucrats want to keep everything exactly the way it was. Their jobs depend on it, after all. We suspect they'll tell the pope that there's only a small group of radicals pushing for a change in ordination requirements. We believe he knows this isn't true, but all his information is getting filtered through a few Vatican officials who manipulate control."

I sensed the emotion in Gene's voice and it made me wary of what might be coming next.

"Yesterday's rally was a step in the right direction. It raises awareness and makes people excited, but it may not get to Pope John. So our group of bishops has been emailing one other, making conference calls and meeting, trying to determine what to do next. They were all watching the rally on television, of course, but thought it better to keep a low profile.

"We're in total agreement that a change must occur, not because of any lofty theological position or injustice towards women, which of course it is. It's that we want to keep the Eucharist celebration available for parishioners and still maintain quality priestly leadership. We need a larger pool of ordained clergy available for the appointments we have to make. Something needs to give. We're running out of priests and we're running out of time. Actually, we've already run out of time. This change in the ordination rules is way overdue. It's time to act."

I agreed with all that he was saying, but where was this leading? What did this have to do with me?

"First let me say that you were magnificent at the rally. You were informative, precise and thorough. You did it calmly, clearly and succinctly. You spoke from your own experience. That was dynamite. It was a powerful message that cannot be ignored. Good for you!"

"Thanks, Gene," I said in response. "That means a lot coming from you. Sorry I didn't stay for the Mass. I was completely spent after I left the stage."

"Yes, I can understand that. You did your part, no more was expected of you," Gene affirmed. Then returning to his task at hand he continued, "Anyway, I'm calling, as they say, from an 'undisclosed location.' Almost all of our group of bishops is here. I flew in last night after the rally. We've been working on a plan that will force the pope's hand. We hope to exert some leverage of our own, you see."

I tried to pinpoint the tenor of Gene's voice. He seemed to be excited, serious and concerned all at once. It certainly had a no-nonsense feel to it.

"Kelly, I hope you're sitting down, because I'm going to have to start from the beginning and go through the whole story. It's important you hear it all because you may be playing a part in it."

"What part!" I exclaimed. "What do you mean 'I may be playing a part in it'?"

"First let me ask you a critical question," Gene inquired. "What I am about to tell you is very sensitive material. No one but the bishops here, and now you, knows this. Can I pledge you to total secrecy, Kelly?"

"Well, yes and no," I responded cautiously, somewhat confused about why Gene was telling me this, but also concerned about its implications and what he might be asking of me. "I'm not sure where you're heading with this, or why you're sharing it with me, Gene, but I must tell you, and this has been going through my head ever since the start of our conversation, I'll need to bounce this off someone else for perspective and insight. I need someone to process whatever you're going to tell me. I can commit myself to secrecy only if you will allow two other people to know the story. Those two would be my husband, Tom, and my good friend and spiritual director, Father Jerry Cross. You know them both. I am absolutely certain that neither of these two will tell a soul. Can you allow me that leeway if I agree to keep what you are saying confidential?"

"Yes, I can live with that," Gene responded thoughtfully. "Actually, that makes very good sense. The more I think of it, the wiser it seems. That's one reason I'm sharing this with you. You have a clear and quick mind, and such good sense.

"Well, let me proceed. Soon after the new pope was elected, we arranged to have this meeting of like-minded bishops. It was to take place somewhere off the beaten track so the rest of the American bishops would not feel slighted and the media would not be alerted. So far we have managed to do that."

"Good for you," I exclaimed. "That in itself shows that you're a pretty shrewd group."

"Thanks, Kelly," Gene said, appreciating the compliment. "Before meeting, we all agreed that some changes in the requirements for ordination must be made immediately, but we had a much harder time agreeing on what those changes should be. Some wanted to open it only to married men because this had been the custom of the church from the beginning. Others of us said that it was unfair not to include women as well. After all, most of the ministering in the church is done by women."

"Thank you!" I interjected. "It's about time we're recognized for all we do."

"Good point," Gene continued in a somewhat more relaxed tone. "There's no doubt many women are qualified, so why not allow them to be ordained? As you might have suspected, the interchange was heated. Then came yesterday's Ordination Rally. It was planned independently of our meeting but it was just the impetus we needed. Your own speech, brief as it was, had a great effect on these men's thinking. I must thank you for your candor. You said exactly what needed to be said. Our parishioners are being shortchanged because we, the leaders of the church, have been timid in making the changes that have been blatantly obvious for years. All the bishops agreed that I should thank you for your clear and moving statement of need. It was Spirit-filled, no doubt about it."

"Thanks, Gene. Thank you all very much," I responded, both flattered and a bit flustered by the praise. "You're right. It did feel as though the Spirit was speaking through me. But that's not the reason you're telling me this, is it? Where is all this leading, if I may be so bold to ask?"

"I love that directness in you, Kelly," Gene responded with a laugh. "All right, let me get to the point. As you might have suspected, I came to the meeting with a proposal in mind, and it involved you.

I found myself sinking further into my chair, afraid to even guess at what was coming next.

"Now this is where it gets critical," Gene went on. "What I have to say next must remain just among you, me and your two confidants. Do you have any reason to believe, Kelly, that someone else could be listening to our conversation?"

"Well, I don't think so." I replied, wondering why anyone would be so intrusive. "I'm in my own home. You don't really think someone could have bugged our phones? Who would want to do that? What on earth could I say that could be that relevant?"

"We have some rather eager and resourceful investigative reporters, you know. After your talk at the rally, I wouldn't put it past them."

"There's a pay phone in the church hall," I replied. "I know that's not bugged. I'll give you the phone number; I can be there in fifteen minutes."

I gave him the number, picked up a tablet and pen for note-taking, made some lame excuse to Tom about going to the church, and escaped to the parish hall to await Gene's call. As I waited for the phone to ring, I prayed to the Holy Spirit to give me ears to hear and an open and clear mind to respond to whatever the bishop would say. Although I was expecting it, the loud ring of the phone startled me. My hand was trembling as I picked up the phone.

"Hello, Kelly," Bishop Gene said with a tone of humor and gravity wrapped in one. "Isn't it crazy having to go to such lengths? I'll bet I'm making you a little nervous right now."

"A little?!" I said with emphasis. "The longer this takes the more nervous I become. My palms are all sweaty. Okay, out with it. Where is all this leading?"

"The plan is this," Gene returned, amused at my impatience. "We don't think the pope will move with this ordination thing unless he's forced into it. That's not a nice thing to say about our new pope, but there you have it. We, as a group, want to do that urging. Eventually, we want him to call an Ecumenical Council to settle the issue, and to call it soon. But we need leverage.

"The leverage is this. Hang on to your hat, Kelly, here we go. As a retired bishop, I have the least to lose. If necessary, I have agreed to ordain a woman to the priesthood. It would be a valid ordination, but not a licit one, meaning that it would not have the blessing of the official church. Others have tried to do this but never before, at least in recent history and to my knowledge, has a legitimate Catholic bishop in good standing with the church ordained a woman to the priesthood. It would, of course, take place in secret."

I found myself catching my breath. What on earth is he saying!

"Before this happens," Gene continued, "one of our members would fly to Rome under another pretext. He would arrange for a private audience with the pope and explain what we're planning to do. The pope would then have one month to call a council. If nothing happens, then we proceed with the ordination and notify him that it's happened. If the pope still doesn't act, then one month later, the fact that the ordination took place would be given to the media. This, we suspect, could become a great embarrassment to the church and this is the leverage we are using to effect a change. We have enough contacts to keep the issue in the press until the pope takes action."

"That sounds a bit like blackmail," I retorted, not mincing my words.

"Yes, it does seem that way," Gene replied, somewhat sheepishly, "but it will be done with great diplomacy and persuasion. It's the way church politics works, I'm afraid. If this were not such a pressing issue, we could use other channels, but we don't have that luxury. There's not enough time for that.

"If the pope agrees to call a council, then no one needs to know about our plan. If he doesn't act, and I go ahead with the ordination, he then has a second chance to respond. If he does respond, it remains secret until it becomes accepted practice to have women priests. Eventually the story could be told and all will be able to rejoice at the news, if they choose.

"If he balks, however, then the ordination becomes public and Plan B goes into effect. That means that I would be the scapegoat and be labeled a rabble-rouser. I suppose I could even be defrocked. The other bishops will have to lie low because they still have dioceses to lead. I'm willing to take the brunt of the impact because, as I said, I have little to lose.

"As for the woman who will be ordained, it will be another matter altogether. It will probably mean the loss of a job in the church, perhaps even the need to go into hiding. It will require great courage and sacrifice, not only for the woman, but for her family as well."

"What exactly is he asking?" I thought as panic began to spread throughout my body.

"I'm hoping and praying this will not be the case." I heard Gene speak as if he were at a great distance. I was shaking so hard that it was difficult to pay close attention. "I can't imagine that the pope is unaware of the urgent need for a change. Hopefully this will put him into motion. The fact that so many bishops are behind this—and we are planning to link up with similar gatherings we heard are occurring in other parts of the world—that it has to sway his hesitant mind and give strength to his tentative nature.

"So, you now know what I am going to ask of you. Every bishop here was more than impressed with your speech and your composure at the rally. They have commissioned me, Kelly More, to ask if it comes to that, if you might be willing to be the woman whom I would ordain."

I sank to the floor beside the pay phone. My head was shaking in disbelief. "No, no, no," I kept muttering under my breath. "No way. Stop this nonsense."

What I said out loud was more like a groan. "Oh, please, Bishop Gene, don't do this to me. I've never wanted to be ordained. It's not my calling. I'm just a pastoral administrator helping in a rural parish that has no priest. End of story!"

"Yes, I know. It's an enormous decision," Gene went on, undeterred by my resistance. "I, of course, don't expect an answer right away. You'll need time to think and pray about this. That was a very good suggestion to include your husband and Father Jerry, now that I think of it. You'll need their wise counsel and unfailing support.

"All that the bishops request at this moment is the understanding that you be willing to think about it and not turn it down outright. That's certainly your privilege. It's asking a great deal of you, and you have much to lose. I hope it won't come to that, but if it does go public, your life will be chaotic. That's a heavy cross to ask anyone to bear, but ask, I must. So what do I tell them? The timeline is short. You'll have a week to decide. If your answer is yes, then our messenger goes to Rome immediately. Depending upon the pope's response, we have a month to make our arrangements.

"So, if you're willing to at least *consider* this request, then I'll return to our meeting and tell them the news. If not, then we'll have to procure another candidate before we leave. So what are your feelings about all this, my friend?"

Still sitting on the floor under the phone, I was unable to speak. "This couldn't be happening," I thought. "First the rally, now this! It's all too bizarre to believe." I sat in silence trying to regain some equilibrium. My mind was a blur. I couldn't even form words to respond.

"Kelly, are you still there?" Gene asked after a long pause. "I can understand why you're speechless, but I must give them some response. Will you consider this? Please let me know by this coming Friday, one way or another. But will you think about it?"

"Yes, I guess so," I responded weakly, my voice shaky, my throat dry. "It's just too overwhelming. Tell them you have one great sucker on the other end of this line. I can't see why on earth you would even think of me. But I'll at least mull it over and get back to you in a week. I make no promises, none whatsoever. You'd better line up some other candidates while you're at it. It all seems too preposterous to me at this moment."

"Oh, thank you, Kelly. Thank you," Gene exclaimed, relieved to hear even this tenuous response. "You're quite a woman. I've always felt that, from the first moment you joined the diocese. You're a very special person. We'll all pray for your discernment this week. Thank you and good luck."

"Thanks, I'll need it. Goodbye." I sat on the floor with the receiver in my hand until the recorded message came through to hang up the phone. I stood with some difficulty and put the receiver back on its cradle, using it to steady my shaking body.

"What am I going to do now?" I moaned. "Where do I turn? My cell phone is at home and I don't have change for the pay phone so I can't call Tom." Without further thought, I went upstairs to the church and collapsed into a pew. "Oh, dear God, help your frightened, trembling child."

FIVE

༄

I STAYED IN CHURCH for a long time after receiving Gene's call. My prayer, when I was able to focus, was filled with foreboding and uncertainty. This was not the peaceful commune with my God that I longed for. The words of Bishop Gene kept running through my mind. "It all seems so enormous a thing to ask . . . I'm afraid I have no choice but to ask that you do this."

Is this really from God, I kept asking myself, or is it just the hare-brained scheme of a group of bishops for which I was the convenient scapegoat? So many other women are better trained, have a desire for ordination, feel a call and have many more years of experience. This is ridiculous to ask me to do it. Something's out of synch here. Besides, I have a husband and three defenseless children to add to the equation. Why not choose a nun who already has this lifestyle? She could pull up stakes and acclimate quickly. But no, they have to call on *me* to be their guinea pig.

I was upset; I could feel myself squirming in the pew. My moods fluctuated between anger and panic, hypertension and exhaustion. "This is going nowhere fast," I finally told myself. "I'd better talk to someone before I go stark raving mad. Watch out, poor husband, here I come."

I rose and headed home to talk with Tom.

"Hi, Sweetheart. What's up?" he called from the family room when he heard me arrive. You left in such a hurry. Nobody knew what happened to you."

"Sorry about that," I replied, "but I need some time with you. May we go for a walk in the park and then have a little ice cream together, just you and I?"

"Sure thing," Tom replied, his curiosity aroused. "This must be important. You have that wrinkled brow, just as you did before your talk in Detroit."

Very wisely, Tom was quiet as we drove to the park on the lake. When we arrived at the park, we walked to a bench and sat down.

Summer was just beginning and the breeze by the lake was cool and refreshing. The sun was warm but not uncomfortable, and the geese were squawking as they came close to the shore looking for a handout. After several minutes, I said, "Tom, do you mind if we just sit for a while?" I took his hand and pulled closer to him. After a few minutes, I began, not sure of my words. "You know that call I got from Bishop Gene this morning? He relayed a most extraordinary plan to me."

I'm sure Tom could feel me squeezing his hand as I said this. I could tell that he took it as a signal to be especially attentive.

"Gene swore me to secrecy but I insisted that you and Jerry should be included—you, as the love of my life and my level-headed soul-mate, and Jerry as my spiritual director and mentor."

I related the entire conversation that I had had with Gene, nearly verbatim. I had no trouble remembering it. It was embedded in my brain. Tom listened intently, surmising where it was heading as I described the bishop's plan. He refrained from giving his impression or reaction. His first instinct was always to "fix" whatever problem I presented, but he had learned early in our marriage to listen and let me tell my story without saying a word, even for clarification. I needed to purge, and as I did so, I could see the situation more clearly.

When I had finished I put my head on his shoulder and sighed, "Why, Tom, why is this happening to me? It's so unreal, so unfathomable. Of all the possible women ministering in parishes across the country, why did they choose me? I just don't understand it."

Tom didn't respond, but now there were two of us who had furrowed brows. He began to massage my neck, noting the knot in my muscles. It felt so good to be with him. The two of us stayed there for a long time. Tom finally asked, breaking the enormity of the moment, "You buying the ice cream?"

"Why not," I responded, accepting his lead that it was time to move.

We got up from the bench. I felt loved and much relieved to have my husband's strong support and understanding. I also sensed that Tom was processing what I had shared and was not at peace. I'm sure he was wondering what this would mean for the family if I said yes to Gene's plan. Many strange events had happened to us over the last few weeks, and this might only be the beginning of more.

The two of us drove to the neighboring town for our favorite cones. Neither of us spoke much about what was on both of our minds. There wasn't much more to be said.

"I guess I'll give Jerry a call this afternoon and set an appointment for Monday," I mused as I licked my moose-tracks delight. "The timeline is so short. I have to have an answer by this Friday, less than a week from today."

When we had finished our ice cream, we headed home. Tom took my hand as he picked up speed. "You know you've had quite a shock to your system this morning."

"Yes, I know. I keep thinking, where will this lead? I do still have a choice, right? I don't have to say yes, do I?"

"Most certainly not. This must be a real choice for you. Promise me, Kel, you'll keep an open mind about this. Let it be neither a yes nor a no for right now. As you could tell, I'm not at all sold on what Bishop Gene is proposing. I'm trying to be supportive, but just because he asked you doesn't mean you have to agree."

"I promise, Tom, really I do," I returned. "Everything is still tentative. I wonder if Jesus ever went through this uncertainty. He must have. Paul was knocked down and blinded. Peter was pulled right out of his boat. But what about Jesus? Before he went to be baptized in the Jordan, did he and Mary discuss it? Do you think he looked at the pros and cons, made a choice, and then headed south? Why did we never hear about *his* decision-making process? It sure would be helpful to know that right about now."

"It never occurred to me," Tom said as we got closer to Sarah. "I suppose it must have happened somehow, sometime."

"Yeah, and look where *that* ended," I exclaimed, not pleased that I had mentioned it.

"Good point," Tom replied, catching my drift. "But that's well beyond our task right now. I suspect you'll need some extra time to think, pray and decide during this week. I want to help any way I can, but right now I have no idea how to do that. You know, of course, whichever way it goes, I'm behind you and I trust your judgment. Even if I may not agree, Kel, I'm your husband and I'll support you no matter what."

"Oh, Tom, thank you. Thank you!" Impulsively I unbuckled my seatbelt and threw my arms around him.

"Hey, careful!" Tom exclaimed with a laugh. "This isn't helping my driving very much."

As soon as we got home I gave Jerry a call. "Hi, Jerry. Sorry to disturb you on a Sunday afternoon, but I need some time with you tomorrow. Is that possible? Something's happened that needs your sage advice."

"I think we can do that," Jerry said. I sensed his surprise at the urgency of my request. "How about eleven in the morning? Meet you halfway if you like. How does that sound?"

"Sounds great. See you at Mickey's Diner, our usual spot. Save room for some of their great pie. My treat."

Relieved that Jerry was free for a meeting, I went back to the family room with new energy and resolve. "It still seems like a dream to me, Tom," I remarked, picking up the Sunday paper. "Did that call from Bishop Gene really happen? And did he really say what I think he said? It seems like virtual reality, like the kids putting on those helmets and thinking they're parachuting from planes or shooting the rapids. But they're really still standing in one place; it's all made up. That's how this feels like for me just now, very surreal."

"That may be how you feel," returned Tom, "but come Friday you'll need an answer for the bishop. Then it won't be so virtual anymore." He said this looking over his glasses at me with a pensive expression.

"You're so comforting! Thanks a lot," I shot back, grabbing the tissues just as a sneeze came on.

Six

✤

I AWOKE MONDAY MORNING with a full-blown cold. Sunday night I took medicine and extra vitamins thinking I could ward it off, but no such luck. Just what I needed for my session with Jerry this morning. Despite my malaise, I was standing in front of Mickey's Diner at 11:00, just as Jerry arrived.

"Thanks for taking the time, Jer. We've certainly seen a lot of each other recently. You know I wouldn't have asked for this extra time unless it was important."

"I could tell from your voice over the phone that it was," Jerry said, holding the door open for me as I started to cough. "Where did you get that cold? It sounds lethal."

"It came upon me all of a sudden yesterday afternoon," I said, stepping into the restaurant. "I think it might be a reaction to what I want to discuss."

As we settled into the booth and ordered coffee, I launched into a full account of Bishop Gene's plan and request. Jerry wasn't as good a listener as Tom.

"You mean," Jerry interrupted, his eyes widening as he grasped the implications of what I was sharing, "that you are supposed to wait in the wings, *just in case* the pope doesn't act? That's rather unfair, don't you think? What's in it for you, other than misery, pain and being labeled an outcast? People have been excommunicated for such things. I don't get it. Why not just orchestrate a groundswell for an Ecumenical Council from all over the world rather than go the route of an underground ordination?"

"Shhhhh. Not so loud!" I said, looking around to see if I recognized anyone from the parish. "Just be quiet for a moment and let me speak. I was wondering the same thing, but from what I gathered, these bishops felt that a groundswell won't do it. No amount of Ordination Rallies will penetrate the defenses of the Curia in Rome. It needs a shock treatment, they feel, and I could be it."

"Wow. I can see their point," Jerry replied thoughtfully. "So what you're asking of me is to help you come to a decision, is that right?"

"Yes," I said with a note of despair in my voice.

"And you have only a few days to do this," Jerry continued, trying to get his mind around the matter at hand. "That's a pretty short time period."

With a fuller grasp of what he was being asked to do, he pulled a pen out of his pocket. "Here, let me use this napkin to map out what we—no, *you*—could do. Today is Monday, right? And you have until Friday. You won't be able to pull up stakes and move to a retreat house or a hideaway in that short a timeframe. So, you'll have to do it at home. It's good you'll be able to touch base with both Tom and me at the end of each day of reflection. This will help you sort what's happening."

"This sounds pretty intense," I said in desperation. "Do you think I'm up to this?"

"Most definitely," Jerry responded, looking up from the napkin and into my frightened eyes. "If I didn't think you could, I would have said so. You know how blunt I can be at times." Then he returned to the napkin before him and continued writing. When he had finished, he handed me the napkin. "It's all here, spelled out day by day. It's just an outline, you understand, but it'll provide a way to come to a good decision. We've talked about discernment before. This should be old stuff to you. You just need to spend some time with The Lord and see what comes of it."

"Whew. This is going to be some week," I replied, looking it over and then putting the napkin into my purse. "You realize, of course, that I don't have the logical mind you have. My brain doesn't work in such neat little compartments."

"Yes, yes, of course," Jerry said, scratching his head. "These are merely suggestions. But it's such an important issue; it needs a careful strategy and some earnest concentration to arrive at a solution. You don't have the luxury of spending a good long time arriving at a decision. You have less than a week to decide a life-changing, history-shaping event. All the more reason to come to it with all the resources you have available—heart, head, emotions, prayer, friends, the works. Say, we haven't even ordered. What about that pie you promised me. Want to join me?"

"No thanks. I've kind of lost my appetite," I responded, amazed at how Jerry could bounce from one topic to another. "You go ahead; I'll watch you devour yours as usual. As you might suspect, I'm not looking forward to this week."

I watched him eat a slice of Boston cream pie, while I was stymied by the prospect of all that Jerry mapped out on the napkin. After Jerry finished and I paid, the two of us stood to leave.

"Pay heed to any swings in mood and keep notes along the way. You'll do just fine, I'm sure of it," Jerry said reassuringly. "It's always great to see you. You are some wonderful person. You know I'll be praying hard for you all week. So, go to it, woman. The fire of the Holy Spirit is in your bones. I feel very special to be included in this process. Stay strong and get over that cold."

The two of us walked to our cars, waved goodbye to each other and drove away in opposite directions. My ride home was somber. I had no trouble keeping my speed under the limit; I didn't really want to get home to begin the analysis. It all seemed overwhelming and insurmountable to me. I pulled out the napkin with Jerry's notes on it and laid it on the passenger's seat beside me. I wondered if I was capable of this task. "Just one step, one day at a time," I told myself. "Don't worry about tomorrow. Just do today's task and leave it at that. Who knows? It might all be clear by the end of the day."

I instinctively knew this would be too much to hope. I turned at the exit for the lake and headed for one of my favorite spots in the park, a common respite during my days off. I pulled into the parking lot and sat quietly in the car staring at the lake for a few moments. Then I walked to a bench. No one was around, for which I was thankful. "Good to be alone," I said out loud. "Now let's see, the first step, he wrote, was to free myself up as best as I can. I wonder what *that* means. Let go of any cares, worries, fears and concerns. A great concept, but he didn't tell me *how* to do it."

I closed my eyes and tried to dismiss any distractions. "How do I feel right now? Dear God, help me know what I'm feeling about all this."

I found myself repeatedly dozing. But in between, I felt more numb than excited or discouraged by Bishop Gene's request. I had no revelation in either direction. It still seemed unreal and farfetched. After half an hour of trying, I gave up and started walking around the lake. "This is going nowhere." I mused. "I don't have any decisive feelings yet. Jerry had asked me to write the results of my prayer, but I still had nothing."

By the time I returned to the car it was getting late. I returned home to prepare dinner for the family. Tom was working on the Internet. "How did it go with Jerry?" he asked.

"I'm not sure. He gave me a process to follow. Part of the plan is to share with you and him what happens at the end of each day. To tell you the truth, I'm ready to chuck it all right now. This is so outlandish. Can't we just escape to some foreign country? Do you have enough frequent flier miles for a long trip?"

"Yes, I guess I do," Tom said, laughing at my desperate suggestion, "but I doubt that was part of Jerry's plan. Let's go for a little walk after dinner and you can tell me what he suggested."

When the meal was over, the two of us went for our walk, leaving the boys to clean up. I told Tom about Jerry's plan, showing him the napkin as we walked along.

"So how did it go after you came home?" Tom asked with some curiosity.

"Nothing, *nada*, zilch—no lights at all," was my reply. "I just felt blah. It's a good thing I have a Plan B for tomorrow. I can't really tell if I'm excited by the prospect or just remotely interested. On the other hand, I can't just say no to all this either. I don't know where I am."

We strolled down the shaded streets without saying much. I drank in the early summer sun, watching as it dropped below the horizon. I returned home feeling refreshed and more centered than I had all day. I called Jerry, as I had promised I would, and related that nothing much had happened. He didn't seem surprised. He was almost expecting it.

"That's fine, Kel," he said. "Now tomorrow, as I mentioned, picture yourself saying yes to Gene, and see how you feel. Identify as many ups and downs as you can in your emotions. Then see yourself saying no to his request and do the same with that. See how it comes out and write down whatever surfaces after you're done. If you can, find some time to do the same thing in the afternoon, maybe half an hour or so. Go for a walk if you feel up to it. I'll talk to you tomorrow night."

"That's it, that's all you have to say?" I exclaimed incredulously. "Thanks a lot. It's easy for you to say. I have to *do* all this stuff. I'm really tired, my cold is getting worse, and it's only the first day. Well, wish me luck," I said and hung up the phone, not feeling very good, either about myself or about Jerry's process.

I got up slowly on Tuesday morning, not relishing the new day. I was still in the grip of the cold, but managed to get the kids to school and to walk to church for some prayer time before starting my day. I settled into my favorite chair in the chapel, closed my eyes and said, "Okay, God, for better or worse, here I am. You're going to have to help me through this."

My mind and heart were much more active than on Monday. I tried to envision saying yes to Gene and how it might feel. A certain thrill and adrenaline rush came with it, but dread and foreboding as well. Then I pictured myself saying no. I was surprised at how much relief I felt, as if a great burden were lifted from my shoulders. "I wonder if that's what Jerry meant by consolation. It sure feels great right now."

As I wrote my thoughts from this reflection, I sensed for the first time a move *away* from rather than toward acceptance. "That's interesting," I thought, putting down my tablet. "I wonder how to decipher this."

The same sentiments returned when I had a little time to reflect in the afternoon. There seemed to be more pleasure and relief in saying no than in saying yes. "Am I just fooling myself here? Whoever would want to say yes to such a thing anyway, although I suppose there must be some women who would? Not I. I don't think I'm the woman for this. I'll have to see what Jerry thinks of all this tonight."

When I called, his response was, "I think we're making some progress. You were paying attention to whatever bubbles up as you thought about each of the choices. That's good. It seems as if there's more comfort in saying no than in saying yes. Is that correct?"

"You've got that right!" I responded eagerly. Then I added with some confusion, "but isn't that understandable? Look at all the risks to which I would subject myself and my family. This could just be taking the easy way out, couldn't it?"

"That's very possible," Jerry said knowingly. "That's why you'll need to take the next step. Put that good, keen mind of yours to work tomorrow. Spend your reflection time thinking of all the reasons *against* saying yes. Write them down as they come to you. Set that aside and then think of all the reasons *for* saying yes. Put the two lists together and see whether one outweighs the other. It's not the longer list that is important, but the one that carries more weight. Talk to you tomorrow night. Good luck. I'm praying for you."

As we were getting ready for bed, I shared my day with Tom, as well as Jerry's reaction. "But I'm not sure I'm making any progress, Tom. I'm as confused and undecided as I was yesterday."

"Ah, but your indecision is going deeper," Tom chided as he gently poked me in the mid-section. "It's down here in your gut now. I can tell. Whatever happens, it will be the right choice. Give it time."

"Time?" I shot back. "That's one thing I *don't* have." I sank into bed with desperation and turned out the light.

Wednesday's task was a little easier for me. At least I had something concrete on which to work. During my morning reflection I diligently wrote one reason after another for saying no to Bishop Gene. It was a long list, including putting my job in jeopardy, perhaps being forced to move and leaving the people I love, being discredited by the church, even being excommunicated. I could lose all I had worked for all these years. There was also the possibility I would be ordained and then not have the chance to exercise my priesthood, and that would be heartbreaking.

I constructed a much shorter list when I wrote all the reasons in favor of saying yes, but the reasons were profound. It could change the course of the church worldwide, it might open ordination to other women, it could force the calling of an Ecumenical Council, the parishioners' needs would be better met with increased clergy numbers.

I spent a long time looking over the two lists. I returned to them and added additional ideas during my afternoon reflection. I was having a difficult time deciding which side offered the stronger case. I reflected on the consolations and desolations from the previous day to see what difference they made. I spent some time talking with Tom, reviewing the lists and seeking his input. When I called Jerry that evening, I was still in a quandary.

"Jerry, I don't know what to think of all this," I said with a long sigh of frustration. "It makes more sense to say no. That side has all the practical and 'safe' reasons. But the yes side has extremely important, significant reasons as well. What do you make of all this?"

"Kel, listen closely to yourself," was Jerry's response. "Yesterday you were leaning more toward saying no, but you were afraid that it was the escape route. Today you said the reasons *for* were more poignant. That's saying something. However, as you say, the risks are very high. You did mention a great relief came over you yesterday as you thought of saying no. The question, I guess, is where is the Holy Spirit in all this. My suspicion is that one way or another, it will soon become clear to you as to which course to follow. So far, all this discerning of yours is still inconclusive. It's time now to watch and pray. Keep your antennae up and active. You know how that saying goes, 'Expect the unexpected.'"

"Oh, great, just bloody great!" I shouted into the phone. "A lot of help you are! It's Wednesday night. By Friday I have to have an answer for Gene. I'm not any closer now than I was when I saw you. And you say, 'Wait for the unexpected.' This is crunch time, Pal. Help me out here!"

"First of all, Kelly," Jerry said, trying not to laugh at my outburst, "you are much farther along than you were at the beginning of the week. You have very clear reasons for and against. You're in touch with your feelings and inclinations. You're going into this with a clear and level head. Few people have that benefit when they have to make an important life decision. Given all that, I'm very confident you'll make the right choice. All I'm saying is that something unexpected might happen to show you what to do. It often does. Something may occur to you, some event might happen—it may be insignificant to anyone else but yourself—and it tips the balance one way or the other. Be patient and be gentle with yourself, and above all, be watchful."

I hung up the phone with more emphasis than I had intended. "What makes him so sure about all this while I'm still completely undecided?" I turned from the phone to look for my other confidant.

"Tom," I said as I came into the living room. "I know it's late but like it or not, we're going for a walk. I have to tell you what Jerry just told me. It sounds pretty ethereal if you ask me. Tell me what you think."

To Tom's credit, he dropped what he was reading and followed me out of the house and down the steps. I'd passed a few houses before he was able to catch me. "A bit worked up, are we?" Tom said as gently as he could. As Tom listened to my description of Jerry's comments, he nodded his head in agreement. "You know, I think he's right. I've been doing some discerning of my own. I, too, can't determine where I stand on this. If you said yes, it could cost me dearly, as you know. But I'm willing to risk it if that's what you decide to do. Only, I can't quite figure which way to turn either. Let's wait and see what happens next, shall we?"

After half an hour, the two of us returned home and made sure the children were getting ready for bed. Then we got ready for bed, both wondering what tomorrow would bring. "Do you suppose," I asked as I climbed into bed, "that the Holy Spirit is on the same timeline as the bishops, I mean, wanting an answer by Friday? Or is it the other way around? Maybe the Spirit has been pushing for a change in the requirements of ordination for some time and we're just now catching up. I don't know," I said with a sigh. "Enough questions. Good night, Love. God bless." I turned off the light.

Thursday dawned and with it, two somewhat confused and expectant people. We both dressed and went about our morning routine. I spent time in prayer, trying to remain open to whatever God was asking. I mulled over the last few days of reflection and discernment, checking my notes and lists, but getting nowhere. It was still the same dilemma, is it yes or is it no?

The rest of the day progressed as any other, including phone calls, appointments and home visits. My cold was still lingering, but one advantage of moving into summer was that there were fewer parish meetings to attend. I remained alert and attentive to what was happening around me, all to no avail. I went to bed early that evening with nothing new to report to Jerry. He was correct in saying that by this time I would be exhausted. I was feeling the strain from the urgency to come to a solution.

"Tomorrow's the day, Tom," I said, as I lay in bed unable to sleep. "What on earth will I tell Bishop Gene?"

"I have no idea," Tom replied. "I wish I could help, but I can't. I guess you'll just have to believe you'll have the right answer when the time comes. I hope you can get a good night's rest. You need it."

THE TELEPHONE WOKE US BOTH from a sound slumber. I glanced at the clock as I reached for the receiver. "My goodness, it's 1:30 in the morning. Who could be calling at this hour?"

"Hello," I said, trying to shake off my drowsiness. "Yes, this is Kelly More. Oh, hello Frank. What's up?"

Tom listened intently, propped on one elbow.

"Sure, I'll be right over," I said, hanging up the phone and swinging out of bed all in one motion.

"That was Frank Casey. He's the cop on duty tonight. He was calling from the hospital. There's been an accident. Three teenagers.

Sounds pretty serious. One is from the parish. The family is there now and they want me to come and pray with them. I'm not sure how long I'll be. Say a prayer for them, Tom."

I got out of bed, into my clothes and raced out of the house. I was pulling into the emergency entrance within twenty minutes of the phone call. I recognized the family as I came into the emergency reception area, although I didn't know them well. They didn't come to church very often. Going to sit with them, I held the mother's hand and asked her, "What happened?"

The story came flooding out amid her tears. The three teens were driving too fast around a corner. The car went out of control and hit a tree. The other two were not hurt badly. They were being kept in the hospital overnight for observation. Their own daughter, Allyson, however, was not so lucky. She was in serious condition. I sat and prayed with the parents and the younger brother, trying to be present and supportive for them. In a short while, a doctor came and said that the girl would be going into surgery soon. He could not offer much information because he was unsure what internal injuries she had sustained. The parents asked me to give their daughter a blessing.

I entered the cubicle where Allyson was being prepped for surgery. I held the girl's hand and said a blessing, making a sign of the cross with my right hand on her forehead. Something about her was vaguely familiar, not from church but from somewhere else. The girl was conscious, a look of panic in her eyes. Allyson realized she was in danger of dying. "Help me, oh please, help me," she said with a pleading look, having trouble speaking. "We were drinking and fooling around. This never should have happened. I'm sorry, so sorry."

"That's all right, Allyson," I said trying to console her and reduce her fears. "God's with you and forgives you. Don't worry. Everything will be well." I felt so helpless. This girl needed so much more than I could give her, an anointing with oil and perhaps absolution. A look from the nurse told me that it was time for the surgery. I walked beside the gurney as the teenager was wheeled to the operating room, holding her hand all the time. I left Allyson at the door wondering what her fate would be. The young girl looked so frail and afraid. I returned to the waiting room wondering where I had seen her before. "Perhaps she's a friend of Nathan's," I surmised.

Once there, I assured the family that I had talked with their daughter and that she was being well cared for. I remained a short while longer and then gave my home phone number to the family, asking them to call me as soon as they knew anything, no matter the hour. I did the same at the nursing station, asking them if they knew how bad it was.

"Hard to say," the night nurse replied, looking at the chart. "There could be lots of internal injuries. It may be quite a while. I'll keep you posted. If everything turns out okay, I'll wait until morning to call. Thanks so much for coming; you made such a big difference. I could see the peace and assurance come into the girl's eyes when you gave her that blessing. I've been meaning to tell you what a great job you do at St. Gabriel's. I don't come but a few times a year. Mostly I'm working on Sunday mornings, but when I do come, you make it worth my while. Good night, now."

I returned home filled with mixed emotions. Although bone-tired, I was shaken by the experience. As I climbed the stairs I instinctively peeked at my own children, thanking God that they were all safely asleep in their beds. I then climbed into my own bed, telling Tom briefly what had happened. Sleep came as soon as my head hit the pillow.

The alarm sounded at six o'clock, waking me with a start. "No second phone call last night," I said to Tom as I rolled out of bed. "That's very good news. I'm so hoping that our girl, Allyson, made it okay. I'll call the hospital to be sure. Funny that Frank should have called me and not Henry. He usually doesn't do that. And why did that girl look so familiar?"

I went into the bathroom to brush my teeth and Tom rolled over for a few more minutes of sleep. The next thing he knew, I was standing over him with my toothbrush in my hand and toothpaste all over my mouth.

"Tom, wake up?" I shouted. "I know who she is! That's the girl who came so close to hitting me with her car a few months ago. You remember, I was coming home from Bible study and stepped out into the street without looking. She came back to see if I was okay. Think of that! Isn't that odd?" I asked, while shaking my toothbrush at my poor bewildered husband. "Is there a message for us here somehow? Could this be 'the unexpected' that Jerry mentioned? I'll still need to do some pretty serious reflecting before calling Gene, but I'm feeling strangely at peace. Get out of bed, you sleepyhead; we have quite a day to live! You know what else? I think that cold of mine is all gone; just like that!"

SEVEN

I PULLED A CHAIR NEXT TO the pay phone in the church hall and dialed Bishop Gene's number. What next, I wondered? Will this cozy little world of mine all change or will it just continue as it has before? This call could make the difference. God, help your people.

That's kind of an odd prayer, I thought to myself, as Gene answered the phone. "I've been waiting for your call," Gene said pleasantly, although I could sense the anxiety in his voice, "I didn't expect to hear from you until later in the day. I've been praying hard for you all week that you might come to a good decision."

"Thanks," I said, feeling a bit tense myself. "I could feel the power of your prayers coming through."

"Before you say anything more," Gene interrupted, "first tell me *how* you made your decision. That will help me assess the result, although I have no doubt about your abilities to come to a good and valid conclusion."

At his urging, I took him through each day, step by step, as he interjected sounds of approval and admiration. "You have done a magnificent job in this process," Gene said when I had finished my account. "I knew you were up to it."

"I'm not so sure about that," I responded with embarrassment, "but when I was at the hospital last night, I knew that if I were going to continue in this work, I needed all the tools and reserves that people requested of me. At the moment, I'm a pastoral administrator in an environment which needs a full-time priest. If what you're asking of me will help revise that, then I say, let's go for it!"

"Good for you, Kelly!" Gene exclaimed, overjoyed with my response. "That's what I call spunk! I'm so happy, for you, for us, for the parishioners, for the whole church."

"Hey, slow down," I protested. "Not so fast, please. You said this was just a preliminary step. Isn't someone supposed to talk to the pope now and persuade him to call a Council? This is just a boost in that direction, right? So what do you think are our chances?"

"To tell you the truth, knowing you and your generous nature, I had banked on you saying yes to my request. Our contact person left yesterday for Rome and was able to speak privately with the pope. Our envoy was pleased to learn to which extent the pope was aware of how acute the problem of a clergy shortage was and how open to change he seemed, but became discouraged when the pope began deliberating about how long it would take for something new to actualize. At one point, the pope took off his glasses and put his head in his hands and sighed deeply. It was as if he felt he didn't have any power to exact changes. This was the most discouraging part of the interchange. We bishops were right. He does feel besieged. In fact, he's frozen. He can't act. The pope has the pastoral disposition of John XXIII, but he lacks that man's decisiveness and perhaps his courage. Our messenger tried to show the pope that he *did* have the power to make decisions, he *could* call for a Council, and that he didn't *need* the Curia's approval. Our contact saved his trump card for last. When he saw that nothing seemed to be swaying the pope, he finally put forth our plan of ordaining a woman to force the issue. Ordaining a married man would not be sufficient, he explained. In terms of justice to women and their ability to be good priestly ministers, and the crying need for more priests around the world, the matter could not be ignored any longer. At the same time, he made it quite clear that nothing would happen for a month. If a Council were called by that time, the planned event would not happen. But if no word was received, then some woman, somewhere, would be ordained a Roman Catholic Priest. He said all this in the gentlest yet most persuasive manner possible.

"At this, the pope became very agitated. Our emissary tried to calm his fears, but the pope kept muttering something in Italian that sounded like, 'Not valid, not valid, not valid.'

"Our man noticed this and said, 'It's not clear whether this ordination would be valid or not. At any rate, if and when it does become public, validity will not be the issue. The media will seize on it and bring it to your doorstep. The damage to Rome's credibility will be done.'"

"The rest of the conversation took a decided turn at that point. On the one hand, the pope was visibly moved, shaking his head in disbelief. On the other hand, our messenger calmly outlined our plan with indications of when and how the pope would be contacted if no Council were called. After thirty days, unless the pope made a move, the ordination would take place. Thirty days after that, it would be leaked to the press. After that, pressure would continue to mount until a Council was called. Our man apologized for acting in this direct and uncompromising fashion, but time was running out. God's people were not being served. A change must occur and the pope was the one to enact it. The envoy made it clear that it would be in the pope's best interest to keep this conversation entirely to himself. The whole interchange took fewer than twenty minutes."

"The consensus seems to be," Gene went on in measured tones, "that we should proceed with our plan. We'll take no action for thirty days. We don't really have much hope that the pope will call for a

Council within that time frame. He's too frightened to act. Because of this, we will have to start preparations now for the next step in our plan." At this point Gene's voice became more somber, almost fatalistic. "What I'm asking of you, Kelly, is that you come to my home within the next few days so we can work out the details of what that next step will be. Could you do that? What we're talking about, of course, is preparing you for ordination."

Those words came as a shock, almost as if a dam had broken in my brain and the torrents of emotion came rushing in. Much as I had prepared myself for this exigency, hearing Bishop Gene say it struck hard. "Prepare you for ordination." Those were sobering and daunting words to hear.

"I'm sorry if I sound a little weak on this end," I said apologetically, thankful that I had a chair to sit on for this conversation. "That's because I am. Yes, I could come on Monday. What should I do to get ready for our meeting?"

"Nothing for now," Gene returned. "We'll work all that out when you get here. Once again, only your husband and Father Jerry should know anything about this. How does ten o'clock sound? I'll have something ready for lunch. This could take a few hours. See you then. Be strong, Kelly. We're getting down to it. It may not be long now. Don't doubt your decision. It was a good one."

"I'll try," I replied as if in a fog. "But what about you? This is a very big step for you, as well."

"Yes, it is," Gene acknowledged, thankful for my concern. "I've always been a loyal and faithful member of the church. I still feel that I am. But if this ever gets into the open, many will not think so. You and I are both in over our heads here. We just have to keep kicking to stay afloat and trust that the Holy Spirit will support us. We're never alone, you know, especially now."

"Yes, I do believe that," I affirmed. "See you Monday."

I put the receiver on the hook and replaced the chair. I did all this in a daze. The words kept running through my head, "Prepare for ordination." "Prepare for ordination." I sat at one of the tables in the hall and stared into space. "He's really serious about this. We're going to prepare for *my* ordination!"

I sat for some time trying to gather my thoughts. After what seemed like a long time, I returned to my office, trying to act as if nothing had happened. But something had happened. It was quite possible that I would become an ordained priest in the Roman Catholic Church.

I knew this had been attempted before. I had read about Ludmilla of Czechoslovakia who was ordained surreptitiously during the Communist regime. I had also seen accounts of women ordained in Europe and Canada by bishops not recognized by the Catholic Church. A number of women had been ordained in the United States as well, but this was different. It was being done by a group of legitimate Catholic bishops to force a change in the system. I was consenting to being a pawn in a much larger chess match. What on earth have I agreed to do? I sat at my desk trying to focus on the work before me, all to no avail.

The next few days went by as a blur. I related my conversation with Gene to both Jerry and Tom. They received the news soberly, both realizing from their own perspective what risks were involved. Tom and I discussed with each other what the children should be told and when. We talked about where the ceremony might take place and who should be present. Jerry asked how we could be sure that it wouldn't become known before it was leaked to the press; someone might discover the bishops' plot. There were so many unanswered questions, so many frightening details to consider as the impending event loomed closer.

I awoke on Monday morning after a fitful night of tossing and turning, coupled with intermittent dreams. "I'm not in the best shape for this," I said to Tom as I headed out the door to pray by the lake before going to Bishop Gene's home.

"What happened to all that confidence and self-assurance I saw last week?" Tom asked as he kissed me goodbye.

"Out the window," I replied with a shrug. "I guess I didn't think it would ever really come to this. Oh, Tom, are we ready for all that might happen?"

"No, but we never will be," Tom replied stoically. "We just have to take it one day at a time. This is one of those days. Good luck today. Hesitant as I have been in the past, you know I'm rooting for you."

"Yes, I do. And thanks," I said as I started to get into the car. Then I stopped and turned back to Tom. "What about you? You must be having some strong emotions of your own."

"Let's just say," Tom laughed in response, "that my prayers of petition are getting longer each day as we get deeper into this."

I drove to the lake and sat on a bench. I tried to keep my mind on prayer but try as I might, I couldn't focus. All I could think was, "Prepare for ordination." It seemed so unreal, so farfetched, but I knew that it wasn't. The time was swiftly approaching for ordination to become a reality. "This is like the birth of a child," I thought. "It seems so inevitable—time marching me closer to this destiny. At one time, I did have a choice but now I don't. I'm a prisoner of my own making."

When my time of prayer was over, I returned to the car and headed out of town for Bishop Gene's residence. I arrived early, a quarter to ten, but Gene was ready for me. "Hi, Kelly. Thanks for coming early," he said as he gave me his usual warm greeting. "We have our work cut out for us this morning. How about some coffee to get us started?"

"Sure thing. But do you have any decaf?" I asked as the two of us headed for the kitchen. "I have enough adrenalin flowing through me now without adding caffeine to the mix."

We retired to the living room with coffee mugs in hand. Gene began the conversation. "I've been making notes for myself. Lots of details to discuss, but first, if you don't mind, I think we should spend a little time in prayer together. This is a big step we're taking. It needs a clear and steady mind. I always find taking a little time to get in touch with the Holy Spirit helps a great deal."

"Sure thing," I chimed in, "fine with me. I need all the help I can get just now."

"I was struck by the first reading for today's Mass," Gene said, pulling out his daily prayer book. "It's from Paul's Second Letter to the Corinthians. 'At an acceptable time I have listened to you, and on a day of salvation I have helped you. See, now is the acceptable time; this very day is the day of salvation.' How's that for providence? This is certainly a special day for us both. Let's be quiet for a while and let those words sink in."

We sat quietly for some time. I thought about everything that had led to this moment of decision. I prayed for stamina and courage for what lay ahead. Then Bishop Gene broke the silence by saying, "What's one thing you would like to pray for today, Kelly? For me, it's a special prayer for our new pope. He's a key figure in all of this. What he does or doesn't do shapes the rest of our actions, perhaps our entire lives. I hope and pray he listens well to the voices within and around him."

"Yes, that's good. For me," I responded, searching for the one petition I wanted to share—there were so many, "it's the people of St. Gabriel's. They're a wonderful group of parishioners and they deserve a full-time priest in their midst. I pray they will have that."

The two of us ended with a "Glory be" and got down to business. "My first concern," the bishop began, "is for you and your family,

Kel. Do you think the children should be included? They must understand that not a word about this can be mentioned to anyone else. Can they do that?"

"I've thought of that, too, Gene. At this point, I don't see how they can *not* be told. That's how we've always dealt with them— honestly and directly. I can give you my word that they'll protect our confidences."

"Good," Gene responded. "I was hoping you'd say that. Now to the task at hand. We have to pick a day and a place. The pope has thirty days to respond, and seven of those are already behind us. Our group of bishops felt that we should wait another week or two to be sure. None of them will be present. This is by design. No one but you and I are supposed to know about this."

"Who will be there?" I asked, suddenly interested in all the details.

"Just you and I and your family. I also thought Father Jerry Cross should be included because he was in on the decision-making process. If we have to go public, however, he should not be involved. I don't want his brilliant career and his unique gift to the church to be jeopardized."

"Yes. I feel the same," I said, digging into my purse for pen and paper so I could keep track of all that was being planned. Looking at Gene, I added, "So, this will be a very secret affair. Where will it take place, in someone's basement?"

"No, nothing like that," Gene laughed. "I think it should be in a church setting to give it credibility and symbolic importance. I will be residing in one of the parishes of the diocese for a few weeks next month while the pastor is on vacation. I've talked to him about using the church for a private ceremony. That's all I said, but I'm sure he thinks I'm doing a marriage validation or something along that order. He's a good man. We'll have no difficulties from that quarter."

"So that will be the place," the bishop continued. "Now the date.

I've been looking at the liturgical calendar for the coming six weeks or more. I thought we should choose a fitting feast or a saint's day for the event. You might have one to our own liking. We have a good list from which to choose. There's the feast day of Mary Magdalene, or St. Bridget of Sweden, or St. James, the Apostle, as possible options. We also have Joachim and Anne, the parents of Mary, Martha from the gospel story of Martha and Mary, as well as St. Ignatius of Loyola at the end of July. This gives us a range of nine days. Does any of these dates appeal to you?"

"Let me think about that for a moment," I reflected. "I'm sure Jerry would choose his founder's day, St. Ignatius Loyola. But how about a married woman like me?"

"That would narrow it to St. Bridget or St. Anne," Gene replied, flipping through his prayer book. "I'm not sure about Martha or Mary Magdalene. We don't know if they were married or not."

"That's not bad. I like Mary Magdalene's spunk," I returned, suddenly getting energized by the prospect. "And she was the one who announced to the apostles that Jesus had risen. And, of course, they didn't believe her until they went to see for themselves. Just like a man. Yes, let's do it on her feast day."

"Something else occurred to me," I added as I made notes on my pad. "When Jesus appeared to Mary Magdalene, she first thought he was the gardener. When she recognized him, she grabbed onto him until he had to say, 'You can't hold on now. You have to let me go. Run off now and tell my disciples.' That was so human and so feminine of her. I love it. Yes, let's do it on her feast day! That finally gives me some positive feelings about this."

"Good for you," Gene replied, as he caught my enthusiasm. "Okay, that's settled then. That puts it on Monday, July 22nd. How is that for you?"

"Perfect," I responded, getting my calendar. "It's my day off. Tom can plan ahead and free up the day, and the kids will be home. Yes, that's a good time. What time of the day will we do this?"

"I would like to find a time when no one else will be there," Gene remarked, casting about for what would be best, at least in recent history and to my knowledge. "The parish is small and people don't use the church that often during the week, especially in the summer. I'd like to do it after the office is closed, but not at night when we would have to use the lights. Let's say six o'clock, while everyone's at dinner. It won't be dark until after nine this time of year."

"There are a few more practical details to settle," Gene continued, "and then we can get to the ordination ritual itself. First of all, I think we should have the ceremony on video, just for the record. We want to be able to prove that this event actually did happen. Do you think Tom or one of your boys could handle this?"

"Sure. We have a good camera," I returned, making another note to myself. "The best one to do it, I think, would be Michael. He's very good with computers and cameras and such."

"The trick will be to keep only you and me in view," Gene cautioned. "I don't want to implicate anyone else if we can help it. Could he manage that?"

"No problem," I assured him. "How long will the ceremony take, do you think?"

"Perhaps forty-five minutes to an hour," Gene replied. "I want to make it a very spiritual and moving experience for us all. It's not something to be rushed. We might even have a little music. Maybe Father Jerry could help with that."

"That takes care of my list," Gene concluded, tucking his checklist into his pocket. "Do you have any questions so far?"

"Other than where's the door?" I shot back . . . "so I can make a quick getaway."

"At the church?" Gene inquired, somewhat confused by my question.

"No, *now*! This is getting way too serious too quickly. We're actually going to do this thing, aren't we?" I asked, looking Gene squarely in the eye.

"Yes, I think we are," he replied with a sigh, "unless we're wrong about Pope John and he surprises us all. In six weeks I'm going to ordain you as a priest in the Roman Catholic Church. There, it's settled." Then Gene took both of my hands in his own and said with some emphasis, "So now let's get into how this whole thing will unfold, with the ritual itself."

The two of us spent the next hour going over the ordination ceremony—old hat for the bishop, since he had ordained many men while he was head of the diocese, but for me, this was a novel experience. I had attended a few ordinations, but I'd never paid that close attention. Each step of the process intrigued me, as I dug deeper into the symbolism of the sacrament.

When we had finished, I leaned back in my chair and drew a deep breath. "It's all so beautiful and rich in meaning and imagery. I had no idea of all that was involved. The image of the candidate lying outstretched on the floor as everyone else prays the litany of the saints, the simple gesture of the bishop placing his hands on the person in silence and then saying the prayer of institution, anointing the hands of the newly ordained with chrism, as well as the bishop presenting the person with the communion plate and chalice to signify the power the priest has for changing the bread and wine into the body and blood of Christ. It's simple, direct, and so profound."

"Yes, it's a beautiful ceremony," Gene replied proudly. "Too bad it's been limited to 'men only' for all these centuries. The more I delve into this, the more just and logical it seems to include women. I'm getting quite excited by the prospect, loaded as it is with risk, intrigue and danger."

"I'm not sure *excited* is the word I'd use, I interjected. "Perhaps *humbled* or *awed* is closer. I still can't believe this is really going to happen, and in such a short time. How will I ever be able to get prepared?"

That night after dinner, Tom announced, "We're on for dishes tonight, your Mom and I. You've got a free one, kids. But before you run away, we'd like to have a family meeting. Something rather important has happened."

That got their attention. Family meetings didn't come often, but when they did, it was always significant.

"What's up, Dad?" Michael asked, changing his mood from 'one foot out the door' to 'this might be interesting.'

"Better let your mother explain," Tom replied. "Only I must tell you before we get started that what we tell you now must never leave this room. You can tell *no one* else about it, do you understand? I'm sorry to lay this on you, but it's essential that you keep this a secret. Can you handle that?"

"Sure, Dad," Nathan said, assuming the status of the oldest and the most responsible. "What's so important?"

"Rachel," Tom spoke with even greater emphasis, "do *you* understand? You can't tell *anyone* about this, not your friends, not your teachers, not the people at church, not anyone, okay?"

"Sure, Dad. Mum's the word," she said, turning an imaginary key over her mouth.

"Okay, children, here goes," I began. "Did you notice this past week that I wasn't acting quite myself?"

Everyone nodded and exchanged knowing glances around the table.

"I had to make a very important decision," I continued. "Bishop Gene had asked me to consider—how can I say this?—well, to be ordained a priest."

"Wow! Mom, you're kidding, right?" Nathan exclaimed.

"Amazing," Rachel chimed in. "How cool! That's really great!"

When?" Michael exclaimed.

"Well, if all goes as planned," I replied, a bit stunned by my children's exuberant response, "in a little over a month. It will be a secret ceremony, just the five of us, the bishop and Father Jerry. No one else is to know anything about this. The idea is to urge the pope to call an Ecumenical Council—a gathering of all the world's bishops. It will be the Council, along with the pope, that will change the requirements for ordination. That's the plan, anyway. Right now the pope is aware this will happen if he doesn't call for a Council within the next thirty days—actually twenty-three days now. The clock is ticking. He doesn't know who will be ordained or where it will take place, only that it will happen if he doesn't act. We don't think he will. So, I'm it. I'm that mystery person."

"Mom, that's really great," Michael piped up. "Will you be able to say Mass at the church then?"

"Theoretically, yes, but that won't happen," I explained. "This is all hush-hush. Once I'm ordained, if the pope still doesn't act, then about a month later it will become known. That's when our lives will change, and change dramatically. I'm sorry about this, but everything will be at risk. Whatever publicity we had from the Ordination Rally is nothing compared to the onslaught we'll feel when this thing breaks. I suspect we'll have to leave Sarah and even go into hiding. I hope it never comes to that, but it could. This is of great magnitude—this is big, really big!"

There was silence around the table as each child tried to fathom what this would mean for them personally. Without knowing what else to do, I instinctively reached for the hand of the person on either side of me as the family formed a circle around the table. "Children, I have no idea why this is happening. I didn't ask for it, *you* didn't ask for it, but there it is. We've been called to do something very special and we just have to see it through to the end. Thank goodness we're all healthy and that we have one another. We're a blessed and wonderful family and no matter what happens, we're together, okay?"

"Okay," came the responses around the table in less exuberant, now more somber tones.

"Now for a few practical details," I said, breaking the circle of hands and pulling a slip of paper out of my pocket. "If we go through with this, it's scheduled for six o'clock on Monday, July 22nd, in a parish about thirty minutes from here, probably followed by dinner somewhere. There will be a practice run for us about a week before-hand so we know what to expect. Michael, I'm going to ask you to do a video of it. You'll have to be careful not to include anybody else's face except mine and the bishop's. Do you think you could do that?"

"Sure, Mom, no problem," Michael spoke up, proud to be singled out for such an important task.

"Good. Any questions?" I asked. "Remember, not a word of this to anyone, *please*. It could destroy a very carefully crafted plan. Let's pray it all works as expected. This is not about your mom, you know, it's about an important and necessary change that must happen soon in the church if the parishioners are going to be served. We're just escalating it a bit faster. So there you have it. The meeting's over. Out you go."

The children scattered, heading downstairs to watch television and discuss the news among themselves. Tom and I began carting the dishes to the kitchen. "How do you think they took it?" I asked Tom, somewhat uncertain whether the children grasped the significance of the situation. "They seemed more pleased than worried."

"They're happy for you, Kel, and very proud," Tom said reassuringly. "They know you are someone very special to be asked to do this. And I totally agree. Where on earth did I find such a woman!"

"Stop that, you crazy oaf!" I protested playfully, taking plates from Tom and stacking the dishwasher as he rinsed them.

The following weeks were routine. I went about my pastoring with a new awareness and perspective. While leading one of the morning prayer services, I found myself thinking, "This could be a Mass and we could be celebrating the Eucharist together. I could be leading worship just as any other priest." I dismissed the thought from my mind, as it was too much for me to fathom.

In my spare moments I studied the ordination ritual, rehearsing each part of the service and contemplating which songs or readings I would like. "The scripture readings from Mary Magdalene's feast day are pretty good in themselves," I mused when I looked at my prayer book. "Maybe I'll stick with those. And the songs should be simple so we can all sing them together. No one will be there to accompany us."

I talked with Jerry frequently by phone. Fortunately he was free on that Monday. I wanted him to be part of this occasion because he was so instrumental in getting me to this juncture. In one conversation he remarked, "Kelly, I can't think of anyone more prepared for this moment. When I was ordained I was all caught up in my theological studies. I had very little pastoral experience. But you have the theological background *and* the pastoral experience. Without them realizing it, your own parishioners are calling you from their midst to be their priest. The closer I get to this, the more sense it makes. Thanks for accepting both the challenge and the responsibility of being ordained."

"Don't get all high and lofty on me now," I chided. "This is challenging enough as it is. Just come and be part of it and help us celebrate afterwards, okay?"

"Okay, but the dinner is on me," Jerry volunteered. "I've been praying hard, but I'm not sure for what. I want the pope to call a Council, of course, but I also want you to be ordained."

"Well, you know both could happen," I suggested with a laugh, "and it would be a lot easier on me. I'm willing to wait a few years after the Council gives the go-ahead if that's what it would take; only now I think I'm convinced I'm *supposed* to be ordained. That's progress, isn't it?"

"It sure is," Jerry assured me. "No longer are you questioning your call. Now we'll have to wait and see what the timetable will be."

The deadline for the pope to make a statement was drawing closer, and still all was silent. The bishops' contact in Rome assured them that nothing had changed. A week after the thirty day time limit, Bishop Gene received a call to proceed with the ordination. He drove to my house with the news.

"We're on," he said, as I met him at the door. Somewhat shaken, I invited him in and we walked to the kitchen.

"We proceed as we had planned," Gene explained. "I've been thinking about the practice session. Is there any time your church might be empty so we could do it there? Doing it in a church would be better than at my home."

"Yes, I could arrange that," I agreed after a moment of reflection. "Six o'clock would be a good time. I'll lock the doors and put up a sign or something. How soon will it be?"

"How about next Monday?" Gene asked as he consulted his pocket calendar.

"That's good," I replied, a bit uneasy about how swiftly the time had come. "I'll alert everyone else."

"Nervous?" Gene said as we sipped tea together.

"Very," I acknowledged.

"It doesn't show," Gene returned.

"It will," I assured him. "Either I'll go on an eating binge and gain fifteen pounds in a week, or I'll lose my appetite and be too weak to walk. We'll see how it goes."

"Fair enough," Gene responded as he stood to leave. "See you next Monday evening."

EIGHT

ON THE NEXT MONDAY, a small contingent of people gathered in St. Gabriel's Church to walk through the ordination ceremony.

"At least we don't have to make programs; that should help," I announced as I stood in the middle aisle waiting to begin the practice.

Bishop Gene explained the steps of the ritual and where everyone should stand. He spent extra time with Michael, making sure he understood what should and should not get videotaped. "You're quite good at this, aren't you?" Gene said as he saw Michael handle the camera angles. "I think you have it exactly the way I had hoped it would go."

Gene then turned to me and said something I wasn't prepared to hear. "You thought this would be only a practice, but in fact, something special is about to happen. I plan to ordain you to the diaconate this evening as the first step to priesthood. Being a deacon means dedicating yourself to a life of service. This you've already done. I'm only confirming a vocation you have been fulfilling for some time."

He went on to say, "Come, Kelly More, and receive the Order of Diaconate, an affirmation of your calling to serve others."

This was a complete surprise to me. I wasn't expecting it, as this was supposed to be a practice, not the real thing. I wasn't dressed for the occasion—wearing slacks and a blouse. This was hardly the attire for an ordination. The main event was going to happen next week, not today!

Yet, here I was, standing in the middle aisle of my own church, surrounded by the people I prized the most. I'd been preparing for ordination to the priesthood and had forgotten about the intermediate step of the diaconate. Now it dawned on me. Yes, of course, I have to be ordained a deacon first. Why hadn't I remembered that? That shrewd Bishop Gene McGovern thought of everything.

As I gazed up the aisle at the bishop, he beckoned me to come forward. By this time he had put on his vestments and stole. I suddenly realized how appropriate this ritual was for me. I had spent the last five years ministering to my flock as a pastoral administrator. I had been their willing table *servant*. Although I hadn't been expecting it, I was ready and equipped for this initial step. My work as pastor and shepherd of St. Gabriel's Catholic community had completely prepared me.

I stepped forward, knelt at the feet of the bishop standing in front of the altar, bowed my head and felt his hands placed firmly yet gently on my head. He kept them there for what seemed a long time, praying silently for me and for my future as an ordained minister in the church. He withdrew his hands, and then I felt a second set of hands on my head. These belonged to Jerry. It was part of the diaconate ritual to have other priests lay their hands on the head of the one to be ordained. Then more laying on of hands followed. Bishop Gene had instructed Tom and my three children to do the same. How sweet of him to include them, and how appropriate. If this had been a public ceremony, I would have asked the entire congregation of St. Gabriel's to lay hands on me. It would be a long process but well worth it.

When all had laid their hands on my head and had prayed for me, the bishop raised his hands over me in a gesture of prayer and said aloud, "Lord, look with favor on you're your servant, whom we now dedicate to the office of deacon, to minister at your holy altar. Send the Holy Spirit upon her, that she may be strengthened by the gift of your sevenfold grace to carry out faithfully the work of ministry."

The momentous deed was accomplished. Somewhat unsteadily, I stood to my feet, turned to face the applause of my family and my friend, Jerry. I was smiling amid tears of joy. "Stop, this is all too sudden," I contested, completely flustered. "There's no need. The truly important event comes next week. I don't know what to say. I wasn't expecting any of this."

I turned to Gene and saw his warm and gentle smile. "You do know how to surprise a person," I remarked. Then, as if affirming my new Order of Diaconate, I said to the assembled group, "Come to the house now for a little treat. If I'm going to be a good deacon, then I'll have to live up to my new calling as *the one who serves*."

After the church "practice" at which I received the diaconate, the entourage went to our house for a repast and celebration. "Bishop Gene McGovern," I exclaimed as the small circle raised their glasses to toast their new celebrity, "You certainly surprised me. In all the excitement I almost forgot to pull down those "Church Closed" signs on the doors. Carol would have been asking me about them in the morning.

"How are you holding up, Kel?" Jerry asked as he poured more wine into my glass from a special bottle he had brought.

"Quite well, really," I replied as I took a sip. "I can feel my face getting warm. It's either from this excellent wine or the headiness of the moment. I have a sense that despite the unexpected turn of events at the practice, this is the easy part. The real challenge comes after the ordination. It's like having children. The birth pangs are nothing compared with the teenage years, right boys?" Their mouths were too full of food to respond.

The rest of the week had a retreat atmosphere to it for me. My moments of prayer were focused on the impending ceremony and what it signified. My conversations with Tom and calls to Jerry were on the same topic. I even shared my feelings with my children, and, to their credit, they listened well and responded appropriately. There was a mystical feel to the week, something like the gathering of Jesus' followers after his Ascension. They stayed in the upper room waiting for the moment of Pentecost. I kept in touch with the movements and emotions within me, trying to prepare for my own Pentecost.

Will this really have an effect? Will it move this monolithic church of ours? Will the pope respond? Will Rome be moved? These are heady questions. Thank goodness I don't have to answer them. That's up to the future. At least God's on our team. "Come, Holy Spirit! Help us through this," I prayed fervently.

On Sunday morning, the family walked to Mass together and helped me do the setup. They had a new appreciation for my service to the community now that they knew I was acting in my new diaconate role. At one point before Mass, as Rachel was handing hymnals to those coming in, Tom had to intervene. Our daughter was smiling at each person she gave a book, saying, "I'm going to grow up to be a deacon, just like my Mom."

Tom overheard someone say, "What did that mean, become a deacon like her Mom? What a strange thing to say. Funny how kids mix up things. She's a cute child, though, so sure of herself."

Tom made his way to Rachel as quickly as decorum would allow. "Here Rachel, let me help you," giving her a stern glance as he took some hymnals from her. She looked back quizzically, as if to say "What's wrong? I didn't say anything about her priesthood."

On the walk home, Tom told me what had happened and I, in turn, gently yet firmly, explained to the children, "Please, no word to anyone, not a living soul, about the practice, or about the diaconate or priesthood or anything. Understand?"

The usually lively Sunday breakfast after Mass was somewhat subdued. Everyone was excited but uneasy as well. They didn't know what to expect from all this clandestine activity. "Let's enjoy this while we can," I said as I poured syrup on my pancakes. "But we have to be careful. Who knows what might happen to us if this goes public? One thing's for sure, I've not lost my appetite! What's getting into me, Tom? I never eat this much."

"Could it be a little nervousness?" Tom said, looking up with a smile. "And how many pancakes is that for you, Michael?"

"I don't know, Dad. They're really good with blueberries," he responded as he reached to stab a few more cakes and put them on his plate.

Realizing that tomorrow was the big day, Tom suggested it might be an opportune time to take a little afternoon trip. Rachel liked the idea and even the boys gave a reluctant assent. They quickly cleared the table and started piling things in the car. I wasn't so sure I would go with them. Having some time to myself sounded appealing, but by the time the car was packed, I couldn't resist the family's pleading. At the last moment, I hopped in the front seat and said to one and all, "Let's go!"

As Tom backed the car out the driveway, he put his hand on my shoulder. "The change of scenery will do you good." Then looking at the three in the back seat, he added, "How about if we check out the lighthouses up north. Maybe we'll find some we haven't seen?"

We found two new ones along the eastern shores of Lake Michigan and returned refreshed and more relaxed. We arrived home late and were all thankful for a bed to flop into. I enjoyed the break; it was just the perfect remedy. For a short while I forgot about what tomorrow would reveal and how it would unfold. "What a good idea that was, Tom," I remarked as we prepared for bed. "I'm so glad I went. I didn't realize how much I needed a diversion."

"You!" Tom exclaimed as he came out of the bathroom. "I needed it more. I was on pins and needles at Mass this morning. I got goose bumps all over when I thought of you up there saying Mass. I needed to get away as much as you did."

"So you're feeling this, too, then," I inquired with some surprise. "You look so calm."

"Look again, Sweetheart. Pleasant dreams," Tom said as he turned off the light.

I awoke the next morning apprehensive but expectant. I wasn't aware of any dreams that I could remember, let alone nightmares. I was happy I hadn't set the alarm. The extra bit of sleep felt good. I could smell the coffee Tom was already brewing downstairs. The kids were all still asleep. I lay in bed for a few more minutes, trying to take in the significance of this day. "Mary Magdalene, stick close by me today. You know the Lord well. Teach me about him and let me do my best."

I made the bed, showered, dressed and went down to join Tom. He was reading the morning paper. "Anything special by which to remember this day?" I asked.

"Nope," Tom replied, not looking up from the paper, but I caught the impish grin on his face. "Just this little story on the back page about some unknown woman being ordained to the priesthood. Nothing important."

"Thanks for reminding me," I retorted as I poured myself a cup of coffee. "How about cooking me a six-egg omelet to get the day started right?"

"Coming up—want bacon, sausage, ham *and* onions?" Tom replied, peering over the top of his paper.

"God help us! Let's stick to an English muffin, lightly buttered," I countered.

The banter between us continued throughout breakfast and until the children straggled to the kitchen. It felt good to have each other to talk to at the start of this big day. I was grateful that Tom had arranged for a light workload so he could spend extra time with me. Father Jerry was coming from Detroit around three o'clock and we would all drive to Gene's church together.

At nine, the phone rang. It was Bishop Gene to say that the coast was clear and he was getting everything ready. He liked the idea of having signs on the church doors. "Do you still have those, Kelly? Bring them along. The weather looks threatening but it's supposed to clear by the afternoon. Better if we don't have to turn on the lights, although I don't know what harm there would be in that."

We had planned a picnic lunch in the park, but it was raining too hard, so we decided to have our picnic on the living room floor instead. We moved the furniture and spread a blanket. We were pouring the drinks and were about to sink our teeth into some country fried chicken when the doorbell rang. Everyone looked up in surprise. "Who could that be, especially in this downpour?" I asked, worried that someone might have heard about our plan.

Nathan went to answer the door. He came back blushing. "Mom, it's Allyson Greenshaw, that girl in the accident. She's out of the hospital, I guess. She wants to see you."

"Well for heaven's sake, invite her inside, Nathan! Don't leave that child at the door, especially in this weather," I exclaimed, amused at how flustered Nathan had become upon meeting this unexpected guest.

Nathan returned with Allyson in tow. She seemed a little surprised at everyone sitting on the floor in the living room. I stood to give her a hug. "We're having a picnic," I explained as Allyson looked at the strange scene. "Want to join us? It was supposed to be in the park, but we were rained out, so we're using the living room instead. You're looking great, Allyson. Are you all healed?"

"Yes, thanks, mostly," Allyson replied, still not sure whether to stand or sit. Nathan stood beside her, also somewhat nonplused. "Some parts of me don't work so well but they say they will eventually. I just came to thank you, Mrs. More, for all you did for me that night in the hospital. It changed my life, it really did. I wanted to come and thank you personally. They told me at the parish office I might find you here."

"I'm glad you did," Kelly said, motioning to Allyson to sit next to her. "Here, have some chicken. Nathan, would you get her a plate, please?"

Nathan went to the kitchen for an extra plate, trying not to stare at Allyson in the process. She was someone he had always wanted to meet but never had the chance. Nathan returned, took a seat on the blanket and awkwardly handed Allyson a plate of food and a drink. Rachel found it amusing.

It wasn't easy for Allyson to sit on the floor, but she refused the chair I offered as an alternative. "I'm fine, really. I'll even be able to attend college this fall. It was touch and go for a while." Then quickly changing the topic, she asked, "Do you do this often, I mean, have an indoor picnic? My family would never even think of it!"

"Only when it rains," I said with a laugh. "I saw you at church yesterday. I'm so happy you're feeling better." The rest of the family was admiring the beauty of this young woman who seemed to have recovered so well from her injuries.

"I'm going to try to come more often if I can," Allyson responded, feeling a little more at ease. "I need to get back in the habit, I guess. It's been awhile."

Allyson stayed for a short time longer but left before the cake, pleading another commitment. "Thanks so much for lunch," she said as Nathan helped her up. "I mean, for the picnic. This was fun. Thanks again, Mrs. More, for getting me started on a new path. It was good meeting all of you. Goodbye."

"Nathan, see her to the door, please" I urged, as he stood frozen beside Allyson. "Thanks so much for coming. That was very sweet of you."

Allyson left and Nathan returned to some gentle ribbing from Michael and Rachel.

"Seems like a nice girl," Tom commented.

"Who learned her lesson the hard way," I added. "How ironic that she should show up on this very day. God certainly has a sense of humor."

"And some pretty good timing as well," Tom volunteered.

JERRY SHOWED UP A LITTLE AFTER three o'clock, as the family was getting dressed for the occasion. "Even though we're going to be the only ones there, I want us all to look our Sunday's best, not like that surprise *practice* last week" I said as I greeted Jerry at the door. "Did you bring the vestments and chalice, song sheets and all the rest of what we need?"

"I have them right here," Jerry responded, admiring how lovely Kelly looked in her black dress and pearls.

"Do you have enough film, Michael?" I inquired as Michael came down the stairs.

"All set, Mom," he assured me.

"Do I have my wits about me?" I added as I looked at my reflection in the hallway mirror.

"Hanging right there between your two ears," Tom quipped, giving me a hug from behind. "You do look great. The black dress is perfect, not that anyone will see it—I mean, it will be under your alb and all."

We all piled into one car and headed out of town. It was crowded, Rachel sitting on Nathan's lap, but I didn't want Jerry driving alone.

"We're all in this together. No stragglers. I hope we haven't forgotten anything."

"Don't worry," Jerry said reassuringly. "Everything will be just fine. All you need is yourself and the bishop to say the words."

We arrived by prior arrangement at the rectory's back door. Thankfully the rain had stopped as Gene ushered everyone inside. "We're alone here and no one's in the church. I just checked. It's nice to have the sunshine for this. God is certainly with us."

We followed Gene through the rectory and along the corridor to the church. He had put some flowers on the altar and the candles were lit.

"Kelly and Jerry, would you come back to the sacristy with me?" Gene asked as he invited the rest to take a seat in the front row. "We can vest there. Remember, Jerry, stay out of the camera's range. I don't want you involved in this. I've asked Michael to focus just on your hands and not on your face during the ceremony." Michael was already busy setting up the camera.

"I'm willing to pay the price," Jerry replied as he put on his robes, "but I concur with your wisdom on this. I'll be careful."

After Gene and Jerry had put on chasubles and I the long white alb, we returned to church to start the service. Michael began filming me as I entered. Despite the anxiety I felt within, I couldn't help but smile at the improbability and wonder of all that was about to take place. "Stay calm, walk with serenity," was my mantra. Over my arm I carried my chasuble and stole in which I would be vested later in the ceremony.

When we reached the back of the church, Jerry led the small group in the opening song, "Holy God, We Praise Thy Name" as the entourage walked slowly down the aisle. Bishop Gene began Mass as he always did, with the Sign of the Cross. He then welcomed everyone to this very special occasion. He did so as if the church were filled with parishioners instead of the small band of six who shared this moment. If this did go public, he wanted it to look as normal as possible. I stood before him in the center aisle. After the opening prayer, I went to the lectern and began by saying, "The first reading is from Paul's Second Letter to the Corinthians." I read the first lesson, which ended with the words, "We no longer look on anyone in terms of mere human judgments, for if anyone is in Christ, that person is a new person altogether. The old is finished and gone. Everything has become fresh and new!" I looked up from the book and announced to those assembled, "The Word of God."

"Thanks be to God," all responded as the reality of the moment began to sink in. Michael kept the camera focused on me as the small group sang the response to the reading, "I will take the Cup of Life, I will call God's name all my days." Then Bishop Gene stood to proclaim the gospel. It was from the twentieth chapter of John about Mary Magdalene's encounter with Jesus. "Woman, why are you weeping?" the bishop read. "She answered, 'Because the Lord has been taken away, and I do not know where they have put him.' She had no sooner said this than she turned around and caught sight of Jesus standing there. But she did not know him. 'Woman,' he asked, 'why are you weeping? Who is it you are looking for?' She supposed he was the gardener, so she said, 'Sir, if you are the one who carried him off, tell me where you have laid him and I will take him away.' Jesus said to her, 'Mary!' She turned to him and said in Hebrew, '*Rabboni*' (meaning, teacher)." Gene continued reading the gospel that ended with the words, "Mary Magdalene went and announced to the disciples, 'I have seen the Lord'; and she told them what he had said to her." The bishop kissed the book and holding it over his head, proclaimed, "The gospel, the good news of the Lord."

All responded, "Praise be to you, Lord Jesus Christ."

Bishop Gene motioned for everyone to sit down, again as if

commanding an entire congregation, as he expounded on the gospel. "Mary thought Jesus was the gardener," he began. "Why? Certainly she was distraught. She had been through a great deal in the last few days. It was quite understandable why she didn't recognize him. She wasn't ready for this turn of events. But suppose Jesus was acting as the gardener on purpose. This was the place of his burial and of his resurrection. Was he doing a little gardening besides? How strange.

"But it's not that strange once you think about it. He had come to show people what kind of God they had, One who loved and forgave and cared for them. He himself had come through death to new life in obedience to that love. Now he had to cultivate the soil and plant the seed of his own resurrection in the minds of his followers. Who better to do this than Mary and the other women? They were the ones Jesus chose to spread the good news of his resurrection to the apostles. It was the *women* who were the first messengers. But the apostles got the glory. Isn't it always that way, the women do the work and the men get the credit?"

At this moment, Michael panned to me to catch my expression as I sat in my chair next to the altar looking at Gene. I was beaming.

"Down through the ages," the bishop continued, "women have been spreading the good news, they have been healing and caring for people, listening to and forgiving sinners, they have been anointing and comforting the sick and dying. But it has been the men who have been ordained." Gene paused as if he were giving his virtual congregation time to absorb this.

Then he added with emphasis, "Until today! You have before you a courageous woman who has been called by God to the ordination of priesthood in the Roman Catholic Church. She has been ministering to her congregation as both leader and pastor for the last five years. Like Jesus, she has been cultivating the soil and planting the seeds in her community. Now it's time to affirm that servant leadership with the sacrament of ordination. In a short time I will lay my hands on her head and will call down the power of the Holy Spirit upon her, and she will become a priest for her people. This is a ritual that has been repeated again and again down through the ages.

"We don't know how many women have been ordained in the past. I'm confident she is not the first. The purpose of performing this ordination now is to make sure she will not be the last. Soon, very soon, my hope and prayer is that legions of men and women, married and single, will follow in her footsteps. They will ascend the altar of the Lord in order to lead people in Eucharist, in a thanksgiving table ministry that Jesus has invited us to perpetuate in his memory. It's our duty to keep this tradition alive. The needs of God's people demand it. Now is the time to expand this ordination rite so that it is inclusive of all who are called by God and are willing to receive it. We have no other alternative but to proceed."

Bishop Gene returned to his presidential chair next to mine and sitting down, prayed quietly for a moment, needing time to catch his breath.

After a short while, once again well composed, he rose, walked to the front of the altar and faced the congregation. He then called me forth to stand before him. Everyone else was standing in the front pew, poised for what was about to happen. Michael was on the side trying to get the best shot of both Gene and his mother.

The bishop then stated in a loud voice, "Let Kelly More, who is to be ordained a priest, come forward."

"Present," I responded, and walked toward him with resolve and determination. Whatever hesitation I felt before had suddenly left me. Only confidence was in my heart as I gave my emphatic response to Gene's invitation.

Jerry, with a voice not quite his own, spoke. "Most Reverend

Father, holy mother church asks you to ordain Kelly More, our sister, to the responsibility of the priesthood."

Bishop Gene, reading from the ordination rite, replied, "Do you know her to be worthy?"

"After inquiry among the Christian people and upon the recommendation of those responsible, I testify that she has been found worthy."

"Relying on the help of the Lord God and our Savior Jesus Christ," the bishop declared, "we choose Kelly More, our sister, for the Order of the Priesthood."

On cue, everyone in the small assembly of five responded "Thanks be to God," and declared their affirmation and support by clapping as long and hard as they were able. The sound of their applause echoed throughout the church and filled me with awe. What a demonstration of God working in strange and wonderful ways.

"Are you willing, Kelly More, in the presence of this assembly," Gene continued, "to undertake this ministry of priesthood, to lead the church's rituals, to preach the gospel and to continue drawing closer to Christ by serving Christ's people?"

"I am, with the help of God." I replied with as strong and resolute a voice as I could muster.

"Then kneel here before me, place your hands in mine and promise respect and obedience to your bishop and his successor." Gene said this as he placed his book on the altar and held out his hands to me. I knelt before him and in a ritual that had been repeated for centuries, I pledged my loyalty to the bishop and to my church.

Then I stood and as I had practiced, walked to the middle aisle and prostrated myself on the floor, face down. (This signified the candidate's humility before God.) While I lay on the floor, everyone prayed the litany of the saints, asking all of heaven to come to my assistance.

Jerry began the litany by singing, "Mary and Joseph," and all responded, "Pray for us."

"St. Anne and St. Joachim,"

"Pray for us."

"Saints Peter and Paul and all the Apostles,"

"Pray for us."

"Saints Martha and Mary,"

"Pray for us."

"St. Mary Magdalene,"

"Pray for us."

"All you holy saints and martyrs,"

"Pray for us."

And so it continued, a canopy of prayer settling on me as I lay in the middle of the church aisle. I felt strengthened by all those who had gone before me and risked their lives for what they knew was right. Mary and Joseph, Mary Magdalene, Francis of Assisi and Clare, Martin Luther King and Dorothy Day—on and on, the list of people protecting me and holding me in their care. It was such a comfort and support to know that I wasn't alone.

"Lord, be merciful, save your people," Jerry sang, then he concluded with "Lord, give us new life." And the little group responded, "Amen."

When it was over, the bishop bent down to tap me on my shoulder, inviting me to rise and come forward. As I stood before him, he solemnly laid his hands on my head and prayed in silence. This is part of the ancient ritual of priestly ordination dating back to the time of the apostles. As Gene had explained to me earlier, it signified the commissioning of the priest to ministry in the church through the gift of the Holy Spirit. I could feel the strength of Gene's hands on my head. It was such a liberating feeling. As he continued his silent prayer, I felt the Spirit coming down on me, into every fiber of my being. Would I be capable of administering this new responsibility? "Help me, God," I continually repeated.

I became aware of a subtle, imperceptible voice deep within that seemed to say, "You now have the power to do what Jesus did; to preach, to heal, to set people free. You now have the power and the obligation to do this."

After what seemed an eternity, I felt the bishop remove his hands and another set of hands rested on my head. Jerry was adding his blessing to the ritual. Michael was careful to film only Jerry's hands. As we viewed the video later it seemed to give the scene an aura of mystery and holiness, to see only his hands on my head.

After Jerry had finished laying his hands on my head, the bishop stood in front of me, extended his hands and said the prayer of consecration. "Almighty God, grant to this servant of yours the dignity of the priesthood. Renew within her the Spirit of holiness. As a co-worker with the Order of Bishops, may she be faithful to the ministry that she receives from you, Lord God, and be to others a model of right conduct. May she be faithful in working with the order of bishops, so that the words of the gospel may reach the ends of the earth, and the family of nations, made one in Christ, may become God's one, holy people. We ask this through our Lord Jesus Christ, Your Son, who lives and reigns with you and the Holy Spirit, one God, for ever and ever."

Jerry and the whole family responded as loudly and emphatically as they were able, "Amen!"

Now I was officially a Roman Catholic Priest. Glowing, I turned around and walked down to the front pew to be vested by my husband and children. Skillfully, Michael kept the camera only on me as Tom, Nathan and Rachel helped put the chasuble over my alb and then the stole—the sign of priestly office—over the chasuble.

I returned to kneel before the bishop who was now sitting in a chair in front of the altar. First he anointed my hands with chrism, signifying Christ's continued presence with this newly ordained person. Then I received from the bishop the paten—a golden plate used to hold the consecrated bread at Mass—and the chalice for the consecrated wine. As he did this he said, "Accept from the holy people of God the gifts to be offered to him. Know what you are doing, and imitate the mystery you celebrate. Model your life on the mystery of the Lord's cross."

He then took me by the hand and gave me a warm embrace. This was the cue for Michael to stop videotaping so everyone could come forward and give me a big hug as a "greeting of peace."

Pandemonium broke out as the pent-up energy of the children and adults burst forth in cheers, hugs and kisses and exclamations of joy. This went on for some time. Already I felt every bit a priest, clothed in chasuble and stole. Tears streamed down my face as I acknowledged the acclaim of my family, Jerry and Bishop Gene.

Finally, Gene motioned to Michael to turn on the camera again, as he and I ascended the steps and stood at the altar. With the others standing on the opposite side of the altar, the two of us concelebrated the Mass. When it was time for the consecration, the bishop and I, now the newly ordained priest, said the words together, "This is My body." And again, "This is My blood." The bishop held the host and I held the chalice for all to see. As Bishop Gene replaced the paten on the altar, and I put down the chalice, he looked into the camera and said, "Let us proclaim the great mystery of our faith." All responded, "Christ has died, Christ has risen, Christ will come again."

As everyone sang this acclamation I had a sense that I was not just reciting the words of consecration with the bishop. My standing there was not merely symbolic. I was a *con*-celebrant with him—the two of us *together* were doing this. Not only that, I now could do this on my own. I didn't need him or anyone else to be there with me. I could now stand before a group of people, a congregation, and *preside*! My words and gestures have power to change the bread and wine into the body and blood of Christ. It will be a *real* Mass, an honest-to-God Eucharist! That was almost too much for me to assimilate.

When it was time for the Lord's Prayer, Michael put the camera aside and we all joined hands around the altar—the table of Eucharist. This is a circle of belief, a ring of ministry, I thought to myself. We are all in this together. All those circling this altar share in my priesthood because of our common baptism. It's a step into an unknown model of priesthood, one freed from clerical control.

After communion the Mass concluded with the final blessing. The experience triggered tears. There I was, laying hands on Tom, Nathan, Michael, Rachel, Jerry, even Bishop Gene. I now possessed a power I didn't have before. I could bless people in a whole new way! It's now sacramental. I could bless them as they lie dying in bed. I could bless them as they come to me for God's mercy and forgiveness. I could bless them as infants in the waters of baptism. I could bless their love in the marriage rite. I could bless them in their losses, their pains and their separations. I could bless them at the end of Mass and send them forth to be a blessing to others. And this blessing is God's blessing. I'm not sure when I would ever be able to exercise this new priestly blessing but I knew I could and I was humbled.

Once the ceremony concluded we all retired to a private banquet room in a restaurant Gene assured us was a safe environment. He had coordinated the beautiful food and beverage arrangements with the owner, a friend of his—who asked no questions. I tried to behave in a dignified manner as one toast followed another. First Tom, then Jerry and Gene, and even Nathan stood to pay a tribute. Michael set up the computer so we could all watch the ordination. It's nice to have a genius for a son, I thought, even if he is a bit wild and unpredictable at times. He did a professional job capturing only Gene and myself. The artful inclusion of other people's hands and gestures was so tastefully done.

Returning home and climbing into bed I reflected on all that happened. "Today was one of *the* best days of my life," I prayed. "Thanks, loving God, for the mystery of it all. I can't believe it happened. Thank You for this day, unfathomable that it is."

I turned to look at Tom, already fast asleep. Good for him, he earned his gold star. He's going to need rest for all that will likely result from this eventful day.

NINE

꧂

THE NEXT MORNING THE FAMILY started to congregate in the kitchen at around nine o'clock. Each child gave their mom some extra attention as they came downstairs for breakfast. For one brief moment they seemed to treat me with new respect and a slight trace of awe. Soon, however, all was back to normal, everyone passing the toast, milk, cereal, orange juice and morning paper.

"I'm so happy I told Carol I wouldn't be in today," I said to no one in particular as I poured milk on my cereal. "I'm not ready to face the real world after yesterday's *out-of-body* experience. It'll take a concerted effort on my part to convince myself that it wasn't all a dream. Kids, did that really happen? Were you there, too? Do you remember it taking place?"

"What, Mom?" Michael said, not looking up from the sports section, but flashing a quick wink at his sister.

Rachel took the clue. "Something happened yesterday?"

"All right, all right, enough already," I threatened, holding a bagel ready to throw at the next person who made a wise crack.

"So now what?" Nathan asked. "We know we can't tell anyone, right, Rachel?" casting an older-brother look at his sister. "But what happens next?"

"We sit on it for a month or more," Tom volunteered, looking at me to be sure he had it right. "Someone important will be talking to the pope, trying to convince him to call a special Ecumenical Council to legitimize what happened yesterday to your Mom."

"So, am I to understand I'm illegitimate?" I protested, putting down my coffee and looking Tom in the eye. "I'll have you know my parents . . ."

"Yes, well, you know," Tom chuckled, enjoying the moment. "Anyway, the whole point is to put some pressure on the pope to make it possible for all who are called to the priesthood—men or women, married or single—to be ordained and start serving in parishes again. It's that simple."

"So, how long will that take, Dad?" Rachel piped up, trying to make sense of it all.

"Not long once the Council is called and they change the current church law. Many people, here and around the world, are eager to become legitimate priests. They're trained and have the experience, just like your mom, but they need the sanction to be ordained."

"So Mom can't be a priest yet?" Michael asked, suddenly more interested in this conversation than in the sports section.

"She is a priest, a fully ordained, real live priest," Tom replied. "That, kids, will take some getting used to, for all of us. But she can't exercise her priesthood yet. If the pope does call a Council, then we maintain secrecy until the Council says it's okay. When that day comes we can take your Mom out of mothballs and have a great ordination party with the whole parish."

"Moth balls!" I exclaimed. "Thanks a lot."

"If, on the other hand, the pope does nothing," Tom continued, ignoring my impertinent interruption, "then it gets a little complicated. The fact that your mom was ordained will be leaked to the press. Then it'll become a big deal. Thank goodness we have a chance to prepare for this ahead of time. It may be a little tough on everyone.

"Your mom and I will be meeting with Bishop Gene to plan our strategy, I suspect. We'll have a chance to discuss this. But it's too soon for all that now. Let's just enjoy the moment and our breakfast together. Whoops. I just remembered. Was I supposed to have you say Grace before we ate, Kel?" Tom said mockingly as the rest of the family started to giggle.

"Will you *stop it*!" I exclaimed in exasperation. "I'm the same person, okay?"

It wasn't long before Bishop Gene called. His tone was more subdued this morning than it had been last night. "Hello, Kelly," he began. "I suspect you knew I'd call. You did very well yesterday. I was proud of you. Now comes the difficult part."

"Yes, I can hear it in your voice. Are you okay?" I asked with some concern.

"I'm fine," Gene affirmed. "It's just that it was a long night. The weight of all this seemed to have come down on me after you all left the house and it gave me pause. Are you sure you're up to this? For me, it's no problem. They can do little to me now that I'm retired. But you—it may get rough. I'm beginning to wonder if we should go through with our plan."

"Too late, Bishop," I quickly responded, trying to raise his spirits. "It's a done deal. You ordained me a priest of God, and as far as I can tell, God agreed. So there's only one way to go and that's forward. I'm ready and willing. Once the decision was made, that was it. Didn't Jesus say something about not looking back once you put your hand to the plow?"

"Fewer than twenty-four hours a priest and already she's quoting scripture to her bishop! Not that I'm really your bishop. I wonder what Patrick Foley would think if he knew he had a new priest in his diocese. That could throw him for a loop. I hope the good Lord lets me see Patrick's face when he first hears the news."

"Anyway, more to the point," Gene continued. I could sense that he was feeling better now that we were having this conversation. "We need to plan our next steps. First, do you think Michael could make two copies of that video he took yesterday? He really did do a superb job. Only two copies should be made and you keep the original. I'll need them as soon as possible. We're sending one copy to Rome in a matter of days and I'll keep the other copy.

"Yes, I'm sure he could. He's very good at that sort of thing."

"Excellent. Now to the second part. You and I should outline some contingency plans."

"I have another idea," I responded, somewhat proud of myself for planning ahead. "Tom and I talked this morning. We think it would be better if everyone who was at the ceremony had a chance to explore our options together. Are you open to that?"

"Oh, a much better idea, much better," Gene replied, obviously impressed with the wisdom of my suggestion. "When?"

"We're thinking about this Friday afternoon. Could you come at three o'clock? I'll invite Jerry and we'll have dinner afterwards. How does that sound?"

"Sounds good. I've nothing planned for Friday. That'll give me some time to formulate some possible strategies. In the meantime, I'll stop by this afternoon for the tapes. I also want to give Michael a little something for his trouble. Will he mind?"

"Not in the least. Aren't you thoughtful? See you soon. And Gene, you did very well yourself yesterday. That celebration was very special. Thank you."

I hung up, happy that Tom and I had arranged a joint meeting with all the players present; a much better way to operate. I hope I remember to do that if and when this priesthood thing takes hold. We've had enough of those exclusive deliberation meetings where not everyone who is affected is included. Actually, I guess I've been doing it all along. I wonder if that's what they mean by the *priesthood of the faithful.*"

I poked my head into Tom's office and told him I was going to the lake to pray for a while. "I'll be back for lunch. Tell the kids when you see them."

I drove to the park and found my favorite bench. On this Tuesday morning the park was deserted. I was happy to be alone. The lake spread before me, azure blue to match a cloudless sky. A slight breeze rustled the pages of the scripture reading I held on my lap. As I began to pray, I thought to myself what a difference *setting* makes. When I have serious reflecting to do, this bench and my chair in the chapel are the two best places. I feel as if I'm coming *home*. I suspect that's why churches are built, as special places of meeting between the human and the divine. Well, dear Friend, I come before you today a different person. You did it all. Whatever happens from here, I know in the deepest part of my being that I'm a real priest. You ordained me for a mission, of this I'm certain. So now it's up to You to see me through."

I closed my eyes and let the reality of my new priesthood seep into my soul and body. I let it touch every particle of who I was. I stayed in this receptive posture for some time. Finally I opened my eyes and looked over the lake and the trees that surround its shore. I guess that's what is meant by *growing into the priesthood*, I thought. It takes awhile for the reality to hit home.

Closing my eyes once again, I returned to my reflective mood and thought about the future exercise of my priesthood. It'll be a long time before I'll be able to minister as a priest. As I thought about this, a strange and unique idea came into my head. Or will it? What about those Hispanic migrants who live in that little shanty outside of town? Could I be a priest to them somehow? They have no one to minister to them. Our outreach group from St. Gabe's goes there only about once a month. The language would be a barrier, but I suspect we could overcome that. What an interesting idea. I think I'll pursue this.

I picked up my Bible and walked to the car with new energy and fresh ideas rummaging through my brain. No one would know that

I'm there; they're so isolated. That little community could be in the middle of Mexico for all the townspeople know. I being their priest was a fascinating concept.

I arrived home and began to fix lunch. "The park was so lovely this morning," I said to Tom as he wandered into the kitchen.

"You're still glowing," he returned as he helped me make chicken salad sandwiches for anyone likely to show up.

"Yes, I guess I am," I admitted as Rachel miraculously appeared to grab the first sandwich. "It's only now starting to sink in, and it'll take some serious concentration before I realize it wasn't just a lovely fantasy. You know, I had thought of going to the migrant community tomorrow. I might be able to practice my priestly ministry out there in ways I could never do in the parish."

"And how, exactly, will you communicate with them?" Tom asked, practical man that he was. He knew that I'd mastered only a few Spanish words, primarily hello and goodbye.

"Not sure yet, but I feel the pull. I may be crazy, but I want to give it a try. Say," I asked, looking at Rachel who was seated at the kitchen counter, "do you know what happened to Nathan. He just up and vanished."

"He didn't say where he was going," Rachel volunteered, "but he did mention something about trying to find out what Allyson Green-shaw's email might be."

"How about that!" I exclaimed, wondering how Rachel always managed to get information before anyone else. "Stranger things have happened. Wonder where she'll be going to college. I'm so happy to know she'll be okay. It still gives me goose bumps to think of that accident and how close to death she was. You be extra careful, young lady. I never want to be on the receiving end of that pastoral care I had to do in the hospital."

The three of us were enjoying our lunch when Gene's visit

suddenly dawned on me. "Oh, my gosh!" I exclaimed. "I forgot all about Bishop Gene coming for the videos." Standing at the bottom of the stairs I yelled upstairs. "Michael, would you make two copies of the ordination video?"

"Sure thing," Michael returned, bounding down the stairs for some lunch, "only they're not really videos anymore, they're DVDs. When do you need them?"

Just then the doorbell rang. I opened the door to find Gene smiling at me. "How's my new priest?" he said taking my hand.

I threw my arms around him and gave him a big hug. "I'm doing just fine, thank you. Come in and have a seat." Then I motioned to Michael to run upstairs and make those copies.

After Michael had left, milk and sandwich in hand, Gene asked, "How much should I give him, do you think? I was thinking two hundred dollars might be right."

"Oh my, that's far too much," I replied. "How about fifty?"

"No, this is too important. It could be seen by thousands of people. I'd rather make this a memorable moment for him. He's really very talented, you know."

"It's your call, but I want to stick around when he sees the size of your check."

Soon Michael came downstairs, copies in hand. As he came into the living room the bishop handed him an envelope. "Here's a little something for your trouble, Michael."

"Oh, you don't have to do that, Bishop" he said, not taking the check. "I had some DVDs I bought on sale."

"No problem," Gene insisted. "You have real talent. Did you ever think about doing more of this sort of thing?" With that, the bishop put the envelope in Michael's shirt pocket and turned to leave.

"I really have to go—a few places yet to visit and a Mass to do this afternoon. Thanks again for the videos. I'll see you next Friday."

"So what did he give you?" I asked Michael with a smile after seeing Gene out the door.

"A check, I guess," he said as he opened the envelope. "Whoa! Look, Mom, two hundred dollars! That's amazing!"

"Now, remember, young man, not a word to anyone about this money," I cautioned him. "We don't want to raise any suspicions. Okay?"

"Sure, Mom. Cool!" and he ran to the kitchen to show his Dad and Rachel.

I laughed to myself as I saw him go. It's going to be hard for these kids to remain silent. Tom and I will have to be watchful.

I WENT TO CHURCH EARLY on Wednesday to lead the Morning Prayer service. I smiled to myself as I said the prayers and led the songs. I could say a Mass instead; if the attendees only knew.

The day was a usual one, filled with people making requests and having special needs, as any pastoral ministry is. The Hispanic migrant community kept coming to my mind and I looked for a moment when I could break away and drive to their community. I suppose I'll have to go in the evening when they're not in the fields, I thought to myself. Perhaps I could even start tonight.

At home, I tracked down Nathan and told him of my intentions. "You've been taking Spanish in school. Here's a chance to practice. Would you be willing to come and help your poor mom?"

"Yeah, I suppose I could do that," Nathan replied, and then volunteered a bit of news. "You know, Mom, I took your advice and called Allyson Greenshaw. I was scared because she was a year ahead of me in school, but she's not at all like what I'd expected. Or maybe she's changed. She's not as snooty as I thought. She was happy that I called and she said she's coming to Mass again this Sunday."

"Good for you, Nathan!" I replied, admiring his courage and surprised that he would share this with his mother. "I'm glad you're making a new friend. Thanks for putting aside your plans and joining me tonight. I really need you to help with the introductions. The migrants would have no idea who I am or why I'm there. We could leave right after dinner. I think it'll take about thirty minutes to get there. I want to be sure to arrive while it's still light."

The two of us drove to the migrant community that evening, pulling alongside a random home just before eight o'clock. We knocked on the door. Unfortunately the family was right in the middle of dinner. I apologized profusely, holding up my hand and saying in English, "So sorry, so sorry," while Nathan added, *pardone, pardone.*

Both the man and woman who answered the door looked perplexed, and they called a young girl about the age of fifteen to help them. Thankfully she knew some English and translated for her parents, as I tried to explain who I was and that I would return at a more convenient time. Instead, the father and mother took us by the hand, and with large smiles led us inside, sitting us at their table. The rest of the family, six children, all younger than our interpreter, made room for us. Everyone was silent at they looked at us; even the youngest stopped crying. Then suddenly a plate full of food appeared before each of us. Our protestations made no impact. We were going to eat what was placed before us. Amen.

I had miscalculated; with long hours of daylight in the summer months, the family would be working in the fields until close to sundown and only then return home to eat their meal. I had no idea how to begin the conversation or what they might understand. I tried to explain my role as the pastor of St. Gabriel's. When I mentioned the parish, it made an impression on the family. They smiled and nodded enthusiastically. Our young interpreter explained that people had come from the parish to give them food, blankets and toys for the children. After trying to eat one more bite, I gave Nathan the high sign that it was time to leave. I tried to explain that I had only come to say hello and that we would like to return at a more convenient time. I had a sense that we were taking food out of the children's mouths by coming during dinnertime. But it was difficult to get away. I promised another visit in a week and retreated to the car, glad to have Nathan there for support.

"That didn't go so well, did it?" I said as we drove out of the compound.

"Sorry that I don't know more Spanish, Mom." Nathan replied, "Thank goodness that their daughter knew some English. I think her name was Maria. I'm not used to how fast they talked."

"I'm not so sure this was a good idea," I admitted. "Somehow I thought I could do some priestly work here, but I'll need to do better than I did tonight. Aren't you just about bursting with food?"

"Yeah," Nathan admitted, "but it was so good. Too bad they kept giving me more when they were holding back themselves. Did you notice? They had hardly anything to eat. They're good people, and they have so little."

The two of us rode the rest of the way home in silence. I wanted to hear more about Allyson, but nothing was forthcoming. Mothers are always the last to know when it comes to teenagers, I guess, but Nathan was more open to me tonight than he's ever been. I hope he and Allyson strike up a relationship; they would be good for each other.

The rest of the week was routine until Friday afternoon. The children had all been alerted about the strategy meeting and they felt very mature to be included in the deliberations. They were also reminded, on a daily basis, not to tell a living soul about all that had happened. Both Jerry and Bishop Gene arrived at three o'clock, and the group gathered on the front porch to talk about options and future steps. After everyone had lemonade or ice tea, Bishop Gene got down to business.

"The video is being delivered as we speak," he began, enjoying the closeness that had developed among us over the last two weeks. "A member of our bishops' group flew to Rome on Wednesday, and he called me when he got there. He's due to have an audience this evening in the pope's private chambers. I've not heard yet what happened. The visit was scheduled some months ago under another pretext. So far no one else in the Roman Curia seems to suspect anything. Let's pray it stays that way."

"Our hope is that our envoy will persuade the pope to change his mind and call a General Council. If our man's initial requests go nowhere, then he plans to show the pope the video as proof of what occurred. This might tip the balance in our favor."

Michael perked up when he heard this just as I looked at him with an admiring nod.

"If not," Gene continued, "and the pope still holds fast, then our emissary will tell the pope of our intentions to go public and inform the world about what has taken place. This last move will not take place for thirty days, so if the pope doesn't act, we have time to plan our next move. That's as much as I can tell you at this time. You now know as much as I do."

Gene finished his report and took a sip of iced tea. It was cool on the porch, but he was sweating, nevertheless.

"And what are your expectations?" Jerry asked. "What kind of person is our pope? Do you think he will bow to this pressure or call your bluff?"

"I'm not sure, frankly," Gene sighed, lost in his own thoughts. "He's always received us with great grace and warmth. He's aware of our group's existence. I suspect there are similar groups of bishops in other parts of the world as well. The pressure on him must be enormous—from both sides—those desiring change and those opposed to it. And to think he's only been pope for a matter of months. He's such a cautious, patient man. No one really knows what he's thinking. Everyone is welcomed and listened to, but nothing happens. I think the Roman Curia is getting as impatient as we are. Everything is on hold while rallies and counter-rallies take place around the globe. It's anybody's guess what will spur him into action or what course he'll take. Those from his own diocese in Italy say it's just the way he is. He usually needs quite a jolt to get going. Once he does, however, our sources say he's unstoppable. But to get to that point, he has to analyze every option from every perspective. Let's just say he's unlikely to act prematurely or impulsively."

"So, from what you're saying," I interjected, as I tried to interpret the conversation, "you're not very hopeful that he'll be coerced into calling a Council of Bishops."

"Yes, I guess that's what I'm saying," Gene admitted. "I've left word with our contact person to call here if he gets no answer at my home. It's six hours later there, so he could be calling any minute. Can you hear the phone from here?"

"Sure, no problem," Rachel piped up, proud to offer her input to such an adult gathering.

"Thanks, Rachel," the bishop responded. Then turning to the group he added," What I'm saying is, don't get your hopes up. Let's presume we'll be unsuccessful and that we'll have to tell the world what we've done. Then what? Let me add that our friend in Rome will not leave the video with the pope. We'll safeguard that until the time comes to notify the press. If we have to go that route, we bishops have already strategized how to get maximum coverage. Sarah, Michigan will become the center of the universe for one brief, shining moment. So, knowing this could happen, how do we respond? And especially how do we best protect all of you?"

"Wow! This is going to be big, isn't it?" Nathan exclaimed, having listened intently to all Gene had said. "We could be famous."

Feeling more troubled and distraught with every word Gene spoke, I asked, "So should we lay low until this blows over?"

"Exactly," Bishop Gene returned. "We won't need you to be present when the news breaks. Best to be incognito, unavailable, sequestered. The question is just how can this be accomplished?"

"Let me get the timetable straight," Tom spoke as he struggled to formulate some kind of plan. "It's the end of July now. The news could break by the first of September, when the kids are back in school. It'll be difficult to get away. About how long do you suppose we would have to be in hiding?"

"I suspect for a month, anyway," the bishop responded, beginning to appreciate the complexity of the situation.

"Okay, so we go underground for a month," Tom continued in an analytical manner. "That means no phones, computers, credit cards, nothing. Otherwise we could be traced and the media would find us. Interesting problem."

"Yes, quite," replied Jerry with a concerned expression on his face. "I hadn't thought of all that."

"But I think we could set up a secure line on the Internet," Michael volunteered, glad to be able to add his piece to the puzzle. "Have someone create an account for us, or perhaps use someone else's. Messages sent there could be read by us. I don't think that could be traced. I'll check it out, Dad."

"Good work," Tom replied. "I think you may be right. We can be kept informed without being discovered. But where could we go? Somewhere no one would suspect."

"Bingo! I think I know where," I interjected with a shout. "The migrants! They're in the countryside all by themselves. Hardly anyone knows about them. Even the farmers don't go into that little community. I suspect, based on our little encounter earlier this week, that they would welcome us with open arms. There must be at least one house they're not using. I remember seeing some empty buildings as Nathan and I drove into the place. They're run down and it would be very simple living, but it would be secure. As for

Internet access, that's something else. I'm not sure anyone there even has a phone."

Nathan broke in, "I'll bet we could offer to get a phone for that family we visited. They might appreciate it. I don't know enough Spanish to explain all that; but maybe their daughter could get the information through to them."

"I could help you," Jerry offered as he joined the enthusiasm of the group. "I know enough Spanish to convey our plan. That really might be just the place! You could start fixing it now, then carry in your belongings and stock it in advance. But you'll have to be very careful so no one around either neighborhood suspects anything."

"Yes, that'll be a challenge," I agreed as I tried to determine how it could be effected. Just then an elderly neighbor waved at us on the porch as she walked down the street. "We could make it look like a service project," I continued, as I smiled and waved back. "Only don't tell a soul what we're doing. Got that, kids? Rachel? Michael? Nathan? Once the press comes around, they'll be mercilessly asking questions of the neighbors. Best not to raise any suspicions. Act like everything is normal, no matter what!"

"But won't the church outreach committee come by?" Bishop Gene asked, still not convinced this would be the best place to go, since it's in such close proximity to home. "How can you avoid that happening?"

"I know their schedule. We can disappear when they come. Will we have our car?"

"Better not," Tom spoke. "It has to look like we just disappeared. Much better to leave the car in the garage."

"But who's going to look after our things?" Rachel complained.

"I think I can get Frank, the police officer who belongs to the par-ish, to arrange that," I volunteered. "I'll explain to him that we may have to be away and we'll need him to keep it safe. Knowing Frank, this place will be as secure as Fort Knox. Do they still store gold there?"

"Not a question that concerns me right now," Tom laughed. "Okay, that's a good idea. Rachel, would you get some pads of paper from my office? We have to start listing all of this. Thanks. Now, about the kids and school. What are we going to do about that?"

"I'll bet we could get our teachers to give us work to do for a month," Nathan said, not sure he liked what he was suggesting but forging ahead anyway. "We could tell them we're going on a trip and we have this great opportunity that only comes along once in a lifetime, and we'll study while we're there. I've seen other kids do this. Why not us? Only we don't tell them where we're going, right, Rachel?"

"I know! I know already. Geez!" Rachel complained. She had just returned from inside the house and was passing pads to all who wanted them.

"Good thinking, Nathan," I replied. "Good for you. This is beginning to sound like quite an adventure. Okay, now let's see. We fix a place for ourselves in the migrants' community. We get Jerry to go there and sort all this for us. We start moving our stuff there a little bit at a time. We add a telephone line and secure a special Internet connection. We arrange for the children to do their studies. What about you and me, Tom? How do we arrange a month's vacation?"

"I think I can do that, especially if I can stay tuned to the Web. I'll not contact the office; only see what they're doing. One month should be no trouble. How about you, Kel?"

"I suppose I can get Deb to handle everything. She did it for the week I was trying to come to a decision about all this. The emergencies can go to Father Henry. I don't like that because he'll try to take over, but for a month, it'll be okay."

"Good. We're getting all of this settled nicely," Bishop Gene stated, feeling more comfortable with the plan as the details became clearer. "This is going well. If the pope doesn't respond in a month to six weeks, we break the story. The media descends on your home and parish, but you're nowhere to be found. Good for you. I think this can work. Now let's move beyond the month you're in hiding. You move back home. The media discovers that and there's a flurry of activity. Not as much as if you'd been here all along, but enough. Kelly, you've had a little exposure to this from the Ordination Rally. It's best to remain quiet as you did then. Just keep saying, 'No comment.' The trouble is with your job. I doubt Bishop Patrick Foley will let you minister at St. Gabriel's any longer, nor anywhere else for that matter. You'll be *persona non grata*."

"A what?" Rachel interrupted.

"A person who's not accepted or allowed to do her priestly work, dear," I explained.

"So, can you folks survive without Kelly's income?" Gene inquired, somewhat embarrassed to be asking such a personal question.

"I suspect I could get a job teaching in one of the public schools," I responded. "I'm qualified, but I'd have to get accredited. I might do substituting. We'll survive. I don't think it'll be a problem. But oh, will I miss ministering to and with the people at Gabe's!"

"Who knows what will happen in a few months," Jerry interjected. "Lots of water will have gone over the dam by then."

"True enough," Bishop Gene responded, both pleased that we had settled on a plan but sad that it would cause this family that he loved such transition and turmoil.

Just then the phone rang. Everyone stopped cold, wondering if it was the call Bishop Gene was expecting from Rome. Rachel shot up to answer it. She returned almost immediately saying, "It's for you, Bishop."

Everyone looked at each other as he went inside to answer it. After what seemed an eternity, he returned to give his report. "Not very good news, I'm afraid," he began, his face having lost the color it had when he went in to take the call. "As expected, the pope was non-committal. Our contact person did have his meeting with the pope without raising any suspicions. They were together for half an hour. That, in itself, is good news. But the report was not very hopeful."

"The pope listened attentively to all that was said," he went on, trying to relay the news just as he had heard it. "His Holiness shook his head in sadness and disbelief when our man said that you, Kelly, had been ordained by me. He watched the ordination with eagerness, but did not react. After hearing the possibility that the media might learn of this in a month, he didn't even blink. It seemed as though he was expecting this, but there was no indication, one way or another, of what he might decide.

"So there you have it. We'd better proceed with all we have planned. I doubt the pope will make a move any time soon toward calling a Council. I'm not even sure this move will have any influence over him. Time will tell. At least we tried. Is there anything more to discuss?" Gene asked. It was obvious to all that he carried a heavy burden. Then, looking around the circle at the younger members, he added, "Remember now, not a word about any of this to *anyone*." The children all nodded in agreement.

"Excuse me, Gene," I interrupted, resigned to what I now knew was going to be our fate, "but I have to check the chicken. Tom, would you please get the cheese tray out of the refrigerator?"

"We've done plenty for one afternoon," the bishop added in a somewhat lighter tone. "It's time to enjoy your home cooking, Kelly."

"Nothing could rival that banquet on Monday night," I responded as I headed inside. "You thought of everything."

"And, thank you," Michael added, remembering his manners, "for that, ah, that check for the DVD. It was awesome."

"You're welcome, Michael," Gene replied graciously. "That work you did might make you famous. Too bad you won't be around to enjoy it. Don't forget to take a television set with you to your new home so you can see what the media does with the video. You may not recognize it after they do their editing and splicing."

"Yes, we'd better start a list tonight of what we'll need," Tom remarked as he returned with the cheese and crackers. "Good thing they have electricity there. They do, don't they, Nathan?" who responded with a nod and a look as if to say, "Well, Dad, of course they do."

"I wonder if this is what the experience of the first Christians was like," Jerry mused as he looked at this small band of co-conspirators. "Only they had to contend with the Romans. Well, come to think of it, so do we."

TEN

꙳

A CELL PHONE BEGAN RINGING in the distance. "Oh, my goodness, that's mine!" I was at church setting up for Mass on Sunday morning, something I had done many times before, but today felt different. This was the first Mass since that life-changing event of last Monday. I ran to the sacristy where I could hear my phone's melodic ring. "I was sure I turned it off. I guess I forgot," I said out loud as I pulled it out of my purse to answer the call. I wonder who's calling me on a Sunday morning. It must be important.

"Hello," I said on the fifth ring. "Oh, it's you, Henry. What's up? I thought you would have been here by now."

"I just got word of an emergency at the hospital," he came back apologetically. "Someone from my parish was in a bad accident. They want me there right away. I'm surprised and glad I was able to reach you. I don't think I can make it this morning. Guess you'll have to do a Communion Service. At least it was your turn to give the reflection. You can do it after the gospel now, as you did before. I'm sure you'll like that," he said with a bit of sarcasm in his voice.

Ignoring Henry's quip, I pressed the off button and put the phone back in my purse. I was both mystified and amused by this sudden turn of events. So, I'm going to be preaching this morning, not just doing a reflection after Communion. *And* I'm going to be leading the service, which I've done before, but this will be very different. God, you do have a sense of humor. Just when I least expected it, you give me this chance to experience my new calling, hidden though it be.

I put on my alb and made the final preparations for the Communion Service. Before processing down the aisle during the opening song, I went to the front of the church to announce that Father Henry was detained by an emergency and would not be here this morning. "We'll hold a Communion Service instead. I think we'll have enough consecrated hosts for everyone. I'll do the gospel and give a reflection. Then, after presenting our gifts, we'll go right to the Lord's Prayer and the Communion Rite. You might even get dismissed a little early, so make up for it by sharing an extra cup of coffee afterwards with someone you haven't fellowshipped with recently."

I could see people smiling as I went to the back of church to start the procession. I sensed they liked this shift as well. "These are my people and I am their pastor," I mused as I walked down the aisle following the book-bearer and the servers. "What they don't realize is that now I'm also their *priest*! I wonder if and when that will become known to them? Won't they be surprised!"

"Let us begin our service in the name of Our Creator, Redeemer and Spirit of Life—Father, Son and Holy Spirit," I began as everyone present made the sign of the cross. The service continued, as would a regular Mass until it was time for the reading of the gospel. I stood to read the proclaiming, a right usually reserved for a priest or deacon. The passage for the day was from Luke's gospel that talked of Jesus sending the disciples out two by two "to every town and place he intended to visit."

I tried to proclaim the gospel with a sense of authority, realizing it was now my right and duty as a newly ordained priest to speak God's Word before the assembly. Only my loving family sitting there in the third pew knew this was the case. Rachel beamed as she looked up at her mother reading the gospel. I caught Tom giving her a sideways glance as if to say, "Don't you *dare* burst out for all to hear, "That's my Mom, the priest!"

After I had finished reading the gospel, the congregation sat and waited expectantly for my reflection. "These were not only the apostles He sent," I began as I walked down the middle aisle so I could connect better with the community, "but many more disciples, seventy, to be exact. They were regular people, like you and me. These were the ones sent by Jesus to spread the good news, people like you, Alice and you, Frank," I said, gesturing to those around me, "and you, Deb and Carol and Greg, yes, even you, my own Nathan, Michael and Rachel. Each of us is called to prepare the ground for Jesus' coming among us. You can't leave it only to the priests and bishops, the ones we think are ordained to do the preaching and teaching. Look at what happened this morning. Father Henry couldn't make it. I had to step in to fill the vacuum. I'm one of those disciples.

"Jesus continues in today's reading, 'The harvest is rich but the workers are few; therefore, ask the harvest-master to send more workers.' No doubt about it." I said as I warmed to the topic. "We're running short these days, at least with the number of ordained priests that are available. On the other hand, there are plenty of people willing to take the challenge to spread God's Word, ordinary people like those first followers of Jesus. What's the solution? Just for a moment, think about this question Jesus presented to us today, 'How are we going to find people to go into the harvest and spread the good news?'"

I paused to let the assembly think about my question. I closed my eyes and tried to envision what I might do. All that came into my head was the irony of me standing before these people as their priest. "If they only knew, if they only knew," I thought. Then suddenly I opened my eyes and discovered people looking at me expectantly.

"Now then," I said, quickly recovering from my musings, "connect with someone next to you and share your ideas about finding people to 'reap the harvest.'"

Slowly people began discussing the issue with one another. The noise and energy level in the church began to rise. I went to the choir and chose one person with whom to share my insights. "There's an easy solution," Margaret, one of the long-time sopranos volunteered. "Just ordain *you*! It doesn't make any sense, really, because we don't need Father Henry; we need *you* as our priest." The woman was so emphatic and sure of herself that it caught me off balance.

"That's all very flattering, Margaret," I said, trying to recover from my shock, "but at the present moment what do we do?"

"Pray for your ordination and many more like you. It's that simple," Margaret replied, as if it made no sense to do otherwise.

"And what will become of those prayers, do you think?" I asked, amazed at the woman's clear understanding of the issue.

"A new and vital church," Margaret declared with conviction. "Keeping the priesthood confined to celibate males is killing us. I've been here a long time and I remember when we had young, energetic and, yes, somewhat naive priests here. We taught them what being a priest was all about. It was a good match. But in those days there were lots of priests to draw on. No more. Now we have to take what's given to us, and it isn't always a good match. When we lost our own priest, I thought it was over. Then you came here and everything changed. You've been a good pastor to us. Ordain *you*, I say. Why can't the new pope see this?"

"You might have something there, Margaret," I said, chuckling within at the accuracy of the woman's perception. "Thank you for sharing. Yes, that makes good sense. Excuse me; I'd better get back to the congregation before this gets out of hand," I said with a broad smile, enjoying the irony of the conversation.

I returned to the center aisle and called the assembly to order. "Any ideas? No long sermons, please, just a word or two from your best insights. Let's make it a collage of solutions about how to find people to send into the harvest."

People spoke from all sides of the church. "Ordain women." "Pray for vocations." "Change the rules." "Bring back the priests who left to get married." "Ordain *you*, Kelly!" "Call an Ecumenical Council."

The people were enjoying the interchange and getting into the spirit of offering ideas. After a few minutes, I brought it to a close by reminding people, "Remember that we're not just talking about the ordained priesthood here. Everyone who is baptized has an obligation to spread the Good News. Despite the shortage of priests—perhaps *because* of it—we all, each of us, must go from here and prepare the ground for Jesus' presence and action in the world.

"One more thing, today's gospel also says, 'Travel light, no extra purse, nor bag nor sandals.' That means no preoccupation with the latest hairdo, suv or designer jeans. We're to be bringers of peace to others. And we're to do it by living simply. That's the trick," I said this realizing that it might be a hard lesson for people to hear.

"We may not be able to solve the shortage of priests, but we can try to reduce the level of violence and anger, of back-biting and gossip, of envy, greed and lust during this coming week. We're going to our own little worlds 'like lambs in the midst of wolves.' But don't worry; Jesus is right there with us. He also gives us a suggestion. 'Find a partner.' Do it *with* someone else. Pair up with a spouse or parent, with a child, friend or co-worker, just as we did here this morning. Whenever and wherever you encounter anger and oppression, abuse and violence, avarice or self-seeking, offer a little compassion, healing and support instead. It's easy to say, but tough to do. That, my friends, is the mandate of today's gospel. Go out there and spread the Good News of peace and love, in both word and action!"

I paused for a moment to make my point, then turned on my heels and returned to my seat next to the altar for a moment of silent reflection. I sensed the congregation had been listening well. Perhaps a few were even moved by the experience. As for myself, I certainly was moved by what Margaret had said with such emphasis. Her words, "Ordain you!" kept ringing in my ears as I sat in the presider's chair.

The rest of the service continued as planned. People offered petitions for those in need and then the collection was taken as everyone sang a hymn. There was no Eucharistic Prayer or consecration. Instead, I led the congregation in the Lord's Prayer and then helped distribute Communion. It wasn't until the end of the service that I got emotional. After the announcements, I stood in front of the altar and said to all those assembled, "May God bless us all, Father, Son and Holy Spirit." I made the sign of the cross, as did the others in church. But to the small band that had witnessed my ordination less than a week before, this was a repeat of my priestly blessing. I made a point of not looking at my family, but I knew what they were thinking. "That's our Mom, the priest, giving the blessing." It was a poignant moment for us all.

The ceremony came to a close and the assembly filed downstairs for coffee. People commended me for my words and for the service as a whole. As one person put it, "I liked your Mass better than Father Henry's."

"But this wasn't a Mass," I tried to explain, to no avail.

"How ironic," I said to Tom as we walked home, "that I was thrust into the role of presider. Is God trying to tell us something here?"

"Just a little gesture of affirmation I suspect," Tom replied, taking my hand. "You did a great job despite the lack of preparation. Very clever of you to get all of us to share like that. You're made for this, no doubt about it."

Sunday breakfast was a carefree meal. Everyone joked with one another about their mom leading the service and laughed when Michael said with a mouth full of waffle, "If those people only knew!"

"Well, they *won't* know," I reminded them. "Please, this is so important. Not a *word*, not a single *hint* of a word to anyone outside this circle."

"Except to the pope, of course," Tom interjected playfully.

The spirit around the table was infectious, but somehow we knew it wouldn't last. At the end of the meal, I announced, "Before we settle into the Sunday paper, let me hereby call a meeting of this family for tomorrow night right after dinner. We have some serious plans to make. Father Jerry and I plan to visit the migrant community this afternoon to evaluate the situation. We'll have more information to report by tomorrow evening."

"Can we come?" Rachel blurted. "I've never been there."

I looked at Tom with a quizzical expression. "What do you think? Will a carload of people be intimidating?"

"We probably should get acquainted as soon as possible," Tom returned, anxious to see our hideout. "It may be our home for a month. I'm kind of curious myself."

"Okay. It's settled," I said, having had my mind changed on the matter. "All comers are welcome. We leave at three o'clock."

THE TRIP TO THE MIGRANTS' COMMUNITY turned out to be an adventure. Because the residents there had no phones, our arrival was a complete surprise. Jerry was a godsend. He connected well with the Sanchez family, the home Nathan and I visited earlier, and they, through him, back to us. Soon the initial tensions from the surprise visit eased and the two families began to interact. Rachel found a playmate and Michael discovered an old computer that he helped the migrant family get working. It even had some games on it they could play. Michael promised to bring some games of his own next time and to find a way to translate them into Spanish. Maria, their daughter, was impressed by his skill. I found it amusing how self-conscious he was in her presence.

Eventually the conversation shifted to finding a place for us to live for a month, without explaining why. When that issue was raised, the Sanchez family got very excited. They took everyone outdoors and marched us around to meet the other fifteen families in the community.

Their homes were plain but serviceable. All had electricity and plumbing, but no phones. One house at the end of the row stood empty. It was in disrepair, but still structurally sound. Tom and I looked at each other, realizing how much work would have to be done in a short while. "Can we get this place into livable shape in a month?" I questioned, pushing open the front door and looking at the broken windows and torn screens.

Jerry responded, "I'll bet I could get some of my students to come next weekend to help. We don't want to attract attention so we'd better not use volunteers from St. Gabe's."

"That's a good point," I said, trying to imagine how a family of five would fit into a house with only two bedrooms. "I could come myself tomorrow to get started," I added. "Jerry, could you ask the Sanchez's how we go about paying for this?"

When Jerry inquired, he discovered that the area farmers owned the houses and rented them to the migrants, deducting the rent from their paychecks. The migrants weren't sure how much was subtracted, because it was managed by the farmers.

"The families will make the arrangements," Jerry relayed to us, "although I certainly would like to know what rent they're being charged. Far too much, would be my guess, or am I just being cynical?"

"Good question," I replied, still trying to understand how this was going to work. "I'll try to ask some questions around the parish without raising any suspicions. A few of the farmers belong to St. Gabe's, but I doubt they ever come to check the renters' living situations."

The trip home was more somber than the drive in. It began to dawn on everyone how great a challenge this would be. "We certainly have our work cut out for us over the next month," I said to no one in particular, "with learning some rudimentary Spanish and fixing the house and all. Be sure, Tom, you don't let your work suffer. This is my baby, not yours."

"Yeah, sure it is," Tom said with a grin. "Think again. We're all in this together, sink or swim. I'll just have to make the time, that's all. That goes for the rest of you kids as well. Let's not let your mother down."

We purchased fried chicken on the way home and then sat on the front porch with cold drinks, good food and a new appreciation for our own home. "I'll miss this place, even if we have to be away only for a while," I said as I retrieved a chicken leg from the box. "It would be so much easier if the pope would come through and say the word. Why is it never simple?"

"Because it tests our mettle," Jerry said, enjoying this relaxing moment and feeling very much part of the family. "In the long run . . ."

"Yes, yes, I know," I broke in. "In the long run it'll all work for the best, but right now, I don't want to budge from this porch of mine, not for all the media in the world."

"You'll feel differently when the news breaks," Tom added as he tried to sort all that he had observed during the visit with the migrants.

"Which reminds me, Jerry," I said. "The media will come immediately to you when they can't find us. They know from the Ordination Rally that we're connected. What will you say?"

"Nothing, *nada*, no comment, have no idea," Jerry said, pulling a make-believe zipper across his mouth.

I laughed at his gesture, but then a thought dawned on me. "But your students, Jerry. Is it a good idea to have them help? They could lead the press right to us."

"Ouch. I hadn't thought of that. Yes, you're right. I'll just come on my own. How about next Saturday morning, bright and early?"

"Sounds great," I responded, trying to think ahead about my calendar for the week.

Saturday was busy for the family. We headed to the migrant community early in the morning, our car filled with tools, cleaning supplies, paint and ladders. Father Jerry met us there and we started working before nine o'clock. The migrants had wanted to help but they were in the fields by the time we arrived, having already put in a few hours of work.

The door of the empty house was unlocked. We tramped into the place with a mixture of determination and hopelessness. "Will we ever be able to live here?" Michael asked as he looked at the broken windows, cobwebs and faulty plumbing.

"We're only talking about a month," I said as a way of cheering everyone. "Think of it as a long camping trip."

"Very long," Rachel volunteered, as she stumbled on an overturned kitchen chair that had been left behind.

There was not much to show for our labors by lunchtime, but by four in the afternoon, our spirits were improving. After much scrubbing, sweeping, a few trips to a hardware store and the start of some serious painting, the place was beginning to assume a character of its own.

At seven o'clock, just as everyone was ready to pile into the car and get some dinner, the little community of families began arriving in a parade of pick-up trucks and vintage cars, waving as they came. When they reached the house, they came inside to see what we had been doing. Amid shouts of acclaim and admiration, they inspected all of our work. We stood by, beaming with pride at what we had accomplished on this first day of renovation. Jerry provided the translation as the migrants insisted that we stay for dinner. This was an occasion for a spontaneous fiesta, they insisted.

More than happy to accept the invitation but somewhat

embarrassed by our sloppy appearance, we all trooped to the Sanchez home to wash up and enjoy a meal. We were treated to an outdoor barbeque and an impromptu concert. As the food was being prepared, people went to their homes to get chairs and benches, guitars and even a trumpet or two. Soon the entire community was gathered in a circle outside the cluster of homes. Adults and children joined in with music and singing, entertainment and dancing.

"How can they be so spirited after a full day in the fields?" Tom asked, clapping his hands to the music and enjoying the sudden change of mood. "Come to think of it, how can *we*, after the long day we just put in?"

Dinner took more than an hour to prepare, but no one seemed to be keeping track of the time. The food was well worth the wait. By nine-thirty, I asked Jerry to explain to everyone that we had to leave, because I had to wake early on Sunday morning to get the church ready for Mass. "You too, Jerry, have a long drive ahead of you. It's time we call it a day."

It took awhile to extract ourselves from the gathering, but soon we were on the road home, the Mores to Sarah and Jerry back to Detroit. The children were sleeping in the backseat while I kept a steady conversation with Tom to help him stay awake. "I'll be a zombie tomorrow," I said, "but what an experience that was tonight, with such gracious and generous hosts. I'm going to enjoy our month there more than I realized."

SUNDAY AFTERNOON, BISHOP GENE called and asked me to see him on Monday morning. As I drove to the bishop's residence the next morning, I thought of all that had happened over the last few weeks. Am I different after my ordination? Will I ever be able to exercise my priesthood and be accepted as a legitimate priest? Right now it seems impossible. Then again, if anyone told me a year or six *weeks* ago, that I would be in the midst of this bizarre intrigue, I would have laughed out loud and told them to get a grip on reality. I suspect others will say that to me when they hear the news.

Bishop Gene greeted me warmly, but I was alarmed to see him looking so poorly. The sparkle was gone from his eyes and his gait was unsteady. "Are you okay?" I asked as we settled down with coffee. "You don't look at all well to me."

"No, no, I'm fine," he assured me, offering cream for my coffee. "I've been having some chest pains that have kept me up at night, but the doctor can't find anything wrong. It must be stress from all this excitement. Enough about me; I have news. I've been in constant communication with our bishops' group. They were very pleased with the video and commented on how well the ceremony went and on your composure and strength in particular. We're planning another meeting in two weeks to put the final touches on our media strategy. I'm glad I don't have to handle that side of our plan; it's all way out of my league."

"So, no word from our pope, then," I asked with more resignation than hope in my voice.

"Nothing at all; it's as if we don't exist," Gene responded, having a little trouble catching his breath. "I know that's not true. We're sure we have his attention, but I suspect he's calling our bluff, hoping we won't go ahead with our plans."

"He doesn't know whom he's dealing with, does he?" I remarked, giving Gene a nod.

"No, I don't think he does," Gene admitted with a grin. "Now, I wanted to explain to you our timeline for going public, so you can orchestrate your own moves. How's it going, by the way? Have you found a place to live? Will the migrant community be a good place for you?"

"Yes, it's going very well," I responded, surprising myself with my enthusiasm. "We spent Saturday getting a house ready. The families are so accepting and welcoming. We'll have no trouble on that end. I suspect in a few weeks we'll be all set."

"Splendid," Gene acknowledged. "That's just what I was hoping to hear. Our target for breaking the news about the ordination is the Tuesday after Labor Day. People will be home from vacations and ready to start the new school year; we should reach a large audience. More importantly, the people at the Vatican will have returned from their traditional month away from the Roman heat. Everything is poised for that day."

"It gives me a sinking feeling when you say this," I said, putting down my coffee mug and looking directly into Gene's eyes. "Our lives will never be the same after that day, will they?"

"Probably not," Gene said with a tone of resignation. "It's like Mary's goodbye to Jesus, as he headed to the Jordan to start his public ministry. I'm sure it wasn't, 'You have a nice time, now,' or even, 'You be careful, you hear?' I suspect it was more like, 'I wish you didn't have to do this, but I know you have no choice, so do it well. I'll be praying for you.' That's how I feel about you and your family. I wish I could make it easier for you, but I can't. You've been called to this, so just do the best you can and God will see you through."

"You're so encouraging," I replied mockingly. "It's like telling poor David to keep his aim straight as he prepares to meet Goliath. 'Good luck, Kid.' But I feel like a David who forgot his slingshot. 'Oh, oh, now what?'"

"Yes, I see your point," Gene laughed, seeming to enjoy my strange point of view. "We're into this so deeply now, we have to see it to the end. Enough speculation, let's get to the business at hand. You now know the date. You'll have to be out of your own house by Sunday of Labor Day weekend. That'll give you a day's grace before the news breaks."

"Can we be at Mass at St. Gabe's on that Sunday?" I asked with concern. "There's no chance of an early news leak, is there? I want to say goodbye to the parish."

"No, that should be fine," Gene assured me. "Then think of moving on Monday morning at the very latest."

"That's easy, since it's Labor Day. The neighbors shouldn't suspect our piling into the car and . . . whoops, no car. That *will* be a problem. Gene, do you think you could help us escape?"

"Sure," Gene replied, grateful to be of some assistance. "Between Father Jerry and me, we should get you there okay. What time?"

"We'll make our last trips on Saturday and Sunday afternoon. Could you come on Monday morning for breakfast, say eight o'clock? I'll need to clean the refrigerator, of course. I'll invite Jerry, too. He can take the kids. We'll make it look like a trip to the lake or something. You can take Tom and me a little later. We should be able to make it look casual."

"Sounds good to me. Will you have a television to watch the fireworks on Tuesday morning?"

"Yes, we're looking into that," I replied, not at all relishing the media attention. "We'll also have a computer with an untraceable connection to the Internet, using a phone line that comes into the Sanchez home. It'll take some doing, but we think we can stay undercover and away from the public's eye for at least a month."

"Such a world we live in," the bishop remarked, shaking his head. "It's way beyond this old noggin's comprehension."

I returned home, my head filled with a million details. "We have to make arrangements with the schools, clue in Deb and Carol about me being away for awhile, see Frank about looking after the house, have a phone line installed, bring a television, check the garage sales for an old refrigerator and washing machine, get enough cash to carry us through the month. There's a lot to cover between now and Labor Day!"

The next few weeks were a flurry of activity. This all had to be done while maintaining an outward appearance of normality. The new house was shaping up nicely. A tour of the neighboring towns uncovered a refrigerator, washing machine, stove and television set. The plan was to bequeath these to the migrant families once the month was over. Everyone in the family was beginning to realize that we would be stuck at this location for an entire month with no transportation and little contact with the outside world. Jerry was able to convey to our new neighbors the reason for our stay and the need for secrecy. They were to act as if this new family was one of their own from Mexico. It took some repeating, but eventually everyone understood.

By the time the Labor Day weekend arrived everything was ready for the move. The schools had been in session for a week and we were able to make arrangements for a four-week absence. My excuse of a family trip—a chance of a lifetime—seemed readily accepted. On Saturday, the final shopping was done, once again in a neighboring town so as not to raise any suspicions.

Mass on Sunday and the breakfast that followed were poignant moments for us as we savored each aspect of the routine that we had taken for granted. The last load of clothes, books and supplies was transported on Sunday. We then treated ourselves to a final meal on the porch that evening.

"When we return," I reflected, exhausted but not wanting to let go of this special occasion, "our world will be different. At least we've had a chance to plan ahead. Most people don't have that luxury. A life-changing event usually happens suddenly, without warning or forethought. Do you think we've forgotten anything, Tom?"

"Oh, I'm sure we have," Tom replied. "But that's part of the adventure, making do with what we have. I'm excited by the challenge of all this. It's going to be fun, and it certainly will unite us as a family."

"It already has," I remarked, looking at the children who could hardly keep their eyes open. "You kids have been real troopers through all this. Thanks for putting up with this adventure your mom has started."

"At least I'll learn some Spanish," Nathan added. "But it was hard saying goodbye to the gang at school and not being able to say where I was going."

"You didn't say anything about all this, did you?" Rachel chimed in.

"No," he said, laughing at Rachel's worried look. "I just said I'm heading out with the family for a month. Tell you about it later."

"What about Allyson, if I may be so bold?" I asked.

"She's still in town. She doesn't head to Michigan State for another week. It was hard not telling her where I'll be. She wanted my phone number. I told her I'll send her a postcard."

"I'm proud of you, son," Tom affirmed. "Who knows, maybe we can have one sent from Mexico."

The easy rapport around the porch was a pure gift. Although exhausted, we were all pleased and happy that everything had been accomplished in a month's time. I sensed everyone was ready to move to our next adventure.

Labor Day morning was a busy one. Bishop Gene and Jerry arrived at eight o'clock as planned. We all had breakfast on the porch, enjoying the donuts and sweet rolls brought by our two chauffeurs. To anyone looking from outside, it would appear to be a simple gathering of friends on a holiday morning. The group itself was not so calm. We discussed last-minute details and final arrangements.

About nine o'clock, the three children piled into Father Jerry's car, loaded with beach clothes and picnic baskets, all prepared ahead of time by design. They waved goodbye to the three of us on the porch and pulled out of the driveway. An hour later, with the night lights set and the doors locked, we got into Gene's car, took one last look at the house and yard full of flowers, and headed out of town toward our new home. "I'm sure glad I remembered to have the lawn mowed and the flowers tended while we're gone. I hired the same crew that takes care of the parish grounds. They never even asked the reason, but were glad to earn the extra cash," I said as I took one last glance back before we turned the corner.

OUR ARRIVAL AT THE MIGRANT COMMUNITY was a joyous one. By now, the people who lived there knew us well. They helped carry the last boxes from the car. Although the new house was simple by our standards, it looked like a palace to the migrants. It was freshly painted and filled with furniture and appliances. None of it was new, but it was better than what the migrants could afford. I was concerned about attracting attention if any of the farmers or, for that matter, members from the parish outreach team visited the area. The migrants assured us that the former never came during September. They were too busy harvesting. As for the parishioners, I was able to sidetrack the committee with another project in Mexico, putting this apostolate on hold for the month.

"I think we have all the bases covered. Only time will tell," I said as we bid goodbye to Gene and Jerry after a late lunch. "Don't worry about us. We'll be fine. We have just dropped off the end of the earth for a month. See you the first of October."

I gave them each a hug, concerned more for them than for us. Jerry, and especially Bishop Gene, would be feeling the brunt of the media pressure, while we would be ensconced in the migrant's compound. "Please be careful of your health, Gene," I said through the open window of his car. "Those chest pains worry me. Are you taking your medicine?"

"And are you my mother?" he retorted with a chuckle as he said goodbye. "I think not."

The whole family waved as the two cars pulled away and swung onto the gravel road. We then turned and entered our new home. "No more running out for pizzas, I'm afraid," I said as I held the screen door open for the rest of the family. "But I do have a scrumptious pork roast ready to go in the oven for dinner. We're not really roughing it here, you know."

The first night in our new home, although a bit strange, was surprisingly comfortable. We awoke to a new routine of taking turns in the one bathroom and not having any morning paper to read during breakfast. Everyone was aware that the news of my ordination would become known sometime during the day.

"We're going to have to set a schedule for school work," I said at breakfast, "so you don't fall behind your classmates. Just remember, your mom was once a teacher. When this is over, you're going to be begging to get back into a real classroom. Who knows, maybe you'll know a lot more than your classmates when you return. This is going to be fun." I said this to calm everyone's anxiety. How the media would broadcast the news was on everyone's mind.

"Yeah, right, Mom," Michael retorted. "I can hardly wait."

"Shouldn't we turn on the television to see what's happening?" Nathan suggested.

"Yes, I suspect we should," Tom responded. "After all, it's the reason we're here."

As Tom flipped on the television, we all recognized something very familiar. We stood transfixed as Michael's video of my ordination filled the screen. "Oh, my goodness, there I am, big as life!" I exclaimed, my hand over my mouth. The announcer was saying that a retired Catholic bishop, Bishop Gene McGovern, had broken ranks and ordained a woman as a priest in the Roman Catholic Church. Following a clip from the video was a shot of poor Bishop Gene before a phalanx of cameras and reporters. He seemed to be holding an impromptu press conference outside his residence.

"Yes, it's true," he was saying, "I have ordained a woman to the priesthood."

Then came a cacophony of questions. "Why did you do it?" "Who is she?" "Is this a legal ordination?" "How will Rome react?" "Did you do this on your own authority?"

Tom and I and the three children were riveted as we watched the saga unfold. It seemed so unreal. There he was, the same gentle, easy-going person we had said goodbye to yesterday now transformed into a media figure.

"The reason I did this," the bishop continued, as evenly as he could despite the crush of cameras and people, "was to raise the issue of the need to change the requirements for ordination. Our people are not being served. The celebration of Eucharist is being curtailed. Many people had hoped that the election of a new pope would make a difference, but so far nothing has happened. What is needed is a special Ecumenical Council—a gathering of bishops from around the world—to settle this issue. My hope is that this action will begin that process. I'm sorry, but this is all I'm prepared to say at this moment. No further comments. Please excuse me." At this, he turned and fought his way back inside. He closed the door behind him, leaving the reporters to turn to their cameras with a final comment before returning to their studios.

I went to the television and flipped through the few channels available without cable. Each of the major networks was focused on the same story. I stopped on one that was reporting, "We have just learned that the person you saw being ordained by Bishop McGovern was Mrs. Kelly More of Sarah, Michigan. For the last five years she has been employed as the pastoral administrator of St. Gabriel's Catholic Church. We have on the line with us now Bishop Foley, in whose diocese Mrs. More is employed. Do you have any comment about this unusual occurrence?"

"None whatsoever," came back his tight-lipped response.

"This should be interesting," Tom muttered.

"Mrs. More has been an exemplary administrator of the parish. If, indeed, this did happen, it's not permitted by the Catholic Church and is condemned by Canon Law. I doubt it's a valid ordination and probably has no legitimacy." He spoke with authority, but his tone was more hesitant and uncertain.

"But it was performed by a Catholic bishop in good standing," the interviewer questioned.

"I have nothing more to say," Bishop Foley retorted.

"Did you know about this happening? Were you given any forewarning?"

"None whatsoever."

"Thank you, Bishop," the interviewer concluded and continued with the story. The next shot was of the front of our own house. "There's our house, Mom!" Rachel shouted as she pointed at the television screen.

"And look at all those people and cameras and television trucks," I added. "Aren't you glad we're here and not there?"

The television commentator continued, "We're at the home of Mrs. Kelly More of Sarah, Michigan. There doesn't appear to be anyone home. We do have word from one of the neighbors that the family was last seen yesterday morning having breakfast on the front porch. A police officer has just arrived. Perhaps he can shed some light on Mrs. More's whereabouts."

"There's Frank, bless his heart," I remarked, happy that he was on the scene to maintain order. "I wonder what he'll have to say. He's such a straightforward guy. Too bad I had to put him in this predicament."

"No, I have no idea where they might be," was Frank's comment. He seemed overwhelmed by the commotion, but at the same time, solicitous for the security of the house. "The last I saw of them was

Sunday at Mass. I'm a member of St. Gabriel's and all I can say is that Kelly More is a wonderful pastor. Hey, be careful over there! Don't be stomping over those flowers."

"Good for you, Frank," I laughed. "This is so bizarre. Let's hope our safety screen holds and no one comes here. It would be bedlam for the migrants."

For the next twenty minutes the television stations remained on the same story. "It must be a slow news day," Tom remarked as he went into the kitchen to make coffee.

"Hey look, Tom," I exclaimed, "they're trying to get a comment from the pope or someone in the Vatican. This should be interesting."

"We haven't been able to get any reaction from Pope John," the commentator remarked. "There does seem to be an indication that a statement will be made later. No, wait, we have word that the Cardinal Secretary of State will make a brief appearance. We now send you to our correspondent at the Vatican."

The camera focused on a stern-looking prelate who said, in somewhat broken English, "I will read a short statement. No questions, please."

He began to read his statement. "It has reached our attention that a retired bishop in the United States has attempted to confer the Sacrament of Holy Orders on a woman."

"Sounds like a disease, doesn't it?" I broke in.

"This is both illicit and invalid. No actual ordination took place. It is not permitted by the church. It never has permitted this and never will in the future. If Jesus Christ wanted women to be ordained, He would have done so in His lifetime. It has never been a practice of the Catholic Church from the beginning. In the mind of the Holy Father, this is a non-event. It never happened and will not change the present requirements for ordination to the priesthood in the Roman Catholic Church."

"Well, that's a positive statement for you," Tom chortled as he returned from the kitchen with a cup of coffee for each of us.

"What does he mean when he said it was a 'non-event,' Mom?" Michael asked with a frown on his face. "I was there. I know it happened."

"So does everyone else, Dear," I responded. "But the authorities in Rome are trying to discredit it so it will go away and not change anything."

"Can they do that?" Nathan asked.

"Not very easily, not in this day and age," I returned, enjoying the incredible reactions my ordination had prompted. "Thank goodness we have your video, Michael, to prove it really did happen. I'm glad we brought it with us for safekeeping. As Bishop Gene mentioned, your DVD is going to be famous. See, there it is again. They're replaying it. They certainly know how to get the most mileage out of a few snippets of tape. They've edited all but a few seconds, the laying on of hands, and the bishop and me at the altar. Very clever. I'm concerned about Bishop Gene. He's all alone in his house, surrounded by the press. I wish we could give him the same relief and assistance as he gave to us."

"Mom, look, the morning show is talking about it," Rachel shouted.

"Looks like they're trying to decide what to call you, Kel," Tom said as he sipped his coffee.

The co-hosts of the program were bantering back and forth, making clever comments about the ordination. "So, do we call her Father Kelly or Mother Kelly, or Reverend Kelly More or what? Sister Kelly doesn't work, and 'Kelly More, the priest' is too long. Interesting question. Let's ask the 'people on the street.'"

"How ridiculous," I exclaimed as I retreated to the kitchen to start breakfast. "We'd better turn that thing off and set up our class schedule for the day."

"Oh, Mom, are we going to have school today?"

"Sure, why not? I want smart kids if I'm going to be famous—or *infamous*, depending on one's point of view."

"So, what *do* we call you?" Nathan asked.

"*Mother* is just fine with me!" I retorted.

Eleven

"THIS IS OUR FIRST BREAKFAST in our new kitchen," I noted as the excitement waned. "Pretty cozy, I'd say." That was an understatement, since the house was small for five of us, Tom and I taking one bedroom, Nathan and Michael the other and Rachel on the foldout couch in the living room. This space also doubled as a study area during the day. "I can't imagine how other families do it," I commented as I unpacked the books. "Some of them crowd nine, ten or even more into a house this size."

"We'll have to devise a routine for the day so we don't get in each other's hair," I continued. "Maybe we could go on nature walks as well. There's a lot to learn from our environment."

"Can we watch a little more television?" Rachel pleaded, putting off her lessons as long as possible. "I want to see what else they say about you, Mom."

"Well, all right," I gave in, "but only half an hour, and *only* about us, not all that other drivel that's on at this time of day."

"I'd like to try our web connection as well," Tom interjected. "We share the line with the Sanchezes, but I suspect they're all in the fields by now. It'll be interesting to see whether Father Jerry's clandestine email connection works."

We delayed lessons for the moment and watched more news

coverage about the ordination. By now there was additional information about my background. My speech from the Ordination Rally was aired, as well as an interview with Father Jerry. He was cordial but non-committal. "He's clever with interviews," Tom remarked. "He seems to say so much, but it has no substance. You don't know any more at the end than you did when it started," he chuckled.

"How very Jesuit of him," I said, smiling and enjoying the coverage more than I realized.

"Look, Mom, there's my class picture!" Rachel exclaimed.

"They must have discovered how many children I have and where you attend school. I suppose the neighbors or the parish supplied that. I feel bad putting any of them through all this."

"Nonsense. I have a feeling they rather like the notoriety," Tom returned. "It makes a person feel important to be interviewed by reporters."

"To a point," I responded. "To a point."

While Rachel and I continued to watch the news, Tom, Michael and Nathan began working on the computer to connect it to the Internet. "Look here," Tom exclaimed. "We have a note from Father Jerry."

As part of the preparations, Jerry had set up a fictitious web account in someone else's name that we could access. He never referred to us, but the message was clearly meant for our family. In part it read, "All is well. We're doing fine. The coverage is great. Rome is scrambling, framing denial after denial. I think we've secured their attention. The media is doing a great job. Watch for the special on tonight's news and a more expansive segment later this week. Don't respond. Catch you later."

"Well, that's working. At least we have an inside resource. The media have some rather clever ways of locating their sources of information, but I think we'll be okay as long as we don't reply to any messages," Tom reminded us, relieved that all was going as planned, at least for the present.

After the initial excitement of the media reports, and the novelty of the new environment, the family settled into a life of 'home away from home.' Both Tom and I contributed to the lesson plans for the children. The teachers had provided a full schedule of readings and tests, with deadlines for each. Added to this were daily Spanish lessons, including conversation CDs and grammar texts. We enjoyed competing with one another while learning vocabulary and syntax.

"What an excellent atmosphere for learning a new language," I remarked as the week progressed. "I just wish I could keep these words in my head the way you can, Rachel. How do you do that?"

"Do what?" Rachel replied, with all the innocence of a nine-year-old and the glee of a winner.

Our new neighbors seemed to enjoy us as much as we enjoyed them. They took turns visiting our home in the evening, which gave us a chance to try the Spanish lesson of the day. Everyone laughed at the clumsy attempts to speak each others' native language. The migrant children grasped the English language more readily than the adults, but they didn't have a solid base for it because they had so little contact with American children their own age. We and our neighbors appreciated the bilingual exchange and the great opportunity for language growth. This month was developing into much more than a necessary retreat from the media. Our family was growing closer— accepting and appreciating one another.

During the second week, I made an attempt to explain to our host family, the Sanchezes, the real reason for our presence in their community. To this point, it was a bit of a mystery to the Hispanic community. All we were able to communicate thus far was that our family needed to *disappear* for a month and this was a good place to come. Regardless, they were more than willing to share whatever they had— home, community, friendship, safe-haven.

Slowly, I was able to explain the extraordinary circumstance of my ordination. The Sanchez family had seen my picture on television, but they were unable to comprehend the reason for my notoriety. Now it was beginning to dawn on them. Expressions of disbelief, wonder and confusion covered their faces as it became clearer to them that I was a *priest, sacerdote*! This revelation didn't fit their mental categories. To them, the *padre* was their leader and confidante, their counselor and parent, all consolidated in one. I didn't fit that role model at all, so it would take some time to accept.

It didn't take long, however, for the little community, all nominally Catholic, to start calling me *Madre*, treating me with deference and devotion not bestowed on the rest of the family. Each of their homes had at least one picture of Our Lady of Guadalupe, a simple shrine to 'the Virgin.' I sensed, with some embarrassment, that I now occupied a position a few notches below that devotion.

As a whole, I found this somewhat amusing until the day one of the women asked me to bless a rosary. I did, but was surprised when the woman, while profusely thanking me, kissed my hands. "No, no, don't do that. *Basta*. I'm just a regular person like you. *No soy special.*"

"*Si,*" was the response. "*Tu es sacerdote!*"

As I reflected on this experience later, trying to clarify what happened, the realization dawned on me. These people believe I am an ordained priest. Their faith tells them so. Perhaps they believe this is who I am even more than I do. What a humbling experience.

The more I meditated on this strange turn of events, the more a vague intuition crept into my consciousness. Perhaps this is where I will celebrate my first Mass. The faith of the people is calling to me. They accept me for the priest that I am. This community of believers, in their subtle way, is asking me to exercise my gift and duty. I *am* a priest, so why not lead them in the celebration of the Eucharist?

I shared my ruminations with Tom to see how he would react. One evening, as the family was out for our post-dinner walk along the dirt road, I dropped behind the children and motioned to Tom, "I need to bounce something off you."

"What's up?" he replied, dropping behind and pleased to have a chance to talk with me alone. The close accommodations didn't allow for many such occasions.

I shared my experience of blessing the rosary and where it led in my reflections afterwards. "Do you think I should offer to say a Mass? I would have to do it from memory—and in English, of course—I don't have a missal along, only my book of daily scripture readings. One of the migrants might have a Spanish Bible we could use. But should I even offer it as a possibility? Am I being presumptuous?"

Tom walked along silently, sizing up the pros and cons in his head. I counted on this quality a great deal. After a pause, he replied, "No, I think you're quite within your rights to do this. It'll be a good experience for all of us, especially the children. They need a little excitement to see them through the hardship of these days."

"Tom, I'm *not* doing this for a little extra excitement!" I stopped and looked at him. "Get serious."

"I am," Tom replied with complete sincerity, somewhat taken aback by my reaction. "This is a huge moment, the first Mass of perhaps the first legitimate woman priest in America. This *is* exciting. But it's also the *right* thing to do. I do think this community of migrants, beyond anyone else, would appreciate the significance of this event, even if they can't understand everything that's being said. They know the gestures and the ritual, and these in themselves will speak to their hearts. I say do it!"

I thought of the Mass possibility during the rest of our walk, then long into the evening. I envisioned how, when and where this event could occur. Thankfully there was wine available. We had brought a few bottles for our own enjoyment. And there was a sufficient supply of pita bread. I was concerned about the ritual prayers until I remembered that one of the books I brought with me did contain a Eucharistic Prayer. I figured I had everything I needed, including the authority to preside at a liturgy. I needed to broach this topic with the Hispanic community to see what they thought.

The next evening, I made the rounds of a few homes, trying to convey my intentions. Some comprehended better than others. I knew they would be speaking with one another, filling in the gaps that were lost in the woefully inadequate translation from one language to the other.

I waited for a few days as the idea continued to take shape. Then I approached the Sanchez family. "Tell me what you think? "*¿Que piensan ustedes? ¿Debamus tener la Eucharistia?*"

"*Si, la queremos mucho,*" they responded. "Yes, Priest Kelly, we have Mass. It be long time we receive communion."

"That settles it. We'll have Mass this next Sunday," I proclaimed, finally coming to the conclusion myself.

As the day approached, everyone in the house was excited. Rachel dressed up for the event and she collected flowers for the altar. Both Tom and I thought our living room was the best place to pray the Mass, until Maria Sanchez came to offer their front yard. She even promised a tarp over our heads if it rained. "Can't do better than that," I exclaimed. "It'll be a Fiesta Mass. Everyone can bring chairs and mats and we can make it a celebration of God's presence in the great outdoors."

Michael was able to put together a rudimentary sound system using his stereo and a tape recorder. By the time Sunday morning arrived, everyone was in high spirits. I wore a long blue skirt and a white blouse, with a simple white stole draped around my shoulders. At ten o'clock, we proceeded from our house to the Mass site, following Rachel and one of the Mexican girls her own age, each carrying candles. An elderly gentleman carrying a cross led the procession. Although the sun was bright, a gentle breeze cooled the morning air.

The place of worship had been decorated with banners, flowers, and a large picture of Our Lady of Guadalupe. A simple table covered with a white cloth served as the altar. Chairs were arranged in a semi-circle, with mats for the children in front. I went to the table, bent down and kissed it, then spread my arms to the assembly and said, "The Lord be with you, *El Señor este con ustedes.*" The people responded, *"Y con tu Espiritu."*

It was a joyous event. The first two readings were in Spanish with a responsorial song in between. I proclaimed the gospel in English while Maria read the same text out loud from a Spanish Bible. I led the prayers and gave a brief reflection on the readings as I had done on numerous occasions at St. Gabriel's. When it came time for the Eucharistic prayer, however, I did not step back in deference to the priest as I had always done at the parish, but now stood front and center and recited, "Loving God, you are holy indeed, the fountain of all holiness. Let your Spirit come upon these gifts to make them holy, so that they may become for us the body and blood of our Lord, Jesus Christ." As I said this, I spread my hands over the two cups of wine and the plate of unleavened pita bread. The small congregation watched, praying with me as the gathered community of the faithful.

I continued, as I held the bread, "Take this, all of you, and eat it. This is my body which will be given up for you." I said this with tears in my eyes. I had no doubt whatever that the Holy Spirit was working through me and was transforming the bread into Christ's body as I spoke the words of consecration. Many in the assembly bowed their heads, folded their hands and prayed quietly.

As the Mass continued, I grew more confident of my priestly powers. I began to realize that I was ordained to perform this sacred duty. I could see in the faces before me, especially in the faces of my dear husband and loving children. They believed in my priesthood as much as I did. This was not play-acting, it was the real thing. It was *of the Spirit*. How this would all unfold in the future was not my concern. I knew, deep in my own being, that I had received the mark of the priesthood. As the scripture says, "You are a priest forever, according to the Order of Melchizedek."

At the end of the Eucharistic Prayer I raised the consecrated bread and wine high in the air and asked everyone to join me, either in English or Spanish, "Through him, with him and in him, in the unity of the Holy Spirit, all glory and honor is yours, almighty God, forever and ever. Amen!"

It was the final *Amen* that kept ringing in my ears as I continued with the Mass. This was an affirmation of all that I knew was true. God was saying, in the voices of this small but significant group of believers, "This is all good and true. It pleases Me a great deal. And you, dear woman, and all who are gathered here with you, are good and holy people."

By the time I invited everyone to join together for the Lord's Prayer, my hands were shaking. Something wonderfully divine and human is happening here, I thought, as everyone prayed, "*Padre Nuestro . . .*"

The intimate gesture of sharing the Eucharistic bread and wine was another high point of the Mass. I distributed the bread while both Tom and Mr. Sanchez held the two cups as people came forward with great reverence and anticipation. For some, it had been many months, even years, since they had received communion. They had little doubt that this was the body and blood of their Savior, and they were very grateful for the strange turn of events that made this Mass and communion possible.

My final blessing and a closing song brought the Mass to an end and signaled the beginning of a festive sharing of food and drink, fun and games. Spirits ran high as old and young celebrated the event. I was given a place of honor and was treated with great respect and deference. I found this almost more than I could bear, following on the heels of the Mass and all the emotion associated with it.

"Mom, you were great!" Nathan said as he brought me some sweetbread and strong coffee.

"It seemed as if you had been doing this your entire life," Tom remarked as he sat down next to me and took my hand. "You looked so natural."

"In a way, I have been doing this for the last five years but without realizing it," I responded. "I've been pastor to the people of St. Gabriel's, only now I have what it takes to pastor completely. At the same time, it does take my breath away. I can't think of a more fitting environment or better circumstance for my first Mass. The pope may not agree with all this, but I know God does. I feel it in my bones!"

"Me, too," Tom said, and gave my hand a squeeze. "You are one great priest—or priestess—or whatever the correct term may be."

"Try *wife* for a change; I still answer to that," I said playfully, so appreciative of Tom's love and support.

The rest of the day was a fiesta. Brunch blended into lunch and lunch into dinner. There was much milling around. Spontaneous games sprang up. Everyone was having a grand time. Finally, as the sun was setting, we made our way back to our little home.

"Already we're more than halfway through this experiment and we're no worse for wear," I remarked as Rachel and I walked hand in hand.

"I never thought I would say this," Nathan volunteered, "but I'll miss this place. There's such a genuine love of life here, despite how little the people own."

"Right you are," Tom said as he opened the screen door for all to go inside. "Crowded as it is at times, we have most of the essentials here. Oh, and Michael, I saw that you were enjoying Maria's company this afternoon."

"Yeah, she's fun—and smart! Too bad that she doesn't get to attend much school, because of all the work she has to do in the fields." I could see that Michael was feeling a bit depressed, probably because he had so little chance to get to know Maria. She was away during the day, had chores at night, helped prepare dinner and looked after the smaller children.

"Everyone, get ready for bed," I mandated, smiling at Michael's obvious captivation with Maria. "It's been a very long day. Snacks first and then line up for the bathroom. It's back to schoolwork in the morning."

"Aw, Mom," came the groans from all three children, although they had to admit their classwork had been fun and they were learning a great deal in spite of themselves.

After making sure everyone else was settled, I collapsed into bed, tired but elated. I kept reliving every part of that Mass, especially the Amen at the end of the Eucharistic Prayer. "Why did that make such an impression, I wonder," I said aloud.

"How's that, Honey?" Tom muttered as he turned out the light.

"Tom, did you . . . Oh, forget it. We'll talk about it in the morning."

"Thanks," came back his weak response. "Good night and God bless."

As I drifted to sleep, the experience of the day stayed with me. I dreamed of being in a large church or an auditorium, and I was at the altar, holding the bread, just as I had done today. Then my dream took a more ominous direction. I was at the bedside of someone I knew, giving the person communion, knowing that this person was about to die. I strained to see who it was. It took some time before I recognized the face. I awoke with a start and sat straight up in bed, tears streaming down my face.

"What is it?" Tom said with alarm.

"I just had a nightmare," I responded, my hands trembling. "It was so real and so terrifying."

"What was it?" Tom rolled over to turn on the light.

"I was anointing someone—or maybe I was giving the person

communion—and that person was close to death. Do you know who it was? Bishop Gene McGovern! Oh, my God, I hope he's okay. How can I find out? This is horrible. I don't want him to die ! Oh, Tom, I'm so frightened!"

"Go to sleep, now. I'm sure it's just all the excitement from today. It's one o'clock in the morning, Kel. I'm sure he's fine," Tom groggily answered as he wrapped his arms around me.

Tom was already fast asleep by the time I settled back on the pillow. I said a heartfelt prayer for the bishop's health and tried to go back to sleep.

The alarm woke both of us from a sound sleep. But the dream was still with me as I got dressed and went to rouse the children. By the time everyone was out of the bathroom and crowded into the small kitchen, I was switching television channels.

"What's up?" Michael asked, knowing that this was unusual behavior for his mother.

"Oh, I had a somewhat disturbing dream last night. I wanted to make sure everyone's okay. It's difficult when you can't call people to check things."

"What was the dream, Mom?" Nathan asked through a mouthful of toast.

"Oh, nothing," I responded, relieved that there was nothing on the news. "You just have a mother with an overactive imagination."

But the emotional impact of the dream haunted me as I went about my daily routine. "I wonder if I should risk borrowing a pickup and going to visit Bishop Gene," I said during dinner.

"May I go? May I go?" all three children piped up in unison.

"Whoops, bad topic to bring up, right?" I admitted as I quickly withdrew my suggestion.

"Right," said Tom, looking a little disapprovingly at me. "Not a good idea. We've done so well thus far, and the commotion is starting to die down. You don't want to kick any dust. The media is still waiting to catch a glimpse of you, Kelly."

"Okay, you're right, Tom. Forget I ever mentioned it. We just have to hang tight, only ten more days to go."

I went to bed that night unsettled but resigned to being unable to make any contact with the outside world. "Dear God," I prayed as I climbed into bed, "keep my friend Gene healthy. I don't know what I'd do if we lost him."

No disturbing dreams plagued my sleep but I still felt uneasy when I woke in the morning. "Something's not quite right here," I mused, as I got dressed. The rest of the day went as planned, filled with schoolwork, Spanish lessons, walks and meals. That evening we all gathered around the television before dinner to watch the news, as had become our custom. "Nothing on the news," Tom said. "You can set your heart at ease."

"Have you looked at Jerry's email, Tom?" I asked, still disturbed by my intuitions.

"Not since this morning. I'll have another look right after dinner," he responded.

When Tom finally did so, he looked at the message in disbelief. "Just got some disturbing news," it began. "Bishop Gene has had a heart attack today. He's at the County Hospital not far from his home. He seems to be resting peacefully at the moment. Too many people there to risk you going to see him. Better to go early in the morning. I'll make the arrangements and pick you up at six-thirty tomorrow morning. Don't respond."

"Kelly, I think you'd better come look at this," Tom said, his voice wavering.

I came to the computer, aware of how pale Tom's face had become. "What is it?" I said, looking over his shoulder and fearing the worst. "Oh my God! There it is, just as I dreamed. I must go to him. What if he doesn't make it through the night?" I exclaimed, clutching the front collar of my dress with one hand and putting my other hand over my mouth.

"Better to trust he'll be okay, Kel," Tom said with as much assurance as he could muster. "Jerry will keep us posted. Wait until morning."

"And keep praying!" I said, tears rolling down my cheeks.

I was in an agitated state the rest of the evening, pacing up and down, realizing that I wasn't very civil with Tom or patient with the children. I could see them giving me a wide berth, to the extent that the crowded quarters of the house allowed.

I tossed and turned all night, worried about my friend, Gene, realizing how much he meant to me and how helpless I felt confined in this small community with no phone or means of transportation.

"I have to trust that God will take care of this," I said to myself as I lay awake, half worrying and half praying that nothing would happen until I could reach out and take Gene's hand in the morning. He's been like a father, as well as a mentor and a pastor to me. He's the one who invited me into the diocese, installed me at St. Gabriel's and had such trust in my abilities to pastor despite my inexperience. He affirmed my gifts and called me, not only to lead the parish, but to the priesthood! What on earth will we do if we lose him? Who will take us to the next stage of his plan? I don't know any of the other bishops in his group. He never mentioned their names, to protect their anonymity. I feel so alone and unprotected without his sheltering care.

These and other thoughts filled my fitful night. By the time the alarm rang at five-thirty, I was ready to get up and get going. Waiting was always difficult for me. I was a woman of action, someone used to taking charge and accomplishing tasks. For the moment I was at the mercy of other agendas and time schedules.

All the family chose to visit Bishop Gene in the hospital, because they loved him as I did, and also because they were a bit stir crazy from being stuck in their hideaway for so long.

Breakfast was quick and quiet as everyone got ready for Jerry's arrival. We had devised a plan to visit the bishop in shifts, while others stood guard in the hallway watching for the press. Jerry's car arrived at exactly six-thirty. He got out and gave handshakes and hugs all around, happy to be reunited despite the trying circumstances of our meeting. Over the last few months everyone in the family had grown closer to Jerry, counting him as a family friend and not just someone I happened to know.

We all climbed into his car and rode to the hospital, about forty minutes away. "I called the nurses' station on Gene's floor and arranged for our meeting," Jerry explained. "We'll go in the emergency entrance to avoid any attention. I've brought the oils for the anointing and Holy Communion as well. I'm not sure what his condition will be, but I wanted to be ready for any contingency."

Although we had not seen Jerry for three weeks, we remained silent for most of the ride to the hospital. "Thanks for the emails, Jerry," Tom volunteered. "They were very helpful. I think we kept our cover pretty well."

"Yes, very well," Jerry responded, minding the speed limit, although his desire was to race all the way to the hospital. "Only time will tell what it will be like once you resurface." Jerry responded.

We drove into the hospital's emergency parking lot and filed out of the car. Jerry knew exactly where to go and how to find the bishop's room. When we entered—all except Nathan, who volunteered for the first watch—we found Bishop Gene sleeping. He didn't appear to be in pain or suffering any discomfort. "Oh, I'm so glad to see him resting peacefully," I sighed as I went to Gene's bed. "I hope we can wait until he wakes so we don't disturb him. How long can we stay, Jerry?"

"Half an hour, maximum," Jerry responded, taking out the sacramental oils and the Holy Communion wafer. "I'd like to get you back to the compound before nine o'clock."

A nurse came to take the bishop's blood pressure. "Oh, you got here, Father Cross. And this is the famous Kelly More, I presume. So glad to meet you. I'm not Catholic, but I think it's great what you're doing. More power to you. If you'll excuse me for a moment, I have to check our patient here."

"How is he doing?" I asked, a little embarrassed at being recognized and wanting to shift the focus from myself to Gene.

"Hard to say," the nurse replied as she looked at Gene's chart. "At the moment everything is stable, but that attack affected large parts of his heart's operation. I'd say he's on borrowed time. It could go either way." The nurse went to the bed and gently called Bishop Gene from his slumber. "You have some early visitors, Bishop. You're a pretty popular guy."

Gene opened his eyes, trying to focus on the faces looking down at him with such concern. As he recognized us, a large smile spread across his face. "Well, well, well. Look who's here. Our phantom family, our notorious fugitives. How are you all?"

"The question is, 'How are *you!*'" I said taking his hand.

"Oh, I'm hanging in there. I can't tell you how happy I am to see your friendly faces; no questions or accusations. I've had plenty of that recently," Gene said, holding my hand as tightly as his strength would allow.

"I'm sorry this fell so heavily on you." Trying to comfort him, I was shocked at how drained his face was and how much weight he'd lost.

"No picnic," he responded with effort.

"We saw your press conference on television outside your home the first day the news broke," I returned. "I felt so sorry for you when you turned and went back into your house alone."

"That wasn't the half of it," Gene replied, grateful that he didn't have to measure his words with his friends. "My phone and fax and email were clamoring for my attention day and night." He paused, trying to catch his breath. "Bishop Foley called immediately and gave me quite a scolding for putting him in such a bad light. Imagine! He was one of my students and twenty years my junior." He paused as he fought the tears. "Then a fax came through from Rome, taking away my faculties as a bishop, effective immediately. It's amazing how swiftly they acted, as if they were prepared for the announcement. I suppose they were worried that I would quickly ordain someone else. . . . None of the bishops from our group called. I suspect they were frightened or cautious, but that hurt." He looked at Jerry. "Thanks for your call; that really helped. Sorry I didn't get back to you. I just didn't have the energy to respond. I suppose all this caused the condition I'm in now." Gene paused once again as he struggled for breath to continue talking. "Those chest pains were an early warning. But the doctors couldn't find anything wrong, so I just kept up my old routine until I dropped. Kind of ignorant of me, I guess."

"But tell me," I said as tears filled my eyes, "what would you have done differently? We should have had you at the migrants' community with us where we could have kept you away from all those meddling reporters and critical authorities. Why didn't we think of that?"

"Because I needed to be the front person to head off the crush of the media. It was all part of the plan," Gene offered.

"And was this hospital bed part of your plan?" I asked accusingly, looking deeply into his sunken eyes.

"Not exactly," Gene admitted with a laugh, "but what a way to go—shaking Rome's foundations like that."

"You're a rebel bishop, no doubt about it, just as the Vatican said." I was shaking my head in an accusatory manner but loving him all the more.

Nathan came into the room and motioned to Michael, "Your turn, coast all clear." Michael slipped away while Nathan came near Bishop Gene.

"Learning a lot of Spanish, I suspect," the bishop said as Nathan came into view.

"Some," was Nathan's reply, surprised at seeing the bishop so pale.

Jerry broke in and said, "I've brought the oils and communion. Interested?"

"Yes, that would be wonderful. Bishop Foley is supposed to come today to do the honors, but I would much rather that it came from you—actually, either of you, now that I think about it. I would also like to receive communion and a blessing from our newest priest," Gene said, looking at me standing by his side.

Squeezing his hand, I blushed and said, "It would be my honor."

Jerry gave me the small canister filled with the holy oil for anointing the sick, and a book with the prayers. I put my thumb in the vessel and applied the oil to Gene's forehead in the sign of a cross as I read, "Through this holy anointing, may the Lord, in his love and mercy, help you with the grace of the Holy Spirit." As he held up his hands, I did the same to his outstretched palms, saying as I did so, "May the Lord, who frees you from sin, save you and raise you up." I sensed there wasn't a dry eye in the room, although I was concentrating on reciting the prayers through my own tears. Gene smiled, looking at me with warmth and acceptance. He was no longer only my bishop, but my willing patient, thankful for the love and care I was able to offer.

As Jerry handed me the small, round, silver pix with the communion host, he broke the sacred moment by saying, "I'm getting a bit anxious that we might be overextending our time here. Before you give Gene communion, Kelly, let me explain what our exit plan is in case we're interrupted. Sorry, Gene, but I feel somewhat responsible for this woman's safety."

"Perfectly correct," Bishop Gene replied, rubbing his hands that had just received the holy oils. "What are the procedures? I'm sure you have it all mapped out," he asked in a teasing tone of voice, his humor still intact despite his weakened condition.

"As a matter of fact, I did ask the nurses about it when I arranged this visit," Jerry grinned, accepting the bishop's compliment. "See that other door? It leads through the bathroom to another room. Everyone escape—through there and then turn left down the hall, go two doors to the stairs and out the exit on the first floor. You'll emerge near the emergency parking. Here, Tom, take my keys just in case. I'll stick around until the coast is clear and meet you later."

"This is all so amusing to me," the bishop said with a smile. "You've been watching too much late-night television, Jerry."

I laughed, and then began the Lord's Prayer as the beginning of the communion service for the sick. Everyone prayed silently with me. I was used to this ritual. I had done it many times at the bedsides of my own parishioners. I took the host and gave communion to the bishop. After a moment of silence, I put my hands on his head and before pronouncing a blessing said with a smile, "I had no idea that I would be putting my hands on your head so soon after you did the same to me." I then called God's blessing for Bishop Gene's good health and peace of mind, when suddenly Michael came bursting into the room.

"Someone's coming," he said in a panic. "We had better get out of here *fast*. They just left the elevator and are heading this way."

Tom took my arm and gently removed my hands from the bishop's head. "We have to scoot. You can finish it later. Come on, kids, through that door."

All of us hustled through the bathroom and into the next room, amid the startled stares of the room's occupants. "Beg your pardon," Tom said as he herded the children and me to the corridor, making sure the hall was clear before we headed for the stairs. We clambered down two flights, out the back door of the hospital, and headed for Jerry's car, happy to have escaped unnoticed. "This is fun," Rachel said. "Just like the movies."

"You can have it!" I said, a little out of breath. "That was pretty close. I didn't even have a chance to say goodbye."

In a few minutes Jerry appeared, a smile across his face. "You just missed Bishop Foley. Do you know why he's visiting this morning? He wants to do a story for the diocesan newspaper, with photos of him and Gene together. He even brought a reporter and a photographer. That smacks of hypocrisy, if you ask me, after what he said to poor Gene when the ordination was announced. Now that Gene's on his deathbed, and can't defend himself, Foley wants publicity."

"Oh, don't say that, Jerry," I exclaimed. "It's *not* his deathbed, surely."

"Sorry, Kel. It's just that I wouldn't hold your hopes too high. The nurse told me last night that it's only a matter of weeks, even days. There's no heart left in that generous body of his. He used it up on others."

"Hey, Mom," Michael interrupted as Tom took my hand by way of comfort, "could we stop at a McDonald's on the way home for an Egg McMuffin or something?"

Tom hesitated, weighing the request in his mind. Turning to me and Jerry, he asked, "What do you two think? It might work, as long as we use the drive-through."

Jerry pulled into the first one he could find, ready to place the order. But while waiting in line, I said to him from the back seat, "Quickly, put the car in reverse and get out of here as fast as you can."

"Why? What's the matter?" everyone asked in unison, fearful they wouldn't get their morning treat.

"Duck, everyone," was my response, as Jerry reluctantly headed for the exit. "That cop car in front of us belongs to Frank from the parish. Didn't you recognize him? I hope he didn't see us. I wonder what he's doing here. It's outside his territory."

"Guess I'd better take the back roads to your hideaway just in case," Jerry said, a bit shaken by this strange coincidence.

We headed out of town and back to our home without using the expressway. The boys kept looking behind them to see if we were being followed. "The coast is clear," Nathan finally said as we drove onto the county road.

"So what if he did see us?" Michael asked. "We weren't doing anything wrong."

"But Frank is the type of fellow who would pull you over just to pass the time of day," I said. "He's a curious sort who would love to get the inside scoop about where we're hiding and then tell the world."

We reached home without further incident. "That was a pretty harrowing experience," I said, trying to cope with my sadness, "seeing Gene and then *Frank*. But I'm so glad we went. I wonder when I can get back to Gene and finish that blessing I started?"

Jerry stayed for the hot muffins I baked to make up for the sudden retreat from McDonald's. He then headed back to his office, leaving us stranded once again. While we were enjoying our belated breakfast, we began to plan for our reentry into civilization. Jerry would return in just over a week to take us home. Then Tom and the boys would return to our temporary home to gather our belongings. We had made arrangements already for a migrant family to move into our renovated home. The level of anticipation and homesickness mounted as we talked of returning to our own beds, front porch and extra bathrooms. "We must get ready for the media," I cautioned. "They'll be after us, but hopefully without the intensity of when the story first broke."

After Jerry left, we settled into our familiar routine for the final week, but our spirits were not as high. The cramped quarters and the isolation were getting to us. Schoolwork and the Spanish classes continued as usual. The evening walks were longer as the nights grew cooler and some of the trees began to change color.

"I know it's been hard and our patience has been sorely tested, but I'm going to miss the peace and tranquility of this place," I said as I took in the evening's sunset. "It's a tradeoff. We've done without some necessities, but gained an appreciation for other unexpected gifts. These walks, for instance. I know I've taken off some pounds," I smiled.

On Monday morning, an email from Jerry mentioned that Gene had been released from the hospital the night before and had returned home. A number of people had volunteered to look after him, but he dismissed them, saying that he was feeling much better and enjoyed his privacy.

As the family returned from our walk that evening, Tom turned on the television to check the baseball scores, one of his regular rituals before going to bed. Instead of the scores, however, a bulletin flashed across the screen. "Bishop Eugene McGovern has just died of an apparent heart attack," it said. "He was found slumped over his desk at home by the police after a caller was unable to contact him by phone. He was 78 years old."

Tom went into the kitchen where I was pouring juice for the kids. "Kel, can you come here for a minute?" He took me in his arms and said, "I hate to tell you this, but Bishop Gene has just died. I saw it on the television."

"Oh, no!" I cried and broke down weeping on Tom's shoulder. "Don't tell me!" Our children looked at him in disbelief.

"What happened?" I wailed, tears streaming down my face.

"Heart attack. He died at home, just a day after being released from the hospital. No word about the funeral."

"Oh, Tom, what shall I do? That dear, dear man. I'll have to go to him. I have to finish my blessing." I said with the pitcher of orange juice still in my hand behind Tom's back.

"Yes, I know," Tom said solemnly. "We'll be leaving for home a little early, children." He let go of me, took the pitcher out of my hand and placed it on the table. Then he said to the children, "It's time."

TWELVE

✢

"WHERE HAVE YOU BEEN!" the next door neighbor asked breath-
lessly. "You missed all the excitement. It was a zoo around here for
a few days."

I listened patiently, not wanting to be rude but anxious to get
inside with the rest of the family. "Yes, we know, Agnes. That's why
we left. Don't worry, the media will return, but hopefully not with
the intensity of a month ago."

I went into the house to survey the situation. Nothing out of kil-
ter, it seemed. The answering machine was full of messages, of course.
I would have to go to the post office to pick up the mail and restart
the newspaper, but surprisingly, everything was in pretty good shape."

By early evening most of our possessions were back in the house
and the family was stowing them where they belonged. We ordered a
pizza, our first in a month, and waited expectantly for it to be delivered. "Oh, it feels so good to be home," Tom said with a sigh, as the
family collapsed in our luxurious family room, or so it seemed, after
the cramped quarters of our temporary home.

The phone rang. Everyone stopped, wondering if they dared
answer it. "Time to face the music," I said as I lifted the receiver.

"Welcome back, Stranger," came the excited voice from the other
end of the line.

"Debbie! How did you know?" I exclaimed, overjoyed to hear her voice.

"A little bird told me," she chuckled, surprised and pleased to have caught me at home. "News travels fast in this little town. Do you have a mountain of mail here waiting for you!" Deb continued. "But that can wait. You first have a ton of explaining to do! What have you been up to, Woman! Good for you. I still can't believe it. You have to come *right now* and tell me every last detail. We had to do a lot of covering for you, you know. Those media people were merciless in trying to dig up every last detail about you. We kept them at bay pretty well."

"Oh, Deb, I am *so* glad to hear your voice," I said, settling into a chair. Although sad and exhausted over Gene's death, I was elated to be talking with my friend and co-worker. "Yes, I know I have a lot of explaining to do. It has been quite an ordeal for the last few months. I'm sorry I couldn't tell you when it was happening. I suspected you knew something was afoot."

"Yes, but not that!" Debbie confessed, her voice so loud I had to hold the receiver away from my ear. "Good gracious, you're a priest! Ordained by a real bishop, God rest his soul."

"What a guy he was, Deb," I said in a more subdued tone, choking back the tears. "I've—*we've* all lost a dear friend. I think it was this last great event—my ordination—that did him in. I certainly hope the funeral will celebrate his whole life and not just this last act of his. He did so much for the church, and he loved it so. As for coming to tell all, I can't do that now. We've just moved back into our home and I have to get my wits about me for tomorrow's funeral. I'm afraid I'll be somewhat the center of attention, although I'll try to stay in the background as much as possible."

"Think again, Girl!" Deb chided, almost bursting with pride at what had happened to me. "Once that press sees you, all the lights and cameras will be turned your way."

"That's what I'm afraid of," I admitted reluctantly. "And I suspect Bishop Foley won't be too happy to see me either. All of that will be going on as I try to pray with and for Bishop Gene McGovern. Can you see now, Deb, why I need some time to get ready for the onslaught? I'll try to come Friday and give you the details, that is, if I still have a job. Bishop Foley may sack me as I come for communion. I suspect it'll only be a matter of time."

"Don't say that!" Deb contested, ready to fight to the end to defend me and my new status. "We need you more than ever. Your being away for a month made everyone realize just how great a pastor you are. This place isn't the same without you. You can't leave us!"

"Don't bet on it," I said, trying to help Deb face the reality of the situation. "Listen, I'm sorry, but I have to go. We're in the middle of a pizza feast, if they left me any. You know what kids are like if they've been deprived of pizza for a month. And there's much to organize before I hit the sack. See you tomorrow at the funeral. It's nice to think I'll get at least one good hug amid the flurry."

"You can count on it," Deb assured me, "and lots more besides. Prepare yourself to be welcomed home as our new priest. My good-ness, I can't believe I'm saying that. Bye, Love."

I hung up, paused for a moment to appreciate Deb's friendship and enthusiasm, and then returned to the others in the family room. All of them, their faces stuffed with pizza, had such contented expres-sions that I'd laughed. "Any left for your poor old Ma?"

"Plenty," Tom mumbled through a mouthful. "We ordered far too much to be sure there would be enough. Dig in. I'll bet that was Debbie? Any news?"

I nodded, still laughing at the scene before me, "Just that she wants the *whole* story, top to bottom, and right *now*! I suspect that will be the request from many quarters. Oh, Tom, what will it be like tomorrow?" my mood changing as I thought about the funeral.

"At least no reporters have shown up yet," Tom said reassuringly. "That's a bonus. Maybe we'll get a good night's sleep before tomorrow's big event."

"Wouldn't that be a welcome gift!" I sighed, settling into a chair and rejoicing at being home.

Thankfully the word didn't reach the media that we had returned home. We spent a long, leisurely evening together and a restful night in our own beds before preparing for the drive to the cathedral in the morning. I limited the children to only two phone calls before bedtime so that the news wouldn't travel too quickly. Debbie's call told me the word was out; Kelly More, the Priest, was back in town.

Thursday morning dawned, promising a bright and beautiful day. Despite the sunshine, it seemed awfully cloudy within. I was still grieving the loss of my dear friend and worried about all I might be facing. "Dear God, help me get through this day," I prayed as I took my shower. Who knows what will happen once I show myself in public? Well, it was meant to be. I owe it to Gene to carry it as best I can. I hope I'll have a little peace and quiet to pray to him during his funeral.

The drive to church was uneventful. We planned to show up just in time—even a little late—so as to reduce the commotion I might cause. Nice theory. As soon as we stepped out of the car cameras surrounded us. The five of us struggled through the crowd and got into church with smiles but no comments. We had worked this all out during the drive.

By prior arrangement, Jerry had kept a pew free for us near the back of church. Thankfully we filed into our seats, gave Jerry a nod and tried to look composed. Faces kept turning to acknowledge our presence. Some of them I recognized. Others were perfect strangers to me, but they seemed to indicate they were long-lost friends. To my surprise, most looked at me with admiration and support—no frowns nor accusations. It almost seemed like hero-worship. For this, I was totally unprepared. "Tom," I said under my breath. "All those people are staring at us."

"Well, what did you expect?" he whispered, looking straight ahead and smiling. "Get used to it, my Dear. It's your legacy from now on. You're their symbol of hope for change."

"Oh yeah, I forgot," I whispered back impishly. "Okay now, one more time, why me?"

"Beats me," Tom replied. "Just look priestly. By rights you should be one of those processing down the aisle right now."

"Yeah, right!" I muttered, shaking my head and wondering when that would ever happen.

The Mass had already begun when we arrived, but it took some time before all the priests taking part in the funeral reached the altar step, bowed and filed into the front pews. The cathedral was packed, although Jerry had no trouble saving seats for the family when he told the ushers whom they were for. Rather than going on the altar with the priests, Jerry opted to stay with the rest of us and help deal with the press.

Bishop Foley was the main celebrant, although a number of other bishops and a few archbishops were in attendance. I looked them over carefully. "I suspect," I thought to myself, "that some of these were part of his treasured group of co-conspirators. Will any of them make an attempt to contact me now that Gene is gone? And what will be the next move, I wonder."

One of the older priests of the diocese gave a eulogy at the beginning of the Mass, telling of all the wonderful deeds of this great man. He had a hard time getting through it. Most of the congregation was in tears by the time he finished. Not so Bishop Foley, I noted, although he looked dutifully somber. What will melt that man's heart? He's the complete opposite of Gene, that's for sure.

The homily after the gospel was delivered by one of the bishops. No mention was made of his last prophetic—some would say, defiant—act, but it was on everyone's mind as they listened to the bishop's words.

The media was kept out of church with the exception of one camera crew whose footage was to be shared by all the networks. On frequent occasions the camera turned to me so I had to be alert. For the most part, however, I was left in peace to pay my last respects to my dear friend and to reflect on how his invitation had changed my life.

When the family filed out of the pew for communion, I was relieved to be heading to a station well removed from Bishop Foley. I knew the priest distributing the hosts and got a big smile as he said, "The Body of Christ, Kelly." This gave me some reassurance and I almost said, *Thanks*, instead of the usual *Amen*.

Communion took a long time—three songs-worth—but the remainder of the Mass went quickly. First the sprinkling and blessing of the casket, an announcement that only a small procession would be going to the gravesite, an invitation for all to gather under the tents outside for refreshments, and then the final blessing and closing recessional.

This was the part I dreaded. I could no longer escape to my hideaway. Now was the time to stand my ground, come what may. Jerry leaned over and suggested that we stay in church while everyone else filed out. As it was, people made a point to stop at our pew and make contact. I was the major attraction, no doubt about it.

Deb rushed over and gave me a big hug, as did Carol and many others from St. Gabriel's. Father Mac, the priest who used to do the Masses at St. Gabe's before Father Henry, stopped to offer his congratulations. "Oh, you are something!" he said with obvious admiration. "I knew you were called to greatness, and here you are, our very own woman priest. Good for you, Kelly!"

"Thanks for your support, Mac, but I don't relish facing that crowd outside."

"Don't worry; we'll all look out for you. Come, take my arm. We'll go to the gallows together," Mac said reassuringly, indicating by his gesture that he wished we were still partners in ministry as we had always been.

"Thanks, but I think I should go with Tom, don't you?" I laughed. "No need adding any more rumors to the mill."

"Right you are." Father Mac said, ushering the family out of the pew. "Well, here goes then."

Our small entourage left by a side entrance but to no avail. The reporters were watching us closely and were there to block our exit.

"Kelly More, tell us what it's like being the first real woman priest?" "What do you prefer to be called?" "How did you feel when it happened?" "Have you been in hiding and why?" "Has the pope or Vatican officials made contact with you?" "Will you be able to say Mass now?"

On and on the questions went. The family and a small group of friends formed a circle around me as we made our way slowly to the refreshments, but the going was tough. "Do you think I should hold an informal press conference right here?" I said to Jerry as he brought me a cup of coffee.

"You'll do better saying nothing for the moment," was his advice as the cameras clicked. "Wait and see what the next few days will bring."

"You're the expert," I replied. I tried to get a sip of coffee as I was surrounded by well-wishers and media. A small group of women made a special attempt to get close and make contact. "We're so glad to meet you," one of them said. "We've come from Detroit just to say hello. You've created quite a stir, you know. The cause of women's ordination has taken a giant leap forward. In fact, it's now a done deal, thanks to you."

I was trying to stay focused on what the women were saying, but was having difficulty because of the crunch of people. Somehow I knew this was important so I strained to listen.

"We helped organize the Ordination Rally," one woman remarked, "and another is planned for November. We want you to be the featured speaker, Kelly. We'll get in touch, but we just had to come and shake your hand. You're an inspiration to us all. Here's my card." At this, the cluster of women nodded and offered their hands in congratulations as if welcoming a hero into their midst. Then they disappeared into the crowd.

This encounter stayed in my mind long after the reception. The family remained at the reception for only a short time. We were glad to get into our car and escape from what had been a trying experience for us all. "I can't promise you," I said on the return trip, "that there won't be more of the same waiting for us when we get home."

As predicted, there was a cable truck waiting in front of our house, set for an impromptu interview. "No, no comment. Sorry," I said from the car window as Tom drove into the garage.

"Thank goodness we can get into the house without having to face them in our front yard," I said, starting to close the blinds in the front windows. "They'll leave soon enough, I suspect. That month away cooled the frenzy somewhat. Okay, kids, we have to contact your schools and see how far behind you are in your studies."

"Or ahead," Nathan quipped, proud of all he had learned over the last month.

"If that media truck outside will let us," I returned, "we can make the tour of the schools this afternoon and see where we stand. Then I have to go to the office and face a mountain of work. Thomas, I don't expect to see you come up for air for days with all you have to do to get reconnected with your work. I hope you still have a job."

"Not to worry," Tom said with obvious pride. "Having Internet access over the last month really helped. At least I know what to expect once I resurface. Actually it gave me time to think up some pretty creative ideas."

Just then the phone rang. "I'll get it," Rachel shouted, so happy to have a phone to answer. "Mom, it's for you," she said, holding the receiver.

"Welcome back, Kelly," a somewhat officious voice began as I said hello. "This is Bishop Foley. I wanted to reach you as soon as possible. Much has transpired since we last talked."

"To put it mildly," I said, fearing the worst. "I suspect you want to see me."

"Yes, that would be correct," Bishop Foley said in measured tones. "When would you be free? We've met on Mondays in the past. Are you free this coming Monday?"

"Yes, I think I can make that." I replied, glad to have the weekend to get ready for the conference. "What time?"

"How about meeting at your office for a change?" the bishop volunteered. "Say, ten o'clock? Would that be convenient?"

"Certainly; I'll see you there," I said in as nonchalant a tone as I could muster. My insides were churning, knowing this would be a most unpleasant occasion for us both. "Goodbye, Bishop."

After reconnecting the children with their school communities, I headed to my office wondering what I would encounter. Although it was late in the afternoon, my two faithful office companions were waiting for me. There were flowers on my desk and two very excited people waiting to hear my story.

"Thank you both," I said as I toured my familiar surroundings. "You've made me feel so welcome. I can't stay too long and it's past quitting time for you, but we can talk for a short while."

The three of us huddled in my office as I recounted the "short version" of all that led to the ordination and what followed afterward. Deb and Carol sat transfixed by my account.

"I thought the Ordination Rally would be the highlight of the year," Carol exclaimed, "but this beats all."

"Oh," I said, "I almost forgot. Bishop Foley, of all persons, is coming here on Monday morning for a *visit*. I suspect he's not too pleased by these recent events. Life may change around here following that interchange."

"We'll be on our best behavior," Deb said somewhat cynically, "but he'd better not do anything to get our dander up."

Carol interjected, "We've sorted the mail and messages. Most of the stuff we've completed, only a few things need your immediate attention." She said this with obvious pride in what she and Deb had accomplished during my absence. "There was a call this afternoon from a woman in Detroit who said you two talked at the funeral. She said it was important. I guess they all are. Most of the other calls we handled as they were received, but this last one had a strange feel. It was a cryptic message from someone who sounded a bit mysterious. He said he'd call later."

"Well done, both of you," I affirmed, giving each a look of admiration and thanks. "You've been good and faithful stewards while I was away. Say, it's time to run home and fix dinner," I said, looking at the clock on my desk. "No communal prayer tomorrow morning; it's Friday. I'll see you both around nine. It's so good to be back in my office."

The rest of the evening was surprisingly relaxed. Tom was right; my return was old news. The media was nowhere in sight when I returned home. I thought about Mass on Sunday and made a mental note to call Henry in the morning to make arrangements. I suspect I'm not needed much anymore. He's probably taken over the liturgy by now, but I do want time after communion to share a few reflections with the congregation. It'll be interesting to see how they will react.

Friday and Saturday were overwhelming days for me as I dug into my office work and juggled the repeated phone and visitor interruptions. It was slow going because I was still grieving over the loss of Gene. Amid the commotion I tried to gather my thoughts for my reflection at Sunday's liturgy. I also connected with Father Henry, who was abrupt and somewhat distant. "So what else is new?" I thought to myself after his call. I suspect he will be very threatened by my presence at the altar on Sunday, but I'm not going to retreat now, not after all that has happened.

When I told Debbie about Henry's response, she replied, "Oh, plenty has happened, all right. You should see how staid and straight-laced our Masses have become over the last month. I'm so happy you're back to loosen things again. We missed your smile and good humor."

I was apprehensive as I prepared to go to church on Sunday morning. I would be facing the congregation with my new identity, one that was now public knowledge. How would they respond?

Any doubts I may have had vanished as soon as I stepped into church. The people had decorated it with autumn colors and had hung a sign across the back of church that read, "Welcome back, Kelly More." I laughed when I saw it. "Nobody, not even my own parish, knows what to call me. Isn't that great."

Slowly people began arriving, first the choir and sacristans, then the ushers and liturgical ministers, and finally the congregation. I stayed in back the entire time, greeting people, shaking hands, receiving hugs and enjoying the lavish homecoming. The parishioners were congratulatory and supportive of their returning pastor. A few people, I noticed, had entered via the side door, perhaps avoiding me as they entered. I suspected my notoriety and acclaim were not shared by all. Father Henry, who had also entered by the side door, had vested and was now looking at the commotion and decorations from the door of the sacristy. He seemed to be seething inside, although his exterior remained in check. He certainly was not joining the spontaneous celebration.

When it was time to begin Mass, Henry and I walked down the aisle as we had done so often before. But this time it was different. I felt his equal, and the reaction from the people reinforced this sentiment. Henry was trying to stay as distant as possible. When the opening song was concluded and before Henry made the sign of the cross to begin Mass, someone started to clap and the entire congregation followed suit. I was stunned. Henry was befuddled. His hand stopped at his forehead as he was about to make the sign of the cross and it stayed there until the applause died. I looked at Tom with an all-knowing glance, but he made a gesture as if to say, "It wasn't me!"

Mass continued as usual. Henry read the gospel and gave a brief homily. I was present at the altar as I had always been, but now the congregation seemed to look at me as deserving new respect and deference. Henry and I were a bit uneasy, but for different reasons; I because I felt self-conscious, not knowing whether I was a concelebrant and co-equal or merely an attendant, Henry because he was unsure about my status—was she or wasn't she a priest?

After communion, everyone sat and waited for my reflection. "Greetings," I began, "and thank you for such a warm welcome. I've missed you a great deal during this last month. I suspect you want to hear the whole story, but there isn't time for that now. I don't know how or when I'll have a chance to explain all that has happened. Briefly, however, I was ordained to the priesthood by Bishop McGovern, on July 22nd, the Feast of Mary Magdalene. You've probably seen a video of the service on television."

People in the congregation nodded in response. Tom looked at Henry and could see him grimace when I said this.

"Bishop Gene," I continued, walking down the middle aisle, "had asked me two months earlier to become ordained, and after much prayer and discernment, I agreed. He was a most pastoral and prophetic individual. He was concerned that God's people were not being served because of the lack of priests. His reasoning was that my ordination might spur the new pope into action and start in motion the process of change that is so needed in our church today. Whether that will happen or not remains to be seen. Bishop McGovern knew that once the news of the ordination was announced, it would disrupt my life and my family's. Under his advice and counsel, we withdrew from the public's eye for the last four weeks. Then our beloved bishop died. That prompted me to return home and wait for what God has in store for me. It hasn't been easy, but I've felt very blessed through it all. We—my whole family and I—have experienced many joys and benefits from this strange turn of events. Finally, let me say that I do feel it has been you, the community of St. Gabriel, which has called me forth for ordination. I was assured of that call in the welcome you gave me this morning. I'm still your pastor and for this I'm forever grateful. Pray for me as I try to discern and accept whatever is God's plan. We're all in this together." I paused and looked at all the faces looking at me with rapt attention. "Amen. End of story," I concluded and returned to my seat.

Everyone gave me a long and booming applause. It reminded me of ordinations I had attended in the past, where the assembly applauded the candidates for priesthood as they came forward. This resounding response was the applause that I missed at my own ordination, although my family and Jerry made up for it as best they could.

People crowded around me at the end of Mass and during refreshment time afterwards. What I neglected to note was the hasty exit of a stranger who had been taking notes throughout my talk. It was no surprise to me, however, to find my remarks quoted on the news that afternoon and evening, and to see them published in the newspaper the next morning. There was even a picture of me that accompanied the article. "When did they take that?" I asked out loud as I read the story. "Amazing how much the media can do without a person knowing it."

On Monday morning we returned to our familiar routine of rushing through breakfast, making lunches and getting to school. Both Rachel and Michael were giving Nathan a difficult time about his renewed relationship with Allyson. She was home from college during the weekend and spent most of Sunday afternoon with Nathan. "Funny," Mike quipped, "how she chose *this* weekend to return home."

"Shut-up!" Nathan said with a glare and rushed out of the house to catch the school bus.

"You'd better run after him, Michael, or you'll miss the bus yourself," I said. Then turning to Tom I added, "How quickly everything returns to normal, whatever *normal* is."

"I hope the meeting with the bishop goes well today, Dear," Tom replied, enjoying his morning paper once again. "Don't let down your guard. He's a smooth operator."

"Don't worry," I assured him, "but I doubt much dialogue will take place. I'm sure he's mentally worked out what he'll say."

I kissed Tom goodbye and then Rachel and I left. We walked to the front door of her school, then I strolled back to church for my hour of prayer in the chapel. With joy and relish I settled into my familiar chair, closed my eyes and let the Spirit's graces flood over me. "Oh, God, help me accept whatever is coming my way this morning," I prayed. "I know in the long run, that only good will prevail. You've shown me that already. But it's difficult to deal with at the outset. Please give me strength and balance today."

I went to my office to get ready for Bishop Foley's visit. He arrived promptly at ten. After exchanging pleasantries with the staff, he and I retired to my office. I had arranged the chairs so we would be facing each other, with no table or desk creating a barrier.

He took a seat and began, "So, much has transpired over the last few months."

"Yes, you might say that," I returned in a friendly tone of voice.

"It came as a great surprise, as you can imagine," the bishop replied with a smile that I sensed did not reflect his true sentiments.

"Yes, I imagine that it did," I replied, saying as little as was possible.

"I, of course, was not pleased," he continued, shifting in his chair and looking away from me. "I didn't share Bishop McGovern's views, as you have probably guessed. When the press called for a comment the day the news broke, I didn't know what to say. It caught me totally off guard. I don't like surprises, you know. Soon after that the Curia in Rome called to ask if it was true and I had nothing to tell them. It put me in a very awkward position."

"Yes, I'm sure it did. I'm sorry to have caused you all that anguish and embarrassment," I replied, but there was no way Gene or I would ask his permission to do the ordination.

"I know it was not your doing; Bishop McGovern put you up to it," the bishop went on with what seemed to me to be a prepared speech.

"Oh, but I did agree of my own free will," I interjected. "I wasn't coerced in any way, if that's what you mean."

"Yes, yes, but I don't hold you responsible, shall we say," Bishop Foley added, fingering the large cross that hung around his neck.

"Oh, but I am responsible," I said with emphasis, looking him straight in the eye. "I chose to say yes to this and I felt it was the right thing to do."

"Well, then," the bishop replied, appearing uneasy because the conversation was not following his script, "what I'm conveying is that Rome has asked that I read you the Rite of Excommunication for your flagrant disobedience and public scandal to the church." With this his tone changed completely. There was no doubt that he was now giving me orders.

My eyes lit up—partly from surprise and partly from the anger I felt over such arrogance and misuse of power on Bishop Foley's part.

Seeing my reaction, the bishop quickly added, "But I have decided not to do this, primarily because I see you more as a pawn in a much bigger power play enacted by people who do not have the best interests of the church at heart."

My stomach churned. I could feel myself getting more upset with each word uttered. One part of me was counseling, "Stay cool. Relax. Don't succumb to his taunting." Another part was seething.

The bishop continued. "To remain here as the pastoral administrator is an untenable position. You can see that I'm sure, can't you?

I made no response. I merely stared at Bishop Foley, my eyes boring into him while not emitting any hint of agreement.

Looking away, the bishop continued. "The reason I chose to come here rather than to have you come to my office is that I wish to formally relieve you of your duties here. The diocese will, of course, honor its financial commitment to you until the end of the calendar year. There's not really any written contract, of course, but at least we're willing to provide proper compensation. There's no one available to take your place just now, so I will have to ask your staff to fill in until we can find a replacement. I would appreciate it if you could have your belongings out of the office by this evening. Do I make myself clear?" He struggled to gain the upper hand but he was not succeeding.

"Perfectly," I said between gritted teeth.

"My wish," he continued, almost as if he were talking to himself, "would be that you find another place to worship. I can't force you to do that, but you might find it easier on yourself if you did. That would be my suggestion, at any rate."

I winced at his condescending attitude while he was taking my job and ministry away from me. "Thank you. I'll take that under consideration," I said coldly, struggling to keep my rising rage in check. "Anything else?" The smiles that began the conversation had long since vanished from both our faces.

"No, I think that will be all," the bishop said, getting out of his chair. "You can bring in your staff now so I can give them the news personally."

During this brief and pointed altercation, Bishop Foley's expression had descended from a pleasant demeanor to a seething frown. My own and Bishop McGovern's acts of defiance had challenged his authority. All of this had happened "on his watch" and he would be held responsible. It probably spelled the end of his episcopal career. Any hopes he had for advancement were now gone. Events outside of his control—even though he had been diligent to do everything expected of him—had changed his life's course. As a result, Bishop Foley was not a happy man. I had the impression that he was thinking, "This woman has done me in." I almost smiled as I thought this. Here I am, getting sacked, and I'm feeling sorry for the one responsible.

The rest of the day was full of tears and sadness for Carol and Debbie. They were so upset and frustrated by Bishop Foley's dictum, that they were not able to function. For me, it was a day of packing. I had sensed this was coming, so it wasn't a surprise to me. The threat of excommunication, however, was devastating.

"I don't know what I'll do if I'm separated from the church I love," I commented to Tom when I called to give him the news. "Can we survive on your salary, Tom? Should we move? What's our best alternative?"

"First of all," he said, attempting to quell the panic he sensed in my questions, "never make any big decisions when in the midst of a crisis. I think it was you who taught me that. Secondly, yes, we can do quite well on my income. Just look at how well we did when we lived so simply at the migrant community. Maybe we should go back there. It sure was a lot cheaper. Not a single credit card slip for the whole month."

"We can't do that," I moaned. "The Mendez family already has our home, remember?"

"Thirdly," he continued as if he hadn't heard me, "you could get a job as a lady bartender and do far more priestly work than anyone else ever does on Sunday morning. Consider the tips you'd get—and could give!"

"Oh, stop, Tom. This is serious," I protested. "I've just lost my job and maybe my church. Do you realize that? Do I, even? Well, you'll have me around the house more these days—just when you thought you'd gotten rid of me so you could do your work in peace and quiet once again."

I hung up the phone and went back to my packing. By dinnertime I had all my belongings in boxes. Then, with Debbie and Carol, who had stayed late to help, I loaded the boxes into our three cars for the transfer back home. "I'm still around, you know," I said as I dropped my keys into Deb's outstretched palm. "You handled everything so well when I was away, you can do it a while longer. It should be interesting to see who will take my place."

"Nobody!" both Carol and Deb shouted in unison with pent up emotion. "No one else could be the pastor that you are to all of us. Let's set up church at your house. You're ordained. Call it Saint—what?—Magdalene!"

"Not so fast," I said, holding up my hand. "I've already angered the bishop. I don't want him throwing me out of my own house as well."

That evening during dinner, I shared the news with the children. All of them were angry about what the bishop had done to their mother, and they felt it an affront to them personally.

"Take it easy, kids," I said, trying to calm them. "It could be worse. He could have thrown me out of the church altogether."

"Can he do that?" Rachel exclaimed.

"Yes, I'm afraid he can," I responded. "I'm sure he had no choice but to fire me. He was only doing Rome's bidding. I wonder what kept him from the excommunication. He was angry enough, surely, but I had a sense there was something else happening behind the scenes."

After dinner, my thoughts returned to those two phone messages Carol mentioned last Thursday. One was from the woman who gave me her card after Gene's funeral. She was inviting me to the next Ordination Rally in November. Should I attend, I wondered? Would it be counterproductive? I don't want to spark a schism. Many people are angry enough to try that. And what about that other call? Could it be one of the bishops in Gene's group trying to make contact, or perhaps a nosey reporter looking for a story? Speaking of story, I should think about documenting all of this on paper. That might take my mind off the sorrow and loss that I feel, to say nothing of wondering what to do with my life.

Throughout the evening and into the next day I gave myself the leisure of allowing my mind to ramble. There was nothing pressing I needed to do, which was a strange experience for me. No more urgent phone calls, pastoral visits or presentations to prepare. As I was mulling this over and enjoying a late breakfast, the phone rang. It was Carol.

"Calls are coming for you, Kelly," Carol said, somewhat apologetically, still considering me as the one in charge. "What should I do, forward their numbers to you?"

"Sure, although you have a real knack for weeding the crazies and the nonsense calls. Send the rest my way. I could use the distraction."

"Okay then," Carol responded. "That woman from Detroit, Susan Jennings, called again. Here's her number."

"Thanks, I have her number already. I'll give her a call. What do you think, Carol? Should we go to another Ordination Rally?"

"Sure!" Carol exclaimed, needing a lift from yesterday's disaster. "That last one was great. We could have a blast in New Orleans. I'd love to see what they've done to rebuild the city."

I laughed, thanked Carol for the message and said goodbye. Then I dialed Susan's phone number. "Hi, this is Kelly More. You called?"

"Yes, thanks so much for returning my call." She sounded relieved to hear from me. "I'm sorry to be a pest, but we're running out of time. The Second Ordination Rally is only a month away. We'd like you to be our guest of honor. You're the one person who encapsulates all we're working toward. We need you there to give the rest of us encouragement and hope. Will you come? We'll pay for your travel and lodging, plus a stipend. Would you agree to preside at our closing liturgy."

"Whoa," I said, overwhelmed with so much information. "That's a little too fast for me. I'll have to talk with my husband and family first. This whole experience has been a bit unsettling for all of us. We need a little while to catch our breath. How much time do I have to decide?"

"Not much, I'm afraid," Susan responded somewhat sheepishly. "How about tomorrow? Sorry, but the publicity is already late, although it looks as if we'll have a really good crowd, even larger than Detroit. The fanfare surrounding your ordination—doesn't that sound good?—has made all the difference. So if you can, please call in the morning. I truly hope you can do this. It would guarantee the rally a rousing success."

"I can't make any promises," I said and hung up the phone with some misgiving. Having Mass with that little community of migrants is one thing. Doing it before a cast of thousands is quite another. Do you really want this, Jesus? Is this really helping the cause? Or is it only sowing more dissension? As people requested when You were alive, give me a sign here, please.

I returned to my new prayer chair in the living room and opened my Bible to see what it might reveal. I flipped the pages to a passage from Luke's gospel, chapter twelve. I read out loud the first thing my eyes saw, "I came to bring fire to the earth. Do you think I have come to bring peace? No, I tell you, but rather division."

Wow, I wonder what that means. Am I really supposed to be a source of division? That's what it says. Well, perhaps I could at least attend at the rally. I wouldn't need to be the keynote speaker or do the Mass, but be present to lend support. I think I could do that. Let's see what the family has to say about all of this. . . .

THIRTEEN

"HELLO," I SAID, AS I PICKED UP the phone that interrupted my prayer time. My mind had been wandering as I tried to imagine what my role would be at the Ordination Rally if, indeed, I decided to go.

"Is this Kelly More?" the male voice asked.

"Yes, this is she," I responded cautiously.

"Good. Sorry to disturb you at home," he said, his gentle voice instilling confidence. "The rectory worker gave me your phone number. I hope I didn't reach you at an inopportune moment." The voice on the other end of the line sounded as if it were an older person, someone who perhaps held a position of authority but possessed a sensitivity and concern for others as well.

"No, no problem," my interest was aroused.

"This is going to sound strange," the gentleman continued, "but I would rather not give you my name. I'll explain why. I'm a friend of the late Bishop Gene McGovern.

Now he had my complete attention.

"He mentioned to you, when he was alive," the caller explained, "that he met with a group of bishops to devise a plan in which you became an integral part. I'm one of those bishops. In fact, I've been designated as your contact person from that group now that Bishop Gene is no longer with us. We sorely miss him, as I'm sure you do, especially his courage and wise insight. I have no doubt that you and I will meet one day, but for now, I would prefer to talk by phone and remain anonymous. This is for our mutual protection. I hope you understand."

"Yes, yes of course," I replied, growing more intrigued as the conversation progressed. I was so relieved to be back in communication with the group again. I had felt not only sad when Gene died, but also abandoned. What would happen to the plan he shared with me that changed my life? Now I might learn what the next steps would be. I strained to not miss a word that this unknown caller was speaking.

"Our small group of bishops has remained active," he continued. "You're still an essential part of our ongoing strategy, more essential than you realize. I'm sure you must feel like a pawn in a much larger game, but this isn't the case. You're the central player. Soon you'll see how vital you are, that is, if our plan unfolds as we hope it will."

"It's strange that you mentioned this," I returned, warming to the conversation and placing implicit trust in a person I had never met. "My own Bishop Foley said I was merely a pawn in a much larger intrigue."

"Yes, I suspect he would say that," the caller chuckled. "As a matter of fact, we've been in contact with your bishop and we're doing a bit of persuasion of our own. I'm sorry you lost your job. It couldn't be helped. We were able to dissuade him from applying a more drastic censure. How are you handling this latest change in your status?"

"You know about all this?" I said, amazed that this person was so well informed.

"Yes, our group tries to stay apprised of events. We also want to be as supportive and helpful to you as we possibly can. For the moment, we'll have to continue to work behind the scenes. We want to assure you, however, that we have your best interests at heart. We're also aware that you've been invited to the Second Ordination Rally in New Orleans. I hope you'll consider accepting the offer."

"My, you *are* up-to-date," I said in amazement. "The call requesting my presence just came an hour ago this morning!"

"But it's been in the works for some time," the caller assured me. "It was the unfortunate death of Bishop Gene that changed the timeline. What was your response, if I may be so bold?"

"I told Susan Jennings I would call her tomorrow morning after I talk to my family," I confided.

"Good response. They need to be part of the decision. However," he added, "we would greatly appreciate it if you would accept the offer. This will help maintain your presence in the news and the pressure on Rome."

"As of now, I'm leaning in that direction," I admitted somewhat surprised at my willingness—even eagerness—to attend.

"Excellent! That is indeed good news. I know how hard this must be for you, but it makes such a difference that you are willing to endure these hardships for the greater good. May I ask, how was your month's retreat?"

"Actually it was a blessing," I said, enjoying this unknown person's concern. "We all grew much closer as a family. The children did well coping with the isolation, excelled in their schoolwork and, as an extra bonus, learned some Spanish. We all did quite well. Thanks for asking. Now let me ask you something. I imagine that none of the group's bishops will be at the rally, correct?"

"I'm afraid not," came the response. "Not that we wouldn't like to attend, but it's too risky if we're going to achieve our desired goal."

"Then will you be contacting me on a regular basis?" I asked, hoping not to be out of touch for long.

"Yes, I suspect we will," the caller confirmed pleasantly. "I'm a little leery about the security of our phone conversations. That's one reason I didn't give you my name. The phone on this end can't be traced. Is there some way you could provide a secure line on your end so we could talk more freely? You're getting to be quite a famous person, you know. Some members of the press have ingenious ways of gathering information."

"Yes, I think there's a way," I responded. "Bishop Gene and I had a plan. Next time you call, I'll fill you in."

"Good. That's about all I have to say for the moment. I just wanted you to know we haven't forgotten you."

"Oh, I'm so grateful," I said with genuine relief. "You don't know how anxious I was. I kept saying, 'There must be a plan here. I won't be abandoned.' But to hear a real live voice, even if I don't know your name, makes all the difference in the world. I can hear your concern and care and that means a great deal."

"Good. We'll continue to be in touch. Just when, I'm not sure. And I'm so glad you're thinking of going to New Orleans. That's an important step in the progression of our plan. I'm sure you'll do very well. You have what it takes."

"Thanks for that vote of confidence," I said, a bit embarrassed by the compliment, "but at the moment all I feel is dread and foreboding. Please ask that group of yours to pray hard for me."

"We've been doing that all along," he assured me. "It's working. You've done a marvelous job so far. Much better than you may realize. The ordination ceremony on that video was superb. Well, Kelly, I've enjoyed talking with you. You're everything Gene said you were. And yes, we'll meet in person sometime in the future; you can count on that."

"Thank you. I'll look forward to it. Goodbye, Bishop."

"Goodbye, Kelly."

I hung up the phone and stared into space. What a strange situation I'm involved in, I mused. My main ally can't even say who he is. Why should I even trust what he says? I guess because his voice sounded so reassuring. It certainly does help to have a new contact in the absence of Gene—although I still sense your presence as well, Gene. You're still here, working your plan, aren't you? We'll not let you down. We'll see it through to its conclusion, whatever it was you had in mind.

I stopped my rumination and shouted down the hall, "Tom, may I interrupt you for a moment? I have some interesting news to share."

After I had recounted the gist of my phone conversation, Tom replied, "Well, that certainly affirms your decision to participate in the rally. Guess you couldn't have any clearer sign than that."

"Yes, I think you're right. Our dinner conversation this evening with the children will be more of an announcement than a discussion. What about you? Do you want to go? It could be great fun amid all the hoopla."

"No, I don't think so," Tom replied after thinking about if for a moment. "If I go, the children go, and that's too much excitement for them after this past month. I'll stay behind and we'll all cheer for you. Why don't you ask Deb and Carol? They'll be a strong support for you, and it would do them good. They need to spend some time with you. This firing business, I suspect, has hit them very hard, perhaps more than it has affected you."

"Yes, I can see your point," I said, taking his hand in mine. "You are so wise, so very wise. Thanks for being you, and for supporting me during all of this. I know you've had reservations about this ordination process, but throughout all of it, you've been a great comfort and ally to me, and I greatly appreciate you."

When I told them of the day's events, the children's response at dinner was, "May we go? May we go?"

"Not this time," I said with a laugh. "One Ordination Rally is plenty. Seen one, seen them all."

"But New Orleans!" Nathan said with obvious relish.

"Ah, yes, New Orleans," I said, casting my eyes to the ceiling. "All the more reason you need to stay and keep your Dad out of trouble."

"What trouble?" Rachel asked.

"I'll explain later," Tom responded.

"*Much* later," I added.

The dinner conversation felt right to me as Tom and I cleared the table. We let the kids watch some extra television and play computer games for a change. They had little homework because they were so far ahead of their classmates after their month away.

"You know, Tom," I said as we finished the dishes, "I would never have guessed what a blessing this ordination thing has been for us as a family. True, I've lost my job, but look at all we've gained."

"A free trip to New Orleans, for one," Tom said jokingly.

"Oh, stop. I'm serious," I insisted. "No matter what lies ahead, I just need to acknowledge all the good that has happened so far, things I could never have predicted."

"Yes, I guess you're right," Tom admitted, changing his tone. "Your priesthood is blossoming in many unexpected places. Which reminds me, how about going to the migrants to do Mass this Sunday? I miss our friends there and I don't really want to face either Father Henry or all those angry faces when they hear that you've been sacked. I could call the Sanchezes, now that they have a phone and let them know we're coming. Besides, Michael has been badgering me to go. I think he has a crush on that cute little Maria."

"Yes, I noticed," I laughed. "But, you know, that would be a great idea! I was wondering what I'd do this coming weekend. Going there would be a real treat."

I went to bed feeling very blessed. I was committed to New Orleans, and now had a place to minister on the weekend. "What more could a body ask?" I said as I kissed Tom good night.

I woke the next morning thinking about what I would tell Susan Jennings. I didn't want to say yes to everything. I needed some parameters and limits so things wouldn't get out of hand. I hoped I'd have some say in all this.

After all the children had left for school and Tom had retired to his office, I dialed my Ordination Rally contact.

"It's good of you to call so quickly," Susan said when she heard my voice. "I hope you have good news for me."

"Yes, I think I do," I said with some hesitation. "I'm going to accept your offer."

"Oh, I'm so happy!" she exclaimed. "It'll make such a difference." There was a brief moment of silence. I sensed Susan was telling others in the office about my decision.

"But I would like to set some stipulations, if I may," I added.

"Tell me what they are and we'll see what we can manage."

"You asked that I preside at the closing liturgy." I said. "Although I left early at the Detroit Rally, I understand that there were many celebrants for the final liturgy. I would feel much more comfortable if I were one of many and not the only person leading the Eucharist in New Orleans. Could you arrange that?"

"Ah," she responded, sounding somewhat disappointed, "that does change things. We had planned to have you there by yourself because you're now the embodiment of an open and inclusive priesthood. Let me contact the organizers and ask what they think. That might well be possible. However we do the Mass, let me ask whether you would be open to doing the homily?"

This was more than I had expected. I thought for a moment, trying to envision how that would feel. As I did so, it somehow seemed right, and it surprised me. "Yes, I think I could do that," I said in response, "only it won't be profound, just the reflections of a simple pastor. As it turns out now, of a *former* pastor."

"Have you lost your job?" Susan asked with a start. "Is that why they had me call your home yesterday? Oh, I'm so sorry to hear that. I'm not really surprised, although it is a difficult burden to bear for accepting the challenge. You realize, of course, this will only heighten our cause. May we include this on the publicity material?"

"No. I'd rather you didn't," I requested, not wanting to become a victim. "Being ordained a priest is enough. I don't want to be a martyr besides. Let's do one thing at a time, okay?"

"I understand," the woman returned, "but I'm sure it will be in the news before you arrive. I hate to appear insensitive, but losing your job does raise the stakes somewhat."

"One more thing," I continued, wanting to affirm that I would not be the only celebrant. "In order to not put so much focus on me, would it be possible to have everyone wearing stoles, not just those around the altar? That's happened at church rallies in the past. It raises the level of interest and participation to have all the participants wearing colorful bands of cloth around their shoulders as an indication of the priesthood of the faithful, not just those who happened to be ordained. People could make their own and extra ones could be given to those who didn't bring one. It would help take the focus off just *my* ordination."

"Interesting idea," the woman replied, not at all convinced it was a good strategy. "We hadn't planned to do that, and it's such a short notice, but we might be able to work something along that line. If we can't do it, you'll still come, right?"

"Oh, I'll be there, all right. I'm committed," I affirmed. "I just don't want to be the center of attention. Ordination is a means to an end, a way of serving the people. This is not about *me*; it's about God's people."

"Well said, but it's a bit unrealistic, don't you think?" was her response. "For the moment, you're 'it' because you're the only woman priest ordained by a legitimate bishop. Like it or not, the spotlight is on you. You'll have to get used to it, I'm afraid."

"That's hard for me to hear," I said, fumbling with the telephone cord. "I'll try my best. Thank you for the invitation. Should I make my own travel arrangements? I'm the only one from my family who is attending, but would the organizers pay for my two former staff members to join me? I'll need someone by my side for support."

"Yes, I think we can handle that," the woman agreed. "You make the arrangements and send me the bill. I'll mail you a letter confirming this conversation, along with a return envelope for your expenses. The hotel room will be reserved in your name. Give me your home address, would you please?"

As I was doing this, I thought of one more thing. "Will Father Jerry Cross be on the program?"

"Yes, of course. People really enjoy his presentations."

"Thank you!" I said, suddenly feeling much better about this whole thing. "It's helpful to know he'll be there, too. I hope the organizing goes well. I'll try to meet your expectations."

"I'm sure you will—you already have. You'll be hearing from me soon. Thank you so much for saying yes. It'll make the rally a huge success. Goodbye."

I was relieved that I could tone down my presence somewhat. "I'm not one for the limelight," I considered after hanging up the phone. How on earth I let myself get involved in all this I'll never know. Well, yes, now that I think about it, I do know. It was Gene McGovern, and I can't even get back at him now. Nice going, Gene!

The rally was on my mind for the rest of the day. Why had I agreed to do the homily? What can I possibly say to all those people? I should keep it simple—nothing elaborate. I'm best when I'm concise and concrete. I'll need help, that's for sure. Won't it be fun going to New Orleans with the girls? I should call them and then make the arrangements right away. I suspect the flights to New Orleans will soon be full.

⌒

"HELLO," I SAID PICKING UP the receiver, still a bit out of breath from rushing to church to use the pay phone in the basement.

"It's me. Sorry for the inconvenience," the caller said apologetically. "We can't be too careful. I called because I've received some information from the organizers of the next Ordination Rally in New Orleans. As you can see, we have a rather thorough communication network. Thank you for agreeing to be on the program. That will help our cause immensely. But now I have a rather large favor to ask of you. Before I ask, let me fill you in on what's been happening on our end.

"Before Bishop Gene ordained you, we had a few important meetings with the new pope. He didn't acquiesce to our request to call an Ecumenical Council and that, of course, is what led to your ordination and the subsequent publicity of the event. The huge petition drive that is taking place in our country and elsewhere is a worthwhile effort, but it will not have nearly the impact as our efforts from within the ranks.

"Our group of bishops has made a few more attempts to sway the pope's mind about all this, but he is still apprehensive about the potential fallout. At the moment there appears to be a split developing within the Roman Curia itself. One faction is adamantly against any change. They refuse to discuss the matter, and are holding firm to the dictates of previous pontiffs about it being a non-negotiable issue.

"Another faction is slowly developing, fueled by the promptings of our group, along with other clusters of bishops from around the world. The publicity of your ordination helped make it visible. The Vatican is now a divided city and the pope is caught in the crossfire.

We need to apply more pressure to tip the balance in the direction of ordination change.

"The pope is a very spiritual person," the caller spoke in a matter-of-fact manner, although what he was saying gave me goose bumps. "He wants to do God's will and what is best for the church. It's all a bit out of his league. He's stymied at the moment and somewhat isolated. Thankfully our contacts in Rome still have access to him, but they're not having much effect."

"And why are you telling me all of this?" I asked, rubbing my eyes as if to better understand what I was being told.

"Because what I'm going to ask of you," the caller continued in a more serious tone, "may be just enough to sway him and lead him into action. We feel we're very close, but something else needs to happen to reach our ultimate goal."

"And what might that be, pray tell?" I asked, not sure I wanted to hear the answer.

"What I ask—and this was the consensus of our group, I might add—is that when you go to the rally in New Orleans, that you *not* be a concelebrant, one of many on stage. Instead, we would ask that you be the *only* one at the altar. *And* the only one wearing a stole. We feel this symbolic gesture will be so direct and so credible that the pope will have the courage to move ahead and call a Council. We realize this is a gamble. It might just push him in the opposite direction, but it's a risk we feel we must take. Except, it is *you* taking the risk."

I felt my knees go weak as I listened to this request. I closed my eyes and tried to envision myself at the altar before this huge throng of people. It felt so foreign, so out of place for me. This was madness! "Are you *sure* the bishops want me to do this? I've already been threatened with excommunication. I could be removed from the church—the church I love and hope to serve for the rest of my life."

"How very shrewd of you. You're quite right," the caller said
with admiration. "Ordinarily, you would be excommunicated
from the church in an instant, but other forces are at work here.
I mentioned earlier that your own Bishop Foley had been swayed
by outside pressures. The same is true for those who call for your
expulsion. There will be many accusations made against you from
the highest sources, but they will not prevail. This I can assure you.
In a sense, there is an ecclesiastical bubble around you, at least for
the moment. This protection will continue after the Ordination
Rally as well, no matter what the press says or what church authorities may insinuate. If you would be willing to say the Mass, I, in
return, can promise you our protection."

"Oh, my! This is all beyond my comprehension," I remarked in
a shaky voice. "Excuse me, but let me get this correct. You want *me*
to stand on stage and defy the legitimate authority of the church, in
front of thousands of people and an international television audience. And despite that, I'll still be able to practice my religion in the
Catholic Church? Is this what you are saying?"

"Yes, that's correct," the bishop confirmed. Then, with an uneasi-
ness that I didn't want to hear in his voice, he continued, "There is
one small hitch, however. After the rally, I'll ask that you not attend
your own church for a few weeks. It will take that long before we
know the reaction of the pope. We have some assurance from sources
close to the pope that he can be convinced, but it's not a certainty.
The odds are about sixty-forty in our favor."

"Whoa. I still don't know your name, although your voice sounds
trustworthy," I interrupted him, my caution antenna rising. "This is
going *way* out on a limb. If the pope reneges and decides against you,
it's *my* church membership that's on the line."

"Yes, that's true," the caller admitted, "but if it *does* go our way,
consider what you've done—changed the entire course of history.

People will look back for centuries on this one moment. What do you say to that?"

"Help!" I said weakly, as I slid down the wall and sat on the floor, just as when Bishop Gene announced that he wanted to ordain me. I also realized that it was too late to turn back. "Well," I spoke after a long pause, "put in those terms, I suspect that I have no choice. What do I do next?"

"Thank you," the caller said with relief. "Go home and wait for a call from the organizing committee. I'll relay to them that you're open to this change. Kelly More, you are a very courageous woman."

"A very stupid woman, if you ask me," I replied, still sitting on the floor.

"Not in the least," he said reassuringly. "I'll be in touch; you can count on that."

"That's what I'm afraid of," I said, the words leaving my mouth before I knew it. Then as an afterthought I asked, "Say, when will I learn your name?"

"If all goes well, soon after the rally," he promised me. "Goodbye for now. All our prayers go with you. Peace." The line went dead.

I stood to my feet and hung up the phone with much apprehension. It's easy for him to ask that I make a fool of myself and jeopardize my whole family, but this is one foolhardy thing I'm doing. Lord, oh Lord, why did I ever let myself get into this? I keep getting dragged deeper and deeper. Where will it end? Where on earth will it end?

Instead of going home, I went upstairs to my old prayer chair in the chapel. This is such a familiar and comfortable place to be, I thought, happy to see that the church was empty, giving me time to evaluate and assess this request. Do I really want to do this? Do I even have a choice?

I closed my eyes and surrendered to the quiet of prayer. This is way beyond me, Jesus—*way* beyond me. You're going to have to take it from here. Then, as I had done so many times before, I rested within God's abiding presence.

⁓

THE TRIP TO NEW ORLEANS was a festive event. Almost everyone on the plane was rally-bound. A few people asked for my autograph, which was disconcerting to me. I looked at Jerry as if to ask what I should do. He just nodded, so I signed my name and thanked them for their support.

The Convention Center was decorated with banners and streamers as people from all parts of the country and beyond marched inside carrying placards and signs of every description. The morning Prayer Service was a fitting beginning. It set a spiritual tone for the day that drew upon the Spirit's presence in the midst of this historic gathering. The lunch clusters were entertaining, small groups of people scattered everywhere, avidly discussing their primary hopes for the future of the Church.

The afternoon speakers described their own desires, including a call for a worldwide Ecumenical Council that would establish an all-inclusive priesthood. As the time drew near for the closing liturgy, the rising excitement in the convention hall was tangible. A large chorus of singers and instruments added to the enthusiasm of the crowd. The stage was set for my appearance.

Meanwhile, I sequestered myself in a room at the rear of the convention hall trying to prepare myself for the liturgy. Jerry had given me instructions about how to say the Mass before such a large gathering—little hints and details about how to better perform the liturgical ritual so that it connected with the people and had an aura of the sacred and transcendent. I reviewed my notes for the homily but nothing made any sense. It was a blur. I tried not to panic, but I was on edge and very close to tears. Fifteen minutes before the Mass, someone knocked on the door and escorted me to where the vesting would take place. Jerry was there to help, as were a few other attendants. I put on the long white alb over my black dress, pinned on the portable microphone, donned the decorative chasuble and finally, put the long white stole around my neck. It fell almost to the floor in two wide strands over the chasuble. I was ready, at least outwardly. But within, it was another matter. "Oh Jerry, I don't know whether I can do this," I said in a panic. "I'm the wrong person entirely. Here, you do this!" I started to take off my stole.

"Sorry, but this is all your show," Jerry said, resisting my trepidation. "Sink or swim, it's your baby. Think of being at St. Gabriel's on Sunday morning. It's the same Mass, just a few more people."

"A few?" I said, almost screaming. "Like a few *million*!"

"And whatever is lacking in you," Jerry assured me, straightening my stole, "The Lord will provide. Have no doubt about that."

Those organizing the closing liturgy appeared in the doorway and motioned to me that it was time to begin. I could hear the beginning of the opening song. There was no turning back. I walked from the vesting room and began the long procession down the middle aisle to the stage, spotlights following my every move. The crowd erupted in applause when they saw me. By design I had not been present for any of the other parts of the rally, so this was the first opportunity the congregation had to see me. The organizers felt this would add to my significance.

I was preceded by liturgical dancers who prepared the way for my assent to the altar. Once I was actually on stage, I stood alone before the crowd. The music stopped, the crowd was hushed as I said in a strong voice, drawing on strength I didn't know I had, "God is here. God is with us. Let us give worship and praise to the God in our midst."

"Amen!" the people boomed back.

"And so we begin, as we do every Mass, in the name of the Father, Son and Holy Spirit."

"Amen!" the people said again in response.

"First, let me say," I said by way of introduction, "I have no idea, none whatsoever, why I am up here and you aren't."

People began to applaud. I put my up hand to restrain the response and then continued, "But such is the turn of events that have transpired since the last Ordination Rally in Detroit. This has been a good day, a very good day. It's fitting that we close it with a Mass of Thanksgiving. For those who are wondering, this Mass *will* fulfill your Sunday obligation," I said with a smile as laughter broke out in the Convention Center.

I continued with the introductory rites and the prayer before the readings. I then sat in the presider's chair elevated beside the altar. People listened to the readings from the Seventeenth Chapter of Exodus about Moses striking the rock and water coming forth, but I sensed that their eyes were on me.

The responsorial song and the second reading from Second Timothy followed, then the Alleluia in preparation for the gospel. At this moment, I rose, bowed my head before the altar and prayed, "May your Word be in my heart and on my lips that I may worthily proclaim your holy gospel." I made the sign of the cross and stepped forward to retrieve the Book of the Gospels from the altar. I held it high over my head and proceeded to the lectern from which I would proclaim God's Word.

"The Lord be with you," I said. I could hear my own voice echoing throughout the large hall.

"And also with you," came back the enthusiastic response.

"A reading from the Gospel according to Luke," I continued, making the sign of the cross on my forehead, my lips and over my heart.

"Glory to you, Oh, Lord," the congregation replied with the same gesture.

"Jesus told his disciples this parable," I began, reading the story in chapter eighteen about the widow pressuring the judge to "give me my rights against my opponent. For a time he refused, but finally he thought, 'I care little for God or humans, but this widow is wearing me out. I am going to settle in her favor or she will end by doing me violence.' The Lord said, 'Listen to what the corrupt judge has to say. Will not God then do justice to the chosen who call out day and night? Will God delay long over them, do you suppose? But when the Son comes, will he find any faith on earth?'"

"The gospel, the good news of our God," I said as I once again held the Book of the Gospels high over my head. The convention hall resounded with, "Praise be to you, Lord Jesus Christ."

I kissed the book, set it on the stand and strode to the middle of the stage. Every eye was upon me as the crowd eagerly awaited what I had to say. Bright lights prevented me from seeing their faces, so I envisioned my small congregation at St. Gabriel's instead and launched into my sermon.

"First, I need to make one thing clear," I began. "I am delivering a *homily* and not just a reflection on the gospel." The crowd caught the significance of my remark—that only the ordained were permitted to preach a homily—and responded with a loud applause of affirmation. They were witnessing the first woman priest speaking with authority in a large public setting.

"Secondly," I continued, "although the gospel for this weekend seems perfectly suited to this event, it is not what you think. I am *not* this widow crying for justice. I'm a happily married woman with three beautiful children."

The crowd responded again, seeming to enjoy the candor of this woman before them.

"You are not the widow, either," I explained. "We are not the ones wearing down the stubborn judge. We have resources, we have alternatives, we have power. We're rich! If we don't like the parish where we live, we get into our cars and go down the road to one that satisfies our needs. We are spoiled. We look for what we want and need and then pursue it. We are, after all, Americans. We solve problems. We get the job done."

The crowd was more subdued now, wondering where this would lead.

"Let me tell you a story," I said as I narrowed my gaze and felt the energy level rising within me. "After I was ordained and notice of this was about to reach the media, my family and I withdrew from the public's eye for a month's seclusion in order to give us a short respite from all the attention. We lived in a migrant community of Hispanics in rural Michigan. It was a simple lifestyle—no car, no phone, no credit cards, and yes, no pizza. The families we lived among worked in the fields all day long. They were loving, caring, deeply spiritual people—Catholics by birth, devotional by nature. When we arrived, none of them had been to Mass or received communion for many months, sometimes even years.

"One of the many blessings of our stay was that we learned some Spanish, not much, but enough to be understood. Eventually I was able to tell my story—that I had just been ordained a Roman Catholic priest. That was all I needed to say, no other explanation was necessary. They embraced my priesthood with generous spirits. It was within that Hispanic community that I said my first Mass, which was a profoundly joyful and moving experience for all. When Jesus asked in today's gospel whether He would find any faith on earth, the answer, based on that one Mass alone must be a resounding 'Yes!' Those Hispanic migrants have faith. Therein lies the widow of the gospel; those are the ones who cry for justice day and night. That is where the focus should be. Not on me, not on you, not on any of us who are fortunate enough to join this magnificent rally. No, the focus should be on the people who have no priest and cannot choose a good liturgy, or *any* liturgy, when they have a need or desire to attend Mass and receive the Body of Christ. The focus should be on those who cannot receive Jesus in communion and have not gathered around the Eucharistic Table for a long time. This is not just a problem we face in the United States; it's a universal problem. And exactly what *is* the problem?—that the leaders of this church we love and cherish do not heed the signs of the times, will not listen to the Spirit in their midst, will not pay attention to the widow that demands justice. 'Give me my rights!' she cries in countless nooks and crannies around the world. It is not the demand for ordination. It is the demand for Eucharist, for reconciliation, for anointing—a demand for priestly servants to minister to God's Holy People.

"We are here today to give voice to their cry. We are problem-solvers. We act when we see a need. We try to fill it. We rally, we petition, we push and we make our power felt. Why? To wear down those judges in our church so they will settle—not just in *our* favor—but in everyone's favor, including the *neglected* people whose voices are not being heard. We give voice to their pleading, and *we - will - not - be - denied!*" I emphasized this last phrase so that each word sank in and made an impact.

At this point the convention hall exploded into prolonged applause. I caught my breath. I could feel my face getting red from the fire within. That power deep within was exploding and I could no longer contain it.

"Pope John xxiv is a good man. He is a spiritual man. He wishes only good for the church, as do we all. But he is a prisoner within a system that does not allow him to act freely or to make decisions which he knows are right and just. We must help him. We must show him the real world. We must tell him that a church without priests is a church left unattended. We must speak for the voiceless people.

Jesus asks in today's gospel, 'Will God delay long over them, do you suppose?' His reply is, 'I tell you, God will give them swift justice!'

"It's time, my friends, it is time. Time for this process of change to be set in motion; time for an Ecumenical Council, a worldwide gathering of bishops; time for an airing of issues from every perspective. *When* this happens, there will be only one solution—a change in these narrow requirements for ordination. Take the burden of being denied the Eucharist and the comfort of the sacraments off the shoulders of the poor and the voiceless. Give them their priests, whether men *or* women, single *or* married. Give them what is their right. Give them swift justice. We have faith that God will do this and we - will - *not* - be - denied!"

I was shaking. My legs wobbled as I moved from center stage and collapsed into the presider's chair. The crowd was on its feet, clapping approval. It went on and on and on. I remained seated, eyes closed, saying to myself, "Thank God, thank God, it's over!"

FOURTEEN
༄

ALTHOUGH THERE WAS A NIP IN THE AIR, Tom was sitting on the porch when I arrived, waiting expectantly for my return. He rose to give me a big hug. "Welcome home, my world traveler and renowned celebrity."

"Please, Tom, I've had enough adulation to last a lifetime," I said, thankful to be home and in the arms of my loving husband. "Any news?"

"Lots of calls and flowers and such." Tom replied, ushering me into the house.

"Really? Flowers?" I said incredulously.

"Yup," Tom affirmed, spreading his arms at the array of flowers throughout the house. "Some people gave me bouquets at church, others came in person. Everyone is very proud of you."

"And hate calls?" I inquired, knowing that not everyone would be pleased with my public display at the Ordination Rally.

"A few rather strong messages," Tom admitted, "but only a few. Your approval rating is off scale."

"Only one really counts," I conceded, "besides your own, of course."

"Rome?"

"Yes, in the long run," I said, enjoying the fragrance and beauty from all the bouquets. "I suspect Bishop Foley will call. I wonder what that conversation will entail."

"As a matter of fact, his is one of the messages," Tom added. "I didn't want to mention it right away, but he sounded pretty hot, not his usual sweet, politically-correct self."

"When did he call?" I had stopped admiring the flowers and turned to look at Tom. "I thought he would have waited until Monday."

"It must have been while we were at Mass this morning," Tom surmised. "We all went together. It was good being there. Everyone was talking about your Mass on Saturday. You'd better not show your face there any time soon," Tom joked. "They'll put a robe on your shoulders, rings on your fingers and a crown on your head. You walk on water for those people, you know."

"No, not really," I countered. "I'm just their recently-fired pastor."

"Think again, Kel," Tom insisted, his arm around my waist. "You're their hero-priest, a world-renowned celebrity whom they know personally, and they are very proud of it."

I laughed and walked to the stairs, wheeling my luggage behind me. I refused Tom's help to carry it upstairs. "Better to do it myself. I could get used to all this attention. My head would be so inflated I wouldn't fit through the door."

I went to my bedroom to unpack. After a while I went downstairs to grab a soft drink from the refrigerator. "Where are the kids?" I called to Tom, who was sitting in the living room.

"Out, I guess. When you're gone, I lose all control," Tom confessed with a chuckle.

"Tell me about it," I returned, coming from the kitchen to join Tom. "And dinner? Any plans? It's past six."

"I told the kids we'll be eating a little later tonight. I wasn't sure when you'd be getting home. We're celebrating tonight—steaks on the grill. Time to splurge."

The children returned one by one as Tom and I began to prepare the meal. "It's funny how they can smell that steak cooking," I said as I set the table. The family gathered for the Sunday evening meal, everyone happy that I was home.

"I liked your story of our migrant community," Michael said. "I miss them. I hope they arrived in Mexico okay."

"Me, too," Rachel agreed, sinking her teeth into the juicy meat.

The phone rang. "Oh dear. Right in the middle of dinner," I said, rising from the table. "I suppose I should answer it."

I lifted the receiver and heard an irate voice say, "Kelly More? This is Bishop Foley. What you did was an outrage! I want to talk to you immediately! Come to my office tomorrow morning, if you can."

Shocked by the sudden outburst, I replied, "Well, I'm not sure." I tried to say this as pleasantly as I could despite his tirade. "I've only now returned home and I'm not sure what's on our calendar."

"This is very important," the bishop continued, not listening to my response. "Please try to make it. I'll be waiting for you in my office at ten o'clock," and then he hung up the phone.

"Oh my," I said out loud as I replaced the receiver. I don't think I've ever received so discourteous a call in my entire life. I wasn't feeling angry; pity was my responsive emotion. I returned to the dining room with a smile on my face.

"Good news?" Tom asked. The children listened to hear what I would say.

"No, not really," I confessed with a hint of amusement in my voice. "Bishop Foley wants me to see him tomorrow morning. He's hopping mad. It strikes me as funny, somehow. The poor man is out of control. That's not his best side. At least the gloves are off. I find this a lot easier to deal with than the facade he's used in the past. At least now I can see his true colors, no holds barred."

"And you're still smiling?" Nathan asked in amazement. His mother's reaction was a complete mystery to him.

"Yes, Nathan, I'm smiling," I said as I resumed my seat at the table, "because I feel sorry for the man. The weight of authority is lying so heavily on his head. I sense he's caught in a much larger political battle over which he has no control. The poor guy. I wouldn't miss that meeting tomorrow for the life of me. I'm tempted to be late and let him cool his heels somewhat, but that would be petty on my part. It's wiser to play it cool and calm."

"Good thinking," Tom said, relieved that the bishop's call had not dampened my good mood. The family turned its attention back to dinner, which at the moment was being capped with chocolate sundaes. "Tom," I complained with a grin, "you are so bad when I leave you alone with the children. Have you all been eating like this the entire time I've been gone?"

"Ya'al?" Tom returned, trying to change the subject. "Three days in New Orleans, Kids, and your mom is talking like a Southern Belle."

I enjoyed the simplicity of the evening, relishing the comfort of my family home after all the activity of the rally. I went to bed thanking God for my life and family and friends. "So much to be grateful for, and the ordination is the least of it," I prayed, as I fell to sleep.

I woke in the morning before the children left for school and then thought about heading upstairs for a little extra sleep. "I'm just exhausted," I said to Tom as I sipped my coffee. "I am *bone* tired. That trip took more from me than I realized. I'm sorry now that I said yes to Bishop Foley."

"As I've said before," Tom replied, "be alert with that man. I don't trust him."

I went upstairs and indulged in a half hour's nap. Although my body craved more sleep, I rose when the alarm rang, dressed and was opening the door when I heard the phone in the kitchen. I thought about letting it ring, but something told me to answer.

"Hello, this is Kelly." I said, wondering who it was.

"Hello, Kelly." came the familiar voice. "It's your mystery caller again. Well done. You were magnificent—all we had hoped for and much, much more. I'm wondering, Kelly, would you be able to go to that other phone so we could talk freely? I have some wonderful news to share."

"Oh, I'm so sorry," I replied with chagrin, "but I'm just leaving to see Bishop Foley. He wanted me to come to his office this morning. Can we arrange for our talk later today?"

"Sure, that will be fine," the called assured her. "How about two o'clock, would that be convenient? I could call the other number then."

"That will be great," I said with relief. "I'm anxious to hear your news."

"As for Bishop Foley," the caller continued, "don't worry about him. His bark will be far worse than his bite today. My advice is to listen to whatever he has to say and not become upset. He's a small fish in a very large pond. I'm sure you'll do just fine."

"Thanks for the reassurance," I replied, somewhat mystified by his comment. "I'll be waiting for your call at two."

I rushed out the door, not wanting to be late for my appointment. All the way to the bishop's office I thought about the phone call. Who is he, I wonder, and what news does he have? And why should he know so much about my meeting with Patrick Foley? It sounds as if he has a lot of connections and a great deal of influence.

I arrived at the chancery on time, and greeted the secretaries with a smile. They acknowledged my presence with great deference but refrained from making any comments. I could feel the tension in the place as I made my way to the bishop's office.

"Come in, please," he said in a more pleasant tone than he had used on Sunday night.

"You wanted to see me, Bishop?" I said as I took the chair he offered.

He closed the door and suddenly his mood changed. "That was a scandalous thing you did," he said as he walked around and sat behind his large desk. "It made a mockery of the priesthood and the Eucharist."

I was about to respond, but I remembered the advice of my mystery caller to hold my temper, so I said nothing. Instead, I looked at him with all the strength and composure I could muster.

"Your ordination is not valid," he voiced in an angry tone. "In the eyes of the church you are not a priest and never will be. Putting on the charade of saying Mass before that crowd and the television cameras was ludicrous. It puts the pope and the hierarchy of the church in a very awkward position. You have much to answer for."

I sat in my chair and felt surprisingly unruffled by his harangue. Now the bishop was spitting out his words between clenched teeth. I could see his neck getting redder as he spoke.

"It is not clear from Canon Law whether your act of defiance merits automatic excommunication," he continued, his hands gripping his desk. "I certainly have it within my power to issue such a decree. People in responsible positions have been clamoring that I do so. It would put you outside the communion of the faithful and make it clear to all that your actions were not sanctioned by the teaching authority of the church."

He paused to see what impact his words had on me. I sat before him looking intently into his eyes but remained unfazed by his outburst. I didn't want to appear defiant or angry and I was nowhere close to tears. Instead, I continued to be attentive to what he had to say. I made no attempt to defend any of my actions.

Somewhat disconcerted, he continued, "I have been in consultation with a number of people in authority, including officials in Rome." He said this hoping it would lend credence to his words. "Although all do not agree with this course of action, it appears that the consensus is not to bring any official censures against you at this time. Excommunication would only fuel the fires of dissent and could lead to a schism in the American Catholic Church."

I sensed that he was making this speech against his better judgment, and that he didn't believe what he was saying to me.

"Rather than be responsible for such a reaction," he went on, "I have decided to pass over this past weekend's travesty without comment or official interdict. But that does not mean, young lady, that you have not committed a grave, serious act of disobedience. You are a cause of great scandal to the faithful. You have much to answer for and penance will be required. As I said at our last meeting, I cannot forbid you to attend church or receive communion, but I can prevent you from ever working as a minister in the church again. From now on, you are forbidden from exercising any function as part of a Catholic parish or mission, whether as Eucharistic minister, lector, catechist, anything! Is that clear?"

A look of disbelief came across my face. I didn't know how to respond. What he said was clear enough, but how could he enforce it? What more could he do? He chose not to ban me from the church, just to keep me from being active. But everything I did was a ministry, from the counseling I did over the phone, to the support and comfort I gave people after Mass. He could try to curtail my involvement, but the harder he pressed, the more my ministry would emanate in other directions. I was ordained to serve, and no one, not even Bishop Patrick Foley, could stop me.

"Well?" the bishop demanded, almost out of breath.

"I'm not sure what to say," I replied in a calm and steady voice. "What you request is clear, but whether it will occur as you wish is another matter." Then, in a more resolute tone, I continued, "This situation is much larger than you or I, Bishop. It has taken a life of its own, and you'll not be able to stop it. We'll have to see how it unfolds. But I do understand what you're saying. I'll try to do as you ask, so far as I am able."

This did not please the bishop. He raised his eyebrows and looked at me in utter disbelief. No one, let alone a woman, had so easily withstood his wrath, which had no impact on me. In exasperation he blurted as he stood and pointed to the door. "Leave! I've had enough of you!"

It was an awkward moment for the two of us. The bishop had committed the one behavior he had struggled not to do—lose his composure. I, on the other hand, was surprised by his command, but I did not fear him. I slowly stood and retreated out the door, looking over my shoulder at the outstretched arm of the bishop. I could see that it was slightly shaking. He was still standing behind his desk as I closed the door behind me. The entire office staff was looking at me as I left. I smiled and headed for the exit. One person clapped quietly as I walked past. The others watched me leave with surprised expressions on their faces. They weren't used to someone withstanding the bishop's wrath with such equanimity.

It's a good thing that I was tired from the rally, I thought as I started the car. I didn't have the energy to fight. Wasn't that the strangest encounter? I hope the man doesn't have a stroke; he was so angry. It was almost as if he were restrained from doing what he really wanted to do—strangle me, for example. Am I ever glad *that's* over. Now what? Well, it's Monday. If I were still working—which according to him I'll never do in the church again—this would be my day off. In the past I would go to the lake and pray. I think I'll do that. It's a little chilly, but it will help me stay awake. This last little exchange did revive me a bit.

I stopped at a drive-through and ordered a bite to eat, then headed for my favorite bench by the lake to spend some time in prayer. "We have a lot to talk about, Lord," I mouthed silently as I sat looking over the lake, pulling my coat around me to stay warm. So how are we doing, you and I? I closed my eyes and tried to connect with the source and center of my being. At times I nodded to sleep, but while awake, it was soothing to have an opportunity to be still and put the past few days' events into perspective. After half an hour, I returned to my car. I was surprised at how peaceful I felt despite the bishop's tirade. It was as if it had no impact whatsoever. Was I insensitive or just tired? Maybe it was a gift from God, and he was shielding me from harm.

I headed to the church hall because it was almost time for my special phone call. The closer I drew, the more curious I became about the *wonderful news* my mystery caller said he had for me. I stationed myself at the pay phone, remembering to bring a chair this time. At two o'clock the phone rang.

"Hello, Kelly," the caller said as I answered. I sensed excitement in his greeting. "I hope you're sitting down. Guess what? It worked! Our sources in Rome said the pope was watching your Mass on television. He was visibly moved by what you said. He's not making any promises, but he seems to be leaning in our direction. The delegation with the petitions people signed at the rally is due to arrive tomorrow. He said he would receive them, something that is viewed as very good news indeed. The Curia is in an uproar. Those who oppose a Council or any change in ordination feel they are losing ground. They are determined to fight to the end. Those in favor are gaining confidence. It's split right down the middle. If you think New Orleans was exciting, you should be here."

"You're in Rome!" I said in disbelief.

"Yes," the caller admitted with a laugh. "It's evening here, a good time to call."

"I shouldn't be using all your money this way," I protested with a mixture of apology and elation.

"No problem. Money is not the issue," he assured me. "But I have even better news to share." I was stunned. What more could he say that was better than what I had already heard?

"Do you have something to write a note?" the caller continued. "You'll need to take some information."

"Hang on, I'll get some paper from the cabinet. Could you hold for a moment?" I ran to the kitchen where the supplies were kept and returned with pen and paper. "All set."

"The news is this," the caller said, hardly able to contain himself. "The pope wants to meet you!"

I was in shock. I shook my head, unable to comprehend what he had said.

"Are you still there, Kelly?" the caller inquired.

After a moment I spoke up in whisper, "Yes, yes I'm here, only I don't think I heard you correctly. What was it you said?"

"The pope wants to meet you," the caller repeated enthusiastically. "That's a very good sign, Kelly. It means he may be closer to a decision. This was better than we had expected. And he wants to see you soon! We need to strike before the opposing forces regroup and force an onslaught."

"It sounds like a war," I replied weakly, still not comprehending what I was hearing.

"It is," the caller affirmed, "and it's being waged in deadly earnest."

"What do you mean by soon?" I said with a gulp, my free hand on my forehead.

"A week, two at the most," the caller replied with emphasis.

"You're kidding, surely," I replied, my head spinning with the news.

"Nope. He wants to see you *now*!"

"So," I said mockingly, "I'm just supposed to go to the airport, jump on a plane and visit the pope?"

"Something like that," the caller admitted, undaunted by my obvious sarcasm. "Here's what I've arranged . . ."

"Wait a minute." I stopped him in mid-sentence. "You've already made arrangements?"

"They can be changed to accommodate your schedule, I assure you, but we can't lose any time."

"Well, that's encouraging to hear," I said, suddenly feeling angry at having no voice in this matter. "Which day am I supposed to be leaving for Rome?"

"If possible, this coming Friday evening," the caller suggested a bit sheepishly. "You would be arriving around noon on Saturday. Sunday is a quiet day for audiences. His Holiness wants a private meeting with you. No one is supposed to know you're here. You'll return home on Monday. Sorry, but no sightseeing. It would attract too much attention. You're quite a celebrity here you know."

"In Rome?" I remarked with surprise.

"Yes, everyone's talking about you," the caller assured me. "It'll be difficult getting you in and out without being seen. We'll give it a try, however."

"Am I going alone?" I asked. I said this more as a reflex. It still had not registered that I would be spending the weekend in Rome.

"No. You can bring someone with you," he responded.

"Realizing that he was serious about all this, I tried to quickly evaluate the situation and decide if this sudden invitation was feasible. "I can't speak for him, but I doubt that my husband, Tom, would want to leave the children alone just now."

"Well then, may I suggest you consider taking Father Gerald Cross? He would be a most worthy companion for conversing with the pope. I understand the two of you are friends."

"Let me guess, you've already booked the two of us on the plane," I said, feeling controlled and manipulated by someone I had initially trusted and admired.

"Well, if truth be told, yes I have. I talked to Father Cross this morning. He laughed when I told him what we were planning. He said you don't appreciate people arranging your life without your knowledge. Is he correct?" the caller said with a chuckle, disguising his concern.

"Dead right," I responded in a serious tone.

"Sorry to have to do it, but time is of the essence. Can you come? Father Jerry said he's willing if you are."

"Do you need an answer right now," I asked, considering what Tom would say about these arrangements being made without his consultation.

"As a matter of fact, yes," the caller admitted hopefully. "That would help expedite matters a great deal."

With exasperation, I surrendered. "Okay, I surrender. Give me the details."

"Good!" I could hear the caller exhale as if he were holding his breath. He continued, "You will need to follow these instructions exactly. Everything will be arranged. Oh, by the way," he said as an afterthought, "do you have a mantilla, a black covering for your head? That's a necessity."

"Yes, one of the migrant women made a black lace veil for me this summer. Any other dress codes?" I said facetiously.

"Something simple," the caller responded, missing my joke, "preferably black. You'll need to blend and look as inconspicuous as possible."

"So, what's the fashion in Rome this fall?" I inquired, not expecting an answer.

"Beats me. Cassocks, I think. Got one?" the caller chided, more relaxed than previously as he joined my humor.

"Nice try. Black it shall be," I said, making a note to myself. "What else?"

The bishop provided the exact details of my flight and connections in Rome. By way of appeasement for such short notice, Jerry and I would be flying first class. "Nice perk," I replied when I heard that part of the itinerary. He described the person meeting us at the airport, our accommodations close to the Vatican, the contact person at the pope's residence, even the length of our audience with the pope.

"You will have twenty minutes with him," he explained. "It could stretch to thirty minutes, but be sure not to overstay your welcome. He speaks English, not well, but you'll have a good conversation. No one else will be present, just the three of you. That is by his request. This is quite a coup. Whatever is discussed should be kept private. It will take place in the early evening so as not to attract attention. Stay away from any public places as much as possible. I know you'll do just fine. That's all I have to say. I'm so glad you agreed to do this. Good luck."

"Wait," I said, not wanting the conversation to end so quickly. "Will I meet you there?" But he was already gone. So much for that. Didn't even say goodbye.

I sat by the phone for some time, trying to digest all that I had heard. I looked at my notes to see if I had it all. What a crazy situation. Me, Kelly More, off to see the pope! Who could have every guessed?" As a lark, I called the airline and asked, "Do you have a reservation for Kelly More and Gerald Cross this Friday heading to Rome, Italy from Detroit?"

"Yes, here it is," came the reply. "First class, returning on Monday afternoon. Any special requests?"

"No, no thank you," I said, somewhat taken back at finding my reservation there. "I just wanted to confirm the flight."

"All you'll need is a passport for identification," the agent assured her.

"Passport!" I exclaimed with sudden awareness. "Oh my goodness, has my passport expired? For how long are they good?"

"Usually ten years," the agent responded pleasantly.

"Whew, I think I'll be okay. This trip is rather sudden, to say the least," I said with relief.

"Have a good flight," the agent concluded.

"Thanks. I hope to. Goodbye."

I hung up, put away my chair, returned the basement key to Carol in the office and headed home. "I have to talk to Jerry as soon as I get home," I said out loud, fairly skipping with excitement. I'll bet *he's* excited. What do I mean him? *I'm* excited. Rome for the weekend! What a jet-setter I've become. Old homebody Kelly—New Orleans one Saturday, Rome the next.

I tried to remain grounded as I walked into the house. "There were some calls for you," Tom said as I gave him a big kiss.

"What's gotten into you? You look like you won the lottery. By the way, one of the calls was from Jerry. He sounded pretty excited. So, how did it go with the bishop?" Tom looked at me quizzically. My mood wasn't what he had expected.

"It was pretty funny," I said, pulling Tom to the couch in the living room. "But that's old news by now. Here, sit with me for a minute. We need to talk about a new development."

I took his hand and told him the story of my phone conversation and the unexpected trip to Rome to meet the pope. Tom's expression was a combination of confusion and humor. "And you're going?"

"Yes, I am. I was upset when I learned that all the arrangements had been made without my knowledge, but now I'm feeling better. Can you believe this is happening?

"Not quite. Are you sure this isn't a hoax?"

"I called the airline afterwards and my name is listed, first class, no less. This does mean that you'll have to take the single parent role for a second weekend in a row. Are you okay with that? I had no choice, really; I had to make a decision on the spot. Those walks we had each evening at the migrants' camp brought us so much closer that I felt confident you would understand."

"Actually I'm quite happy about all this. Something rather extraordinary is happening here, isn't it?" Tom held my other hand and turned to face me on the couch. "You go see the pope and be just as convincing as you are with me."

"Thomas, you are so great! Thanks for putting up with me over these last few months. And there's more. My mystery caller has booked Jerry on the same flight. Apparently he could be an asset when I see the pope. I have the feeling that those bishops have thought of everything. I'm certainly glad they're on our side."

We were both feeling more relaxed about the trip when the phone rang. "That's Jerry, I'll wager," Tom said. "He has a knack for good timing."

"Oh, hi, Jerry," I said, happy to hear his voice.

"Wow!" Jerry started, full of excitement. "Some surprise, huh?"

"I'll say so," I replied, getting caught in his enthusiasm. "Tom and I were just talking about it. This ordination business certainly has some unexpected twists and turns?"

"Yes, indeed," Jerry responded. "This is all so sudden. I don't have anyone to take my class on Monday morning, but this takes precedence over everything else."

"Can you imagine, Jerry. We're going to Rome! It's where that little guy in white lives." By now was I beginning to realize all that was happening and to rejoice in my blessings.

"From what I understand," Jerry continued, catching my elation, "all we have to do is arrive at the airport and off we go. I was given very detailed instructions about all the arrangements."

"Me, too," I added, looking at the piece of paper on which I had jotted the schedule. "We can compare notes on the way. I'll drive to Detroit on Friday and meet you at the airport at four-thirty; our plane leaves at six-thirty."

"What a crazy church we have, sending us to Rome, first class, no less. It must have cost a fortune. I doubt either of us will have a relaxing week. I hope it's worth the trip. I'll meet you at the ticket counter. Goodbye."

I hung up the phone and turned to Tom. He had a smile on his face that said something like, "I should have known what I was getting into when I married this strange woman." I went to him, pulled him to his feet and put my arms around him. "Oh, Tom," I said lovingly. "Thanks for understanding. Your support means everything to me."

Say," he asked, as he remembered my earlier appointment, "you never said anything about your session with Bishop Foley. How was it?"

"Forget about the bishop," I responded, my arms tight around my husband. "I'm going to the *top*! No lower-level management for me. Can you *believe* it, Tom—Rome! This should not be happening to a little girl from Kansas—or even Michigan. But, hey, who's complaining?"

When Friday finally arrived, I was on the road early, hoping to beat the afternoon rush hour in Detroit. I arrived at the airport ahead of schedule, parked the car and was at the ticket counter as Jerry arrived, looking dapper in suit and tie. "I thought this would be fitting attire for the Vatican," he said, feeling pleased with himself. "I was told to look inconspicuous."

"Then why not your Roman collar?" I inquired playfully. "It's named for the place we're heading."

"Because no one wears such a thing there," Jerry informed me. "Cassocks or civvies are the rule. While in Rome, you know. Come to think of it, I've used that phrase before, but for once, it really fits."

"I love it; you are so *wired*!" I exclaimed, laughing at his humor. "This is going to be quite a trip. But let's not overdo it. We have to remember that we're on a mission here. It isn't supposed to be a vacation."

We stepped to the counter and gave our names, showing the agent our passports. "Here you are," the agent replied. "Two first class tickets to Rome, Italy. You're all set. Have a good trip."

"We hope to," Jerry responded, and we headed for the departure lounge.

"What on earth are we going to say to the pope, Jerry?" I asked as we went through security.

"Wing it, I say," was his response. That didn't soothe my nerves one bit.

"Great! 'Wing it,' he says. Where did you get your degree, Upper Michigan Polytech?"

"Rome, if you must know," Jerry said smugly.

"Really?" I said with surprise. "So you know this place,"

"Very well, indeed," Jerry admitted. "It's going to be hard not to show you the town. The food is magnificent. But I was told to keep you under wraps, so maybe next time. I'll say one thing, in all my travels to Europe, I've never gone first class. This will be a treat."

The flight was all we had hoped. We were wined and dined across the Atlantic and landed in Rome at noon on Saturday, local time. Per instructions, a young man met us as we left customs, holding a sign that read, 'Hildegard,'—our code word. He drove us to the hotel, carrying our bags into the lobby. He was a seminarian from Ohio who was studying in Rome.

"I'm not sure what your business is, but I was told not to ask any questions," the seminarian said as he took his leave. "I'll meet you here on Monday morning at eight o'clock. That will get you to the airport in plenty of time. Pretty quick trip."

"Yes, somewhat," Jerry confessed, trying to act nonchalant. "Thanks so much for your help." Jerry handed him a twenty-dollar bill for his trouble. "Have a little dinner on us."

"Wow. Thanks," the seminarian said with relish. "I just might do that. See you Monday morning. Good luck."

"We'll need it," I said as I turned to survey the hotel lobby. "Pretty fancy, I'd say."

"Yes, our contact person chose well," Jerry said with admiration. "I'm getting the feeling that we're dealing with someone rather high up the Vatican food chain. This place is a little too steep for us Jesuits."

"Well, that's a surprise," I said in jest. "Say, do you have the feeling, as I do, that we're being watched?"

"Everyone has that feeling in the Vatican, and we're right next door to it now," Jerry said, looking around the lobby. "It's probably an accurate feeling. Kel, if you don't mind, I think I'll take a nap. I'm a little weary and we have an important day ahead of us tomorrow. Besides, it's the custom here, you know."

"My sentiments exactly," I agreed. "I didn't get much sleep on the plane, with the movies and dinner and all. One could get addicted to that sort of thing."

The two of us headed for our rooms, agreeing to meet in the lobby and then have something to eat at a secluded restaurant Jerry remembered from his previous days in Rome. "We can plan our Sunday there," Jerry said, enjoying the recollections of his old haunts. "I would love to take you to see the Gesu—the Jesuit church—for Mass. It's big enough that I'm sure no one will notice us. There are other places in the city that we can enjoy without being seen. Our only commitment is to be at the pope's residence by six o'clock Sunday evening. Otherwise, we're on our own."

"But let's be careful. We don't want to blow our cover. Too much is riding on this. I'll see you later." I retired to my room and went immediately to the phone. Using the calling card Tom had given me, I called home.

"We're in Rome, Tom!" I told him. "I still can't believe I'm here. The trip was grand, but now I have to get serious. I wish you were here to give me good advice and keep me focused. I could easily get distracted by this beautiful city. But I sense that everything is coming to a head. We're playing for all the marbles. My ordination, a call I never imagined or expected, got this started. Now I'm about to see the pope to plead the case that the ordination of women should be accepted as a legitimate part of the Catholic Church. Pray hard that it all happens according to God wishes and that I'm up to the task."

"That I will do. I've been at it ever since you left. I'm so proud of you, Kelly, really I am. You are being transformed by this, and I like what I see."

"Thanks, Tom. It's happening to both of us. I wonder if the kids are beginning to be concerned about us."

"They always have."

We talked for a while longer. The kids were still asleep; it wasn't quite eight o'clock on Saturday morning. "Don't wake them, just give them a hug for me," I said and bid my husband goodbye. Then, after setting my alarm, I settled down for a much-needed nap. As I dozed, I murmured, "Dear God, what on earth do You have in mind—last week that huge crowd and this week the pope?" I faded into oblivion with the question still looming in my thoughts.

I awoke early, just because it was difficult to stay still. I put on my simple black dress and headed toward the lobby. Although it was only five o'clock, an hour before they agreed to meet, Jerry was waiting for me.

"Here, have some of this delicious coffee," he suggested. "I just couldn't sleep the afternoon away knowing all that awaited us. We should go for a little walk before dinner. People eat much later here than they do in Sarah, Michigan," he quipped.

I sensed that Jerry was in a different mood than I. Returning to a place he knew well, he was looking forward to sharing some of his favorite spots. For me, the city was incidental to the reason we came. It seemed important to stay focused on our mission.

Although it was November, the air was still warm. As we left the hotel, we could recognize the dome of St. Peter's in the twilight just a few blocks away. We decided to stroll to the huge square in front of it. Without realizing it, I had just stepped into Vatican City. "The seat of all that ecclesiastical power and prestige," Jerry reminded me.

I stopped to admire the scene, thinking of all that this place represented. "Imagine," I said to Jerry, "I'm about to see the pope to plead for women's ordination. Who am I to challenge a two-thousand-year-old tradition? How I ever came to be here is a complete mystery to me."

"I think the word is destiny," he replied, taking in the majesty of St. Peter's Square and the colonnade that surrounded it. "The time has come for a radical change. You happen to be the one God has chosen to get the proverbial ball rolling. We can't stop it now that it's heading down the hill and gathering momentum. Watch out, Your Holiness, here she comes!"

"Stop it, you crazy man," I pleaded. "It's not like that at all. This is very serious business. You are my spiritual director, in case you've forgotten. Pray me through this, give me some of your sage advice. I think this city is pulling you in another direction."

"Yes, I think you're right, Kel. Sorry. I am so excited about being here that I'm acting more like a tour guide than a spiritual companion on a journey. Thanks for reminding me. I'll do better."

We walked to a small café that Jerry remembered from his student days and feasted on wine and pasta prepared as only the Italians can do it. Returning to our lodgings, we bid each other good night. I let myself into my room and succumbed to the impulse to give Tom another call and to say hello to the kids. They wished me well and wanted to know all that I had seen. "Not much, really. I'm not supposed to be seen here, remember? I'll tell you all about it when I get home on Monday." I hung up feeling both lonely and fortunate to have such a loving husband and three wonderful children. I closed my eyes and tried to pray, thanking God for all these blessings and asking guidance for what tomorrow might bring.

The next thing I remember is waking, still fully dressed and on top of the covers. I wasn't sure where I was or what I was doing. "Oh, yes, I'm in Rome," I said to myself sleepily. I sat up in bed and said in a much louder voice, "Oh, my goodness, I'm in Rome! I'm here to see the pope!" I glanced at the clock and was grateful that it was still early, plenty of time before meeting Jerry in the lobby at ten. After a shower and redressing I settled into a chair by the window to spend some time in prayer. "Let's see, it's Sunday, "I said to myself as I pulled the daily scripture readings from my bag. It's almost the end of the church year, with just a few weeks to Thanksgiving and the beginning of Advent. What a year this has been—a new pope in April, the Detroit Rally in June, my ordination the 22nd of July, the month of September with the Hispanics, the second rally just last week and now here in Rome the middle of November. I know one thing, I'm not the same person I was last year at this time. I can't help but think of Moses, flawed and ill-equipped, yet called to lead the Israelites to freedom. Here I am, flawed and not feeling up to the task, but about to have a private audience with the Sovereign Pontiff and perhaps change the entire direction of the church. For the next hour I prayed hard, asking for help, humility, strength, courage to speak the truth, acceptance, endurance, wisdom, and most importantly, not hinder this much larger plan of which I was only a small, but apparently, essential part. "Keep me focused, Jesus, throughout this day and help me stay under control as we spend our twenty minutes with the pope. It could lead to something wonderful."

The rest of the day was uneventful, except for a chance meeting at the Jesuit church after Mass. Jerry and I were leaving the Gesu by a side entrance when a voice came echoing from the body of the church, "Jerry Cross, what are *you* doing here!" Instinctively I slipped behind a pillar as an American about Jerry's age rushed forward and threw his arms around him.

"You should be in Detroit, right? Taking a little break, are we? It's so good to see you! How about a little lunch?" Then putting his arm around Jerry's shoulders, he walked him out the door leaving me hidden, but also stranded. Now what? I left my purse at the front desk of the hotel for safekeeping. I had no money, no passport, no notion of where I was.

Ten tense minutes passed before Jerry reappeared. As he explained, still smiling at the coincidence of it, one of his classmates from theology was in Rome doing research. Jerry was able to dodge the lunch invitation, pleading a prior engagement. He may have been laughing, but it took some time before my panic subsided. "Jerry, no more surprises, okay? Let's just lie low and get ready for this audience. Nothing else is as important as that. We can walk for a while, but I'll need to return to the hotel by four, so I can get dressed and compose myself. I'm already as nervous as Rachel before a piano recital."

At five o'clock, we headed for a private entrance to the pope's residence behind St. Peter's. Jerry had heard of this place but had never been there. When we reached our destination, I put on my black mantilla, while Jerry handed a card with our code name, Hildegard, to the guard at the door. He glanced at it and escorted us inside as if he knew who we were and was expecting us. In silence, we followed him up a flight of stairs and entered a large reception hall. The guard led us across the room and into a smaller chamber with a warmer, more relaxed atmosphere. Our escort indicated that we should have a seat and then left the room. It was ten minutes to six. We sat on a large couch without saying a word. My eyes traveled the room, noting the pictures and furnishings. It was at once an ornate and yet simple room, filled I was sure, with many priceless antiques.

Promptly at six o'clock, a door opened at the opposite end and the pope entered, holding his arms in a welcoming gesture, wearing a wide smile on his face. He was shorter than he appeared on television, and leaner, even Spartan in appearance. His face was clean-shaven, his cheeks a bit sunken, as if he didn't sleep enough. He was dressed in a floor-length white cassock, a wide sash at his waist, a skullcap over his thin, white hair. His eyes were dark and penetrating, but friendly, nevertheless. He reminded me of Father Mac, my partner at St. Gabriel's before Henry's arrival, because he exuded such a welcoming, pastoral manner. I couldn't help but feel drawn to the man as soon as he entered the room. He took our hands as the two of us rose from our seats.

"So good of you to come on such short notice," he said in passable English, acting as if he had known us his entire life.

"You must be Kelly More," he continued as he motioned for us to be seated. "You've caused quite an uproar these last few months," still with a smile on his face.

I wasn't sure whether he was being accusatory or just stating a fact. I sensed it was more the latter.

"I realize this not something you chose," he went on. "It was given you. I understand. This happened to me also. Here I was, being good archbishop, and all of a sudden, puff, here I am, pope! It come as big shock. 'Why me?' I ask. 'Why me?'"

"Yes, I know the feeling exactly," I replied, laughing in spite of myself. I felt very relaxed and at ease with this man. I also felt sorry for him. The world's weight on his shoulders must be enormous.

"And you, Father, are Jesuit scholar, no?" the pope said, turning to Jerry "You investigate historical facts, yes?" He spoke in English but with a thick Italian accent.

"Actually, someone else did the research," Jerry admitted hesitantly. "I've only put some of the pieces together."

"Si, but you say is 'priesthood greater than present interpretation,'" the pope replied with an expansive gesture.

"It seems so," Jerry replied, feeling confident enough to speak his mind before this man.

"So, what are we to do?" the pope asked, looking back at me. "We are in divided city, divided church. Everywhere, people upset, not act as Christians. How we come together? What does Spirit want? Constant prayer in my heart 'what is proper action?'"

Both Jerry and I could see the anguish on his face. The pope looked off in the distance and shook his head. "Is mystery what to do. Too late to turn back. No good to say 'Don't discuss—this ordination of women.' Too late to say, 'No change requirements for priesthood.' Here you are, priest, ordained by Catholic bishop. Was he good man, holy man?"

"Oh, very holy and very loyal to the church," I replied, nodding my head as I thought about my friend Gene and all he meant to me. I still missed him deeply and my face showed it.

"Then why he do this? Not permitted," the pope asked, greatly perplexed, shaking his head.

I hesitated, wondering if this was a rhetorical question. I decided to take the risk of replying. "Because he was concerned for his people," I suggested respectfully. "They were not being served. He felt a change was needed."

"So he take it into his own hands?" the pope said with raised eyebrows.

"He felt compelled to do it," I said honestly, somehow encouraged by this man of God to speak my mind. "For some reason, he asked me to be the one to receive Holy Orders."

"Ah, si, you run parish," the pope replied, giving the impression that he knew a great deal about my background and ministry.

"I was, in effect, their pastor," I added without apology, looking straight into the pope's eyes.

I could sense that Jerry was surprised at how forcefully I had said this, but he could see that the pope took it well, a look of bewilderment but not reproach on his face.

"You knew needs of your people," the pope continued, looking intently at me as he asked this, "needs you not be able to address without being priest? Is that it?"

"Something like that," I said, gaining confidence as I sensed an invitation from the pope to speak freely.

"I very much want to meet you in person, Kelly More," the pope said, taking me off guard, "I see person you are. You now pass test." I could discern a twinkle in his eyes as he looked at me. When he said this I looked at Jerry with surprise and some embarrassment.

"I want to see," the pope continued, "if you really be called by God for this or something you want. I see now, by your concern for your people, that it be a response to call. To you, Kelly More, others come first. That very good sign. I, too, am pastor. I am one ever since being ordained. My being priest is to be with the people. I am not of Vatican. I am—how you say in English?—at odds with some here. But must not lose their good will. Is big problem. One people want me make changes, other people tie my hands." He said this making a gesture of tied hands, revealing his frustration and consternation. Then he looked at me and said, "Something good about you, Kelly More, something I trust. Maybe it is honest way you talk. How do you Americans say? 'Just do it!' It can be trouble, much trouble. But not now, I feel. Tell me, Kelly More, what you do if you pope?"

I again looked at Jerry, seeking his counsel, but received no hint from him about what to say. I closed my eyes for a moment, summoning my courage to speak what I felt. I could feel the color rise in my face as I remembered both the parishioners at St. Gabriel's and the migrants who were without a priest for so many years. A transformation came over me. I was no longer the pastoral administrator of a parish but an ordained priest calling for change in a church that was not taking care of her people.

After a long pause I looked at the pope and said, "Call a Council,

Your Holiness. Call the church together to discuss this issue. Gather representatives from the entire church, people from all over the world, not just Vatican officials. Call together holy leaders who know what is needed, who have direct experience with those who have been abandoned and are without shepherds. Bring them together and listen to what they say. Let them help you solve this problem."

I sensed that Jerry almost fell off the couch when I said this. People do not usually talk to the pope this way. I looked at Jerry who himself was looking at the pope to see how my demands had been received. To his surprise, the pope seemed pleased; he was nodding his head thoughtfully.

"Good, Kelly More! I like you, you speak from heart," the pope responded, putting his hands out to me. "The Spirit, too, I think. No one else speak like that to me. Is too bad. I no like talk behind back. But I go now. Others wait. Pray for me. I must come to decision soon. It not easy, but you help much. Your travel good?"

"Yes, excellent," the two of us spoke in unison. "Thank you for seeing us," Jerry added hesitantly. "Thank you for your time."

"No, no, pleasure mine," the pope objected pleasantly. "I hope meet you again soon. I much enjoy." With that he stood, gave us a simple blessing with the sign of the cross, shook our hands and walked out the door, leaving us standing in amazement at how natural it was to talk with him, and how quickly it was finished.

"Oh, dear, oh, dear," I finally said, shaking my head. "I hope I didn't offend him. Was I too direct, Jerry, was I too blunt?"

"No, not at all," Jerry assured me, seeking to comfort me. "You were marvelous. It was vintage Kelly More. You were at your best—no beating around the bush, no coyness or holding back, just speaking the truth directly and letting the chips fall where they may. I was proud to have witnessed this interchange. It made an impact, believe me."

Catching my breath and blowing my nose I said, "Do you really think so, Jerry?"

"No doubt about it. Mark my words, you have made a difference."

With that, our ubiquitous guide returned and escorted us from the residence. By six-thirty, we were making our way back to the hotel, somewhat in a daze, wondering if we appeared as awestruck as we felt. The entire episode with the pope had lasted fewer than twenty minutes. Its aftermath, however, would last much longer.

Fifteen

༄

"HERE'S TO YOU, OUR VERY OWN CATHERINE!" Jerry said as he raised his glass of wine. We were enjoying dinner at a small café less than an hour after our audience with the pope.

"Catherine?" I asked quizzically as I clicked my glass with his in response.

"Yes, Catherine of Siena," Jerry returned with a grin. "You know, the one who called the pope back from Avignon. You were just as forceful, and I loved it."

"Oh, Jerry, thank you for your support. I felt I had no choice. I prayed hard that I would find the right words, say the right thing. This was my only chance and out it came. You're sure I wasn't too blunt, too arrogant. You seemed to be surprised by my directness."

"Yes, I suppose I was," Jerry responded, savoring the wine and the recap of the audience. "But he asked you a question and you responded. It's as simple as that."

"It's never that simple and you know it!" I protested, wondering if my words to the pope would make any difference.

We would be heading home in the morning, but for now, all we had to do was enjoy the moment and reflect on our experience of meeting the pope. "Kelly, you and I should document all we can remember about this day. It could have historical significance." And with that, Jerry took a small notebook from his coat pocket and began to write. The two of us discussed all that had transpired as we shared our meal. It helped me to see the interchange with the pope from Jerry's perspective. I was surprised at the confidence and self-assurance I felt in the pope's presence. This was no idle conversation. He was evaluating me to see if this was from God or not, and I was trying to determine if he would initiate the change. It was an exchange among equals, something that will always be mystifying to me but an event I cannot deny. How on earth did I ever arrive at this point? This is all God's doing, along with that risk-taker and instigator, Bishop Gene McGovern.

"Jerry," I interrupted as he scribbled in his notebook, "write that Gene was in that room with us today, telling us what to say and urging the pope to be open to our words."

After dinner, we walked to our hotel in good spirits. I headed to my room to call Tom and share the day's events. I was exhausted but elated with all that had transpired.

"It sounds as if you had a very frank exchange," Tom said, sensing my optimism but also my weariness.

"You can say that again. Oh, Tom, I so wish you were here with me right now. I miss you something awful. I can't wait to see you tomorrow. Give the kids a big hug for me. *Ciao*."

I was about to turn in when the phone rang. "Hello, Jerry."

"Actually no, it's not Jerry," the person on the other end of the line confessed.

I recognized that distinctive voice at once. "Oh, it's you!"

"Yes, your mystery caller again. I hope it's not too late. I just want to congratulate you on an excellent meeting this evening. You did *very* well. In fact, you were magnificent, if I can be so bold."

"You've already heard?" I exclaimed in amazement.

"News travels fast in the Vatican, especially news that is supposed to be private," the caller said with a chuckle. "I trust all the arrangements were to your satisfaction?"

"By far," I confirmed. "They were wonderful. Everything is perfect. Thank you so much."

"I called to wish you a pleasant trip home," the caller replied, seeming to enjoy my obvious appreciation. He continued in a more serious tone, "I'll be getting back to you in a week or so. I have much to do in the meantime. This is a most critical period. A great deal lies in the balance. Pray for the success of our adventure."

"Yes, of course," I agreed as I tried to imagine all that was transpiring behind the scenes. "I tried to ask when we last spoke whether I would see you in Rome."

"Not this time, I'm afraid," the caller admitted, "but it will happen, I'm sure of it, especially if all goes as planned. I do hope you can take some time for yourself when you get home. You've had a busy schedule of late."

"Yes indeed I have!" I said, finding the conversation both relaxing and affirming. I had long ago forgiven him for making all the sudden and unilateral arrangements that brought me to Rome. "Thank you, Bishop, for your support. I'll look forward to your next call."

"*Ciao.*"

I climbed into bed and reflected on the day. "Ah, so much for which to be thankful. Please, dear God, bless Your servant, Pope John XXIV, and this strange church of ours. We do seem to get ourselves into some serious predicaments. Stay close; we need Your strength and Your guidance." With that, I fell into a deep slumber, happy to be alive and also aware that somehow I was an integral part of God's all-wise and encompassing plan.

AFTER THAT SPURT OF ACTIVITY, life did quiet down for me. Thanksgiving weekend came and went, followed by the pre-Christmas rush. With what little time remained, I made an attempt at writing my account of my ordination and all that led to it and followed thereafter. Without the duties of a regular job, I was able to complete projects that had waited on the back burner for years, including reading, decorating the house and studying my Spanish. I also completed an application for a substitute teacher position at the local elementary school, hoping to begin part-time employment after the new year.

Our meeting with the pope invaded my mind at the most unexpected times, prompting a prayer for his well-being. I also wondered when my mystery bishop would call again. Nothing had happened for over a month. But with the celebration of Christmas, that call receded into the background.

I answered the phone on the Feast of St. Stephen, the day after Christmas, in the midst of cleaning the house after the holiday onslaught. Without even saying hello, the caller said, his voice full of jubilation. "I have wonderful news! Our plan has worked—we are victorious! Congratulations, Kelly! Your words, plus some gentle persuasion from our side, did the trick. The pope has agreed to call a Council! Can you imagine that?"

"Oh, my goodness," I shouted, jumping up and down. "You can't be serious! I don't know what to say. I'm so excited; I don't know what to do!" Putting my hand over the receiver, I yelled down the hall, "Tom, Tom, come quickly, the pope is going to call a Council."

"The news will break this evening," the bishop continued, laughing at my reaction as Tom came to the phone. I held the receiver so he could hear. "Watch CNN around four o'clock your time. We're all thrilled! The pope has reached way beyond what we were seeking. Get this; there will be *three* sessions, each two years apart. All the details will be announced at the press conference. Your visit with the pope last month was so vital to our entire effort. Ever since that day his attitude changed. He took on a new resolve, a more pastoral tone, a willingness to take risks. Your words had a definite impact."

"I'm so glad to hear that," I exclaimed, "but much of the praise belongs to Bishop Gene for his daring fortitude. It cost him his life." I paused; "Are you still in Rome?"

"Yes, for the moment," he said. "I travel back and forth with some regularity these days. Our group of bishops sends its regards. I suspect you'll have a chance to meet us in the not too distant future."

"Oh, I hope so," I shot back. "I would love to hear your side of the story."

"As much as can be told," the bishop acknowledged. "I must leave you now. There is much to do before this evening's news conference. This place is a flurry of activity. You'll be pleased by what you hear. Oh, one last thing; could I ask for the time being that you keep a low profile? The victory is ours, but we don't want to flaunt it. Reconciliation is the theme now, reuniting all the different factions, as far as possible."

"Certainly. That's fine with me," I agreed, "But oh, this is such good news. Thank you for calling and letting me know. I'll just pray and wait for further instructions."

"It sounds strange when you phrase it like that," the caller laughed, "it's like being a lieutenant in the army. But that seems best for the moment. I had to call because you played such an important role in this whole scenario. You needed to hear about it before it went public. We'll be in touch. Goodbye, Kelly."

"*Ciao*, as the Romans say," I replied and hung up the phone.

I looked at Tom, my eyes dancing as I blurted, "The pope is going to do it, he's calling a Council! The bishops of the world will finally have a chance to debate the ordination issue and come to a conclusion. Oh, Tom," I said, grabbing his hands, "I have no doubt what the outcome will be. More women will be ordained and they will be honest-to-God legitimate, official priests."

I suddenly stopped my rejoicing and looked away. "I wonder what will happen to my own ordination. Will it be recognized as valid? Will I be able to return to St. Gabriel's and continue to do what I love best—be their pastor? What a blessing that would be." Then looking at Tom I continued, "The news will break at four o'clock. I'd better get on the phone and alert people about the announcement. They won't want to miss this!"

Tom and I were seated in front of the television exactly on time. A special bulletin flashed across the screen about a significant event coming from Rome. The pope himself was before the cameras, speaking in surprisingly fluent English reading from a prepared text. He looked as I remembered him, dark, welcoming eyes, a wisp of white hair under his scull cap, thin, friendly face, only now he seemed to possess more determination, more self-assurance. With him were five cardinals, all dressed in red, plus a few other prelates. The pope began, "Today we wish to announce our decision to call an Ecumenical Council. It will have three sessions, each in a different location. The first will take place here in the Vatican and is to open about a year from now. The theme of this first session will be church leadership. It will deal with such issues as the requirements for ordination, decision-making in the church and vehicles of collegiality and consultation. The second session will take place two years later at a location yet to be determined. The subject will be on marriage and relationships. It will treat such subjects as sexuality, human relationships, marriage and annulments. The third will follow two years after the second. It will have health, justice and the earth's well-being as its theme. It will treat such topics as bio-ethics, global warming and care for the poor. It, too, will take place in a location yet to be announced.

"The five cardinals who have joined us this evening will serve as the organizing committee for the first session that will be convened a year from January. While this does not provide much time for preparation, the issues are urgent and need to be addressed. Each of these illustrious men is from a different continent. They will introduce themselves in a moment. This is a worldwide gathering of bishops, observers and *periti*, or resource experts. The attempt will be to hear all sides of the issue of church leadership. It will be an open forum, involving both general assemblies and separate working sessions. We do not know what the final outcome will be, but our hope is that the combined wisdom and prayerful insight of those attending will produce a solution to the critical shortage of ordained leadership experienced in the church today. Now to our distinguished organizing group."

As I watched the screen I was amazed at how confident the pope appeared as he addressed the world. The cardinals approached the microphones each in turn. One was from Germany, another from Africa, the third from South America, the fourth from Asia, and the last from the United States. When the cardinal archbishop from the States stepped forward, I gasped.

"Oh, my God!" I screamed. "It's him, he's the one! I would recognize that voice anywhere!"

"What are you so excited about?" Tom asked as he took his eyes off the screen to see me frantically pointing at the television.

"That's my mysterious caller," I stammered. "That's my contact person from the bishops' group. He wasn't just a bishop; he's Cardinal Stevens, one of the most influential prelates in our country! He's the one who was so pleasant and solicitous over the phone. I should have known. I've heard him give speeches. I never made the connection. Imagine that! He was one of those in the inner circle. He was part of Gene's plan from the beginning. That was no average group of bishops. I wonder who else was involved. So, that's who you are. I hope you call again. This time I'll know your name!"

Tom laughed at my delight in discovering who my mysterious caller had been. "You only deal with the top—the head honchos," Tom joked, squeezing my arm, "first a cardinal, then the pope. And to think I once knew you only as Kelly, my wife."

"Very funny, very funny," I said, giving in to his chiding. "And I'm still your wife! In fact, our cardinal friend told me to lie low for a while. That pretty much settles what I'll do with those requests to give talks and workshops at Catholic gatherings and conventions. 'Sorry, can't do it. The cardinal says no.'"

"As if you always followed instructions," Tom quipped.

"I do when it suits my fancy," I smirked and returned my attention to the television. The press conference was finished; only the commentators remained on the screen as they repeated all that the pope had announced. "I better start getting dinner ready," I said, turning off the television. "That really is good news. January is just a little over a year. Do you think it can happen that quickly?"

"It can if the pope says so. He's the boss," Tom replied.

The newspapers and television were full of the news about the new Council. People didn't know what to call it. Vatican III was one option, but it was more than that. World Council seemed to be the favorite. Suggestions for the other two sites included South Africa, Brazil and the Philippines. Some were even suggesting a location in the United States. "Wouldn't that be wild!" I said over dinner. "An Ecumenical Council we could actually attend. The pope said it would be an open meeting. How will they handle all those who want to come? It could be like the opening of the Olympics, the bishops of each country filing in around the track with flags and banners. Wouldn't *that* be awesome?"

"Will you be invited, Mom?" Rachel asked after I announced the news.

"I doubt it," I confessed, enjoying this biggest Christmas present of all. "I'm a minor player in that crowd. You and I can sit and watch it from the comfort of our family room, Rachel. How's that?"

"Oh, but I want to go," Rachel whined. "I want to see you with all those bishops."

A few days later Jerry called. "I'm sorry I didn't phone when the news of the Council broke. Pretty big stuff, huh? I honestly think you had something to do with it, Kel. Well, I have some news of my own that has kept me from calling. I got an email from our Jesuit headquarters in Rome. It seems that the organizers selected me as one of the resource people for the first session of the Council."

"Oh, Jerry, I'm so pleased to hear that," I exclaimed, happy for his good fortune. "Good for you! You *should* be there. You can add so much to the deliberations."

"I'm going to have to give up teaching for at least the next semester, maybe more. In fact, everything will be on hold to make room for the preparations. The timeline is so tight that I'll be burning the night oil from now on. Get used to not hearing much from me."

"I figured as much," I replied, realizing how drastically both of our lives had changed this year. "There's no telling what the new year might hold for us.

"How about yourself? Has anyone contacted you?" Jerry inquired, wondering what part I might be playing in all this.

"Not about attending the Council," I admitted. "If they did request my presence, I would decline. It makes perfect sense to have you there, but not me. I may be a symbol, but I'm not an expert."

"All the more reason that you should be there," Jerry announced. "We need symbols to focus our activities, to tell us why we're doing this."

"No, symbols do not make decisions," I reminded him. "You can do quite well without me. I do have some interesting news, however. Remember Cardinal Stevens from the United States on the news conference? Well, he's my contact since Gene died! Isn't that amazing?"

"Wow!" Jerry replied with surprise. "Well, it figures. I knew your mystery caller was anxious for change, but I didn't realize he was involved from the ground floor. No wonder that group of bishops had contacts in Rome. The cardinal has been a constant companion of the pope since the beginning. It helps to have friends in high places. Next time I need anything, I'll give you a call."

"As if I knew how to reach him," I quipped. *"Don't call me, I'll call you* sort of thing. I am pleased to hear your good news, though. So, it's back to Rome for you. Can you tell I'm a bit jealous? One of these days Tom and I are going there to take a good look at the city I visited but missed seeing. I'll let you go, you have work to do. Congratulations, Jerry."

"Thanks, Kel. Pray for me as I try to keep all these plates in the air."

"As always. See you in about ten years."

"Very cute. Until next time—*Ciao.*"

"*Ciao*, yourself."

"So, Jerry is a *periti*, an expert at the Council," I said out loud as I hung up the phone. "He'll do well. He's in his element. And me? I'm in mine as well, in my own home, with my own family. That's plenty to keep me happy, thank you very much."

On the next Sunday, the feast of the Holy Family, we all attended Mass at St. Gabriel's. Everyone in church was excited about the news. "A Council! The pope is calling a Council! We finally did it," Deb said as she greeted me at the door. "Maybe this will mean you can come back as our pastor."

"Don't hold your breath," I laughed, enjoying Debbie's optimism. "The Council is still a year away, and even if they do make a change, imagine how long it will take to make all the arrangements, including me."

"As a matter of fact," Debbie admitted with some hesitation, "the bishop has sent me a letter offering me your old job, the position of pastoral administrator. Should I accept it?"

"Why, yes, of course," I said, congratulating her. "Good for you, Deb. You'll do well. Be sure to ask for a big salary. Then hire someone right away to replace yourself as director of religious education. You can't keep doing both jobs, you know." I said this with as much interest as I could muster. I was surprised at the lump in my throat when I heard that Deb would be replacing me. It hit me harder than I expected. Suddenly I felt cast aside and quite alone.

"Thanks for the advice," Debbie replied. "I'm getting awfully worn. But as soon as the changes in ordination are in effect, you can have your job back. People loved you as their pastor."

"Thanks," I replied, appreciating Debbie's compliment. "That's sweet of you. We'll see what develops. In the meantime, let me know if there is anything I can do to help."

Our family filed into our usual row of seats. I loved worshiping with my friends and fellow parishioners. This community was such a comfort to me, although Henry was hard to tolerate sometimes. He was aloof and officious whenever he interacted with me now, which wasn't often. But it was still my parish and I owed it to the community to remain in close contact with the congregation.

The New Year came and went with little fanfare. I began my substitute teaching, finding it a challenge to teach whichever grade was needed. I found myself in Rachel's fifth grade classroom one day, to the delight of both of us. As Easter approached, preparations were intensifying for the first session of the World Council. Diocesan and regional Councils were taking place in preparation for the larger gathering in Rome. When he was able, Jerry called to keep me informed. There were no calls from my cardinal contact. I imagined he was overwhelmed with the task of preparing to convene the Council on time.

During the summer, our family had a quiet celebration for the first anniversary of my July 22nd ordination. We made frequent trips to the migrant community to visit our friends. On one occasion, Michael gave everyone a scare when he *borrowed* the family car—without a license—to take Maria Alvarez for a ride around the country roads.

When they returned an hour later, both Tom and I, as well as Maria's parents were furious. Nothing like this had happened before. Michael's plea was, "I only wanted to take her for a ride. Lots of the boys here drive without a license. We didn't do anything. And I was home before dark. What's the problem?" But Mr. and Mrs. Alvarez were extremely upset.

"What am I to do with you, Michael?" I asked with disappointment. "I expect more from you. Besides being dishonest, you betrayed the trust of the families who have been so good to us. Our customs and ways of relating are not their ways. Go and apologize to the Alvarez family. And you know, of course, that you are grounded for the rest of the summer."

Other than this episode, summer blended into fall with preparations for the Council behind schedule. The opening day was supposed to be January 25th, the Feast of the Conversion of St. Paul, but that deadline couldn't be met. The logistics required to gather all the bishops in one place for meaningful discussion was daunting, even in this technological age of instant communication and simultaneous translations. Changing the requirements for priesthood was proving to be complicated. Who controlled the leadership of the church needed to be determined. If opening ordination to married people, both men and women, it would be more difficult to reassign priests from one parish to another, in addition to providing salaries which could support an entire family. The issue of the episcopacy, if bishops be allowed to marry, needed to be addressed. And, might there be women bishops?

Position papers on all of these topics were being circulated to bishops around the world and these served as the focus for the regional Councils. The position papers required translating responses which had to be incorporated into revised drafts. On and on the circle continued. Finally, on March 19th, the Feast of St. Joseph, the first session of the World Council commenced. My entire family watched the opening ceremonies on television, trying to detect Jerry within the vast throng of bishops, observers and resource experts.

"Would you prefer to be there?" Tom asked, watching to check my reaction.

"No way. I'm fine just where I am," I replied, pulling Rachel to me on the coach so we could enjoy it together.

"But don't you feel you *should* be there?" Tom insisted. "In some small way you helped start it."

"Perhaps, but this job belongs to the bishops and the pope to ascertain how this change will occur and to work through the details. This is their show, not mine."

All of us fell silent as Pope John xxiv intoned the opening liturgy. Finally I interjected. "This is an important moment, kids. It could change the course of history. The Second Vatican Council paved the way for this. Now it's time to finish what the First Council left undone. From now on everything could be different. I certainly hope so. Look, is that Bishop Foley? It sure looks like him. I wonder what he's thinking right now."

As the Council developed, Jerry sent an email each week to his friends and colleagues about its progress. He sounded as if he were being pulled in many directions, but he remained optimistic about what was happening. I responded each week, offering my support and prayers, and telling him to pace himself.

It became clear early that this first session of the Council would not be finished in a couple of months. "Three, if we're lucky," Jerry said in his last epistle. "But we are making headway. Soon we'll be able to write a final draft on ordination and offer it to the bishops for their approval. It calls for an open priesthood, no limits to marital status or gender, only adequate training and sufficient spiritual maturity and motivation. It's a real breakthrough."

I could sense his elation despite his exhaustion. I was heartened by what I read. "Maybe I'll be able to say Mass again," I said to Tom one day. "I miss my ministering so much. I wonder if I'll ever get my job back as pastor. It seems a distant possibility."

"That's a tough one, Kel," Tom responded. "It's too bad you can't do what needs to be done in the church. You do it so well."

"Someday, someway," was my response as I longed for my days of ministry in the parish.

Then one day, as the Council was well into its third month, I received an unexpected call.

"Hello, Kelly," the caller said as I answered the phone.

"It's you!" I exclaimed, overjoyed to hear his voice. "I know your voice and now I know your name. You're Cardinal Stevens, aren't you?"

"Yes, I confess you've found your man," the cardinal admitted, relieved that he had been identified.

"It is so good to hear from you," I said, delighting in the opportunity to talk with him once again. "You must be going crazy trying to keep this Council on track."

"You might say that. Sorry I haven't called earlier. I've had a number of concerns."

"I can imagine. Why are you calling now?" I inquired, full of curiosity. "What's on your mind?"

"I have an important request," he said. I could sense the rising energy in his voice.

"Oh, oh, that makes me a little nervous, judging from our past conversations," I replied, bracing myself for the unexpected. "What is your request?

"We've made great progress at the Council, Kelly," he went on. "The logjam has been broken and we're close to voting on the document for an open ordination. You were a key figure in this effort. My request—are you ready for this?—is that I want *you* here when the vote takes place. I want you among the observers. In addition, the pope has specifically requested that you be among those present when he ratifies the document with his signature. Do you think you can arrange that?"

"Am I to understand that you are calling me to Rome for a *second* time?" I interjected, trying to get my thoughts straight.

"You've got it," he replied.

"Whoa. I can hardly believe it. How soon?" I asked, as my adrenaline surged.

"One week, actually," the cardinal responded, enjoying my exuberant reaction. "Things are moving very swiftly here. We'll need you here by next Wednesday."

"And this is Thursday! Are you serious? That's so soon!"

"You've always come through in the past. I'm sure you can do it again. I'll even let you tour Rome for a change."

"May my husband come with me this time?" I asked expectantly, crossing my fingers.

"Absolutely, all expenses paid," the cardinal assured me, relishing the excitement he heard on the other end of the line.

"All right!" I shot back. "Thank you so much, Cardinal! Tom will love it! You've made me a very happy woman. Judging from past experience, I suspect you've already made the arrangements."

"Yes, as a matter of fact, we have," the cardinal said with delight.

"And will I have a chance to meet you, at long last?" I asked cautiously.

"Even better," he returned. "You will be the guest of honor for our bishops' planning group. We all very much want to meet you. That's part of the bargain."

"Wonderful!" I responded, hardly able to contain myself with all of this good fortune. "I don't know what to say, you've been so kind. Wait, let me get a pad of paper so I can write the information. Excuse me if I'm a little slow. I don't operate very well when I get excited. Black dress and mantilla again?"

"No. Be as colorful as you like," the cardinal chuckled. "You're going to be our showcase."

"Like a dog and pony show, right?" I quipped.

"Like the priesthood of the future," the cardinal responded with a note of admiration.

"Oh, yes," I acquiesced, appreciating the compliment. "And with women priests, it could be colorful indeed. Now tell me, please, what I need to know."

My fingers could hardly write the flight arrangements, I was so nervous. "This is heady stuff," I thought as I copied the itinerary. "Imagine, a whole week in Rome! Tom and I can discover it together. Maybe Jerry will have time to be our guide." My mind was racing with possibilities.

"There, I think I have it," I finally said in response to Cardinal Stevens' directions. "Will you be seeing Father Jerry Cross? I'll try to email him about our trip, but he may not see it."

"Better yet, I'll make sure he meets you at the airport," the cardinal assured me. "You'll be arriving next Wednesday around noon. I've scheduled nothing for you until Thursday evening. That's when you'll be the guests at a special banquet of our bishops' group. If all goes according to plan, the final vote on the Ordination Document will be on Friday, and we want you there for that. Sometime over that weekend there will also be a special ceremony with the pope. Get some rest; you're going to be a busy person during that week in Rome. That's enough for now. Your tickets are waiting for you at the airport, just as last time. I'm looking forward to seeing you one week from today."

"Yes, one week from today!" I repeated, still trying to comprehend this sudden turn of events. "And thank you for making all the arrangements. You have been a most worthy host and ally."

"The feeling is mutual. See you shortly. *Ciao*."

"*Ciao*, yourself," I said and stood with the receiver in my hand long after the line had gone dead. Rome! For a whole week this time—*and* with Tom. What blessings, what unexpected, undeserved blessings. Thank you, God, for being so good to your servant. Oh, my goodness, what about Michael and Rachel? I wonder if Nathan could come home from his summer job for a week and look after them. If not him, I'm sure we can find someone. After all, it's not everyday I'm asked—no, escorted—to Rome to dine with bishops, witness an historic vote and meet the pope. And my cardinal friend said, "Get lots of rest." Who's he kidding? It will be hard to get a wink of sleep with all that's going through my head.

"Tom! Drop everything and come here for a minute," I shouted down the hall. "And bring your passport!"

Tom looked out his office door and said, "What? You seem excited."

"Excited! Wait until you hear!" I ran down the hall and threw my arms around him. "We're going to Rome—you and I—this coming Tuesday!"

I told him the story as the two of us stood in the doorway. He laughed at my exuberance and tried to get me to sit, but I wouldn't stop talking. "You are as giddy as a teenager who just got invited to her first dance." Then with a devilish grin he added, "Let me check my appointments to see if I'm free."

"You'll do nothing of the sort! Grab your jacket," I demanded. "We're going for a hot fudge sundae. This demands a celebration!"

The rest of the week was a flurry of excitement for the two of us. This time my trip to Rome was no secret. I could tell the world—and I did, at least the world of St. Gabriel's. Everyone was happy for me because they knew the year of inactivity had been difficult for me. They also had hopes that I might be returning to my old job. Deb was especially ecstatic. "We need you back," she said. "I can't do this job as you do."

"Perhaps we could be a team, do it together," I suggested, not wanting to encroach on Debbie's turf. "We'd be unbeatable," I added, giving Deb a boost to her ego.

Nathan was glad to come home and look after his brother and sister for the week. He had to admit that he missed them during his first year at college, as they missed him. Being away for the summer was equally difficult. As he explained to his boss, "This is a family emergency. I have no choice except to go home and help." By Tuesday afternoon Tom and I had packed our bags, bade farewell to our little town of Sarah, and were on our way to the Detroit airport. We took the overnight flight to Rome as Jerry and I had taken a year-and-a-half earlier, arriving in the early afternoon. Jerry was waiting as we passed through customs, smiling from ear to ear. I ran to give him a big hug. "Oh, Jerry, it's so good to see you. I've missed your spiritual direction this last year."

"I missed you, too. Detroit seems like ancient history right now," Jerry admitted, delighted with the reunion. "Tom! So good to see you! This is going to be an exciting week for you two. Beginning tomorrow it will be non-stop activity, one function after another. At least you can sleep late tomorrow morning. Ready for a little repast?"

"*Little* is the operative word," I said as I took the arms of the two most important men in my whole world and headed through the airport. "They served us one meal after another on the flight."

The evening was festive as the three of us shared our latest stories. Jerry explained the Ordination Document news that was being submitted for a vote. He was proud to have played an integral part in its formulation. Tom and I were returned to our hotel a little after ten that evening, tired and feeling a bit light-headed as well.

At ten the next morning, Tom gently nudged me awake and said, "Don't you think we should act like responsible adults and greet the morning before it eludes us altogether? Jerry will be here to take us to lunch in a little over an hour."

The two of us dressed, had coffee and a roll and waited for Jerry's appearance. He was uncharacteristically late. "I'm sorry about that," he apologized. "I had to take care of some last-minute details regarding the Ordination Document. We're nearing the end. Come, let me show you a few of the pleasures of Rome. Your big dinner isn't until eight."

"Are you coming to the dinner?" I asked, enjoying my old friend's company after such a long absence.

"I wouldn't miss it for the world," he replied with a smile, "although I'm a bit of an interloper. You're the person they want to see."

"How many of the group will be there?" I asked, a bit uneasy about being the center of attention.

"About thirty," Jerry guessed as he reflected on the group. "A few had other commitments and some couldn't make the trip. The original group numbered close to forty when Gene was alive."

"Will I recognize any of them?" I inquired, wondering what the evening would be like.

Most, I should think," Jerry assured me. "They're a very distinguished lot, many you've seen on the news recently. There are two cardinals, a number of archbishops, and the rest are bishops and auxiliary bishops."

"*Two* cardinals! I'm impressed," I said with surprise.

"And they're impressed with you, as well," Jerry returned with a smile.

"How do you know that?" I asked, doubting Jerry's statement.

"I've been working with them, side by side, for months. They often mentioned your name and how influential you were in developing this," Jerry affirmed.

"Me?" I responded incredulously.

"Yes, you!" Jerry said, poking his finger at me playfully. "That little *talk*—should I say *speech*?—you had with the pope has made the rounds."

I narrowed my gaze at Jerry, not sure I liked having my words make the rounds.

"Well, they didn't get it from *me*, believe me," Jerry shot back. "I think the pope spread the story himself."

"Then I guess that's good," I concluded. "He really is a delightfully humble man."

Jerry chose a quiet restaurant for lunch and then showed us some of the highlights of the Eternal City—the Catacombs, the Spanish Steps, the Coliseum, the Trevi Fountain, as well as a number of churches. We returned to our hotel room by six to take a nap, dress for the evening and then join the bishops for their special banquet. I was so nervous I could hardly dress. Tom helped me get ready.

"What will I say to all those bishops?" I pleaded in a panic.

"'Hello,' would be good for starters," Tom joked as he ushered me out the door.

The restaurant reserved for the occasion was within walking distance. Jerry met us in the lobby and we walked together. As we entered, the bishops all stood and applauded. I was embarrassed by the acclaim. Then Cardinal Stevens stepped forward and pinned a large orchid on my dress. "Welcome to our gathering, *Priest* Kelly More," he said, amid greetings from the others. "It's a pleasure to meet you at long last. And this must be your husband, Tom. Welcome!"

I was speechless. I stood with a grin on my face, receiving the adulation of the group. I was seated at the head of the circle, with chairs on either side for Jerry and Tom. It wasn't as large a room as I had imagined, but small and cozy. Chairs lined the outside of a circle of tables with the waiters on the inside pouring wine.

"Come," Cardinal Stevens said. "Have a seat so we can begin the toasts. Allow me to introduce everyone." He circled the room giving each person's name and diocese. As I tried to remember each name, I realized it was equivalent to a "Who's Who" of the American Catholic church.

"You were all in this from the onset?" I asked after they were introduced. The group all nodded, reveling in their disclosure as accomplices. "We did exercise a certain amount of influence, you might say," Cardinal Stevens remarked facetiously.

The meal progressed, course after course, wine-toasts accompanying each. I tried to pace myself with just a sip for each toast. As the evening waned, I became more comfortable and at ease. They seemed to enjoy my company as well. The bishops solicited my side of the story with a barrage of questions. Both Jerry and Tom added embellishments of their own. Finally, one of the bishops asked, "Do you have any questions for us?"

"Yes, as a matter of fact I do," I admitted. "Tell me: at the second Ordination Rally in New Orleans, as I was leaving the convention hall, there was a crowd of protestors who had placards and banners condemning my ordination. One of the signs read, 'Look up Canon 1378—you're out of here!' When I got home, I did look it up and it bothered me. It said, if I can remember correctly, that any person who, not being an ordained priest, attempts to celebrate Mass, incurs a *latae sententiae* interdict. Did that mean I was automatically excommunicated? Is that what Bishop Foley was referring to when he called me into his office?"

The entire room exploded in laughter. "You hit the nail on the head, Kelly," Cardinal Stevens said with glee. "That wasn't the only Canon with which we had to contend. We grappled for weeks over how to interpret what we could and could not do. In the case of the one you mentioned, we finally agreed, 'Well, she *is* an ordained priest, so she can say Mass at the closing liturgy.' This is what we used to persuade Bishop Foley. As a matter of fact, you'll find him a changed man after his experience here at the Council."

"Now we have a question for you'" the cardinal said. "It's actually more like an offer. Once the Ordination Document is signed and we all return home to enact it, we plan to establish a national office for the implementation of this new decree. We would like *you* to head that office. You don't have to give us your answer right now, but the offer stands."

"What about my own ordination?" I asked, humbled by this offer but wanting to clarify my confusion. "Will I be able to function as a priest?"

"Yes, indeed, you'll be one of the first," was the response.

"Then, before you continue further, I think I know the answer to your question." I squeezed Tom's hand under the table. "If I had my way, my request would be to return to my own parish of St. Gabriel's and finally be their priest. That is my hope and joy. If I can do that, then all my needs and desires would be fulfilled."

The room erupted in loud applause which unnerved and confused me. "Why are they clapping?" I asked Jerry.

"Because they admire your dedication and loyalty to your home community," he returned.

When the commotion died, Cardinal Stevens spoke, "Then you shall have your wish." and the company of bishops stood to give Kelly one final toast.

The walk to the hotel was a hilarious affair. The three of us were accompanied by a small contingent of bishops who wanted to make sure "their Kelly got home safe and sound." Tom and I bid them good night at the elevator door, thanking them profusely for "an evening I shall treasure forever," I said as the door closed.

"Oh, Tom, wasn't that grand!" I said as he put his arm around my waist. "Can you imagine them offering me that job? It was tempting, but you and I—well, we belong in Sarah, Michigan, don't we? It's our home, and St. Gabe's is our parish. Not only will I be their pastor, now I will be their *priest!*"

~

ST. PETER'S SQUARE WAS CROWDED as the three of us made our way into St. Peter's for the Mass of Thanksgiving. The Ordination Document had been approved the previous day and we were given special tickets for this liturgy. The pope presided, surrounded by those most responsible for the success of the World Council's first session. I was glad we were so close to the front. I could see not only the pope, but Cardinal Stevens as well. "They're all such good men," I thought. "But I'm glad that in a short while it won't just be men up there. Women need to balance it."

At communion, the pope himself distributed the Eucharist to the section where the three of us sat. He smiled as I held out my hand. I smiled back, remembering well the brief but significant encounter the two of us had more than a year ago.

After the Mass, Jerry, Tom and I made our way to the pope's residence for the signing ceremony. We were surprised that more people were not in attendance. "I had no idea that this was going to be such an intimate affair," Jerry said as we took our seats. As I looked around I estimated fewer than a hundred people would witness this momentous event. Television cameras lined the walls, while those invited filled the chairs that faced a long table in the front of the room. Most were cardinals and bishops, although about a quarter of the gathering were men and women from various parts of the world. Some were wearing colorful outfits from their native lands. Eventually the pope entered. He walked around the room shaking hands and greeting people. Cardinal Stevens and a few others from the bishops' group were there. When the pope stood before us, he took my hand and said in English, "So, we meet again, Kelly More. More words for me today?" He said this with that distinctive twinkle in his eye. I couldn't help but love this man.

"No," I replied deferentially. "You have fulfilled my deepest hopes and desires. Thank you so much for all you have done. And thank you for including us in this ceremony."

"You must not leave when is over," he insisted, still holding my hand. "Stay here. I have favor to ask."

"Of course," I said, somewhat surprised. After the pope had moved to the next chair, I looked at Jerry and Tom inquisitively, but they were equally bewildered.

After the pope had met everyone, he took a seat at the table while attendants brought copies of the Decree on Holy Orders for the pope's signature. He began by saying to those assembled, "English not easy language. We use it now so more people be able to understand as we address whole world. We use prepared speech, yes?"

He then nodded to the camera crews and they began their coverage of the event. "This is an historic moment in the life of the church," the pope began, reading from his text as he sat at the table. "For centuries the priesthood of the Roman Rite has been limited to celibate males. There were good historical reasons for this, and the tradition lasted for many years. Now there are other, more important reasons for opening the priesthood to include not only celibates, but married men as well. This had been the custom for the first thousand years of our history and is still an option for other Catholic Rites within the church. We are now restoring this ancient custom. Our first predecessor, St. Peter, was married and Jesus himself cured St. Peter's mother-in-law." The pope said all this with a great smile on his face. He was not rotund like his namesake, Pope John XXIII, far from it, but he exhibited his same warmth and disarming manner.

"The next step," he continued, "is to open the priesthood to include women. This was not part of the tradition of the church. But new evidence has come to light in recent years that suggested it may have been a practice of the early church. There has been some excellent research done in this area, including that performed by one person in our midst, Jesuit Father Gerald Cross.

As the pope indicated where Jerry was sitting, the cameras turned to film his smiling and somewhat embarrassed, face.

"He has suggested," the pope continued, "that St. Paul himself may have ordained women priests."

I looked at Jerry and gave him a wink of recognition as the cameras returned to the pope.

"Whether or not this was the case is not as important as a new awareness in our present age of the equality between men and women. This equality should be manifested in our church leadership as well. The first session of the World Council has debated this issue and has seen fit to present us with a document that states that the Sacrament of Holy Orders on all three levels—diaconate, priesthood, episcopacy—should be open to all. This is a momentous day. We gladly sign this decree and place our stamp of approval on it." He said this as he pressed his fist on the table with emphasis, his face beaming with pride.

At this, the gathered prelates and dignitaries erupted in heartfelt applause. As the acclamation quieted, the pope continued, "Before we do this, however, allow us a slight digression. There are here— from around the world—special cardinals, bishops, priests, deacons and lay people." He stretched his arms and the cameras panned around the room.

"Each played a part in the development of this decree in its final form. We cannot acknowledge them all, but we would like to single out a few."

As he said this I started to get the sinking feeling that maybe I shouldn't have attended this event. It could become very embarrassing. I sank into my chair so as to not to be conspicuous.

"First," the pope said, reading from his prepared text, "there was a group of bishops from the United States of America who tried to persuade me on this matter. I do not consider myself easily pressured, but this group convinced me to schedule a debate on the subject." With that he raised his eyes from his papers and gave Cardinal Stevens a wink and a smile.

"Please, cardinals and bishops, you stand," the pope insisted, gesturing to the contingent I had met on Thursday evening. Ten bishops and two cardinals stood, somewhat uneasy at being identified as "pushing the pope into action."

"I wish to thank them," the pope looked at the standing prelates, still smiling broadly, "for their courage and persistence. It is risky business to challenge the pope, no? But they were successful in the end."

Returning to his text, he continued, "Let us also acknowledge Bishop Eugene McGovern of happy memory who died two years ago, but who was a key figure in the implementation of the bishops' plan. He was the one who took it upon himself to ordain a woman to the priesthood, a most unorthodox move," the pope contended, shaking his head with mock seriousness, "but one that has now been blessed in the decree that we will sign today." Everyone laughed and applauded his humor.

"The person he ordained is here with us today. Could we ask Mrs. Kelly More to please stand?" the pope requested, turning to face me directly.

Panic flooded my body. "No, not me, please."

With some prodding from Jerry and Tom, I stood and tried not to look too self-conscious. I tried to quickly resume my seat but the pope, his hand outstretched in my direction, continued, "No, please, not sit down.' Then turning to the cameras he explained, "Over one year ago, Mrs. Kelly More was here, also Father Jerry Cross—you stand, too, please?"

Now it was my turn to nudge Jerry. While we stood, the pope went on to say, "We must admit that we were of two minds about the ordination of women." The pope said this as he pointed to himself. "Our predecessors were strong in their opposition. They did not want any discussion. What right did we have to shift directions so quickly? Then we met Kelly More. She spoke so clearly, so forcefully. She said, 'Call a Council. Let people discuss it.' It was as if the Spirit were speaking through her. We were not able to resist. Soon we changed our mind on the issue." The pope then pointed to where we were standing with a humorous gesture that suggested he had no choice but to relent. I was overwhelmed by what he was saying about me. My face flamed red with embarrassment.

"Thank you," the pope concluded and the two of us gratefully resumed our seats. The pope acknowledged others in the room. One was the head of an international group of inactive priests who had asked that they be allowed to exercise their priesthood as family men. The Decree on Holy Orders welcomed all those who were once active to return to ministry if they wished. Another was a small contingent of the Roman Curia who had advocated change and had been courageous in standing firmly against the considerable opposition in the Vatican. Finally, representatives from Asia, Africa and Latin America were asked to stand as they were acknowledged for their long and persistent requests for a more inclusive priesthood. "For far too long," the pope read from his speech, "the people of your lands have gone unattended because there were no priests to serve or to provide priestly leadership. It was a scandal that is finally being addressed at this late hour. We pray we have not waited too long." the pope added, shaking his head.

Then the moment came for the signing. The pope asked all those in attendance to stand behind him so that the television audience could witness this signing of the decree as an act of solidarity with Catholics from around the world. The three of us found ourselves close to the center. We watched with approval as the pope put pen to paper. Nathan said when we talked with the family by phone that evening, "We were all watching as the pope signed the document. We could see you right there behind him. It was amazing. Rachel was so excited, she jumped up and down, pointing at the television and yelling, 'There they are, there's Mom and Dad, and Father Jerry, too.' It was awesome."

After the signing, people were ushered from the room, except for the few who had been asked to stay. Tom, Jerry and I were part of that select dozen. The pope came to the small cluster of people. "Large crowd of people outside in Square," he explained. "They are there long time. Is customary I go and wave, give blessing. They cheer in support of this signing. Balcony not very large, only few people at once. Please, would like some of you to join me. The rest please wait, no? It take only a moment. Just smile; receive shouts and waves from crowd. Yes?"

The pope chose a few from the group and escorted them to the balcony window. I was one of the first to be chosen. I looked back pleadingly to Jerry and Tom, but they only motioned me to follow the pope to greet the crowd. I shrugged and turned my attention outward.

I was stunned. The entire Square was jammed with people. "*Il Papa, Il Papa*," they chanted again and again. The force of the crowd's chanting almost pushed me back into the room. The pope, in his gentle way, urged me forward. He took my hand and raised it high in the air. The crowd broke into sustained applause. I tried with all my might to smile, but I was visibly shaken by the intensity of the experience. I seemed in a daze.

"Smile, Kelly More, smile!" the pope was saying as he took my hand in his and raised it over our heads. I looked at him in surprise. "Oh," I said, and did my best to recover, forming a smile as tears streamed down my face. From Psalm 118 came "This is the day the Lord has made, let us rejoice and be glad." I returned to the room, fell into my husband's arms and wept for sheer joy.

SIXTEEN

"LOOK AT THIS, TOM," I said as we returned to our hotel room after my experience with the crowd from the pope's balcony. "There's a letter under our door. I wonder what this could be."

I opened it and read the name. "Bishop Foley, of all people," I said as I read the note. "Can you believe that?! He's inviting us for dinner tomorrow night. Will wonders never cease? We're to call him at his hotel if we're free. What do you think, Tom? Should we go?"

"Maybe he's calling a truce," Tom suggested somewhat halfheartedly. "Remember what Cardinal Stevens said when we met with his group of bishops, that you'll find Patrick Foley a changed man. Do you think that's possible?"

"I'm willing to go if you are," I said, although not entirely sure it was a good idea. "But I would hate to have an unpleasant experience after all the joy and happiness of these days."

"Life is a risk," Tom returned. "He's offering an olive branch. I think we should try to meet him half-way. It could make a difference for your future employment."

"Good point," I acknowledged. "Yes, I think I'll give him a call right now."

I went to the phone to accept the invitation, wondering as I did so what he had in mind.

When Bishop Foley answered the phone, he sounded delighted by my response. We arranged to meet in the lobby at eight o'clock the next evening. I was amazed by the tone of his voice. "We're all set," I said to Tom, somewhat mystified by what this could mean.

"How did he sound?" he asked.

"Different, very different," I admitted, searching for a way to describe it. "He seemed to be more human, somehow, less—what?—officious."

Tom and I spent a quiet Monday after the excitement of the previous day. We had lunch at an outdoor café and then walked along the Tiber. By eight o'clock that evening, we were dressed, ready to meet the bishop and curious to see how the evening would develop. Bishop Patrick Foley was in the lobby to greet us, which he did in a most civil manner, quite unlike the last time he and I had met when he ordered me to leave his office.

"Thank you for accepting my invitation on such short notice," he began. "Thank you for even agreeing to meet me. I've treated you very poorly, I'm afraid."

I glanced at Tom, looking for advice as to how to respond. "Apology accepted," I finally said, not in a very friendly manner, however.

"There's a nice, quiet restaurant not too far from here," the bishop suggested. "Are you willing to walk a few blocks?"

"By all means; I need all the exercise I can get," I replied, starting to like this adventure. "These Italian meals are deadly."

"Excellent. I have much to share," he said as he escorted us from the hotel and into the mild summer evening. "It needs, however, a good bottle of wine to give it the right flavor."

The two of us followed the bishop to a lovely restaurant that had only a few tables, all beautifully decorated. "I asked for a quiet table in the back, so we're not disturbed," he said as the waiter led us to our table.

He ordered a bottle of choice wine and began what appeared to be a well-rehearsed speech. "This is not easy for me," he said. "It has demanded some deep soul-searching on my part. I was quite wrong to treat you the way I did, Kelly. I am very sorry and ask your forgiveness. But first, let me give you some background.

"When Bishop McGovern took it upon himself to ordain you, I was stunned. He was my teacher and idol. I felt betrayed. And all this happened in *my* diocese, so I also felt responsible. I'm a loyal son of the church. I'm not a risk-taker. My job, as I saw it, was to maintain order and discipline. Everything else was secondary. The ordination destroyed all that. What would Rome say? It all happened on *my* watch. I would surely be removed. Your presence in my diocese, Kelly, was a threat. I wanted to act swiftly and with authority. I thought I had to get this place back to normal.

"But Rome did *not* call. Instead, Cardinal Stevens called. That totally surprised me. My diocese was not even under his jurisdiction. Why was *he* involved? We had a nice chat. The gist of it was, 'Don't do anything rash or foolish. Sit tight. Any public statement or censure at this time would only cause more problems. Let it be for now.' His advice stunned me.

"Then Bishop McGovern died. In my final visit with him at the hospital he did not recant or apologize. He merely told me to act justly. I wasn't sure what that meant. I was confused. Something was taking place behind the scenes and I had no idea what it was.

"Then you came out of hiding. At the very least, I needed to cease your ministering. It was too much *in my face*. I needed to show people I was still the bishop, still the one in charge. The manner in which I did it was poor, this I now realize, but I wasn't acting very rationally during those trying days.

"Next came the Ordination Rally in New Orleans. When I saw you on television I became irrational. There you were, standing before the whole nation, defying me and Rome and the pope—everything I had worked my whole life to protect. I fumed about it the entire day. By Sunday morning I could tolerate it no longer. I called your home, knowing you weren't there. But I had to *do* something, anything to put a stop to the madness and frustration I felt.

"That Sunday afternoon, however, Cardinal Stevens called me again. I'd never had any dealings with him before, but here he was, calling for a second time. He told me that there might be some precedent to excommunicate you and lay heavy censures and strictures on you for your actions. But the Code of Canon Law was not clear on this point. He again counseled me not to do anything rash for the time being. I was of two minds on all this. I was so confused. But when he said he had it on the highest authority not to take any action against you, I realized I was way out of my league. It was common knowledge that he was a friend of the pope. Who was I to buck that level of power?

"However, I was still so angry at you for doing this. I should have stopped and regained my composure, but I didn't. It gnawed at me all day and all night, so that by the time you came to my office, I was totally out of control, as was obvious."

I nodded my head in agreement. This entire conversation—monologue, really—was completely unexpected. What I was experiencing was an entirely different side of Patrick Foley. He was, in effect, confessing to me. He was like a child who had done wrong and was now repentant and asking for forgiveness.

"I'm so sorry for my behavior," he continued. "Your reaction was heroic. You withstood my rage as no one has ever done before. My temper is my downfall. I try hard to keep it in check, but it keeps rearing its ugly head. You deserved much better from me, and I will try my very best to make it up to you.

"At any rate, to continue with my story . . . here, both of you, have some more wine," and he reached to fill our glasses. I could tell that Tom was still withholding judgment, but I was beginning to feel sorry for the bishop. I was quite willing to forgive and forget. He seemed so fragile; there was much anguish bottled inside this man.

"This Council was announced and all of us bishops gathered here in Rome," he continued, taking a sip of wine and growing more at ease as the wine took effect. "It was an eye-opener to me to hear what the bishops were saying. Loyalty and conformity were not being rewarded and reinforced to the same extent as were innovation and creative responses to concrete needs. It was as if the lid had been removed and we were now free to offer our opinions and to think independently. This isn't my strong suit but I tried to adjust. You know I have a desire to do what is right and what is expected of me.

"I began to recognize that the Curia officials who had held sway for so long were being replaced by new leadership, by more pastoral people who were in touch with and sensitive toward what was occurring in the world at large. When I arrived for the Council, people I respected told me that a new climate was taking hold, one that was similar to the tenor of the last Vatican Council. It's been quite awhile since this sentiment predominated in the church. This was difficult for me to accept, although the discussions we had in the English-speaking clusters were very exciting. I began to envision the future possibilities of the American church and all the good that could result if we clerics would loosen our grip a little and give the Spirit free rein. It was exhilarating."

Tom and I listened in amazement. Could this be the same man who pointed his finger at me in his office and said, "Leave! I have had enough of you!"?

"So, as you can see," the bishop said, "I'm somewhat of a changed man. Earlier I said I would like to make it up to you for the wretched way I've behaved. Here's my surprise." He pulled a letter from his breast pocket. "This is for you, Kelly" he said as he handed it to me.

"What is it?" I asked with a combination of surprise and curiosity.

"Take a look," the bishop coaxed with obvious relish.

I opened the envelope. Inside was an official document. On top was the word, "Indult." What followed was a statement that the person in question—Kelly More—was hereby officially recognized as a priest in good standing in the Holy Roman Catholic church. It was signed by the pope himself. Stunned, I showed it to Tom and then looked to the bishop for an explanation. "What does this mean?" I said, my voice shaking with emotion.

"It means," he said in response, "that you don't have to go through the regular process for your ordination to be validated. According to the new Decree on Holy Orders, all those who have previous claims to ordination must go through the proper channels to have their status regularized. This is primarily for those men who left the active priesthood, but it applies to you as well. The pope has just granted *you* an exception, that's what it means," the bishop said with delight.

This was the first time I had ever seen a genuine smile on Patrick Foley's face. It was not artificial or contrived, it was genuine. I now was confident about this man's change of attitude.

"So does this mean that I can say Mass—I mean, right now, anywhere? And that it would be okay? It would be a valid, legitimate Mass?" I asked, hardly able to contain the joy rising within me.

"Yes, that's exactly what it means," the bishop affirmed. "This first session of the Council will be over in a matter of days. The closing liturgy will be on Sunday. Will you still be here?"

"No, we're leaving Saturday morning," Tom interjected, wondering what Patrick Foley had in mind.

"Ah, a pity," the bishop replied sadly. "Well, it can't be helped. I'd hoped we could arrange for you to be one of the concelebrants at the Mass, right there among the rest of us. At any rate, when I return home I want to plan a special Mass for the entire diocese. All the

American bishops will be saying similar Masses in their own dioceses, one way of promulgating this new Decree on Holy Orders. I would also like to use that opportunity to reinstate you as the pastor of St. Gabriel's parish; that is, if you still want your old job."

"Do I!" I exclaimed, taking the bishop's hand. "That would be wonderful!"

"When I say 'reinstate you as pastor,' I mean installing you as the priest-pastor there," the bishop explained somewhat awkwardly in response to my taking his hand. "Father Henry's services would no longer be required, you understand. You would do it all. You would be the pastor. It's *your* parish now. I would like to use the diocesan-wide Mass as the time for ratifying your assignment. How does that sound?"

"Better than I had dared to imagine," I said, not believing the words I was hearing. "St. Gabriel's is where I belong. It had always been my fondest hope that I could remain there as the pastor. Those are the people I love." I paused to catch my breath. Then my eyes flashed as an idea came into my head. "Let me ask you one more thing. I'll be home this weekend. Would it be possible for me to preside at *this* Sunday's liturgy?"

"Of course," the bishop responded, thinking for a moment. "I don't see any reason why not. I could call the chancery and have them tell Father Henry that you'll handle it. If he has any questions, you can show him this Indult I just gave you. You are, as of this moment, the priest-pastor of St. Gabriel's parish. No need to call others from outside to preside at the Masses. You're it."

"Oh, thank you, thank you! What a wonderful surprise," I responded, my eyes filling with tears. "The congregation will be so thrilled!" At this I leaned over and gave the bishop a kiss on his cheek. He turned scarlet and smiled sheepishly.

"Thank you, yourself," he stammered. "Well, sermon over. Let's dig in and enjoy this meal. It's one of the best places in the city."

The rest of the evening was relaxed and rewarding. I gave the Indult to Tom for safekeeping. "It's like having your license on your wedding night," I said as we got ready for bed. "All is right with the world—the sky's the limit."

"You can say that again. Come over here, Your Holiness!" Tom said as he turned out the light.

Saturday morning dawned as Tom and I packed our things for the trip home. Jerry met us at the door of our hotel room to help with the luggage. "Too bad I can't go with you," he said, "but I have to be at the closing Mass. It's a command performance. Cardinal Stevens was wise to arrange your trip for today. By Monday there won't be a seat available on any airline leaving Rome. All the bishops will want to return home as soon as possible."

Jerry drove us to the airport in a car borrowed from a local Jesuit community. "It's nice to have connections," I teased as we arrived at the airport.

"It does help," he replied as he pulled our bags from the trunk. I took my carry-on and was heading for the counter when a voice from behind asked, "May I help you with your bag, Madam?"

"No, thank you," I said without turning. Then I realized that the person who spoke didn't have an Italian accent. I spun around and there before me stood Cardinal Stevens. He held a large bouquet of flowers in front of him. "I simply had to wish you bon voyage," he said as he handed me the flowers.

"Oh, you are so sweet," I said, smelling the bouquet. "Did you come all this way just to see us off?" I said, deeply moved by his gesture.

"Indeed I did," he responded. "Because I made your arrangements, I knew when you would be leaving. I've not had a free moment since last Sunday, but this morning I canceled my appointments to say goodbye. Was the Indult delivered into your hands all right?"

"Yes, perfectly! You thought of everything. And thank you for getting us on this flight," I said with deep appreciation. "Did you hear? I'll be home in time to celebrate Mass with my community on Sunday morning. I'm going to surprise them. Thank you for all that you have done. I am so happy!"

"No, thank *you*, Kelly More," the cardinal countered. "Your part was important to our success."

"And Gene McGovern's, bless his soul," I added. "Please come visit us sometime."

"The invitation is mutual," he assured me. "I would love to meet your whole family."

"That you shall. Our oldest is in charge right now," I said, not wanting to say goodbye but knowing I must. "All the more reason to return soon."

"Goodbye, Kelly. I'll miss you," and he gave me a large *embrasso*.

"I, too," I admitted. "I wish you well on Sunday. I understand you'll be the main celebrant."

"Thank you. It will be a great honor. *Ciao*."

"*Ciao!*"

I turned toward the counter with tears streaming down my cheeks. "Without him," I said to Tom as we handed in our passports, "I would have had no advocate. Who knows where I would be now. Instead, I'm heading home with a certificate that says that I'm a real live, honest-to-God, validly ordained Catholic priest!"

Our trip home was a celebration of all the monumental events. Tom and I compared notes on the plane, recording all we could remember so we could tell our children and anyone else who might be interested.

The plane arrived in the early afternoon. We were already pulling into our driveway by five o'clock. The kids ran to greet us. We all retired to the family room to open gifts and share stories. Nathan had been a worthy caregiver during the last week. As Rachel said, "I'm so happy you're home, Mom. Nathan makes us do our homework every night—no television until we're done. He was *strict!*"

"Great!" Tom said, giving his eldest a nod.

"Can you three keep a secret?" I asked with an air of mystery.

"Yes!" they said in unison, knowing this was part of the established pattern. They were good at it by now.

"Well, tomorrow morning we're all going over to St. Gabe's for Mass," I began as if I were telling them a bedtime story. "I'm going to call Father Henry tonight to see if he received the message. Guess what? Your Mom, now a legitimate Catholic priest, is going to do the liturgy all by herself. Imagine that!"

"Wow!" Michael said. "You can do that? I thought you weren't allowed."

"That's no longer the case," I said with a big smile. "Go ahead, Tom, show them the Indult. Tom pulled the official paper from his pocket and passed it around.

"What's an Indult?" Rachel asked, trying to read the fancy script.

"A permission slip, Dear," I replied. "It says that by special favor of the pope—see, that's his very own signature—I can say Mass, and do everything else an official priest can do. We met with Bishop Foley in Rome and he gave me my old job. I'm the pastor once again; except now, there is no Father Henry."

"Great!" Michael said. "I never liked his Masses all that much. Yours are much better, Mom."

"Well, thank you, Son, but don't be too hard on Father Henry," I cautioned. "He was only doing his job as he saw fit." Then changing the subject I asked, "So what should we have for dinner?"

"Pizza!" screamed Rachel. "Nathan wouldn't let us have any until you came home."

"Good for Nathan. He knows what's best for you," Tom

confirmed, giving his son a compliment and leaving himself open to my kidding about his own choice of menus when I was gone. However, I let it pass, which greatly surprised him.

The family gathered around a homecoming pizza, not of the same caliber we enjoyed in Rome, but even more rewarding.

"It feels so good to be home," I said to Tom as we got ready for bed. "It's really three in the morning, Rome-time, but I feel wide awake. I'm ready for tomorrow. It should be quite a surprise and a great celebration. It's been a long time coming."

"I wouldn't miss it for the world," Tom added. "And we must do something special for the kids. Without their willingness to play this game, you wouldn't be looking to lead that Mass tomorrow morning. Rachel is *so* excited; I hope she can keep the secret until your announcement."

"She'll be fine. She's growing up all of a sudden," I mused as I turned out the light.

Early the next morning, before the sun, I was up and raring to go. "Only six?" I said as I looked at the clock. "It feels like noon."

"It's not, Dear, believe me," Tom assured me sleepily. "Try to relax. Mass is still a few hours away."

"I'm so nervous," I confessed as I started to get dressed. "I think I'll go downstairs and prepare the homily."

"You'll do fine," Tom affirmed, "but suit yourself. Just keep it short. The Mass will be long enough as it is."

Eventually the children awoke and everyone was ready for church. We all walked together, Tom and I enjoying the early morning air. People were surprised and pleased to see me. "You're home already?" one person asked. "I just saw you with the pope last Sunday. We were *so* proud of you, Kelly."

"Thanks, but we had to come home and be with all of you for Mass this morning," I replied.

As Mass time approached, we took our usual seats a few rows from the front. Nearly everyone attending greeted us. The choir was ready with the opening song, but Father Henry was absent. He had called me the night before and suggested that he not attend, in order to heighten the drama of the moment. I was pleased with our conversation. "He, too, is softening," I thought.

I heard Debbie asking the ushers, "Where is Father Henry?" as she readied to process with the priest. At five after the hour, she came to the front and announced to the congregation that she had tried to contact Father Henry by cell phone but to no avail. At this, I lifted my hand and motioned to Deb that I had something to say. I strode to the front of church, took the microphone and said, "Father Henry is intentionally not here today. He and I spoke last night and made other arrangements."

With raised eyebrows people began questioning one another. Then I held the document I had received from Bishop Foley. "This, my friends, is a special Indult from Pope John xxiv." People strained to see what it was but they couldn't read it. "It stipulates that I am exempt from ordination validation processes, and effective immediately, I am an official priest in good standing with the Roman Catholic Church."

People were confused about my words. Then they began clapping. "Yes!" "Good for you, Kelly," various sections of the church called.

"What's more," I continued with calm determination, "I have the authority to say Mass this very morning."

"Hallelujah" one of the choir members shouted out spontaneously.

"In addition," I continued, looking at the choir with a smile, "We have no need of visiting priests, since Bishop Foley has appointed me as your legitimate pastor and priest."

Once again the congregation applauded, this time standing to welcome their former pastor and newly appointed priest. "So if you'll be patient for a moment, I'll go dress in my priestly garments and we'll celebrate Mass together." Then, as an aside to Debbie, I added, "Sorry, Deb, but I wanted to surprise everyone, including you. Come with me and we can process in together."

People held out their hands in congratulations as I walked down the aisle to the sacristy. They were still in an uproar as I signaled to the choir to sing the opening song. Everyone smiled as Debbie and I walked to the front of congregation and bowed. I then kissed the altar to begin Mass. I turned toward the congregation, making the sign of the cross, and said, "In the name of our Creator, Redeemer and Spirit of Life—Father, Son and Holy Spirit."

"Amen!" everyone chanted back.

As I sat in the presider's chair for the first two readings, I looked at the contented faces and said a prayer of thanks. "I don't know how this all happened, but here we are, just two years from when this exciting adventure began. And now it has come to pass, far beyond my wildest imaginings. You are a wonderful and mysterious God, and I love you."

When it was time for me to read the gospel, everyone stood to sing the Alleluia with a new burst of enthusiasm. I proclaimed the Sunday's gospel from Matthew chapter 18, about what to do if someone has wronged you. "Go and tell him his fault between you and him alone," Jesus said, "if he shall hear you, you have gained your brother." The gospel concluded with, "Again, I say unto you, that if two of you shall agree on earth as touching anything that they shall ask, it shall be done for them of my Father in heaven. For where two or three are gathered together in my name, there am I in the midst of them."

I concluded the reading, kissed the Book, set it on its stand and came to the middle aisle to address the congregation. "Have you been praying for me?"

"Yes we have!" Carol shouted as others nodded.

"So there you have it, two, three, ten, a hundred, praying together in God's name. You would not be denied. You have kept the faith and it has now been released. Good for you! Special thanks to you, Deb, for pastoring in my absence. She has done very well, hasn't she, folks?

Everyone gave a round of applause to a blushing Debbie.

"And regarding Father Henry," I continued. "His was not an easy job, but he remained steadfast. Be sure to give him affirmation when you see him. Once Bishop Foley returns, there's going to be a big Mass either in the Cathedral or in the convention center. You are all invited, so you may see Father Henry then.

"And that last part of today's gospel, 'where two or three are gathered . . .' is right here where we are gathered together in God's House. There's no doubt that Jesus is beside you and me, smiling and enjoying this extraordinary moment. This is just the beginning. There is no end to what we can accomplish as a parish. My dream is that St. Gabriel's becomes a beacon, a magnet, a model in the diocese and surrounding community. As a parish, we stand for healing and reconciliation, for caring and loving service to all. We've had enough division among us."

"Yes, we have," someone shouted out from the back.

"Now is the time to be all we can as a parish. I'll be the prod and support, I'll be the bearer of your dream, but it's in your hands, it's your dream. I have been called to this priesthood not as an honor, or symbol or to achieve a higher status or position. I have been called to the priesthood to be your leader of change and hope and possibility. This is our parish; you and I together with Jesus. Let's see what we can do with it. Wherever two or three are gathered together in Jesus' name, we can do astounding things, way beyond anything you or I could possibly imagine or accomplish on our own. Look at me here. Could you ever imagine this would happen? No, nor could I. So, my friends, let's dream big! We have achieved only a small part of what we are called to become, the very reign of God in our midst. Now that's something worth praying for!"

"I must level with you," I said, walking down the middle aisle. "I am just too excited to continue with Mass at this moment. I suggest we do the Greeting of Peace next. I am hereby moving it to this point in the Mass. The peace of Jesus Christ that is flooding into our hearts at this very moment be with you all."

"And also with you!" came the congregation's thundering response. People stood and gave me a long and sustained applause. I tried to subdue them but they persisted. I hugged Tom and the children, then Deb and Carol. For ten minutes people moved throughout the church giving one another God's peace and congratulating themselves for their good fortune in having their very own pastor, and priest, back in their midst.

I returned to the altar and said to the congregation, "Join me around the altar. Crowd in as closely as you can. *We* are the church! Let us celebrate as one family, with Christ in our midst. Then let's go spread this experience to the world around us, for this is, indeed, Good News!

EPILOGUE

IT WAS AFTER TEN IN THE EVENING when I looked out on the porch. Bishop Patrick Foley had been sitting in the same chair all afternoon and evening reading my manuscript, not uttering a word. I offered him dinner but he refused, so I placed a sandwich and a glass of milk on the wicker table next to his chair. He thanked me without looking up.

Now when I looked through the screen I could see that he was holding the manuscript close to his chest, his eyes closed as he rocked back and forth shaking his head. I was concerned how he would react to my account of our interaction. I spared no words in my description of him, recounting as well as I could my experience.

"Would you like to come inside for a nightcap, Bishop," I gently suggested, not knowing whether I should disturb his contemplation.

"Yes, I think I would, Kelly, if you don't mind—and if you'll have me. Our reconciliation in Rome was so healing for me, but now having read your account I had no idea what you had to endure as a result of my bombastic and rigid behavior. Can you ever forgive me?"

"That's over and done. Your gift of the Indult resolved all of that. Being able to surprise the parish with that Mass was more than recompense for what happened between us. I am a little concerned though. That manuscript will be published soon and it will not cast you in a very good light. How do you feel about that?"

"I'm okay, really I am. At least I redeemed myself at the end. Thanks for including that chapter of the story as well. Maybe this will serve as a model and prod to my fellow bishops to recant their clerical ways and act as servant leaders instead of thinking they are people who deserve prestige and privilege. You be sure to call me to task whenever I slip into my old behavior patterns. I'm sure it will happen often enough."

"And, for your part, Bishop Foley, please be sure to also confront me anytime I fail to be a faithful and loyal priest of your diocese. I have a great deal to learn about priesthood, you know. Now come inside so Tom can fix you a drink and we can talk about your thoughts and insights. We have a very special Italian cordial that we brought back with us from Rome. It won't be a match to the wine you served us at that choice little restaurant, but to us simple folks of Sarah, Michigan, I know it will be enjoyable."

"My dear Kelly More, you are the last person in the world I would ever categorize as simple folks. You are a strong, stubborn, determined and persistent woman—no, *person*. And do you know what? I've grown quite fond of you. I hope you can see your way to feeling the same about me some day."

"Done!" I exclaimed. The two of us put our arms around each other and marched into the living room to the utter surprise and astonishment of my dear husband, Tom.